Other Titles by David F. Stevenson

Mission to Ramalon – A Brandon Brothers Adventure in Space
The Pirates of Pegasus – A Brandon Brothers Adventure in Space
In His Own Words – The Edited Papers of Richard F. Hinton
Kidnapped – Book and Lyrics for the Musical
What Colour Is God's Skin? – Collected Poems and Lyrics

With Jane Hinton
The Girdwoods of Muiravonside and Polmont

Edited with John F. Stevenson
As I Remember – The Autobiography of Richard F. Hinton

© Copyright 2005 David F. Stevenson.
All rights reserved. No part of this publication may be reproduced, stored in a retrieval system, or transmitted, in any form or by any means, electronic, mechanical, photocopying, recording, or otherwise, without the written prior permission of the author.

Note for Librarians: A cataloguing record for this book is available from Library and Archives Canada at www.collectionscanada.ca/amicus/index-e.html
ISBN 1-4120-6869-x

Printed in Victoria, BC, Canada. Printed on paper with minimum 30% recycled fibre. Trafford's print shop runs on "green energy" from solar, wind and other environmentally-friendly power sources.

Offices in Canada, USA, Ireland and UK
This book was published *on-demand* in cooperation with Trafford Publishing. On-demand publishing is a unique process and service of making a book available for retail sale to the public taking advantage of on-demand manufacturing and Internet marketing. On-demand publishing includes promotions, retail sales, manufacturing, order fulfilment, accounting and collecting royalties on behalf of the author.

Book sales for North America and international:
Trafford Publishing, 6E–2333 Government St.,
Victoria, BC v8t 4p4 CANADA
phone 250 383 6864 (toll-free 1 888 232 4444)
fax 250 383 6804; email to orders@trafford.com

Book sales in Europe:
Trafford Publishing (UK) Limited, 9 Park End Street, 2nd Floor
Oxford, UK ox1 1hh UNITED KINGDOM
phone 44 (0)1865 722 113 (local rate 0845 230 9601)
facsimile 44 (0)1865 722 868; info.uk@trafford.com

Order online at:
trafford.com/05-1780

10 9 8 7 6 5 4

THE Frosts OF Winter

David F. Stevenson

For Jane and All Our Family

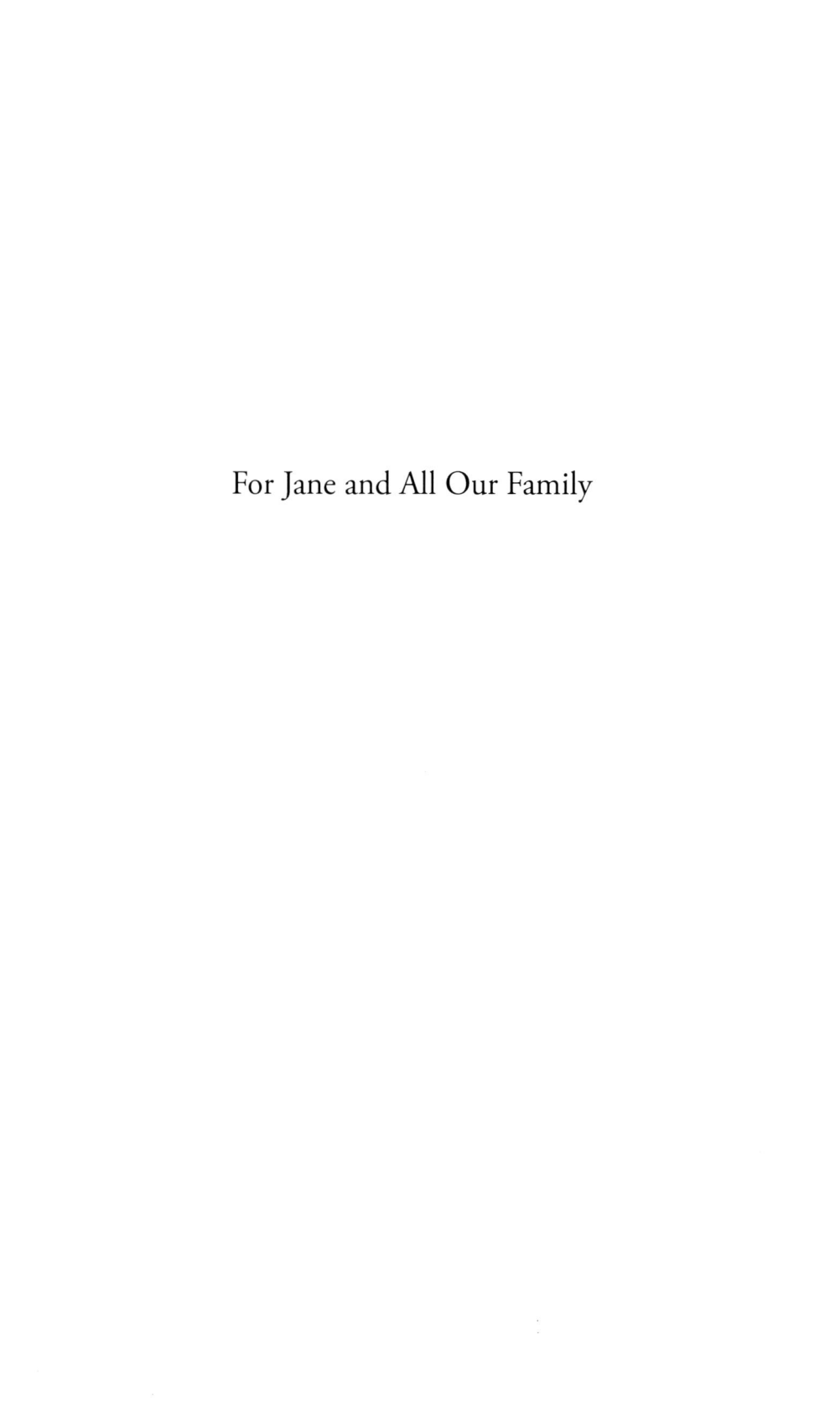

Acknowledgments

This novel started as a research project to try to understand why the American west was opened up with such violence and the Canadian west with so little. I found an explanation in the lives of four individuals – Crowfoot, Chief of Chiefs of the Blackfoot Confederacy; Colonel James F. Macleod, Commissioner of the North West Mounted Police; Sitting Bull, Grand Chief and Medicine Man of the Sioux Nation; and Lieutenant-General Philip H. Sheridan of the United States Army. In piecing the story together I thought that rather than a research paper, it would make much more interesting reading as a novel. That is how *The Frosts of Winter* came into being.

In an attempt to make this story as historically factual as possible I would like to acknowledge my debt to the following sources:

Stephen E. Ambrose's *Undaunted Courage* – the matchless telling of the Lewis and Clark expedition.

Dee Brown's *Folktales of the Native American.*

Edward Cavell's *Sometimes A Great Nation* with its superb collection of vintage photographs.

Dean Charters' *Mountie 1873-1973*, for the remarkable collection of photographs, maps and stories of the first years of the North West Mounted Police.

Alister Cooke's *America.*

David Cruise and Alison Griffiths' *The Great Adventure*, their epic depiction of how the Mounties conquered the West.

J. Clarence Duff's *Toronto Then and Now.*

R. Douglas Francis', *Images of the West.*

W. G. Hardy's *From Sea Unto Sea.*

A. L. Haydon's *The Riders of the Plains.*

Richard B. Howard's *Colborne's Legacy, Upper Canada College 1829-1979.*

Robert Knuckle's *In The Line of Duty.*

R. G. MacBeth's *Policing The Plains.*

Grant MacEwan's *Fifty Mighty Men* with its portrait of Crowfoot.

Sherrill McLaren's *Braehead,* for its remarkable and detailed description of the James Macleod family.

John McLean's *The Indians – Their Manners and Customs,* written in the late 1800's as he lived in the emerging North West.

RCMP – The March West, published by the Royal Canadian Mounted Police as part of its 125th Anniversary.

Carl Sandburg's *The War Years,* his classic history of the American Civil War.

Edward Smart's *History of Perth Academy.*

Robert M. Utley's *Custer Battlefield National Monument* for its detailed reporting of events leading up to and including the battle at the Little Bighorn.

I owe a special debt of gratitude to Sub-Inspector and Adjutant E. Dalrymple Clark of the NWMP. He was present at the signing of Treaty Number 7, at the meeting between Lt. Col. Irvine and Sitting Bull and at the meeting of Commissioner Macleod, Sitting Bull and General Terry. He took verbatim notes of the discussions and conversations through an interpreter. These notes are printed in full in *Opening Up The West, Being The Official Reports to Parliament of the Activities of the Royal North-West Mounted Police from 1874-1881* and are the source for the descriptions and conversations that took place during these events.

David F. Stevenson
Toronto
July, 2005

The Redcoats have protected us
as the feathers of the bird
protect it from the frosts of winter.

Crowfoot
September 22, 1877

1

Having a fleet, sleek horse under him made James Keyden feel about as happy with the world as anything could. They had left the city a mile or so behind and he could see the river that the stableman had described crossing their path up ahead. It was a broad, dusty road, busy this bright, spring Sunday morning with buggies full of well-dressed couples and their children and individual riders like him all out enjoying the warm sun.

James smiled as he thought of old Donovan at Taylor's Livery. Stablemen were all the same, tall, bent, thin hair uncombed, loose shirt tucked into old trousers that were always too big, hanging just below their waist from worn suspenders. Their life was spent mucking out stalls, brushing down horses and moving hay. There was no possible way to get the stable smell out of their clothes or their pores. But Donovan still had his pride. James saw it when he handed the old fellow the note from Mr. Martland saying he could borrow his horse. Donovan had taken the note, opened it as if it were an important official document, pretended to read it though James could see that he was holding it upside down, folded it as he had received it and handed it carefully back to James.

"Augustus is right this way, sir," he had said.

Augustus – what a name for a horse! But what could you expect from a classics master.

James thought back to his five years at Perth Academy and three more at St. Andrews. The last weeks of his last year seemed to never end. He was so ready to leave the college that he never went back for convocation. When it was all over he would have been even happier if he had had some idea of what to do next.

They reached the road running alongside the river. The bank was crowded with couples walking, families sitting on the grassy slope to the water, parked buggies with their horses tied to wood rails and children running about. The women wore long white dresses, their hems brushing the dusty boardwalk. Broad brimmed hats shielded their pale faces, leftovers from the long, dark winter. The men pranced in their dark coats and trousers, high collars and top hats. They carried umbrellas as canes though there was not a suggestion of rain. To his left, towards the lake he could see a large, white wooden building that looked like a hotel. Through the trees he glimpsed a raised platform on which couples were dancing. The tunes of the fiddles wafted through the branches, thick with buds about to burst into leaf.

A young boy attempted to throw a stone to the opposite bank. The momentum of the effort threw him off balance and he fell like a fallen tree into the muddy water. A young woman near him hurried to his aid. She walked into the shallow edge of the river wetting her shoes, stockings, dress and whatever was underneath up to her knees. Surprisingly, she was not at all angry, but helped the boy to his feet as they both burst into shouts of joy.

Interesting country. If that had happened on the banks of the Tay some father would have jumped up and given the lad a clout across the head.

He had noticed the difference almost as soon as the boat left Greenock. All the passengers seemed to share his feeling of expectation. He was relieved to leave the old behind and excited and a trace fearful of what lay ahead. When he landed in Montreal the fear was gone and he was overcome with a sense that the world was open to him. Everything was new even though some of the buildings would not have been out of place on the streets of Edinburgh. He couldn't take his eyes from the window on the train riding up the valley of the St. Lawrence, past Prescott, past Kingston and into Toronto. But where were all the people? Mile after mile he studied the small farmhouses and plots of land robbed from the forest.

The road he was on now paralleled the river as it ran north from the lake. Trees rose from the bank, their branches forming a screen to the afternoon's falling sun. James turned Augustus and touched him with his heels.

"Do you think you can handle my horse?" Mr. Martland, the classics master had said to James. "He was an excellent jumper but he just needs a light workout. Don't run him too hard."

James hadn't been on a horse since he had left his father's home six weeks previous. He felt like riding hard. He let the reins out and smiled as Augustus picked up the pace. There was a couple riding slowly ahead and he knew he frightened them as he raced by. When a field opened up beside them he wheeled Augustus to the right and dug his heels in sharply. The horse's long strides carried them quickly across the hard, unsown field towards a low fence made of stones piled on top of each other. Augustus took the fence with ease much to James' delight. There was a rail fence further on, twice as high as the stone wall. They raced for it and James checked the horse's speed to time the flight.

Augustus enjoyed it as much as James. They ran down a gentle slope to a large pond, around it, back up the incline on the other side, found three more rail fences to jump and finally slowed to a walk and headed back to watch the ducks swimming on the still water. James swung out of the saddle and led Augustus to the edge of the pond. The horse dipped its long neck and vacuumed up some of the cooling liquid. James stroked its damp shoulder, glistening with the sweat of its effort. James felt contentment. He had ridden horses before he had walked. It was one of the advantages of having a father who was the colonel of the Scots Greys.

James' mind went back to the stable behind their old stone home in Gask. He could feel the flat stones of the floor, smell the soiled straw heavy with wet dung. He knew the slats on the sides of every stall. Whenever life had been too much he had retreated to an empty one, sat in a corner and listened to the horses munching, stomping and pooping around him.

Augustus had his fill, raised his head and shook it vigorously from side to side, swung it around to nudge James and slobbered over the side of his jacket. James ruffled the hair over the horse's eyes playfully, gathered in the reins and swung back into the saddle. Augustus didn't wait to be told. He turned away from the pond and galloped up the hill towards the open field.

The sun was lower behind James' shoulder. He held Augustus at a steady run and they took the low stone walls, the rail fences and whatever stood in their path. A road ran beside them on the other side of a row of tall trees to their left. James nudged Augustus for one last run. They raced down the field beside the line of elms, over a series of fences and came to a walk so that they could pass through a narrow break in the foliage onto the road. If James had it right they were headed back towards the city.

"I say there," shouted a voice from behind them as they turned onto the road.

James wheeled Augustus around and saw two riders – or rather one rider and a man standing beside his mount. The man on the ground was waving an arm.

"I say there. Can you help me?" the man standing on the ground shouted again.

James nudged Augustus with his heels and headed for the pair. The man standing on the ground was a stately looking gentleman, middle-aged, medium height and a little paunchy. He wore a long black riding coat and breeches, a tall black hat and beautifully polished high riding boots. To his surprise, James saw that the rider beside him was an attractive young woman. She wore a black riding jacket like the man but with a lace scarf at the neck, a tall hat and most surprising of all, she sat astride the saddle wearing men's riding breeches that tucked into the top of her high brown riding boots.

"My horse is about to lose a shoe," said the man with annoyance. "Do you think there is something you could do to fix it?" He was a man who wouldn't have thought to try to do something about it himself.

James swung out of the saddle. "Would you mind holding these?" he said to the young woman, handing her the reins.

The loose shoe was on the front left hoof. James pulled on the fetlock and raised the leg, positioning himself so that he could rest the hoof on his knee. Two of the nails had come loose from the wall of the hoof and the shoe was askew. Another nail had broken off taking a chip with it. James worked the shoe back and forth but the other nails held. He did not want to break off another piece of the hoof.

"Can't you just pull it off?" asked the gentleman, his voice sharp with annoyance.

"Not without damaging the hoof," replied James. "You'll have to walk him to the nearest farm house. They'll have the tools to remove the shoe."

"I don't have time for that, young man," growled the man. "I need to be back in the city forthwith."

"This horse can't be ridden even with the shoe off," said James. "Not until he gets another shoe."

"He can't be ridden?" exclaimed the gentleman.

"My father has an important dinner engagement this evening," interrupted the young woman. "He's very anxious to get back to town."

James put the horse's foot down gently. The man's face under the top hat was red with impatience.

"Why don't you ride my horse back to the city," James suggested to the fuming man. "I'll deal with the shoe and return your horse to you later this evening. I'm in no rush to get back to town."

"That's very good of you," said the gentleman. "I don't recall seeing you around town."

"I arrived only a couple of weeks ago," James told them.

"Sounds like you're from the Old Country."

"Perthshire."

"I'm from Glasgow, but some years ago. What brings you to Toronto?"

"Visiting my sister," replied James. "She's married to a teacher at the College."

"Upper Canada College? What's his name?

"Arthur Jackson."

"I'm sure I've met him – very athletic as I remember."

"That's him," replied James.

"Is this his horse?"

"It belongs to another teacher, Mr. Martland," replied James. "He was busy today and he let me exercise him."

"I've heard of Martland too," replied the man. "It's very good of you to offer. Do you know your way back to town?"

"I'll just follow this road and I'm sure it will get me there eventually."

"That's right, straight ahead. It will take you about an hour."

"Father!" said the young lady with a slight edge in her voice.

"Well, maybe a little longer," said the man. "You should be back before dark."

"Where shall I leave your horse, sir?" asked James.

"My name's McLennan. Oh, yes and this is my daughter."

James shook the man's hand and touched his cap to the young woman.

"James Keyden," he replied.

"Merrie McLennan," said the young woman, holding out her hand to James.

"Pleased to meet you both," said James as he shook her hand lightly. "I'm sorry your father has had this trouble."

"Our home is quite close to the school," interrupted Mr. McLennan. "I'm sure your sister will know it. The stable's behind the house. Morgan looks after it for us. Just leave the horse with Morgan."

"Why don't you leave this horse with Morgan too," suggested James. "I'll take him back to Taylor's after I get back."

"Thank you," said McLennan. "Yes, I'll leave it with Morgan."

James took the reins from Merrie and handed them to her father.

"What do you call your horse?" James asked.

"His name is Nevis, but I call him Ben," McLennan replied with a smile. "And yours?"

"Augustus, after the Caesar," said James. "But he answers to Gus."

2

Merrie was right. It took James a lot longer than an hour to get back to the city. He found a farmer who helped him remove the loose shoe and file down the hoof around the edge where the chip had broken off. It was a warm evening and a pleasant walk. He was in no hurry though he knew his sister Fiona would be concerned and probably Donovan too.

The sun sank behind the trees making great splashes of red and orange, and purple and blue. Birds sang in the trees and a V of geese winged northward overhead introducing James to their characteristic honking. There were flickering yellow lights in the windows of the farmhouses and curious cows peering over the fences watching him pass. There were dogs barking in the distance. He heard someone chopping wood. Occasionally a farm wagon passed in the other direction. The driver always lifted his hand in silent greeting.

There was no difficulty finding McLennan's house. The first person he asked knew it well. It wasn't a full-scale mansion but almost. It could have been a country house in Scotland. Built on the high ground of a large lot, it was a laird's two-storey stone structure, built by Scottish masons, James was sure. A stone wall surrounded the grounds. There was an impressive entranceway with a covered portico flanked by two large windows. There were four windows across the front on the second floor. Two large chimneys towered over each end of a black slate roof. There was a long circular driveway up to the imposing front door with a side road branching off beside the house to the stable in back. A chandelier, blazing with candlelight, hung from the ceiling of the portico.

James led Ben up the driveway and followed the side road around the back. Morgan heard them coming and was waiting in the doorway of the stable.

"Evening, sir, you've had a long walk."

"Pleasant enough," replied James. "Harder on Ben than on me."

"See you got the shoe off im all right."

"The hoof's chipped – should be all right with a little more trimming."

"I'll see to him in the morning," replied Morgan as he took the reins from James and turned for the stable.

"I'll take Augustus back to Taylor's," said James.

"Saved you the trouble," said Morgan over his shoulder. "'Figured you'd walked far enough so I took him back to Taylor's myself. Donovan and I go way back. I told him what happened to you. He thought Gus looked better than he had for a long time."

"Thanks."

"No trouble," said Morgan, as he disappeared into the stable.

James walked out the driveway, glancing at the windows as he passed. They were heavily curtained and he couldn't see behind them. It was a short distance to King Street then west where his sister and family had an apartment in one of the school's boarding houses.

Fiona was not at all surprised to see him come in so late.

"Sorry, Fiona…" he started.

"I know," she interrupted. "We had a caller – Merrie McLennan. She dropped by to let me know that you would probably be quite late for dinner."

"She did?" replied James

"So, you've had quite an afternoon," said Fiona with a smile.

"Augustus is a fine jumper," said James, as he sat down to the place Fiona had waiting for him. "Best ride since I left home."

"James," said Fiona, "you weren't jumping?"

"Couldn't hold him back," replied James with a smile.

Fiona put a hot, thick soup and fresh bread in front of James.

"Looks great," he told her. "Who's this Mr. McLennan?"

"Angus McLennan is a banker – the banker in this city," explained Fiona. "He's the head of The Dominion Bank and one of the powers behind the Liberal Party, which, for your information, is in power in Ottawa."

"And Merrie's his daughter?" asked James.

"His one and only," replied Fiona, "a very sad story, really. His wife died several years ago. He's never married again. He dotes on Merrie. She's his hostess now for parties at their home."

"I think there's one going on there now," James told her. "The front of the house was all lit up when I brought his horse back. I guess that's why he was so anxious to get back."

"Tonight was the first time I met Merrie," said Fiona, glancing over at her brother. "She told me they had seen you racing over the jumps before they met you on the road. She seemed quite impressed."

"Was she still wearing riding breeches when she called?"

"No," replied Fiona. "James, she wasn't wearing riding breeches!"

"Yes, she was."

"You must have made some kind of impression. She left a letter for you."

James took the unaddressed envelope, turned it over in his hands and opened it.

"She remembered your first name was James," Fiona explained, "but she couldn't remember your second name. She thought it looked a little strange to write plain 'James' as an address so she left it blank"

James read the note to himself and smiled.

"It's not from Merrie, it's from Mr. McLennan," James told Fiona.

"What's he say?"

> *In thanks for your kindness, it would give me great pleasure if you and Mr. and Mrs. Jackson would join me at a reception in honour of Mr. R. W. Scott at my home this coming Wednesday evening at 7:30 PM.*
>
> *Angus McLennan*

"Who's R. W. Scott?"

"Our Member of Parliament and Secretary of State in Alexander Mackenzie's Cabinet."

"Okay if I wear my tweed jacket?"

"Do you have anything else?"

"No."

3

James walked with Arthur and Fiona up the tree-lined avenue towards the McLennan's. They could hear the party before they saw it. There was the buzz of a large crowd and the faint strains of a string quartet. Interested spectators were strolling slowly up and down the road watching the goings-on.

Though the sun was still above the horizon, lanterns had been lit and were scattered around the spacious lawn where the crowd, gathered in small groups, was sipping from tall crystal glasses. Two militia officers in dull grey-green uniforms stood on either side of the entrance gate. They let Arthur and Fiona pass but on seeing James in his tweed jacket, asked to see his invitation. Fortunately, he had Mr. McLennan's letter in his pocket.

His was the only tweed jacket among the black coats and long dresses. He had tried on one of Arthur's long black jackets but it was so obviously too big for him, and the sleeves so short, that even Fiona agreed it wouldn't do. He had, however, put on one of Arthur's high collars and ties, large as they were, making his neck look small, and Fiona had pressed his trousers – their first attention since leaving Gask.

There was a bit of the showman in James. He smiled at the stares that his clothes invited from the dark-suited men and their ladies in finery. His brother-in-law and sister had been drawn into a circle of friends while his attention had been elsewhere so he walked towards a table of glasses and was offered one by a serving woman in black dress, white apron and cap. Another offered him a warm pastry and with his hands thus occupied milled through the crowd expecting to meet no one he knew. There were a few men in uniform, the same as those who guarded the gate and he guessed from the drabness of their uniforms that they were militia rather than regular officers. A notable exception was a tall officer in a bright red jacket, black trousers with a blue stripe and a white helmet. He was enjoying the company of a young woman whom, as James approached, he recognized as Miss McLennan. He changed course to avoid them but Merrie noticed him and guided her officer friend towards him.

"This is the person I was telling you about," Merrie said to the officer. "I'm sorry I don't remember your last name," she said to James.

"Keyden, James Keyden." He moved to shake her outstretched hand but with a glass in one and a pastry in the other he had to make do with a slightly embarrassed smile.

"This is Captain Channer," she went on. James smiled and nodded. "I'm sure you two can find something interesting to talk about. Richard," she said to the captain, "I'll see you before you go." There was a glint of disappointment in the captain's eyes as they followed Merrie's retreat.

"Regular army?" James asked.

"Yes, assigned to Mr. Scott's staff for the duration."

"Mr. Scott's staff?" queried James.

"He's just been given responsibility for the policing of the North West. I spent two years out there and I guess they think I will be of some help to him."

"The North West?" James asked, trying to appear not too ignorant of this new country.

The Canadian west – the thousand miles of prairie from the Red River to the Rocky Mountains. You've heard of the Mounted Police?"

"No," said James honestly. "I've not even heard of the North West."

"You've heard of the Hudson's Bay Company?"

"I've heard the name."

"Until six years ago it owned all the land from Hudson Bay to the Pacific. Canada, after it became Canada, bought it from them. I was out there with a party to survey the border between us and the United States."

"And you did that?"

"We did. Three hundred and eighty-eight piles of prairie sod with spikes in the top, three miles apart from Lake Superior to the Rockies."

"Father, this is Mr. Keyden." It was Merrie who interrupted, her father in tow. James felt the banker's unapproving eyes as they noted his oversized collar and his tweed jacket. But he seemed to shrug off his concern and smiled warmly as he shook James' hand free now that the pastry had been eaten.

"I'm glad my daughter thought to invite you tonight, Mr. Keyden. I'm very grateful for your help the other day and I'm glad for the chance to thank you in person. I see you've met Captain Channer. He's a very fine horseman, like you. He can tell you some fascinating stories about his last few years in the North West."

"I've just begun to hear some of them," James replied.

"What are your plans in this country, young man?" asked McLennan.

"No plans, sir. I'm here to spend a couple of months with my sister and her family, then see what's next after that."

The banker and Merrie were engaged by another couple and turned away.

"So you ride," said the captain, following on from the bankers's remark.

"Since before I could walk. My father was the Colonel of the Scots Greys."

A spark flared in the captain's eyes. "I joined the army hoping to get into a cavalry regiment. Only trouble is, this country doesn't have one. I had to settle for the infantry."

"No cavalry, in a country this size?" said James incredulously.

"Mounted police is as close as we get," replied the captain, disappointment in his words.

James and the captain were still talking as the sun disappeared below the horizon. Chatter, broken by the occasional shrill laughter, washed over them. The maids in black and white filled their glasses and a little of their stomachs. The lanterns cast a warm glow over the broad sloping lawn. The captain pressed for stories of his father's regiment. James' interest grew in his stories of the International Boundary Commission and life on the Great Plains. They didn't notice the crowd thinning until Merrie returned. Over her shoulder he noticed his sister and Arthur taking their leave from friends. He excused himself, thanking Merrie for the invitation and telling the captain he hoped to meet him again and walked to join them. They found Mr. McLennan and Mr. Scott together near the gate bidding goodbye to their guests and stopped to express their thanks. The banker was complimentary in his comments about James to the cabinet minister who smiled politely in spite of the tweed jacket and ill-fitting collar.

As they turned onto the road towards home James glanced back at the scene of the party. Light glowed from all the windows and from the array of lanterns across the lawn. Shadows accentuated the square cut stones of the facade. It was an elegant dwelling. There were still a few groups of well-dressed men and stylish women conversing. The maids busied themselves cleaning up. His last glimpse was of the backs of the banker and the politician as they disappeared through the front entrance.

4

Restlessness was setting in. James had thought he might stay a few months with Fiona and that the change from life in Scotland would invigorate him. But after two weeks he wasn't sure. He had covered most subjects with his sister, walked through most of the streets of the city and for miles along the lakefront. He wished he had a horse and could get out into the countryside.

The party at the bankers had been an interesting diversion. A few days after it had taken place he returned home from a long walk to find a letter waiting for him. He needed a surprise. It was from Captain Channer – an invitation to go riding. What could be better.

They met at a livery beside the armory of the militia. The army may not have had any cavalry but they had some fine horses used for ceremonial purposes and the two that were being saddled for them caused James' heart to jump. James appeared in the same tweed jacket, trousers and oxfords, but a loose tartan shirt had replaced Arthur's high collar.

"Would you like some riding boots?" Channer asked him.

He declined, even though the captain hinted that they might get in a little jumping. James watched the stableman tighten the saddle and fit the bridle. When he was handed the reins he went to the horse's head, stroked it between the eyes and down its nose and rubbed its neck. Once up on the saddle he had the stableman shorten the stirrup leather a notch.

They walked and trotted the horses to the north edge of the city. When they were warm the captain picked up the pace. They galloped along a dusty road, which wound its way among the farms. At times James sensed that the captain wanted to race. Whenever he drew alongside him, the captain spurted ahead to keep in front until the horses were running hard. When they got to a large pond, they dismounted and gave the horses a chance to drink and rest.

"When did you start riding?" asked the captain.

"Truly, I can't remember," was James reply. "My father used to sit me ahead of him on his horse with his arm around my chest. I must have been quite young. I can't remember the first time I was on a horse by myself."

"You ever fall off?"

"Lots of times but never seriously."

"Do you jump?"

"Yes."

They bantered back and forth about riding, horses and cavalry. They sat on the bank surrounding the pond and the captain quizzed him about life in the Scot's Guards.

"Did you ever ride with the cavalry?" he asked.

"All the time."

The horses were rested. They mounted up and set off over the farm fields. Again the captain led. James politely swung in behind him though he was aching to let his horse loose and fly over the countryside. They took several small stone walls and rail fences and drew up at the edge of a wide meadow.

"You okay with the jumps?" the captain asked.

"Fine."

"There's a good view of the city and Lake Ontario behind it from that hilltop over there," said the captain pointing to a rise a mile or so through the fields to their right.

James took that as their next destination and not wanting to get stuck behind the cautious captain turned in the direction of the hilltop and touched the horse's flanks with his heels. He thought he heard the captain shout but pretended not to as he shot across the field and over the first rail fence. Beyond the next field he saw a line of trees and a steep bank beyond. He cleared the barriers to the trees and slowed to maneuver through the underbrush. There was a shallow stream. He found a flat crossing in the streambed, splashed through the water and started up the embankment. There was a narrow trail which the horse had little difficulty navigating. When they reached the top he turned again towards the hilltop and sped across the open fields. There were several high fences that he guided his horse towards. It rose to meet them and cleared them easily. Having taken the last fence before running for the summit of the hill, James turned to see how the captain was making out. He was nowhere to be seen. James thought of turning back to look for him but knew he could look after himself and headed for the hilltop. It was his last chance for a fast run. If the captain were not there he would go back to look for him.

The horse was winded but James coaxed him up the steep slope. They reached the top and the captain had been right. There was a breathtaking sweep of the countryside, farms stretching away to the east, the city ahead and to the right and the bright blue waters of Lake Ontario shimmering beyond them. They walked to the edge of the hilltop. A road sloped gently to the southeast. Far down it he could see the captain galloping towards them.

"I thought you meant us to go through the fields," said James, when the captain arrived, knowing in himself that it was a half-truth.

"Too hard on the horses," replied the captain, with a note of irritation. "But I see you made it all right."

"Good exercise for them," James replied with a glint in his eye. "It'll make them into good cavalry mounts."

"Don't I wish," replied the captain, regaining his good humour. They rested on the horses surveying the scene in front of them. Finally they turned and followed the road the captain had taken back towards the city.

After they arrived at the armory and had handed the horses back to the stableman, the captain invited James for a drink. They walked to a small pub nearby and enjoyed cool ale.

"What do you do besides ride horses?" asked the captain.

"I like writing," replied James, "one of the reasons I like history and philosophy so much. It gives me something to write about."

"What do you want to do with it?" prodded the captain.

"Not sure yet," answered James with a touch of caution. "I just arrived. I'd like to look around a bit and see what the possibilities are. I'm not sure yet whether I'll stay over here."

"Something interest you in Scotland?"

"Not really. I'm rather discouraged by what I see of the future over there."

"Ever thought of going to the North West?"

"I hardly know anything about it."

They finished their glasses and a second one. James appreciated the diversion from his family visit and the chance to trade stories with the captain. They talked easily of horses and the military and James found his experiences of the two years with the Boundary Commission exciting.

"Would you like to ride again sometime," asked the captain, as they parted outside the pub. James felt a touch of disappointment. He sensed the captain had more on his mind than he had let on, but it hadn't surfaced.

"Anytime," replied James.

5

After dinner that evening James walked with Fiona, Arthur and the children, William aged seven and Hermione aged five, through the grounds of the school. James sat on a bench with his sister and chatted while Arthur tried to extract the last bursts of energy from the children so they would go to bed peacefully.

"I was very surprised when I heard you say that you don't want to join father's regiment," remarked Fiona as they watched the children.

"I'm not sure what I want to do," replied James, "but I'm pretty sure what I don't want to do – and that's join a regiment. It's too restrictive."

Arthur wore out before the children did and James took his place, chasing and being chased, throwing and kicking a ball and swinging them by their arms in great circles. The children had grown to love their newly arrived uncle and when Fiona announced that it was time for bed they pleaded to play a little longer. James made a game of chasing them among the trees and in so doing led them back towards the apartment and finally in the front door. When the children were finally settled in bed, Fiona joined them in the sitting room.

"Would you two like a glass of port?" Arthur poured the drinks while Fiona and James settled in front of a cold fireplace.

"What does father think of you not joining the Greys?" said Fiona, picking up the conversation.

"He was quite furious at first," answered James, "but he cooled down soon enough. His last years in the army were not particularly happy ones for him and he's relieved to be out of it."

Arthur arrived with the port.

"As father tells it," James continued, "the British army has gone steadily downhill since the day Wellington defeated Napoleon. How far down was painfully obvious during the Crimean War. He still gets angry when he talks about it. Thank God he was wounded before Sevastopol or between the high command's incompetence and disease he probably would never have made it home."

"I knew he was unhappy," commented Fiona. "But I never understood why."

"You don't know why he was never made a general like grandfather?" asked James.

"I thought he couldn't afford it or something like that," answered Fiona.

"No, it wasn't that at all," James told her. "He was critical of preparations for the war with Russia. He made no secret that he thought the army and particularly the cavalry weren't ready for it. The war proved him absolutely right. But he had made a lot of enemies in high places and after he was wounded, instead of moving him up to general, they retired him."

"Is that what happened," said Fiona. "I didn't realize that. I thought his wounds were so bad he couldn't continue."

"The war was a disaster for the army and they didn't want anyone as vocal as father around during the inquiries."

"I expect he was very disappointed."

"Less than you would think," said James. "He misses some parts of army life, but not others. He and mother have adapted well. They've never had so much time together and they're enjoying it."

"Now I understand his feelings about you and the army," said Fiona.

"There's more to it than that for me. Warfare is changing and so are weapons. Father was a great student of the American Civil War, particularly the cavalry units. He shuddered when he told me about the carnage in those battles. There was certainly no glory or honour, only slaughter. Then came the Franco-German war with its new technology, old tactics and horrendous casualties. In father's judgment all the glory has gone out of war if there ever was any. He thinks that before long there won't be any role for horse cavalry."

Fiona caught Arthur's eye. She had never heard her brother speak this way. He had still been a boy when she and Arthur had left for Canada. It was years since she had seen him and was impressed with his determination to find his own way.

"I'm not even sure I want to stay in Britain," James continued almost talking to himself. "Disraeli's made Queen Victoria Empress of India to try to revive our imperial stature but it's not working. British greatness is dying. I see its decline in father. The economy's flat and we've been in a recession for three years. I want to be part of the new, not the old."

James looked at Arthur. "Why did you come here?" he asked.

It was Arthur's turn to reflect.

"For many of the same reasons you're expressing. I'd finished my graduate work. Most of the positions in education that really interested me were open only to those with status, wealth or rank – which I didn't have. I could have taught in one of the academies, like Perth, but I can't say that the prospect excited me."

Arthur sipped his port.

"George Cockburn, the Principal here at Upper Canada College, was a few years ahead of me at the University in Edinburgh. I knew him by reputation and was surprised to find out that he knew of me. After he was made Principal he wrote and offered me a position in the Classics department. I was bowled over. I had never considered coming to Canada. He made a strong and convincing case. The educational system in English Canada is in its infancy and the College is setting the standard. It's pioneering work. It certainly wasn't the money – which is barely adequate – that convinced us to come. The job had some of the elements you were speaking of – the challenge of building something new. That appealed to me. Still does."

"And raising the children in a country where the opportunities seem limitless," added Fiona.

There was a long silence. The glasses were empty. James told them of his ride with Captain Channer and their conversation in the pub. In telling them his excitement grew. The captain had something in mind with all his questions and he wished he knew what it was.

James was lingering over a third cup of breakfast tea when there was a knock at the door. Hermione dropped the scissors and cloth she was cutting into small pieces and followed her mother to the door. It was Captain Channer. The bright red jacket of the dress uniform was replaced by one of dull grey-green. He had the black officer's hat with the bronze badge tucked under his arm.

"Sorry to disturb the household so early," he said to Fiona, "but I have a message for James from Mr. McLennan. He has invited you and me to dinner this evening at his home and apologizes for the short notice. He wanted to get this message to you early in the day."

"I'm very happy to accept," James replied surprised by the invitation and excited by the opportunity.

"It's for seven o'clock", the captain said and added, "James, it's a beautiful day. How about a short ride in the country before dinner?"

"I'd like that."

"The armory at three then?" suggested the captain.

"Fine."

"See you then," and the captain was gone.

"Looks like you've found a friend," Fiona remarked, sitting down beside James at the table.

"There's more to this than friendship," he said to his sister. "There's something on his mind."

They had the same horses as the previous day. The captain did not set the pace, lead him over the fields and fences or race to the height of ground. They rode side by side, talking. The captain was full of questions.

"Yesterday he wanted to see if I could ride," thought James. "Now he wants to see if I have any brains."

James played along. The captain asked him to describe the countryside they had ridden through the day before, particularly the rough country through which James had ridden to the hilltop. Did James enjoy hiking? Yes, he had often ridden alone for days through the Scottish hills. Could he shoot? Yes, about as well as he could ride. Did he know much of the history of Canada? No. The United States. A little. His father had followed the course of the Civil War closely, particularly the role of the cavalry. What about his father? Where did he serve? Had he any political affiliation. No.

They reined their horses to a halt in front of a small hotel. They were on a narrow dirt road beside the Humber River not far from where it emptied into Lake Ontario. It was the road he had travelled on his first outing.

"All right," said James looking the captain straight in the eye. "Something's on your mind?"

"Just an interesting possibility," Channer replied., "but I can't say more for the moment. Let's have a pint before dinner."

They left their horses with the stableman and went in. James remembered the first thing he had learned about the captain. He was on the staff of Mr. Scott. Why hadn't he gone back to Ottawa with the cabinet minister? Why was he still in Toronto? He would continue the game until his patience ran out.

They had a drink at a table beside the window looking out on the broad lake. There was a gentle swell pushed by the breeze. Sailboats skimmed to and fro. Conversation was light but James instantly recognized when the probing resumed. What were the subjects of his papers at the university? The Crimean War – his father had been there and he himself thought at the time that his career lay with the Scots Greys; the American Civil War – his father, after his retirement, had made a thorough study of it which made it easy for James to find the information he needed. Try as he might, or infer from the questions, James could not conclude where the questioning was leading.

They rode at a trot back to the armory without more than a few words passing between them. James mind was racing at what the captain's motives were.

"You planning to be in town long?" James asked.

"Depends," was his vague reply.

7

JAMES FOLLOWED CAPTAIN CHANNER TO the front door of the imposing McLennan residence. They had walked the short distance from the Armory along King Street and north up University Avenue. The sun had fallen behind the trees and a half moon could just be seen rising low in the east. As they waited for their knock at the door to be answered, they were bathed in the light of the chandelier hanging over their heads.

A short, cheerful, middle-aged woman wearing a starched cap and crisp white apron over a black dress opened the door.

"Please come in. Mr. McLennan is waiting for you in the dining room."

They stepped into the brightly-lit foyer. There was a long broad hallway in front of them leading to the rear of the ground floor. On the right of the hallway was a wide staircase leading upstairs. James noticed through a doorway on his right the dining room. The long polished table was set with candles already lit on the table.

"This way please," she said, guiding them into the dining room where Mr. McLennan rose from his seat at the far end of the table to greet them. James was surprised to see Merrie sitting at the opposite end of the table.

"Good evening," Mr. McLennan said cheerily. "Please join us."

They talked casually through a steaming chicken broth but when the maid served the roast of beef with fresh garden vegetables and warm bread, which must have just come from the oven, Mr. McLennan turned to James.

"Mr. Keyden, you seem to have a fine way with horses."

"My father was the colonel of the Scots Greys…"

"Fine regiment," interrupted Mr. McLennan. "Some say the best cavalry at the Battle of Waterloo."

"My father wasn't at Waterloo," replied James. "But my grandfather was, same regiment. It runs in the family."

"And what did he do after beating Napoleon?" inquired the banker.

"They made him a general and assigned him to the Imperial Staff in London," James replied.

"And you'll be the next family cavalryman?"

"I'm not sure of that, sir."

"What then?" he asked.

"Something challenging, but not in the cavalry although I love to ride."

"You must have some stories about riding with the cavalry," Merrie broke in.

James looked at her and at his host as if seeking permission.

"Go on, Mr. Keyden," urged Merrie. "I'm sure we would all like to hear one."

James warmed to her smile, paused to gather his thoughts and began the story.

"Once a year, generally in September, my father took his regiment into the hills north of Dunkeld to test the skills of his men and their horses. A course was designed with low fences, and high fences, and streams and pits, steep hills to climb and steeper ones to go down and mud flats along the river. The men set off over this course two by two, several seconds apart with the officers posted along the route to judge each man's performance at various points of difficulty."

James looked quickly around the table and caught Merrie looking at him intently. He saw he had their attention and continued.

"My father was at the starting line watching the pairs set off. For some reason he took me with him. I must have been thirteen or fourteen years old."

"My father had taken two of his horses," continued James. "He was riding one and I was sitting on the other behind him, watching the excitement. One of his officers rode up to him and must have given him a message of some sort because they rode off together. I moved forward to get a better view of things and just as the next pair went off my horse started after them. I made a half-hearted attempt to stop him but he had made up his mind and I thought, 'Why not? This could be rather exciting.' So off we went.

"My father always had wonderful horses – this one's name was Raj. He had served in Bengal and although past his prime, was still a magnificent animal. We took off down the course behind the two and before I knew it we had passed them and were moving up on the next pair. Raj flew over the fences and was up and down the hills hardly losing speed. We must have passed two or three pairs before we finished."

"As you can imagine I was pretty excited when we crossed the finish line," continued James. "I was cheering and patting Raj on the neck – until a lieutenant came up to me and in a voice that meant no nonsense, said, 'Follow me.'

"He took me back towards the starting line where a tent had been erected for some purpose. My father was inside with some of the other officers. He hadn't seen me go down the course and didn't know about it until the lieutenant took him aside and whispered in his ear. My father wheeled around, came out of the tent and saw me sitting on his horse with a big smile on my face. My smile disappeared when I saw the look on his face as he came over to me.

"I don't remember what he said but it was loud and ended with the words 'I'll speak to you later.' But he never did."

"What else have you done with your young life besides ride horse, Mr. Keyden?" asked the banker.

"I've played a lot of rugby," added James with a smile, "and cricket and tennis."

"Where was that?"

"Perth Academy and St. Andrews," replied James.

"You graduated from St. Andrews?" asked Mr. McLennan.

"Yes, sir."

"Difficult for a father on a soldier's pay," commented the banker. "You must be scholarship material."

"Yes, sir, full tuition from my first school, the Free Church School in Auchterarder."

"And your field of study?" pried Mr. McLennan, "My guess is Classics and Mathematics."

"No. English and French Literature and History," explained James, "and a little Science."

All the while Captain Channer was listening and watching the conversation intently.

"Fine preparation for the cavalry, I'll be bound," said the host sarcastically. "And what do you plan to do in Canada, young man?"

"I'm not sure yet," answered James. "I just arrived. I'd like to look around a bit before making up my mind."

"Would you like to stay in this country?" asked Merrie.

"If something catches my interest," replied James, smiling at her.

"Have you considered going to the North West?" asked Mr. McLennan.

"Not really," answered James. "I know little about it."

They had finished the deep apple pie with thick cream when the host suggested to Merrie that she take James into the drawing room and show him some of the paintings on the wall.

"I need a few minutes with Captain Channer. We'll join you in a minute or two."

Merrie led James into the drawing room and towards some large oil paintings on the wall. There was one painting particularly that caught James' interest and he moved towards it to have a closer look. It portrayed an Indian chief in a long colourful robe, a long spear, one end firm on the ground held in his right hand, sharp tip pointed skyward, a round shield circled in feathers in his other. Behind him were five of his warriors and behind that a tepee, a grazing horse and a wild sky. James looked at the name plate on the bottom of the frame: "Paul Kane, Big Snake, A Blackfoot Chief Recounting His War Exploits."

"What do you think of it?" asked Merrie

"Intriguing," was James' reply. "It's a view into another world."

Mr. McLennan looked into the drawing room from the hallway.

"I'm sorry to cut the evening short but I have another engagement to go to."

James reached to shake his host's outstretched hand and was surprised to see that it held a calling card.

"Mr. Keyden," he said firmly, "Would you be good enough to drop by my office at nine o'clock tomorrow morning? There is a matter of some urgency I would like to discuss with you."

8

James made his way through the crowded Toronto streets to Mr. McLennan's office. The breeze off the lake was cool but the morning sun warmed him. The Dominion Bank building, with its solid granite façade and imposing columns would not have been out of place on a busy street in Edinburgh.

The man polishing the brass grillwork on the massive front door stepped aside to let James through. The entrance hall was paneled with white marble. There was an elaborate chandelier hanging over a gleaming hardwood floor. James was greeted by a middle-aged gentleman in a morning suit, stiff white collar and black tie. In these surroundings he was conscious again of his tweed jacket over a Shetland sweater.

"May I be of service, sir?" asked the porter.

"I'm here to see Mr. McLennan."

"You have an appointment, sir?"

"He asked to see me at 9 o'clock."

The porter raised his eyebrows at the word 'asked'. "And your name, sir?"

"James Keyden."

"Please wait in here, Mr. Keyden," ushering James to a large, black stuffed chair inside the main banking hall.

The huge room took up most of the building. The ceiling was three storeys high, with narrow windows running the full height up each wall. More chandeliers, this time of cut glass, dominated the ceiling. Around the walls on three sides of the ground level were offices enclosed in rich oak paneling. Along the fourth was a long polished oak counter.

The porter emerged from an office at the far end of the room.

"This way, sir?"

James followed him across the floor and was ushered into a small office where a woman sat in front of one of the new typewriting machines. She wore a severe black dress.

"Please sit down," she said, looking up at James. "Mr. McLennan will see you shortly."

She dropped her head and returned to the machine. James had never seen one before and was fascinated to watch the multitude of arms hammering against the paper as the woman's fingers raced over the keys.

James felt a knot of excitement forming in his stomach. He had regarded the questioning of the captain rather casually but realized now that the probing had led to his sitting where he was. McLennan and Scott were colleagues. Channer must have been working under their instructions. Now, here he sat outside the office of one of the country's leading bankers, where he had certainly never expected to be.

There was the tinkling of a bell from the inner office and Miss Severe Dress was on her feet ushering James towards it. He was not totally surprised to see Captain Channer standing with a smile on his face, back to the windows, while Mr. McLennan rose from his chair behind a massive desk. Mr. McLennan's office was what James expected, dark oak inlaid ceiling and paneling, large bright windows along one wall, three large black chairs arranged around an ornately carved table and portraits in heavy dark wooden frames on two walls. A large wall map hung on the other.

"Good of you to come at such short notice," said Mr. McLennan gesturing towards one of the large chairs. "Of course, you know Captain Channer. Please sit down." The tone in Mr. McLennan's voice was all business.

"There is an assignment that might interest you," said Mr. McLennan, without further pleasantries, his dark eyes drilling into James'. Captain Channer thinks you may be the person we are looking for."

James glanced at the captain and met his smiling eyes.

"Before I tell you what it is let me give you a little background. The dinner engagement, which you so kindly made possible for me to attend after my horse threw a shoe, was with Mister Scott who is the Secretary of State in the cabinet in Ottawa. We are friends of long standing and I did what I could to help him win in the last election. It's the country's good fortune that he and his party did. As I'm sure you are aware we are engaged in this country in the noble task of nation building. Since we became a country less than ten years ago we have made some great strides forward. We have also made our share of mistakes."

James wondered what the mistakes might be but Mr. McLennan did not elaborate.

"The opportunities are immense," the banker went on, "but we are still a fragile, vulnerable collection of old colonial provinces and new territories. The Dominion stretches from the Atlantic to the Pacific but there is a great gap in the middle which is largely unknown to us."

"The Great Plains?" asked James.

"Or as we call it, the North West."

The knot in James' stomach tightened.

"We have yet to tie this country together, but we will – with a railroad. The steel is already reaching towards the west but has not yet crossed the plains. We mean to do that, then push it through the mountains to the Pacific."

James was fascinated at the thought.

"Financing an undertaking of this size is a staggering challenge for a small country like ours," Mr. McLennan continued. "It's far beyond what we can do on our own. We need money from abroad. The North West is a mystery to British investors – in fact it scares them. They're frightened of an Indian uprising. They fear it would scare off settlement which the railway needs to make it pay."

James felt the banker's eyes looking right through him.

"Which brings me to why I've asked you here. Mr. Scott and his government have asked me to raise the money to extend the railway from Winnipeg to the mountains – across a thousand miles of prairie. It's home to millions of buffalo, something like thirty thousand Indians and about the same number of half breeds."

James looked puzzled.

"French speaking half-breeds," Captain Channer added. "They're the offspring of French voyageurs from the fur trade and Indian mothers. There are small settlements of them scattered across the prairies but most of them still move about the same way the Indians do."

"Mr. Scott has just been assigned responsibility for law enforcement in the

North West," Mr. McLennan continued. "You may not know, but two years ago we sent a small force out there called the North West Mounted Police. They have done admirable work but they are a very small group. There are less than three hundred of them. That's one Mountie, as we call them, for every one thousand square miles of prairie. Not much protection if there is a serious uprising."

James nodded in agreement.

"There are two threats in the North West which concern us deeply," the banker went on. "If either one of them materializes it could have very serious consequences for our plans for the railroad and for the country. The first is an Indian uprising. The second is an incursion into our territory by the American military, using the pursuit of renegade American Indians as an excuse to enter and occupy our prairies."

James' eyes were fixed on the banker who rose from his chair and paced the floor. He turned back to James.

"Mr. Scott, Captain Channer and I all agree that what we need, and need urgently, is information on what is really going on out there. The reports Mr. Scott gets deal with police matters – thieving, smuggling and the like. They reach him months after they are written."

James sensed what was coming next and could hardly contain his excitement.

"We need someone in the North West right away to assess the situation with our interests in mind and get back to us quickly, someone with no other priority than to keep us up to date. We need to know what is happening with the Indians. Do they present a threat? What are they thinking? Where are their loyalties? What are the possibilities of an uprising? What is the likelihood of the Americans crossing into our territory? We need to know. Keyden," said Mr. McLennan forcefully. "On Captain Channer's recommendation, I want you to go to the North West and do this job for us."

James' spirits leaped at the thought, but he controlled his enthusiasm and waited as the banker continued.

"Your reports will come directly to me. I will pass them on to Captain Channer who will be sure that Mr. Scott sees them. Although you will be an employee of the Dominion Bank, Mr. Scott has agreed to appoint you to the North West Mounted Police for the duration of this assignment. Captain, anything you would like to add?"

Captain Channer moved to the large map on the office wall and motioned for James to join him.

"This is Fort Macleod," said the captain, placing his finger on the map. "It is sixty miles north of the American border and forty miles east of the Rocky Mountains. It is the center of our concern."

James studied the point on the map and noted the emptiness around it.

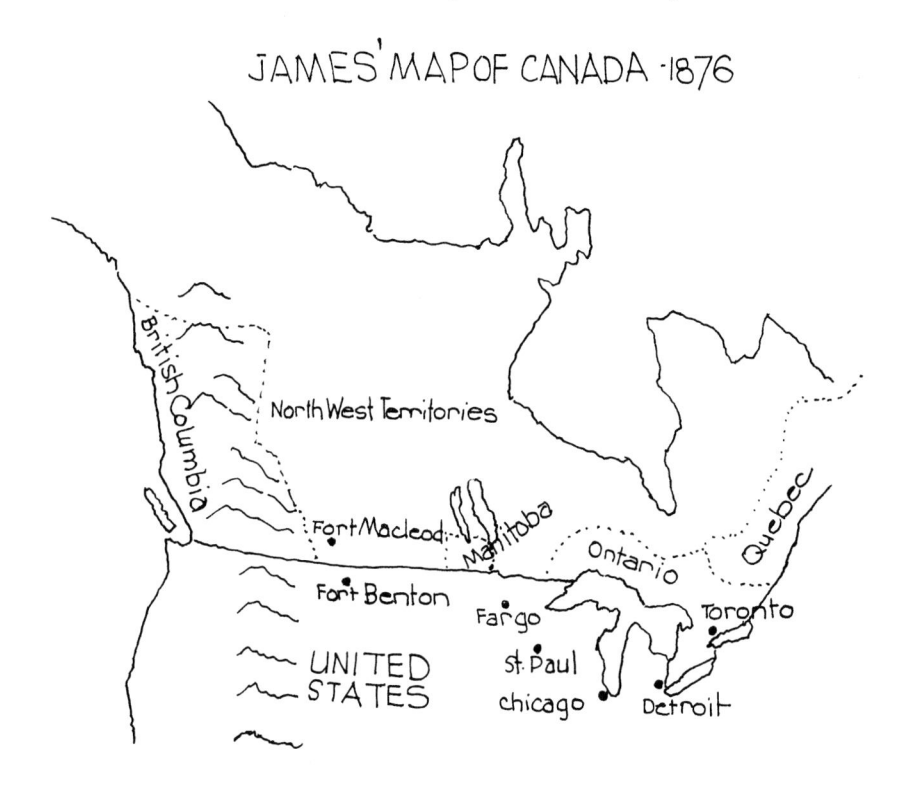

JAMES' MAP OF CANADA - 1876

"You would send your reports through Fort Benton in Montana Territory," the captain went on, moving his finger to a bend on the Missouri River. "It's about a hundred miles south and east of Fort Macleod. It's the closest telegraph and postal service available. Now you understand why we want someone who can ride. It's the fastest way to get around."

"How long would I be out there, sir?" asked James, his heart pounding.

"Twelve, fifteen, eighteen months," replied Mr. McLennan, "until the situation appears stable."

James absorbed the thought of eighteen months in the Canadian west.

"Does it interest you, Keyden?" interrupted the banker.

"Very much sir."

"I realize this has come to you rather suddenly and that you don't know much about the North West. But Captain Channer is available to answer all your questions. He knows about as much as anyone around here what it's like out there. And Keyden," continued Mr. McLennan, "I want someone out there right away. Could I have your answer on Monday? It will give you a few days to talk with Captain Channer and think it over."

It was early Thursday – four days to make up his mind.

"Yes, sir," replied James. "I'll let you know on Monday."

"Then nine o'clock Monday morning here?" confirmed Mr. McLennan.

"That would be fine," answered James.

"I have an office in the armory," added Captain Channer. "I should be back there within an hour."

As they were leaving, Mr. McLennan caught James by the arm.

"You're a fine horseman, James."

First time he's called me James, he thought with surprise.

"For some time," Mr. McLennan went on, "my daughter has been pressing me to allow her to take some instruction to improve her riding. She would like to learn to jump but up to now I've discouraged her from that. As I was leaving this morning she suggested that I might ask you to give her some lessons while you are in our city."

"I'd be happy to do that, sir."

"My daughter was not born on a horse as you were," McLennan went on. "I am not happy to think that she might race across the fields as we saw you do or take anything other than the smallest jumps. But if you can help her gain more confidence in her riding, without endangering her, I'd be grateful. You can use one of my horses."

"Thank you, sir."

9

Merrie was in the outdoor kitchen at the rear of the house with her hands in a large tub of water. The sun was streaming in through the vines that covered the latticed framework that enclosed it. Spring was advancing towards summer. The coolness in the air was quickly giving way to the heat of the sun. She was washing some rectangular glass plates.

She faintly heard the sound of the knocker on the front door but gave it little thought until Clare appeared.

"Mr. Keyden would like a word with you, Merrie," said the housekeeper. "What would you like me to tell him?"

Merrie stood up from the tub, water dripping from her hands. She had expected she might receive a note from James later in the day, but certainly not a visit this early. She was wearing one of her oldest dresses because the chemicals on the glass plates she was cleaning left stains when they splashed on her clothing, just as they had stained her hands and arms now. Strands of hair had fallen over her face.

Merrie had noticed her father handing his card to James the previous evening. She had asked her father about it after the guests had left. He had told her of his meeting with James the following morning. She had risen and dressed earlier than usual to be sure to see her father before he left for his office. She wanted him to ask James to give her some riding lessons. She wasn't at all sure he would pass on the message. But he must have. James was at the front door.

"He said he would only be a minute," added Clare.

Merrie was torn. She wasn't sure she wanted him to see her looking like this.

"Please show him back here, Clare."

Merrie took a cloth and wiped her hands and arms. She tried to push back the hair that had fallen over her face but it wouldn't stay. She tried to smooth her dress but it didn't make any difference.

"Mr. Keyden," Clare announced and left them.

"Good morning, Miss McLennan," said James cheerily. "I'm sorry to have called unannounced but your father said you were anxious to do some riding. I wanted to see when might be a convenient time for you."

He was amused to see Merrie in her working clothes. He hadn't pictured her this way. He found it a marked contrast to her appearance the night before and he smiled at the thought.

Merrie caught the grin.

"Forgive my appearance," she said apologetically, "I wasn't expecting anyone. This is the way I amuse myself."

"What are you doing?" asked James.

"Washing photographic plates," she explained. "I'm really interested in photography. I've started taking pictures and developing them myself."

"That's wonderful," exclaimed James. "I'd like to see some of your prints. I became quite interested in photography while I was at St. Andrews."

"You did?" replied Merrie with interest.

"Yes, we had a very active Photographic Society there. We used to go down to Edinburgh to see some of the exhibitions. I got quite fascinated."

"Did you ever do any printing?" she asked.

"No," replied James. "I've watched others do it but never done it myself."

"Father took me to London last year," Merrie told him. "I visited a number of the galleries and museums. It was the first time I came across the work of Julia Margaret Cameron. I couldn't get over it. It's what made me want to get into photography myself. Do you know her work?"

"Yes," answered James. "I remember seeing her photographs of Tennyson's *Idylls of the King.*"

"It's her portraits that I think are so wonderful," said Merrie. "They're so alive."

"Edinburgh is quite a center of photography," James went on, racking his memory for anything intelligent he could say on the subject. "Do you know the work of Alexander Gardner?"

"Remind me," she said, impressed that James was at least knowledgeable on what was becoming her favorite subject.

"Portraits of Abraham Lincoln. Scenes of the American Civil War."

"When I think of those images I think of Matthew Brady," she replied.

"After Gardner left Edinburgh twenty-five or so years ago he came to America and worked with Brady," continued James pleased that he remembered. "In fact, he ran Brady's studio for years."

"I didn't know that," replied Merrie.

"Gardner followed in the tradition of Hill and Adamson," James went on, hoping to impress Merrie with his knowledge. "They were the real pioneers of photography in Scotland back in the 40's and 50's."

"You know quite a bit about photography," Merrie commented.

"Not really," he replied. "I've never actually made any images like you have. Can I see some of your work?"

"Most of it is in an old cupboard in the stable," she told him. But there is one piece upstairs. Father had it framed and hung it in the hall. But another time."

"Then what about riding?" said James.

"Did my father speak to you this morning?" she asked.

"Yes," said James. "He said you were hounding him for lessons – that you wanted to learn to jump."

"He didn't say 'hounding'," she contradicted with a smile

"You're right," he laughed. "I think he used the word 'pressing'…but he did mention that you wanted to learn to jump."

"He said that?" she said, her voice full of surprise.

"Small jumps," James corrected himself with a smile. "Nothing that would endanger you."

"That sounds more like him," said Merrie. "How was your meeting with him, if I may ask?"

"Interesting, extremely interesting," said James. "Did he tell you what he had in mind?"

"No," she replied. "But I'm interested if you want to tell me."

James began to give Merrie an account of the conversation he had had with her father.

"Just a minute," Merrie interrupted and poked her head into the kitchen.

"Clare, would you please bring two glasses of cider to the back porch along with some of your good oatmeal cakes? We might as well be comfortable," she added to James.

They settled into two straight-backed wooden chairs on the back porch. Clare brought the cider and cakes. James continued with the story of their meeting and was glad for the chance to do it. It helped him recall the details and sort out his own thinking. He was impressed with Merrie's interest in what he was saying and her comments. She knew of the North West Mounted Police. She had watched them parade to Union Station two summers before when they had boarded the train west. She thought they looked marvelous in their scarlet tunics but she thought the pillbox forage caps were a little ridiculous. Their horses were wonderful, she told him, each division outfitted with ones of a different colour. She had heard her father speak of Colonel French but not in very complimentary terms. In fact, he thought there was a strong possibility that he might be reassigned.

She knew a great deal about the railroad, which she must have picked up from her father. She knew the names of the financiers and she knew how desperately in need the government was for the money to continue building it. She told James the story of the scandal surrounding the railroad's financing that had led to the defeat of the Macdonald government and the election of Alexander Mackenzie, much to her father's delight.

"Father wants you to make up your mind by Monday?" Merrie asked.

"We're already scheduled to meet at nine o'clock."

"What will you say to him?"

"I like almost everything about it," he answered.

"What don't you like?"

"It has all happened so suddenly," replied James. "I'm trying to get used to the idea of a year or more out in the North West."

"When are you going to see Captain Channer?" she asked.

"As soon as I leave here."

"Then riding is out for today," she said. "Do you have any plans for tomorrow?"

"None," James answered. "Would you like to ride tomorrow afternoon?"

"Let's," she replied enthusiastically. "How about two o'clock?"

"Fine with me."

"I look forward to it," she replied

"So do I.

10

JAMES FOUND CAPTAIN CHANNER IN the cavernous, ugly armory just north of the center of the city. It was a large Victorian structure of red sandstone that looked completely out of place among the stately houses surrounding it. The captain had a spartan office stuck off in a corner of the drill hall.

"It will probably be most helpful if I start by telling you about our tour through the North West last summer," the captain began. "After I got back from two years with the Boundary Commission, I was assigned to travel with General Smith, chief of our militia, on an inspection tour of the entire area from Fort Garry to the Rocky Mountains. Until you see the prairie, it's hard to imagine. I grew up in Nova Scotia and the prairie reminded me of the ocean. In parts it's as flat as a calm sea. In other parts it's rolling like an Atlantic swell. When the wind sweeps across the plains the grass sways in waves. It's like standing on the shore and watching the surf. On the prairies like on the ocean, there are no trees."

"No trees?" questioned James.

"There are some in the coulees," said Channer.

"Coulees?"

"River valleys, sometimes a mile across and several hundred feet deep with rivers winding through them. Trees grow along the riverbanks. But up on the plains – none at all."

James was familiar with some treeless highland areas, but he found it hard to imagine vast plains without a single tree.

"The North West is nature magnified," the captain continued. "You've never seen so much sky or such sunsets. It's bone dry for weeks with the dust sticking in your throat. Then there's a lightning storm that crashes around you for hours. It lights up the prairie for miles and soaks you to the skin. For a short time the rain comes down in torrents. It turns the parched prairie soil into mud so thick horses can't pull a wagon through it. The next day every sign of the rain has disappeared and you're back to breathing choking dust. In winter there are snow drifts over the tops of tepees and cold that freezes your face in a minute."

"Tepees?" asked James

"Indian lodges," explained Channer. "Round and come to a point at the top. They're made of long poles with buffalo hides stretched over them."

"I've seen them in pictures," remembered James.

"The vastness is hard to imagine," continued the captain. "Let me show you."

Channer walked to the map hanging on the wall.

"This is the area we're talking about," he said, placing his finger on the map and tracing the territory with his finger. "From Fort Garry here," jabbing the spot on the map with his finger, "to the Rockies over here." Another jab. "That's a thousand miles, east to west."

The captain ran his finger across the 49th parallel of latitude on the map.

"This is our border with the United States that the Boundary Commission marked," he went on. "From it to the North Saskatchewan River," he said tracing the river, "is three hundred miles south to north." James took a closer look at the map to follow the course of the river.

"Until seven years ago," continued the Captain, "this whole area was owned by the Hudson's Bay Company. For more than 200 years they traded with the Indians for furs and robes. They traveled up and down the rivers but they never got into the southwest corner.

"Why was that?" asked James

"Not many beaver for one reason; Blackfoot Indians for the other. The Americans call their Sioux the 'Tigers of the Plains', but the Blackfoot are every bit as fierce. They've fought the traders and explorers from the moment they first showed their white faces."

"No settlers?" asked James.

"None. Add a handful of missionaries and that's it," continued the captain. "There was no law and order until two years ago when the North West Mounted Police arrived."

"The Mounties," said James.

"The Mounties," repeated the captain.

"And before that?" asked James.

"Roaming bands of buffalo hunters, wolfers and whiskey traders from the American side – a wild bunch – disappointed gold seekers, renegades from justice, deserters from the Civil War and opportunists of all kinds."

"Wolfers?" questioned James.

"Hunters for wolf pelts. They're a valuable commodity in the American East. Hunters sprinkled strychnine on the carcasses of dead buffalo after they took their hides. The wolves ate the tainted buffalo meat and died. The hunters skinned them for their pelts. Tens of thousands of buffalo hides and thousands of wolf pelts are shipped down the Missouri from Fort Benton every year."

"Are the wolfers still operating?" asked James.

"Not many wolves left," explained Channer.

"What about the whiskey traders?"

"They're worse than the hunters," answered the captain. "Both the Hudson's Bay Company and the American government outlawed the sale of liquor to the Indians in the 30's. But that didn't stop the whiskey traders from operating in the North West. They brought it into Canada from Fort Benton and set up a chain of whiskey trading forts just inside our border."

"Trade for what?"

"Hides, pelts, horses, Indian women," explained Channer. "Whiskey is devastating for them. Some Indians will do anything for whiskey. It makes them crazy. When they're drunk they attack each other and shoot their own wives and children. There has been any number of killings and burnings. The truth is that between whiskey and small pox, in the last ten years, over half the Indian population has been wiped out."

"You can't be serious," said James.

"If it weren't for the Mounties putting a stop to the whiskey trade the Indians would be well on their way to extinction by now."

"If the Mounties have done away with the whiskey trade what's the problem now?" asked James.

"The Indians are nomadic, their whole existence depends on the buffalo. They follow the herds wherever they go. So do most of the Metis – the half French half Indian people. But the buffalo are disappearing fast and, understandably, the Indians are feeling threatened. Besides the vanishing buffalo, the Indians see more and more whites appearing. And we're confining the Indians onto small patches of land we call reserves," he went on. "They aren't too keen on this and you can't blame them, after centuries of moving across the plains whenever and wherever they pleased. The government wants them all on reserves in the next few years."

"And the Metis?"

"Politicians won't admit it but the government badly misjudged the Metis when it took over the North West from the Hudson's Bay Company."

"How was that?"

"There has been a settlement of your Scottish countrymen in the Red River Valley for over sixty years. Lord Selkirk brought a number of families over after they were forced out of their homes during the Clearances. Their Red River settlement grew to include hundreds of Metis families who had been living there for years."

"French-speaking," added James.

"And Catholic. When Canada took over the territory no one bothered to tell the people of the Red River what was going to happen to them and their land. The first that they knew was seeing government surveyors running lines right through their farms. Of course they felt threatened and still no one bothered to tell them what was going on. So they took matters into their own hands and established a provisional government. They passed their own laws and established their own justice system. Things got a little out of hand and unfortunately on one occasion they executed a man, who happened to be an Orangeman."

"Protestant," added James.

"Yes. This infuriated the English in Eastern Canada. Ottawa ordered Colonel Wolseley and the army to the Red River to put down this so-called rebellion. By the time the colonel got there, the Metis had moved hundreds of miles northwest to the valley of the North Saskatchewan and that was the end of that."

"They resettled?" asked James.

"Some did, but I don't think they'll ever forgive us Easterners for forcing them off their Red River land," said the captain. "They live very much to themselves. They have much more sympathy for the Indians than they do for us in this part of the country. They don't even relate any more to the French speaking people in Quebec."

"But they don't cause any trouble?" inquired James.

"Not at the moment," answered the captain. "But we have a more serious concern."

"What's that?" asked James.

"The Americans," answered Channer.

"In what way," asked James.

"We signed a treaty with them in '62, formally recognizing our common border. We thought that would end any threat of them moving into Canada, but there are still Congressmen, especially in border states like Minnesota, agitating for their cavalry to just keep traveling north and take our prairies. They've got settlers filling up their west and the pressures on to take some of our land."

"What about American Indians?" asked James. "Are they setting up reserved land for them the same way we are?"

"Just the same," answered the Captain. "They call theirs agencies or reservations. Some Indians have moved onto them and some haven't. Those that have they call 'friendlies'. Those that haven't they call 'hostiles.'"

"Hostiles?" asked James.

"The American cavalry and the Sioux had been fighting for years," explained Channer. "Finally they signed the Treaty of Laramie in 1868. It guaranteed the Sioux all of the Dakota Territory west of the Missouri. The Sioux were pleased because it included the Black Hills which is one of their most sacred landmarks."

"And?" asked James.

"Three years ago someone struck gold in the Black Hills. All of a sudden they were swarming with gold seekers from the East."

"But it is Sioux land," said James.

"It was supposed to be Sioux land," replied Channer. "The army had promised to keep the white man out but they didn't try very hard. They made some half-hearted attempts but they couldn't stop the hordes of gold-crazy miners."

"So?"

"The American government offered to buy the Black Hills from the Sioux but they wouldn't sell. So the government withheld the rations they had promised to the Sioux as part of a tactic to force them. When that didn't work they sent in the cavalry and ran them out."

"Just ran them out?" asked James incredulously.

"They sent in a flamboyant Indian fighter called General Custer with his cavalry and he forced them further west out of the Black Hills."

"And the Sioux?" asked James.

"They're back at war with the Americans," answered the captain.

"And they're still at it?" asked James.

"They've been at it for three years now but the American government is losing its patience. Last December they sent runners out to all the hostile tribes like the Sioux and the Cheyenne. They warned them that if they didn't get back to their reservations by the end of January they would be attacked and forced onto reservations."

"What's happened?" asked James.

"They refused."

"And?" asked James.

"The word we have is that the American military is planning a major offensive. They're going to turn their cavalry loose on them."

"And drive them back to their reservations," added James.

"Or wipe them out," replied the Captain.

"You mean kill them?" asked James.

"If they have to," answered the captain. "But there's another possibility that really worries us."

"What's that?" asked James.

"Indians don't stand and fight like we do. They're too smart and too mobile to do that on the open prairie against superior forces and weapons. They hit and disappear in small groups. Often in the past when the Sioux have been under pressure they have escaped north over our border, the Medicine Line, as they call it. The Indians know that if they can escape into British territory they are beyond the reach of the American cavalry."

"Is that true?" asked James.

"It has been up to now," replied the captain. "We think the American commanders are mad enough and determined enough this time that if the Sioux flee into Canada, as they have in the past, they'll order their field commanders to disregard the border and chase the Sioux wherever they go until they capture or kill them."

"Will we let them?" asked James.

"Can we stop them?" replied the captain. "With a few hundred Mounties? Not a chance."

"What about the Canadian Indians?" James went on.

"That's another thing that scares us. If the Blackfoot join the Sioux we are in really serious trouble. The Blackfoot alone, if they chose to, could wipe out every Mountie in an afternoon. Combined with the Sioux, they could control the whole North West. It would take us months to get a strong military force out there and we'd have to move it through American territory to get it there quickly. Our railway is still a year at least from reaching the Red River and the Blackfoot are a thousand miles beyond that."

"Would a military force from here be able to deal with the situation?" asked James.

"Probably not," said the captain. "We'd need a large cavalry force and we don't have one in this country. We'd probably have to ask the American cavalry in to help us and nobody in our government would consider doing that."

The captain stood back from the map. James fell silent as he absorbed what he was hearing. Both men were staring at the map but their thoughts were in the North West.

11

As he walked back to his sister's place, James ran through his mind the new words he had learned: Sioux, Blackfoot, tepee, prairie, coulee, Metis, Red River, Saskatchewan. He recalled what he could from his growing up about Indians and the wild west – illustrations of missionaries tied to stakes being tortured by a circle of screaming Indians, their bodies painted with streaks of colour. Indians on ponies, more painted bodies, chasing each other with upraised tomahawks trying to bash each other's heads in.

As James closed the front door behind him young William raced down the hall and jumped on his back. He threw James' hat on the floor and grabbed a handful of his hair.

"Ahhhh," he screamed. "I'm an Indian and I'm going to scalp you."

Later that evening James took the opportunity to talk to Arthur about the assignment in the west. Arthur was more of a mind that the future of the country lay in the east and although a railroad to the Pacific was important, he thought it would be years before it became a reality. To Arthur, the most important development for the country was the expansion of the rail lines in the East, supporting settlement throughout Ontario and with it the growth of agriculture and industry. There were a number of risks in going west, he thought, particularly at this time with the unrest among the Indians, but he wasn't against the idea of James going at all. In fact, he sounded almost envious.

"If you plan to settle in this country," he counselled James, "you should find a position with one of the railway companies or the banks that are financing them. Mr. McLennan, I'm sure would help you with that."

"Mr. McLennan wants me in the North West," answered James.

"Then by all means take him up on it," said Arthur. "Who knows what he might offer you after that."

James passed the time waiting to call on Merrie by taking a long walk along the lakeshore. On the east side of the city he found a beach where a few families with their children were playing in the sand and splashing with their toes in the shallow edge of the still cold water of the lake. He found a place where he could sit leaning against the seawall and still be in the warmth of the sun.

There were a number of sailboats crossing in front of him. He noticed one particularly that was making its way into the wind, tacking to port, tacking to starboard, tacking to port. It was a little like the direction of his life. Perth Academy had been the natural next step after the Free Church School. St. Andrews had more of the courses that interested him than Edinburgh did so it was an easy decision to go there.

But what next? He was clear that he did not want to join the Scots Greys or any other regiment. When he had the idea of visiting his sister in Canada He seemed a convenient way to avoid making a career choice. But he hadn't considered very deeply what he might do when he got here.

The sailboat tacked to starboard.

Accepting Mr. McLennan's offer meant committing to staying in Canada for over a year. He could accept that. Going west – it was a very exciting prospect. There was no question. He would accept the offer.

The sailboat tacked to port.

12

MERRIE WAS TALKING WITH MORGAN in the courtyard between the house and the stable when James walked up the driveway. She was holding the reins to Rob Roy and Morgan to Ben, the horse that had thrown the shoe and which James had escorted on their long walk back to town together.

"Good afternoon," said James, "isn't that your father's horse?"

"Yes, it is – and with new shoes. Father asked Morgan to saddle it up for you. He needs exercise."

They rode up University Avenue and into the rolling countryside on the north edge of the city. They walked and cantered, trotted and galloped in intervals. James was relieved to see that Merrie was comfortable in the saddle even if a little stiff and a touch fearful.

James noticed a flat farmer's field where the grass was low. In the distance were a few bushes and trees surrounding a large pond. Across the field were a series of low stone walls.

"Let's go in here," suggested James. "This looks like as good a spot as any. Ready to give it a try?"

"I've been wanting to do this for a long time," she replied eagerly.

James got off his horse and asked Merrie to do the same. He handed his rein to her and took Rob Roy.

"Let's see what he can do," he said as he swung up onto her horse. He walked Rob Roy slowly for a few steps, then ran him towards the stone wall. It wasn't a thing of beauty but Rob Roy was over without much trouble. He had done it before but not for a long time. James took him back and forth a few more times until Rob Roy felt comfortable in the rhythm of the jump.

"Your turn," he said, handing Rob Roy back to Merrie. James explained the shifts in balance as the horse took the jump – the weight in the stirrups, lean forward on takeoff, lean back on recovery. "Rob Roy knows how to jump. You just have to go along for the ride," he said with a grin. "I'll go first."

They walked to a position a little distance from the wall. James knew she was anxious about the first jump but she didn't say a word. He ran Ben towards the wall and over. Ben was comfortable. It wasn't much of a challenge for him. Now Merrie. He turned to coax her on and found that she was already heading for the wall. He watched her go over. She was sitting up a little too straight as the horse leaped but she leaned forward in mid air and her face almost touched the horse's neck as it touched ground – but she was still on.

"Yeah!" she yelled as she reined in and drew up beside James.

James gave her a few more pointers and led her several times over the wall. Her second time was not much better than the first but after that she improved steadily. When James finally suggested that they had had enough she didn't want to stop.

"You may not be tired but the horses are," he said stretching the truth a little. He wanted her to stop at the height of her excitement and not get to a point of fatigue where she might fall off. "Let's give them a rest down by those trees."

They tied the horses to branches near the large pond and found a grassy slope beside it with a fallen tree trunk for a bench.

"That was fantastic," she exclaimed. "I love doing that. I'm not sure father would be particularly pleased but my mother certainly would have been."

"Your mother?" asked James.

"Even though my mother was an invalid all the time I knew her," said Merrie, "I remember her as an amazing woman."

"You remember a lot about her?" asked James.

"She was always encouraging me to do new things," Merrie continued as they looked out over the pond. "She was an artist. Before I was born she had been a really talented oil painter, although she didn't do much after she got sick. She always kept a sketch pad beside her bed and pencils and chalks and sticks of charcoal. When she had the strength she would sketch what she saw around the room, and she would try to get me to sit still long enough to sketch me."

"I can't imagine you a fidgety girl?" said James sarcastically.

"I was a very fidgety girl," replied Merrie. "When I got restless she would give me a pencil and paper and say, 'Merrie, you sit by the window and I'll sketch you and you sketch what you see out the window'. And I would. I would finish before her and she'd say, 'Show me, Merrie, Show me.' And she'd always say, 'That's marvelous, really marvelous.' Then, 'Here, Merrie, take these chalks and give it a little colour.' And I would. And again she'd say, 'That's marvelous. That's really marvelous.'"

Merrie picked at the grass beside her as she remembered the moments.

"When I was tired of sketching," Merrie continued, "she'd have me fetch a book and we would read together for hours. And she'd say, 'Merrie, what did you do exciting today? Did you help Clare bake? Did you ride in the carriage? Did you go with Father to the office? Is he going to take you to Montreal next week? Merrie, be sure to ask him to take you to Montreal next week."

Merrie pulled the strands of grass from her hand and let them fall beside her. James watched her sympathetically.

"I came home from somewhere one afternoon," Merrie went on. "It was the end of winter and most of the snow was gone. When I walked in the house I saw my father and two or three other men talking in the hall. When my father saw me he came to me and scooped me up in his arms. He didn't do that often. He carried me into the drawing room and whispered, 'Your mother's very ill.' I said,

'Can I see her?' He said, For a moment.' He carried me up the stairs and into her room and let me down beside her bed. She was sleeping. I ran my finger across her cheek but she didn't move. Father picked me up again and said, 'Say good-night to your mother.' 'But it isn't dinner time yet,' I answered. He said, 'Just say good-night to your mother,' and when I looked at him there were tears in his eyes. It is the only time I ever saw my father cry."

James reached over and touched her on her arm, but said nothing.

"She died that night," said Merrie, her voice breaking slightly. "Next morning my uncle and aunt took me to their place in the country. We'd been there several times and I loved the place – still do. They have seven children, two about my age and we played in the barns and with the animals and they never once mentioned my mother."

Merrie paused. Some birds flew by in front of them and she watched them until they were out of sight.

"Then, just as suddenly, I was taken home," she continued. "Clare was there to cook and look after me and I started school. I missed my mother terribly but I was soon caught up in other things. I was quite young and I guess it didn't affect me then as deeply as it did my father."

Merrie was silent again.

"I don't think he has ever recovered from it," she said quietly. "Sometimes I go into the drawing room in the evening and he's sitting in his favourite chair, feet up towards the fire, staring at the flames. I know he is thinking about her."

They watched some ducks swimming along the far side of the pond. There were several of them dodging in and out among the reeds including a mother and her several ducklings.

"James, you're a great listener," she said looking at him. "Forgive me. I don't have anyone I can really talk to and it all just came spilling out."

James saw that she was near tears. "Talk all you like," he said.

They watched the ducks bob up and down, swim into the rushes and disappear.

"Have you made up your mind about going to the North West?" asked Merrie.

"Yes, I'm going to go," he said firmly

"James, that's great," she exclaimed. "What an opportunity. I think it must be destiny that brought you to this country. You do believe in destiny, don't you?"

"I've definitely been spared for some reason," he replied.

"Spared?" she said. "What do you mean, spared for some reason?"

She had been open with him and although he didn't like talking about himself he carried on.

"You were six when your mother died," he began. "I should have been killed when I was about the same age."

Merrie looked over at him. "What do you mean?" she asked.

"When I was about seven," James began, "I was playing at the far end of our fields. They bordered on a stream that flowed for a few miles before emptying into the river Earn. My friend Ginna was with me."

"Who's Ginna?" Merrie asked.

"Ginna was the daughter of the woman who worked for us. They lived in a small apartment attached to the stables behind the house. She was a year older than I was."

"What happened?" Merrie asked.

"It was a warm evening in spring," James began, "and the water in the stream was higher than usual. It was flowing quite swiftly. There was a rowboat tied to a post on the bank that the local people used to cross the stream when it was too deep to wade, as it was then. Someone had used it recently and the knot in the ring on the post was not tied too tightly. I climbed into the boat and began slapping at some bugs swimming on the surface of the water with a stick. Ginna climbed in the boat with me and we were laughing as we splashed. We kept splashing and laughing until I looked up and saw the shore drifting by us."

"What then?" asked Merrie.

"I thought it was kind of fun," continued James. "I said to Ginna something like, 'Don't worry, we can paddle to shore anytime we want to.' Anyway, we drifted down the stream, through the neighbours' fields, past the ruins of an old castle, under the arched stone bridge carrying the road into our village."

James paused to recall some of the details he hadn't thought of for some time.

"I looked back at the bridge," James went on, "and I remember I was looking right into the sun which was just touching the trees. There was a man on a bicycle who had stopped to watch us on the bridge. The sun was almost directly behind him and I couldn't make out who he was. I remember him yelling, 'You best be getting off that stream and heading home children,' and I recognized the voice of one of the men who worked for our neighbours. 'Okay, Mr. Young,' I said. Then I said to Ginna, 'Let's paddle to shore.'"

Merrie was caught up in the story and looked at James. He was staring across the pond, his eyes lost in the past.

"I stuck my stick which must have been about an inch thick into the water and started paddling for shore. Of course, it didn't do a thing. 'Use your hands, Ginna', I suggested and paddle same as me.'"

"We stroked together," he went on, "two hands slapping the water on the right side of the boat, which paid no attention whatever and kept drifting down the center of the stream, sometimes bow first, sometimes sideways. The stream began to widen and the sun fell behind the trees and still we paddled, getting more frantic by the minute."

"What did you do?" asked Merrie.

"'Maybe we should swim,' Ginna suggested and I said 'No, it's too cold.' I looked ahead and saw that the stream was just about to join the River Earn. The banks were getting farther apart and the current stronger. And it was almost dark."

"What happened then?" asked Merrie, aware that he could remember every detail of the story. 'He must have played it over and over in his mind a hundred times', she thought.

"Ginna was just about to jump over the side and swim for the nearest bank," James went on. "The current of the stream had pushed us quite close to the left bank of the river and there was an old road running alongside. Ginna was a much better swimmer than me and in truth the thought of jumping in frightened me. So I said, 'No, Ginna, the current's too fast. Let's try to grab a branch, or something, or maybe we can steer towards shore.' I moved to the back of the boat and put my stick in the water behind the stern, like a rudder, but it made no difference."

James paused again to recall what happened next.

"We floated like this for some time until night fell and we were alone with the rush of the water. If there were branches sticking out into the river we'd never see then. We could hardly see the water ahead of us. Then I heard the sound of horses galloping hard down the road beside us and as they got nearer the sound of someone calling my name. It was my father.

"I yelled with everything in me," James continued. "He heard me and shouted back, 'Is Ginna with you?' and I yelled 'Yes, we're here. Over here.' 'Keep to the other side of the river,' he yelled back. 'Paddle with your hands, hard. Move the boat to the other side.' 'But we want to get near you,' I yelled back. 'No, no, move the boat to the other side. Do it now, use your hands and paddle hard.'"

James' voice grew softer.

"It was so dark we could hardly see each other," he continued. "Father yelled out, 'Where are you?' 'We're here,' I yelled. 'You need to be further over. Paddle harder.' At that moment we hit something solid in the middle of the river. I bounced from my seat near the back of the boat, falling over Ginna who was also thrown to the floor. The boat had been turned around and was gathering speed moving stern first. We tried to sit up. Then we jerked to a stop, which sent us sprawling again to the bottom of the boat with the water rushing past us. The side of the boat was banging against whatever it was that we had hit.

"I heard my father calling but I was too terrified to even yell," said James. "Finally I screamed, or cried or something, 'We're here, we're stuck on something.' Then for the first time I was aware of the sound of rushing water and a great grinding noise ahead of us. Ginna heard it too and I felt her hand grab my foot and then both her hands tight around my ankle. I reached down and grabbed her wrists. The boat was shaking in the current and crashing against the stone wall beside us."

"James, what did you do?" asked Merrie.

"I looked down the river towards the grinding noise and saw three lanterns moving slowly toward us. They looked like they were moving up the middle of the river. I pointed them out to Ginna. She turned her head but she wouldn't let go of my ankle. They got closer and closer.

"I saw by the light of the lanterns three men hurrying towards us and one was my father. They were on a narrow pier that stuck out into the river directing part of its flow towards that terrifying noise ahead of us.

"The two men with my father had long poles with hooks on the ends," said James, with a haunting look in his eyes. "They put their lanterns on the pier and one hooked the ring in the front where the rope was tied and the other grabbed the stern. The rope was stretched tight, the end away from the boat disappearing under the water. It had caught on something, swung the boat around stern first and held us there. The men held the boat firm alongside the pier where my father was on his knees. He grabbed my arm and began to lift me out but Ginna wouldn't let go of my ankle. One of the other men grabbed Ginna's wrist, and we were lifted from the boat."

James paused, reliving the relief he had felt at the time.

"I threw my arms around my father's neck," James recalled. "I must have almost strangled him. He knelt there with one arm around me and one around Ginna for a long time not saying a word. I remember as if it were yesterday, one of the men saying to the other, 'It was providence what saved them. The last person that went over that millwheel was a sorry sight.'"

The ducks had reappeared on the far side of the pond. James watched them swim among the reeds.

"So that was it," James said, looking back at Merrie. "Our lives were spared by a six foot piece of rope that got snagged on an old stone pier in the middle of a flooded river."

Merrie was thoughtful. "Whatever happened to Ginna?"

James paused, reflectively. Now was not the time, he thought, to get into that tragic story.

"That's a story for another day," he told her.

"And yes," he continued, "to answer your question. I do believe in destiny or fate or whatever it is."

13

The meeting Monday morning in Mr. McLennan's office was short and to the point. The porter in the black morning suit was in his regular place as James entered the bank. Miss Rossiter, the lady in the severe black dress, directed James into the inner office before he had a chance to sit down. Captain Channer was there again as he expected.

"Good morning, Mr. Keyden, and what is it to be?" said Mr. McLennan before James had a chance to shake his outstretched hand.

"I accept your offer," said James firmly, "and I appreciate the opportunity."

"Fine, fine," replied Mr. McLennan shaking his hand warmly. "We were sure you would."

They had anticipated James' acceptance. Without hesitation, the captain spelled out the details. Mr. Scott would write a letter introducing James to Lieutenant-Colonel James F. Macleod, Assistant Commissioner of the North West Mounted Police and the senior officer of the Force in the west. Mr. Scott would be sure that Colonel Macleod fully understood James' role. The captain would spend the next few days providing James with as much background information as he could absorb and outfit James in the uniform and equipment of a Mountie constable.

"We want you in uniform for this assignment," said Mr. McLennan. "It will give you some authority and respect. We can't have you looking like just another fortune seeker on your way west."

James was to be ready to leave by the end of the week.

"That's four days!" thought James, shocked by the suddenness of his departure.

"There's a train leaving Friday morning for Windsor," the captain told him. "You cross the border at Detroit and go on to Chicago. There you will catch a train to Fargo then on to Bismarck in Dakota Territory. From there we would like you to travel by fast stage rather than slower steamboat up the Missouri River to Fort Benton. We'll telegraph for someone to meet you there and take you to Fort Macleod. We want you on the scene as soon as possible."

James' mind was racing to keep up with the captain's instructions.

"You will have to pick up a few things in Fort Benton," Mr. McLennan continued, "a horse for one. We will work out the arrangements for payment and let you know what they are later in the week."

"Anything else, Captain?" asked the banker.

"Not at the moment, sir. I suggest Mr. Keyden meet me at the armory in an hour and we can begin the briefing."

"All right with you, Keyden?" asked the banker.

"Yes, sir," replied James, dazzled by the speed of events.

The banker turned towards the door and James knew that the meeting was over.

"Mr. Keyden," said the banker, as he shook hands with James, "I'm pleased that you have accepted the assignment. If you carry out your duties satisfactorily, as I am sure you will, it will be the first of many opportunities for you in this country."

14

"You're a lucky man," Captain Channer said to James when he walked into his office "It's an exciting time to be going to the North West. What happens out there in the next few months will be very important for the future of the country. I offered to take the job myself but, unfortunately, Mr. Scott wants me with him in Ottawa."

They discussed the best way, over the next four days, for James to learn as much as he could about the North West. The captain suggested that it would be useful to cover the history and the geography of the American as well as the Canadian west, and James agreed. The captain had already gathered several books, articles and maps which were sitting on his desk.

"Start with these," he suggested, selecting some of the material. "It's all useful background. It will give you a good idea of what you're getting yourself into. Take them home and bring them back when you're finished. After that we'll start on the maps."

James took the large pile of books, reports, clippings and files under his arm and walked back to Fiona's.

"What in the world are all those?" asked Fiona as he walked in the door.

"My reading material for today," he grinned.

James placed the pile of documents on the dining room table near the window and began going through them. He lay them out in the order of their publication dates. Fiona watched as he read some of the titles:

"Journals, Detailed Reports and Observations Relative to the Exploration of British North America," John Palliser, 1859.

"Narrative of the Canadian Red River Exploring Expedition of 1857 and of the Assiniboine and Saskatchewan Exploring Expedition of 1858", Henry Youle Hind, 1860.

"North West British America and Its Relations to the State of Minnesota", James W. Taylor, 1860.

"The Confederation of the British North American Provinces; Their Past History and Future Prospects, Including Also British Columbia and Hudson's Bay Territory", Wedd Rawlings, 1865.

"The North-West Passage by Land; Being the Narrative of an Expedition from the Atlantic to the Pacific", Viscount Milton and W. B. Cheadle, 1867.

"Ocean to Ocean: Sandford Fleming's Expedition through Canada in 1872", George M. Grant, 1873.

"The Wild North Land: Being the Story of a Winter Journey, with Dogs, Across Northern North America", William F. Butler, 1873.

"Saskatchewan and the Rocky Mountains", Earl of Southesk, Edinburgh, 1875.

The last report caught his attention. It was published in Edinburgh and was the most recent. He sat down at the table and began reading. It wasn't long before he was completely engrossed. He continued reading through lunch and the afternoon. Over dinner with the family he told them some of what he had learned. Even the children listened in rapt silence.

"I can't get over how few people there are in that huge area," James commented.

"Most of us from Europe have the same reaction," answered Arthur.

"Is it really as cold in winter as it sounds?" James asked

"If it's anything like it is here, every bit as cold as they say. It's colder than Aberdeen in May with a sharp wind off the North Sea," Fiona added with a grin.

"Will you be fighting Indians?" asked young William.

"I'm sure I'll be seeing them," answered James.

"Will you be living in a tepee, Uncle James?" asked Hermione.

"I'd like to if I get the chance," he replied with a thrill running through him. The idea had never crossed his mind before her question.

After the children were tucked into bed James sat by the fire with Fiona and Arthur.

"Has your captain mentioned Colonel Macleod?" asked Arthur.

"I'm to report to him when I get out there."

"Did you know he graduated from this school?" asked Arthur.

"Really?"

"It was a few years ago," Arthur continued. "From what I've heard he was an outstanding student. There is a teacher here, Mr. Wedd, who I'm sure would remember him. Perhaps we should invite him to dinner so that he can tell you about him."

"I would be interested in that."

James read well into the night and was at it again early in the morning. He finished in the early afternoon, gathered up the documents and headed back to the armory.

"Well, what do you think?" asked the captain as James laid the pile on his desk.

"Breathtaking," said James with enthusiasm. "The more I read the more excited I am."

"Wait 'til you get out there," replied the captain with envy in his voice. There were a number of maps and charts of various sizes laid out on his desk.

"There's an empty office down the hall that you can use," said the captain. "Take these down there where you can spread them out. But let me show you something first." He motioned James to the wall map.

"It's a clear stretch from here," said the captain, putting his finger on Fort Garry, "to here," moving his finger north to south down the Rocky Mountain chain. "If the earth were flat you could climb a tree beside the Red River and see the Rocky Mountains with only a few bumps in between. It may help you get your bearings on the whole area if you start with the rivers."

The captain placed his finger on the source of a river near the mountains and traced it to Hudson's Bay. Then he traced another and another. James missed the names.

"I'd better spend some time with these maps," James said walking back to the desk. He gathered them up and followed the captain down the hall to the empty office. He laid the maps on the desk and settled in.

"Is there something I could write on?" he asked the captain as he left the office.

The captain returned with a writing pad and James started in. He took the captain's advice and began defining the vast North West by the river systems. Starting in the north, he traced the North Saskatchewan, rising in the Rockies west of Rocky Mountain House, past Fort Edmonton, Fort Saskatchewan, Fort Pitt, a long stretch to Fort Carlton and northeast to the top of Lake Winnipeg and on to Hudson's Bay. Moving south he ran his finger along the South

Saskatchewan, starting in the mountains as the Old Man's River, soon joined by the Belly and the St. Mary's Rivers, swinging northeast to join the main South Saskatchewan near Chesterfield House and continuing a long sweep to just east of Fort Carlton where it joined with the North Saskatchewan. Then there was the Qu'Appelle River, rising in the heart of the plains and flowing due east to Fort Ellice where it joined the Assiniboine River which then went on to join the Red at Fort Garry on its long run to Hudson's Bay.

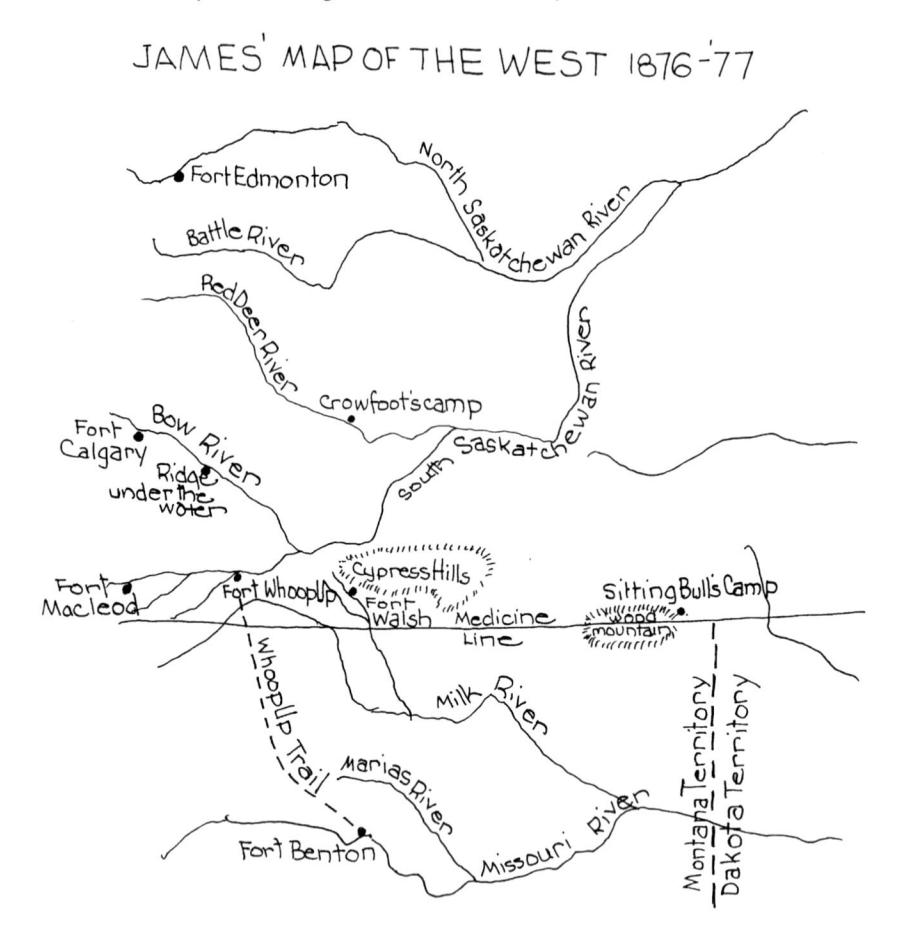

JAMES' MAP OF THE WEST 1876-77

Hand-drawn map showing: Fort Edmonton, North Saskatchewan River, Battle River, Red Deer River, Bow River, Fort Calgary, Ridge under the water, Fort Macleod, Fort Whoop Up, Crowfoot's camp, South Saskatchewan River, Cypress Hills, Fort Walsh, Medicine Line, Sitting Bull's Camp, Wood mountain, Whoop Up Trail, Milk River, Marias River, Fort Benton, Missouri River, Montana Territory, Dakota Territory.

James took a piece of paper and drew a line down the middle, north to south, and a line across the middle, east to west, representing the border between Canada and the United States. He labeled the upper left quadrant, "North West

Territories", upper right, "Manitoba", lower left, "Montana Territory", lower right, "Dakota Territory".

"Now for the rivers," he said to himself.

Putting the maps aside he drew, as best he could remember, the rivers running west to east across the Canadian plains. He checked what he had done against the maps.

"Not bad for a first effort," he thought checking where he had made mistakes.

He took another piece of paper and went through the same exercise again. More satisfied this time, he moved to the river systems south of the border. He picked up the Missouri far south of Winnipeg and followed it north and west. He was amazed at its length.

"This river drains the entire American North West," he thought in amazement, tracing again its full length.

James followed the Missouri from its various sources near the Rocky Mountains. There were the Jefferson, Madison and Gallatin Rivers, which started far to the south, flowing north and joining to form the Missouri. He traced the Missouri downstream and memorized the names of the rivers that joined it as it flowed first north, then northeast, then east, then south east – Sun, Teton, Marias, Milk, White Mud Creek, Musselshell. He stopped at the Milk and traced it upstream to where it crossed the border into Canada. He was intrigued to discover how close the Milk River came to the St. Mary's.

"If I stood looking east between the St. Mary's and the Milk and spit to my left it would end up in Hudson's Bay. If I spit to my right it would end up in the Gulf of Mexico," he thought.

He traced the Missouri all the way to the Mississippi and down to New Orleans. He retraced the route and ran his finger upstream along the Yellowstone and discovered it to be a giant drainage system on its own. Strangely enough, the Yellowstone started not far from the Missouri near Fort Ellis but moved directly east, picking up the Big Horn and Powder Rivers before joining the Missouri at Fort Union. He found two smaller rivers adding to the Missouri. The Little Missouri River flowed north out of the Black Hills, the Cheyenne River south before both joined the mighty Missouri further downstream.

James went back to his paper and sketched out the systems. He did it over and over until he got it right.

"Now let me get the Indian tribes straight," he thought. He started in Canada and worked from east to west – Assiniboine, Plains Cree, Woodland Cree, Cree and Blackfoot. The Blackfoot Confederacy was made up of five tribes – the Blackfeet, Bloods, Peigans, Stoneys and Sarcees. When he had memorized the Canadian tribes he started on the American side, east to west – Sioux, Mandan, Gros Ventre, Blackfoot and Nez Percé. To the south, the Cheyenne.

Again he went back to his paper, placing the tribes within the river systems, doing it again and again. He went through the major geographic features – Turtle Mountain, the Dirt Hills, Wood Mountain and the Cypress Hills in Canada, the Black Hills and the Alkali Flats in the United States.

He did the same with the forts on both sides of the border. Invariably they were located beside the rivers. He traced the route of the Great March of the North West Mounted Police from Fort Dufferin to the whiskey forts near the mountains. He studied in detail the area around Fort Whoop-Up where the Great March had ended.

"The Whoop-Up Trail," he thought as he memorized the route from Fort Benton north to the infamous whiskey trading post. "I'll be there before I know it."

His concentration was broken by a knock on the door. It was the captain.

"How are you making out?" he asked, noticing the sketches that James had made. "Looks like you're hard at it."

James had not been aware of the passage of time. Out the window the sun was fading.

"I'm learning," he answered.

"I've got your uniform laid out in my office. Do you want to have a look at it?"

James picked up the maps and his work papers and followed the captain back to his office. An array of clothing and equipment was laid out around the room.

"Here it is," said the captain, going through the items one by one. "The Prime Minister insisted on scarlet jackets," he explained, holding up the colourful tunic. "He wanted to distinguish the Mounted Police from the blue uniforms of the American army. Some of the Indians were used to the red uniforms of the 6th Regiment at Red River. They think soldiers of 'The Great Mother,' as they call Queen Victoria, always wear red."

James picked up the Norfolk jacket. It was a brilliant red with a touch of gold at the collar and the cuffs. There was the single white chevron of a staff constable on the left sleeve. The jacket had a row of shiny brass buttons down the front. On each button was the head of a buffalo and the words "NWMP Canada".

"No fuss and feathers on these uniforms was the Prime Minster's order," said the captain, as James examined the jacket.

There was a wide, brown leather cartridge belt, a white helmet with shiny brass spike and chin-scales, breeches of navy cloth with broad white stripes down the sides. There was a beautiful pair of brown riding boots, which laced up the side, with spurs. There was also a round navy coloured forage cap with a gold band around it. It had a leather strap to hold it in place. The captain noticed James examining it.

"You'll make good use of the strap," commented the captain. "The wind blows all the time out there."

In addition to the dress uniform there was a set of fatigues of brown duck. In another pile the captain had placed the winter uniform – a fur cap, buffalo skin coat, buckskin mitts, moosehide moccasins and long woolen stockings. James picked up the buckskin mitts and tried one on.

"I hear it gets pretty cold out there?" he said to the captain.

"I won't scare you with the stories."

There was a Snider carbine and a brown leather bandoliers for its ammunition. There was a revolver in a smooth brown leather holster, which was worn reversed on the left side of the cartridge belt. There was also an impressive looking sword in a shiny metal scabbard.

"Ever used one of these, constable?" grinned the captain holding it up.

"Never!" replied James. "I've never fired one of these either," he added, picking up the revolver. "I'm okay with the rifle, but I'll need some practice with this."

James took the sword, drew it out and tested the blade. It was sharper than he had expected.

"Never been used," said the captain with an amused smile as he watched James struggle to put it back in its scabbard.

"I'll try these on at home." James packed the dress uniform and the fatigue jacket in a duffel bag. "I'll take these to show the kids," he added, packing the moccasins. "They'll get a kick out of them."

"There's a saddle for you in the store room as well," continued the captain, "but I didn't bring it out. Word is that our style hasn't proved very satisfactory out west. You might be better to pick up a Western one when you get your horse."

"Sounds like a good idea," replied James.

"There's a trunk in the storeroom. We can pack all the things you don't need on the train and send them along with you in the baggage car."

James filled the bag with the final items, including the sword, to take back to the house.

"There are a few things I would like to do around town tomorrow morning," he told the captain. "I'll try to drop by again after lunch."

"Come any time."

He smiled as he watched James wrestle the sword into the duffel bag.

15

William and Hermione were almost in their beds when James arrived at the front door. They ran out of their rooms and each wrapped their arms around one leg as he stepped into the front hall.

"What's in the bag?" they asked, their voices high with expectation. Fiona and Arthur came to see what all the excitement was about. When James told them he had his new uniform they all wanted to see what he looked like in it.

"Put it on, put it on," they shouted, William's eyes big as he saw the sword come out of the bag.

"Okay, give me a minute," said James, carrying the bag into his bedroom. "William, bring the sword."

William sat on his uncle's bed as James took the items, one by one, out of the duffle bag. James put on the dress uniform – stockings, breeches, boots and spurs.

"Hey, what's this?" shouted William with glee picking up the shiny leather holster with the revolver tucked into it.

"I'll take that young man," said James firmly. "I'll show you that later."

James put on the jacket and the belt. He struggled to insert the holster and position it on his left side. He struggled again to attach the sword. Finally he put on the white helmet which, fortunately, fit him well.

"Okay," he said to William. "Let's see what the others think."

James stepped out into the hall with William behind him. The three who were waiting broke into howls of laughter and clapped their hands with amusement. James had suspected that the jacket was a little big but not that big.

"You look wonderful," said Fiona coming up to him and inspecting the fit. But James," she added, "it needs a little taking in." Arthur was laughing and pointing at the sword.

"James, my boy, I don't think you've ever worn a sword before." James looked at his sword. It was hanging straight down from his belt to his ankle.

"You look like one of William's toy soldiers," he said breaking into a loud laugh. "It's supposed to be slung so it angles behind you."

Arthur went behind James and found the second fastener on his belt through which the scabbard was supposed to have been threaded.

"May I?" he asked James.

Arthur unclipped the sword and threaded it properly. It hung at a jaunty angle, as it should, just below the holster.

"That's more like it," confirmed Arthur. "Now you really look like a soldier."

"I'm not a soldier, I'm a policeman," corrected James lightly. "In fact, I'm not even a policeman."

"What then?" asked Fiona.

"I'm an employee of the Dominion Bank of Canada dressed up in a policeman's uniform," James explained. "I'm really just a reporter. I hope I never face a situation where I have to act like a policeman. I'm not sure I'd know what to do."

Fiona inspected the jacket and breeches, deciding what she could do to make them fit.

"Hermione," said James "there's something on my bed I want to show you. Run in and get them." She ran off with William close behind her and came back with the moccasins held in triumph in front of her.

"Look at these!" she exclaimed, holding them up to her mother and father.

She kicked off her slippers, put them on her feet and skated around the room. "These are beautiful," she said. "Can I have them?"

"Afraid not," said James. "But I'll send you both a pair when I get out there."

"Yes, yes," they said, grabbing him by the legs again.

Finally the children were off to bed and Fiona went about measuring and fitting the jacket and breeches. James told them about his day and some of what he had learned about the North West. Fiona and Arthur looked at each other and smiled to see his obvious excitement.

"James," said Fiona, as she walked over and gave him a soft kiss goodnight, "Father will be very proud of you."

16

That night James hardly slept at all. The house was quiet. He didn't want to move around and wake the children. He lit a candle and started a letter to his parents. It was his first since he had left Gask. The writing of it gave him his first chance to fully evaluate events of the last weeks – the ocean crossing, becoming reacquainted with Fiona and her family, the chance encounter with Mr. McLennan, his subsequent meetings with him and Captain Channer. He thought of mentioning Merrie but he didn't. There was the decision to go to the North West and the fact, which he found almost unbelievable, that in less than two days he would be on his way there. He described some of what he had learned about the western plains knowing that his father would be interested. As he wrote, James was almost overwhelmed with the speed with which his life had taken a new turn. He had to fight down the doubts that grew in the night.

"It's difficult," he thought, "when the choice of one fork in the road means you don't go down another."

The doubts subsided and his excitement returned. He ended the letter with a growing confidence within himself that this was the perfect next step for him. He concluded the letter by saying to his father and mother that he regretted that he would not be seeing them for over a year but he promised he would write frequently. "Your loving son, James."

James spent the morning talking with Fiona while she made the alternations to his uniform. It was a bigger job than she at first had thought. Between fittings he shopped for the few things he needed for the journey and was back in time for a quick lunch. More fittings confirmed that she was making good progress and she thought the uniform made him look more handsome than ever. He was deciding which items he would take back to the armory to pack in the trunk when there was a knock at the door. He rose to answer it.

"Who is it?" asked Fiona, raising her head from the sewing.

"A package from the Dominion Bank," answered James, "for me." Inside were three large, sealed envelopes. The first, addressed to Staff Constable James Keyden, he opened. In it were a bundle of Canadian banknotes, another bundle of American banknotes and a letter.

It was another letter written on Miss Rossiter's new Remington typewriter. There were two copies.

> *Toronto, June 7, 1876*
> *Staff Constable James Keyden*
> *North West Mounted Police*
> *Sir:*
>
> *Enclosed with this letter you will find Canadian banknotes totaling $100 and American banknotes totaling $200. These funds are to be used in the fulfillment of your assignment in the North West.*
>
> *There is a second envelope which contains a railroad ticket from Toronto to Bismarck, Dakota Territory and an additional sum of $50 American which should be sufficient for your transportation and expenses from there to Fort Benton via the Montana Stage.*
>
> *The third envelope is a letter of authorization from the Dominion Bank to the I. G. Baker Co. in Fort Benton, Montana Territory. It is for an amount not to exceed $300 American, which will cover the purchase of a horse and equipment for your use as well as the postal and telegraphic expenses you will incur.*
>
> *May I remind you how important it is to us that you report regularly. I expect to hear from you not less frequently than once every two months. For your services you will be paid the regular Staff Constable salary of $1 per day in addition to your room and board. As well, there will be assigned to an account in your name with this bank the sum of*

$20 for each report we receive from you whether by telegraph or post during the period of engagement. Would you please sign both copies of this letter and return one to Miss Rossiter.

I regret that business calls me away to Ottawa and that I will not be able to see you before you leave Friday next. I wish you well on your journey and look forward to your first report.

Angus McLennan
President

17

By the time James found himself walking once more towards the armory he had delivered the signed copy of the letter to Miss Rossiter. As he walked he watched the low clouds moving overhead from the northwest. He could hear birds chirping in the low branches and looked at the maple trees lining the street ahead of him. He reached up as he walked and picked one of the small pointed maple leaves that were just emerging on the branches.

He looked around at the low buildings, the wide streets, the newness of it all, the people and the trees. He was swept with a flash of panic.

"My god," he thought to himself, "I'm about to go three quarters of the way across this gigantic country on some wild adventure and I just got here."

18

Fiona had fed the children and was preparing the table for their dinner with Mr. Wedd when James arrived home. In all the excitement he had forgotten that the professor was joining them that evening. William and Hermione hurled themselves on him as he came into the hall. They had become very fond of their uncle during his visit. During the last few weeks he had taken them on walks and played games with them in the grounds of the school. They had chased each other among the trees until the children collapsed with exhaustion.

"How about a quiet story before bed," suggested Fiona from the kitchen.

"Tell us a story about Indians," shouted Hermione.

The children sat, one on each side of James, as he made up a story about the Blackfoot. He used all the new words he could remember from the maps. He wove the names of tribes and rivers into a tale of Indians and buffalo and tepees. The children didn't want the story to end. Finally they calmed down and were ready to go off to their rooms.

James and Arthur sat by the fire waiting for Mr. Wedd to arrive. William Wedd, Arthur explained, was the head of the Classics Department at the school. Arthur and Mr. Martland, owner of Augustus the horse, were the other members of the department. Both families lived in apartments in that same building. William Wedd, Arthur explained to James, had been on the staff for over twenty-five years. He was highly respected by the faculty and community as the foremost classics scholar in the country. He was much loved by the boys and, though he never raised his voice or threatened his students, never had a problem with discipline.

"The boys call him 'Billygoat,'" said Arthur with a smile, "because of the shape of his whiskers."

James saw how apt the name was when Mr. Wedd stepped through the front door. The teacher had the high forehead of a scholar. He wore a long jacket over a vest and a white shirt with a tight collar and wide necktie. He had a pair of small eyeglasses perched on the bridge of his nose.

Arthur had warned James that at this time of year there was a great deal of work for the teachers to do. Mr. Wedd, he had said, would not be able to stay long.

Fiona had the meal on the table promptly. But when Mr. Wedd heard that James' father had fought in the Crimean War the conversation went off in that direction. James found the classics master fascinating and entertaining. He had a wide range of knowledge and a keen interest in every detail. They covered military history, the politics and economics of the Old Country and were just beginning on renewed British Imperialism when Arthur interrupted.

"I know you're busy William," he said, "and can't stay long...."

"Always time for stimulating conversation," said Mr. Wedd. They continued with Disraeli, Gladstone, India and Queen Victoria.

Finally Mr. Wedd said, "I hear you're headed for the North West, young man."

"I'm leaving Friday morning,"

"He'll be serving under Colonel Macleod," added Arthur. "We thought you might be able to tell James something about him. You probably taught him while he was a student here."

"I certainly did," answered Mr. Wedd. "He was a very intelligent boy from a very interesting family. In fact, my wife and I were out at the family home not more than a month ago. It's still a very lively household. They have a tradition of after dinner music and song. All the children play one instrument or another."

"Why don't we sit by the fire," said Fiona. "I'll serve tea in there."

The three men settled in the drawing room and Fiona went to the kitchen.

"James Macleod – fascinating fellow," William began. "He was born and raised on the Isle of Skye. His father, Martin, was the cousin of Norman Macleod the head of the clan."

Mr. Wedd paused and looked into the fire.

"James," he said, "you mentioned your father was in the Scots Greys. Martin Macleod served with the Moiras Regiment. He was one of eight brothers who joined the British army. They served in India, the Caribbean and North America. Seven of them died from disease and Martin was the only one to return to Skye."

"What a tragedy," said Fiona, who had brought the tea and joined them.

"Martin vowed that none of his sons would ever join the army," Mr. Wedd continued. "In fact, that's one of the reasons he brought his family to Canada."

"What was the other?" asked James.

"He believed there was no future for his sons cooped up on that tiny rock of an island," he explained.

"There's something to that," added Arthur.

"Martin brought his wife and eight children, four boys and four girls to Canada," Mr. Wedd went on. "James was the seventh. I think he was about nine years old at the time. They bought land about twenty miles north of here in Richmond Hill and over the years it has become a great estate. They call it 'Drynoch' after the village they came from on Skye."

"Macleod's family still lives there?" asked Arthur.

"Martin and his wife died some years ago," William continued. "The two eldest sons, James' brothers, and their families live there now."

"What about James?" asked Fiona.

"He started here in the lower grades," William told them. "The family ran into some kind of financial difficulty and James was taken out of school. Their fortunes must have improved. James returned for his final year and graduated, with honours, as I remember. He was a fine athlete and a very free spirited young man."

"And after that?" asked Arthur.

"He went to Queens in Kingston. His first years there were a bit of a disaster. He became the typical rebellious son away from home for the first time. He was more interested in the social and military life of the university than he was the academic life. His father wanted him to do law. As I recall, he failed his first year and maybe his second, I can't remember."

Mr. Wedd paused to recall the details.

"He was drawn to the military life at Fort Henry," Mr. Wedd continued. "He was even granted a commission, much to his father's horror."

"Did he join the army?" asked James.

"Only the militia," replied Mr. Wedd. "He continued his studies but he loved the glamour of a soldier's life. He used to wear his full dress uniform to dances and parties against regulations. It finally got him into a lot of trouble with his superiors. I think they even tried to dismiss him from the service."

"His father would have been pleased with that," added Arthur.

"He and his father had a serious falling out," Mr. Wedd continued. "I think it was over money and career. There were years when they hardly spoke to each other."

"Did he finish at Queens?" asked Arthur.

"Eventually. He graduated in law and was called to the bar. He practiced in Kingston for a time with Sir John A.'s old firm. He must have tired of that because he moved to Bowmanville. Then for no reason, he dropped from view for a couple of years and no one really knows where he went. He loves to hunt and some people think he just went off into the wilderness by himself."

"That must have concerned his family," commented Fiona. "Did he ever make up with his father?"

"Never fully," William replied. "Eventually he appeared again and practiced law for a few years. But his heart was never in it. He was always a bit rebellious."

"How did he get out West?" asked James.

"His brother Norman told me the story when we were out there recently. Norman said it was the rebellion in Manitoba six years ago that finally got James on the right track. It provided the opportunity he had always been looking for. He was made a Colonel in the army under Wolseley and ordered to raise two brigades to go to the Red River."

"Riel?" asked James, remembering his conversation with Merrie.

"He was the leader of the Metis and the Provisional Government," explained Mr. Wedd.

"And was the rebellion put down?" asked Fiona.

"In a manner of speaking," answered Mr. Wedd. "To hear Norman tell it, James selected good men, trained them to peak fitness and led them through some of the roughest country in the land. They dragged their boats up rivers that had never seen anything bigger than a canoe. They pulled their equipment and supplies around rapids and waterfalls. To hear Norman tell it, the morale of the men never flagged. They thought his brother was the best officer they had ever had."

"Why was that?" asked James.

"Norman said he would carry the heaviest loads over the portages. He would never ask his men to do anything that he wouldn't do himself."

"Led by example?" added Arthur.

"I expect that was it," replied Mr. Wedd. "He was daring too, from all accounts. Not so much in the face of the enemy, but in tackling the wilderness with intelligent courage and a sense of adventure. He asked his men to do things that British soldiers had never been asked to do and they seemed to love him for it. Wolseley was so impressed with his leadership that he recommended him for the Cross of St. Michael and St. George."

"Did they catch Riel?" asked James.

"By the time they got to Winnipeg, Riel and the Metis had fled," replied Mr. Wedd. "They entered Winnipeg without a shot being fired."

"What then?" asked James.

"The troops came home to the East and James stayed on in Winnipeg as second in command. He was very happy to do it. He loved the frontier life and besides that, for the first time in his life, he fell in love."

"With whom?" asked Fiona.

"A girl called Mary Drever," answered William. "To hear Norman tell it, she is every bit as courageous and daring as James."

"Do you know anything about her?" asked Fiona.

"Norman told me a little," Mr. Wedd explained. "Mary Drever's father was a veteran Hudson's Bay Company trader. Her mother had been governess to the children of the only judge in the territory. After they were married their home became the social center of the community for years – parties, dances and singing. They were friends with the Indians, the Metis, the English – everyone."

"What about Mary?" asked Fiona.

"Norman told me several stories about Mary. Let me try to remember."

He paused to recall what Norman had told him.

"There was a Sioux uprising in Minnesota in the early sixties," he began. "Some of the renegade Indians crossed the border and ended up in Red River. One night they broke into the Drever house and threatened the family. It was Mary who blocked their way and told them to leave. And they did."

"Some woman," said Fiona.

"I think Norman said that she was only sixteen at the time," added Mr. Wedd. "She was known for her fiery temper and I guess it showed itself on that occasion."

"Anything else?" asked Fiona.

"During the rebellion the Drever house was the center of the loyalist group against Riel and his men," he went on. "When some of their friends were imprisoned by Riel, Mary baked bread and hid files in the loaves so the men could cut their way out. Her father was one who escaped that way. It was mid-winter and he fled back to their home in his bare feet. From that day on he could hardly walk."

"What happened to Mary?" asked Fiona.

"I don't remember whether it was because of that event or something else," Mr. Wedd went on. "But on one occasion, Riel got so angry at the family that he had his men place a cannon in front of the house and threatened to blow it up."

"And?" said Fiona.

"The family refused to move. Mary stood in the window directly in the line of fire. Riel backed down and had his men haul the cannon back to the fort."

"I hope to meet this woman," said James.

"There's one more story about her I remember," said Mr. Wedd. "During the height of the rebellion it was Mary who ran the messages between the loyalist forces. Time and again Riel's men stopped her but they never caught her. The rebels were good Catholics and didn't think to search her clothes where she had hidden the messages.

"Sounds like she's a good match for James Macleod," said Fiona.

"They were engaged that winter he was out there. But James was ordered back to Toronto and she refused to leave her old father and family so they broke it off."

"How sad!" said Fiona.

"Norman told me the engagement is back on again," Mr. Wedd replied. "But they still haven't managed to get married."

"That's terrible," said Fiona. "They've been engaged for nearly six years."

Mr. Wedd took out his pocket watch and checked the hour. It was long past the time he had meant to leave. The fire had burned to a glowing smolder. Arthur, Fiona and James saw the teacher to the door.

"When you see Macleod," said Mr. Wedd, turning to James, "please pass along my greetings. Tell him I remember him well and follow his exploits with great interest."

"I certainly will, sir," answered James. "I'm sure he remembers you as well."

18

JAMES SPENT HIS LAST MORNING in Toronto at the armory putting the finishing touches on his packing and preparing the trunk for shipment. During the previous night, when again he had difficulty sleeping, he reviewed the maps he had studied in his mind. The mountains, rivers, tribes and forts were becoming fixed in his memory. He recalled Mr. Wedd's stories of Macleod and looked forward to meeting him. He finished packing the trunk and returned to the office to thank the captain.

"I wish it were me going on this assignment," said the captain. "You're in for a real adventure."

James said good-bye to Captain Channer, found a dray and rode on it with his trunk to Union Station.

"I'll check it as far as Windsor," said the baggage master looking at his ticket. "After you get to Detroit, you can check it on to Chicago and from there to Madison, St. Paul, Fargo and Bismarck. You'd better check at each station to be sure it's still with you."

19

Shortly after he returned home there was a knock at the door. James answered it and found Clare, the housemaid in the McLennan home standing there.

"I have a letter for you, sir, and I'm to wait for your reply."

James invited her in and walked to the window where he opened the letter.

> *Dear James,*
>
> *Before he left for Ottawa my father gave me two tickets to a concert at the St. Lawrence Hall this evening. I would very much appreciate it if you would escort me to it. I realize it is your last evening in Toronto and that you might wish to spend it with your family but if you are free I will send the carriage for you at seven o'clock. Would you please give Clare your reply?*
>
> *Merrie*
>
> *PS If you are able to come would you please wear your new uniform. People generally dress up for these occasions and I am anxious to see how you look as an officer of the North West Mounted Police!*

"What is it, James?" asked Fiona.

"It's from McLennan's daughter, Merrie. She's inviting me to a concert tonight. Would you mind if I went?"

"Not at all," replied Fiona. "Enjoy yourself on your last evening."

"She wants me to wear my uniform."

"But it's hardly ready, but it could be if we hurry."

James told Clare that he accepted the invitation and would be ready at seven.

"I'd better get busy then," Fiona said making James try on the breeches and the jacket one more time. The breeches fit him well but Fiona was not satisfied with the jacket. James took the opportunity to practice walking with his sword. He put on his boots, that fortunately fit him, and his belt. He attached the sword in the way that Arthur had shown him. He marched up and down the hall and into the small drawing room with William and Hermione trying to keep in step close behind him. He would stop suddenly and they would bump into him. Then they would all have a good laugh and do it all over again.

"If I practice walking with this thing," he said, touching his sword, "maybe people will think I know what I'm doing."

When Fiona was finished with the adjustments to the jacket she had James put the whole uniform on including the white helmet. She walked around him, smoothing here and fussing there.

"James," she said, standing in front of him and looking him up and down, "you look fantastic."

James, with his left hand grasping the hilt of his sword, raised himself to his full height and, looking very serious, gave her a very proper British officer's salute. The children howled with laughter.

20

When seven o'clock arrived, Fiona, Arthur, William and Hermione escorted James out of the apartment and onto the street. They watched with wide grins as the coachman held the door open for him and he stepped up into the carriage. He acted the part and pretended to be most serious which made them smile all the more. Even the boys on the street who were kicking an old ball around had stopped to watch him. James felt like the Duke of Something-or-Other riding in the open carriage in his scarlet jacket, white helmet with the shiny spike on top and the awkward sword by his side. He smiled thinking what he must look like and what his father and mother would think if they saw him at this moment.

James listened to the clip-clop of the hooves of the carriage horses on the paving stones. They were a beautiful matched team of blacks with a touch of white on their faces. The oiled harness shone, the brass fittings gleamed. Morgan wore his driver's jacket, breeches, boots and cap. A coachman similarly dressed sat beside him. It was a carriage with one wide cushioned seat facing forward and another facing it. It had low sides, two small wheels in front with the driver's seat over them, two large wheels in back. The carriage was balanced on springs, which gave it a smooth, elegant ride.

Morgan brought the carriage to a halt in front of the McLennan house. The coachman jumped down and opened the door. James stepped down, careful not to trip on his sword. Clare opened the door before he reached it, welcomed him and gestured him to step inside. He took off his helmet and tucked it under his arm. Clare gave him a broad smile and showed him into the drawing room. James was sure she smiled because he looked so outrageous.

The drawing room was elegantly decorated with rich wallpaper and dark, heavy maroon curtains. They were drawn over the windows on each side of a massive stone fireplace but open facing the front of the house revealing deep window casings finished in polished oak. There was a thick carpet covering the hardwood floor, stately furniture and oil paintings on the walls. A chandelier hung from the centre of the high ceiling, its light bouncing off the polished woodwork.

James drew closer to the Paul Kane oil painting he had seen earlier, the one with the Blackfoot Chief. He studied it with care. There was intelligence in Big Snake's eyes that startled him. For the first time he was struck with the thought that Indians were actually people. He studied the other figures in the painting, the chief's people, his home, his horse, the wild sky. He had never considered Indians anything other than wild savages. Big Snake didn't fit the description at all.

"Do you like it?"

He had been so absorbed that he had not heard Merrie enter the room.

"Fascinating," he replied, his mind still sorting through his fresh impressions.

"Thank you for coming, and on such short notice. By the way, you look absolutely wonderful in your new uniform."

James thought she looked absolutely wonderful herself and said so. She was wearing a white gown that nearly touched the floor. It was square cut under her neck with puffy short sleeves and a ruffle around the bottom. She had on long silver earrings and a silver necklace with a blue stone hanging from it. She had a wide yellow ribbon around her waist. A smaller ribbon of the same colour was in her long black hair, which shone in the light of the candles. She was wearing white gloves.

"Shall we go," she said, taking his left arm. As he offered it, the hilt of the sword swung around and banged against her hip. They both burst out laughing.

"Mr. Keyden," she said. "I do believe you have never worn a sword before."

"I do believe you're right, Miss McLennan" he replied and they laughed again.

Merrie moved to his other side and they walked to the front door together. Clare was waiting with a broad smile on her face.

"Well," said Merrie to her, "what do you think?"

"Very charming, I'm sure," she replied as she helped Merrie wrap a black mink cape over her shoulders. "You'll be the most colourful couple at the concert."

"Colourful, certainly," replied Merrie. "Hilarious, if we don't learn what to do with the sword."

James was enjoying every moment of the carriage ride. People looked at them as they passed, as well they might, she strikingly attractive in her white dress and cape and his the only scarlet uniform in sight. It was five years since the British had moved their regiments out of Canada leaving behind only a few militiamen in the dull grey uniforms he had seen at the garden reception. In the failing light of dusk the stone mansions and office buildings along the route looked impressive. They seemed more formidable and permanent than he remembered. He was losing the perception that this was a colonial city. These buildings were certainly here to stay and radiated more energy and potential than the cities of Britain. He could get used to living in this country.

"Morgan, put the horses away when you get back," Merrie said as they pulled up in front of the Hall. "We'll walk home when the performance is over."

"You sure, Miss Merrie?" asked Morgan. "I don't mind waiting up."

"No, it's all right, Morgan," she told him firmly. "It's a pleasant evening and besides," she said looking at James, "I'll have a police escort."

Their seats were in the center section, second row on the aisle. Heads turned and people whispered as James, with Merrie on his arm, made their way towards the front. Merrie took her seat first. James followed. He had a few tense moments figuring out what to do with his sword. He managed to be seated without embarrassment much to the relief of both of them.

It was a concert of the combined talents of the Toronto Philharmonic Orchestra and the Metropolitan Choral Society. James enjoyed the Mozart and the Bach, but he wasn't looking forward to the Requiem in the second half.

At the intermission they walked up the aisle to the lobby. Merrie introduced him to some of her friends and some of her father's colleagues.

"May I introduce Constable Keyden," she would say. "He leaves tomorrow on a special assignment to the North West."

She placed extra emphasis on the words 'special assignment' and 'North West', which gave an air of mystery to this scarlet jacketed officer beside her. James thought she was being a little melodramatic until he caught her eye. There was just the touch of mirth that told him she was teasing both him and her friends ever so slightly.

The remarks of her friends were the most interesting part of the evening's performance for James.

"Oh, Constable Keyden, how exciting," said one woman. "My husband and I are dying to go west. We're waiting for the completion of the railway so that we can go in luxury."

"I say, Keyden, I hope you will deal firmly with those half-breed renegades," added her husband. "If you ever get your hands on that Riel fellow, hang him from the nearest tree."

Obviously, thought James, he doesn't know that there aren't any trees out there. He didn't bother to correct the old gentleman, but smiled politely.

"I hope you won't lose your scalp out there, Constable Keyden," giggled another wife. Then turning to Merrie, she added in a loud whisper, "He's very handsome."

An usher rang a bell summoning the audience back into the Hall for the second half.

"I'm not in the mood for a Requiem," Merrie said to James. "How would you like do something else instead."

"What do you have in mind?" asked James.

"One of my friends is in the same frame of mind. She's leaving early too and has invited us back to her place. There will be a few others there as well. It will be a much more enjoyable send off for you than staying here."

"Wonderful idea," James replied. "Let's go."

She slipped her hand under his arm. They stepped from the lobby, crossed King Street and started through the park.

"I hope you won't lose your scalp out there, Constable Keyden," mimicked Merrie. They burst out laughing.

James saw another side of Merrie. They laughed about the silly things her friends and acquaintances had said, chatted about trivialities and pretended to look very proper as they passed older couples who were also strolling in the park. Merrie was pleased with how she looked and was thoroughly enjoying the company of the handsome officer in the bright scarlet uniform beside her. James felt strong and protective.

There was a wooden bench off to the side of the walkway and Merrie steered James towards it.

"Let's sit here for a minute," she said rather hesitantly. "There's something I need to ask you."

"What could that be?" asked James.

They sat on the bench next to a bed of flowers looking towards the lights of the avenue.

"Tell me about Ginna."

"You don't really want to know about Ginna," he replied.

"You mean, you don't really want to tell me about Ginna," she said with a note of defiance.

James hesitated and then began.

"Ginna was my best friend growing up," James began. "We chased each other around the fields, threw straw at each other in the stable, even pushed each other into the manure pile."

"Did you ride together?" she asked.

"Never," replied James. "Nobody thought to teach her how to ride."

"Why was that?"

"She was a servant's daughter," he explained. "Servant's daughters don't ride their master's horses."

"Oh. You're right, they don't."

"My father had a younger brother," James went on. "He was an officer in the army like my father but not the cavalry, the Gordon Highlanders. He spent most of his career in India. While he was out there he caught a disease of some kind and died."

"I'm sorry," said Merrie.

"Some months after he was buried in Bengal," James continued, "my father received a letter from India. It was not signed. The writer thought my father should know that his brother had had a mistress in India and that there was a child. Since the father's death, the mother and child were living under the worst possible conditions."

"Ginna is Indian?" asked Merrie.

"Her mother is Indian. Her father was my uncle which makes her my cousin."

"Oh," said Merrie almost to herself somewhat relieved. "How did she get to Scotland?"

"My father knew a number of senior officers in India," James went on. "He wrote one and asked him to look into the matter and let him know. The answer came back that the story was true. My father brought the mother, whose name is Rupa, and her child, Ginna, to Scotland to live with us. They've lived in an apartment beside the stable since then and Rupa has been our housekeeper for as long as I can remember."

"Where is Ginna now?" Merrie asked.

James paused to decide how best to tell the rest of the story.

"When I was ten," he continued, "I was sent as a boarder to Perth Academy. Ginna never went to school at all. Everything she learned was from her mother and my mother. My father could hardly afford to have one housekeeper let alone two and he tried very hard to place her with another family in the area. But nobody wanted an Indian girl."

"She is quite dark?" asked Merrie.

"Yes."

"Would you say she was beautiful?" prompted Merrie.

"She seemed to me to become more beautiful the older she got," James replied thoughtfully.

Merrie glanced at him to try to gauge his feelings for Ginna.

"My father couldn't find a position for her anywhere so she stayed on with us. Father used to entertain other officers at our home from time to time and eventually there was a young lieutenant who took a strong interest in Ginna. He asked my father if he could take her out on Sunday afternoons. After speaking with Rupa, Father agreed. The lieutenant would arrive in a buggy and off they would go."

A look of concern crossed Merrie's face.

"In due course," James continued, "the lieutenant asked my father, who I expect he regarded as her guardian, if he could marry her. My father talked it over with Ginna's mother and, as Ginna was very excited at the prospect said yes. The lieutenant gave her a ring and they talked of setting a date. Several Sunday's came and went and the lieutenant failed to show up. Finally my father made some inquiries and discovered that the lieutenant had come to the end of his service with the army, had decided not to reenlist and as far as anyone knew, had left for America."

"Poor Ginna," said Merrie.

"A short time later," James went on, "it was obvious that Ginna was expecting a baby."

James paused stung by the memory.

"I don't mind telling you," he said to Merrie who was watching him intently, "that when I came home from school that summer I cried to see how shattered Ginna was by the experience."

"Where is she now?"

"Still at our home," replied James. "A servant just like her mother. I expect she'll be there for the rest of her life."

"Your parents are very special people to have helped them both like that," said Merrie.

James was thoughtful.

"They are very special people," he replied. "I remember my father saying to me once, 'I've been part of enough killing in my day. It's high time I did something for the living.' I expect that helps explain why he did what he did."

Merrie took James by the arm and together they left the bench and continued on their way until they reached the entrance to the grounds of an imposing mansion situated well back from the avenue. Lights were blazing from the front porch and from the windows on the ground floor. A wrought iron fence ringed the property. The gates were swung back and they turned in and up the long flagstone walk to the front door. Wings of the building stretched out to right and left. A butler in a black suit, high white collar and black bow tie greeted them at the front door.

"Miss McLennan and guest to visit Miss Graham," Merrie told him.

"This way, please."

The butler led them across a spacious lobby with granite floor and dark, high beamed ceiling to a wide doorway. He stopped at the side of the entrance and gestured for them to enter. It was a very large sitting room with a huge bay window at the far end. Two crystal chandeliers hung from the beamed ceiling, their blaze of candles casting a bright light throughout. The floor was covered with a thick rug. Soft chairs and sofas formed a circle on the perimeter of the carpet. There were several couples standing at the far end, sipping from crystal glasses. One of the young women walked over to greet them.

"Merrie, wasn't it a dreadful concert," she began, glancing over at James.

"Louise, this is James Keyden. James this is Louise Graham."

"What a marvelous uniform," Louise replied, holding out her hand to James. "I could have used that sword on the contralto tonight. She was abysmal. Come and meet the others."

As they met and chatted, a maid served them a light, dry sherry and before long a number of other couples joined the party. James' uniform was certainly the center of attention and he was plied with questions about his imminent departure for the North West. He soon realized that the others knew as little as he had a few days earlier about the people and circumstances in the country's western half. Merrie was by far the most knowledgeable. The girls expressed their excitement for him. The men said they were envious but James surmised that they were far too comfortable in their present situations to think seriously of abandoning them for the hardships of the western frontier.

Two men entered the room carrying violins and Louise broke away from the group to speak with them. She directed them to a corner of the room and spoke to one of the maids who quickly disappeared. She returned in a few moments with the butler and another houseman and together they pushed the furniture to the walls and rolled up the large, heavy rug, moving it back to create a large open space on the gleaming hardwood floor.

"James, I hope you like dancing," said Merrie taking his arm. "We're all mad about it."

"Depends on how you dance over here," he replied.

The fiddlers began and the couples formed up.

"Wait a minute," said James in a voice that rose over the music. He went to a chair near the wall and removed his shoulder belt and with it the sword and holster and laid them on the chair beside his helmet. "Okay, now I'm ready."

The music started and a reel of eight formed. James, who reveled in Scottish country dancing recognized the movements at once.

"James, you're good!" shouted Merrie across the line.

"This is primitive when you're used to the real thing," he chided her.

"James, you're a snob," she shot back jokingly.

Each couple went through the sequence three times. James infused Merrie and the others with his flare and enthusiasm and they reeled and twirled until some of the dancers began to flag. Finally the fiddlers brought the music to a conclusion and James, Merrie and the others clapped and hollered their approval with shouts of "More. More."

The fiddlers started up again and Merrie took James' arm.

"This is ridiculous," he said, "these boots are not made for dancing."

James sat down on the floor and unlaced the high boots.

"Wait for us," Merrie shouted to the others, kicking off her own shoes.

James wrestled with the boots, scratching the immaculate floor with one of the spurs in the process, threw them over so they landed near the rest of his equipment and jumped up to join Merrie.

"Much better," he said as the music began. The dancing went on and on. They switched partners and Merrie's friends all wanted the opportunity to dance with the handsome constable with the scarlet jacket, except that before long the scarlet jacket had joined the belt, boots and helmet in a pile near the chair. So had Merrie's shoes and the shoes of most of the other dancers and all the other men's jackets. The yellow ribbon in Merrie's hair had come loose and was waving from behind her head as she twirled and spun.

The glasses were continually filled. With the exhilaration of the dancing and the effect of several glasses, James began to feel slightly dizzy. At the end of a particularly energetic jig he put his arm around Merrie's shoulder to steady himself and he felt her arm around his waist. It was only then that he noticed the two distinguished looking gentlemen at the door watching them with expressions of disapproval.

"That's Louise's father," whispered Merrie, waving a hand in their direction. And behind him was Captain Channer. The father was glaring straight in his direction and Captain Channer's expression was not much different. James waved heartily but it didn't change the expressions on their faces. Then it occurred to James that with his shirt hanging out and most of his uniform in a pile on the floor he didn't look like the model of a responsible reporter for the Dominion Bank. He was standing there in his stocking feet, in a white undershirt, thick suspenders holding up his heavy breeches with his arm around Mr. McLennan's daughter.

"Oh, oh," James said to Merrie, as the music stopped. "I think I've made Louise's father angry. And Captain Channer is probably questioning his judgement in selecting me for this job."

"One more," shouted Louise above the chatter. Some of the dancers cheered and some of them moaned. The fiddlers started up again. Merrie took James firmly by the arm and led him to the floor.

"Don't worry," she reassured him. "The decisions made and that's that."

When he looked back at the entrance, the two men were gone.

Under the bright chandelier of the Graham's portico James and Merrie said goodbye to their hostess and walked with some of the other departing guests to the avenue where they separated in their various directions. It had been a struggle to get his boots back on but James was respectable again, sword in place, helmet on, but he was still sweating hard from all the exercise and he left the top buttons of his jacket undone.

Merrie led the way back to her house and they walked slowly up the quiet, tree-lined streets. When they reached her home they turned in and walked together up the driveway. By the light of the portico James saw for the first time the name "Afton" carved in a stone at the corner of the house.

"Afton?" questioned James.

"My mother was born near Afton Water, she explained. They named this place after it. She loved it here and so do I."

They lingered in the shadows by the side of the house.

"Thank you for a wonderful evening, James," she said looking up at him. "You are a very good dancer."

"Depends who I'm dancing with," he said with a smile.

"And thank you for teaching me to jump. I never would have had the courage if you hadn't helped me."

"You're a fast learner," he replied, "and you have no shortage of courage."

"I'll miss you," she said quietly and leaned up and kissed him softly on the cheek.

James was caught by surprise but recovered quickly enough to put his arms around her and hold her closely to him.

"I'll miss you, too," he replied, surprising himself that he truly meant what he said.

"When does your train leave?"

"Bright and early tomorrow morning."

"That soon?" she answered with a touch of regret. "You know, I wish I were going too. I'm ready for an adventure."

"I'll tell you all about it when I get back."

20

It was early the next morning when James arrived at Union Station to catch his train. He had said goodbye to Arthur at the apartment before the teacher went off to his classes. Fiona, William and Hermione had accompanied him to the station, proud to be walking alongside a scarlet-jacketed officer of the North West Mounted Police who wore a sword and carried a haversack over his shoulder. The children were sad to see their favorite uncle leave but were excited to be going to the train station. They were fascinated and frightened by the great puffing engine with its large smokestack and other bumps along its back. Escaping steam hissed from its powerful cylinders.

The train to Windsor was loading beside the platform. The baggage was being handled into the express cars next to the engine and the passengers where climbing the steps into the coaches. James walked the children down to the engine where they could see it up close. Hermione held his hand while William scurried around. James was relieved to see his trunk inside the baggage car as he passed the open door. William wanted to go closer and touch the drive wheels, which were taller than he was. James held his hand as he approached and William squealed with pleasure as he patted the cold steel.

As they turned to walk back James was surprised to see Merrie talking with Fiona. He had not expected her to come to see him off. The children ran on ahead, William chasing Hermione. They dodged around Merrie and their mother, one trying to tag the other.

"Good morning, Miss McLennan. I'm surprised to see you here so early in the morning."

"Good morning, Constable Keyden," said Merrie, with a smile. "As my father and Captain Channer were not able to see you off themselves I thought the least I could do is represent them and give you this as a parting gift."

She handed James a thin, rectangularly shaped package, carefully wrapped.

"It's not everyone who appreciates the new art of photography," she added.

"It's one of your images," he guessed, smiling his appreciation.

"Open it on the train and see what you think."

The conductor yelled, "All aboard." The last passengers were making their way to the door.

"Don't go! Don't go!" shouted the children as they grabbed James' legs.

James ruffled William's hair, which annoyed him, and he lifted Hermione up and hugged her. Putting her down, he kissed his sister lightly on both cheeks.

"Thanks for taking such good care of me, Fiona," he said to his sister.

Merrie held out her hand to him.

"Thank you for my gift in advance," he said, holding on to her hand.

"Safe journey," she replied.

He found a window where he could look out on Fiona, the children and Merrie. The engineer blew two short blasts from the whistle. The engine huffed and coughed and the train jerked forward. James waved and they waved back until they were lost from sight. He was on his way to the North West.

21

James lifted his haversack into the rack above, settled into a seat next to the window and watched the city slide by. Before long he noticed out the windows on the opposite side of the coach the hotel where he and the captain had chatted over lunch. He pictured Captain Channer questioning him at the table by the window as they watched the sailboats. He had passed the test whatever it was. He also pictured the captain at Louise Graham's and hoped he hadn't disappointed him too much. In a moment the hotel had disappeared behind them.

He had been holding the package that Merrie had given him. He opened it to find a photographic print in a light metal frame. It was an image of Morgan sitting on a stool at the corner of her home where she had kissed him. Morgan was holding a pipe to his mouth. Behind him was the stone with the word "Afton" carved on it. The image was blurry around the hands but the eyes were clear and the dark background of stone set off the features of his face and hair. James remembered the first time he had seen Morgan when he was returning Mr. McLennan's horse after their first encounter – the incident that started it all. James turned the print over. In a flowing hand Merrie had written, "Hurry home, Merrie."

22

Although the excitement of the journey was still with him, James found it a long, slow trip. The train stopped at every village and crossroads. Baggage was loaded off and more baggage loaded on. One or two passengers and sometimes none would board or leave at each station.

What continued to amaze him was the distance and space. He was traveling through the countryside hour after hour with only a farm, a village, a town, more farms, another town, but nowhere great concentrations of people as he was used to in Britain. Detroit and then Chicago gave him a different perspective. These were sprawling, noisy, chaotic cities.

There was another sensation that was growing in him. It had to do with the distinct differences he felt in the people as he crossed the Detroit River into the United States. After all he had heard and read about the United States of America, he had finally reached it. Maybe it was what he had always expected to find. Maybe there was something to what he sensed. He couldn't define it exactly. It had to do with the pace at which people moved, the volume level of their voices and their directness. In Canada almost everyone looked at his brightly coloured uniform but almost no one spoke to him. In America he was approached continuously by people who wanted to know who he was, what the uniform meant and where he was going. The openness and lack of restraint was foreign to him.

James had never in his life seen such a variety of faces and costumes as he did in these great American cities. There were men in tall hats and black coats that reminded him of Mr. McLennan. On the same street were men who looked like they were farmers, women in black shawls and heavy black dresses and children in rags. He had never seen so many black people. In the stations he heard conversations in any number of languages. Wherever he went he was stared at as if he were a character out of a picture book.

The numbers of people and settlements thinned out as the train made its way north from Chicago towards Madison. It was open, farming country and there was so much of it. The trees had been cleared over large sections of the land. The fields were planted with a variety of grains. There were endless herds of cattle.

At the station stops he watched the people, trying not to look too conspicuous which in his scarlet jacket was a little difficult. But there seemed to be no hesitation in people who wanted to come up and talk with him. They just did it. They had none of the reserve that he had grown up with. He began to adjust to it and found himself starting up conversations with people near him. Many laughed at his accent.

"Accent? They're the ones with the accent," he thought to himself.

He studied the faces in the coaches and tried to make some order out of what he was seeing. There was no order. They were from everywhere. He tried to guess where they were from and where they were going. There were whole families, fathers, some prosperous looking, others not, mothers with anywhere from one to six or seven children. There were even some men in uniform whom he recognized from photos he had seen as American army officers.

Most people had brought their own food for the journey. James noted with surprise how at ease they were eating, sleeping, talking and drinking among themselves as though they were alone in the world. On the whole, the children were well behaved. The young ones would continually run up and down the aisle and stop by his seat, stare at his uniform, his revolver, his sword and say, "Can I see that?" He would let them touch the handle and they'd run off to tell their parents who would smile back at him. Then the children would run back and do it over and over again. It helped to pass the time.

There were bunks that folded down from the ceiling but James hadn't thought to reserve one. It was mostly the women and their children who slept up there. The bunks were open, with no privacy, but that didn't seem to bother them in the slightest. Fortunately, the swaying of the coaches made James sleepy and after the many near sleepless nights in Toronto, he found he just had to close his eyes and he'd be off.

It was more difficult at night when he was supposed to sleep. The seats were hard and straight. He had to sit upright or lay across them which he did when there was no one beside him. Sometimes the seat opposite him was empty and he could put his feet up which helped. After a time he began to take his boots off at night. He knew his father would be horrified to see an officer with his boots off but it helped him relax and sleep. Many of the other men seemed to get through the night by drinking and playing cards.

Usually at the larger station stops there were people outside who were selling apples or sausage or bread. He was intrigued with the variety and had tried different things. Unfortunately, somewhere after Madison and before St. Paul, he had eaten something that had made him feel quite ill. He kept one eye on the lavatory at the end of the coach and hoped it would not be occupied if he had to make use of it in a hurry.

As they arrived in St. Paul it was announced that this was the end of the line for that train. He had a few hours before another train would leave for Fargo and on to Bismarck. He checked with the baggageman, to ensure that his trunk was being transferred to the Fargo train, then left the station to stroll through the town. He noticed some other men in uniform who looked like they had stepped out of an Alexander Gardner photograph of the Civil War. They were wearing swords as well so he didn't feel quite so conspicuous. Their long jackets were dark blue, their breeches grey with a navy stripe and they wore black, wide-brimmed hats. His scarlet jacket, white stripe down his pants and white helmet still stood out.

James walked briskly up and down the main street of the town. After sitting for days in the train he was glad for the exercise and the chance to stretch the muscles in his legs. The fresh air revived him and seemed to settle his stomach.

St. Paul was a busy town. There were horses and wagons everywhere and crowds of people walking purposefully up and down the streets. He was surprised at the warm reception he received, the greetings and smiles from people he passed. One man even said, "Glad to see you back in town," and invited him for a drink.

With no other plan in mind and in the spirit of his newly discovered American informality James accepted. His new friend led him to a tavern a short distance down the street, held open a swinging door for him and led him to a table. As they sat down his friend yelled at the bartender, "Mike, beer," and held up two fingers. James noticed three blue uniforms sitting together across the room at another table. They were eyeing him as he sat down.

"How did the other Redcoats make out on their trek across the plains?" asked his new friend.

"Other Redcoats, trek?" James asked.

"Yeah," answered the friend. "Bye the way, the names Andersen, Aage Andersen."

"James Keyden," he replied, "Glad to met you."

"Me too, Jim," said Aage. "I've only seen a few in your uniform since the gang that landed here two summers ago with all their stuff."

"You'll have to forgive me, Mr. Andersen…."

"Aage, Aage, A-A-G-E…."

You'll have to forgive me, Aage," replied James. "I'm new to the Force."

"Two summers ago, right about this time," Aage told him, "a whole bunch of your guys arrived on the train. Must have been a hundred or more – with all their gear, horses, wagons, cannons, you name it. Spread it all over the ground fresh from the factory. It was a hell of a mess, all in boxes, all in pieces. Well, the whole damn town was out watching them clean up the mess. We were sure it'd take them two weeks to get it straightened out and on their way. They were headed north and then planned to march clear across the country to the mountains. They were after whiskey traders they told us."

"Must have been the recruits for the Great March," said James.

"Well, they sure as hell fooled us," continued Aage. "They worked day and night and you know what, in two days they had straightened out the whole damn mess, got their wagons loaded and were headed out of town. We couldn't believe it.... Fine bunch of men....Fine bunch of men. Paid us well, too, for the stuff they bought."

James, whom Aage insisted on calling Jim, and his new friend talked for an hour or more. Aage had come to America from Norway and had lived in the area for nearly twenty years. He had been a farmer but moved his family into town during the Indian troubles of a few years back and now owned a local livery stable. It was a hard life but a good life.

"I haven't seen any Indians in the town," remarked James.

"You're gawdam right you haven't and you won't around here, either," he answered with some heat. "Not since the Uprising of '62. Them Sioux sons of bitches rampaged through this country and killed every white person they came across. Came damn close to getting me and my family. The cavalry got them good and proper though. Hanged a bunch of them and chased the rest off. Some of them ran off to your Red River country. We were damn glad to see the last of them."

James heard a series of whistles from the locomotive and noticed the blue uniforms leaving.

"I think that's my train," James said to Aage as he rose to leave. "Thanks for the beer. I enjoyed talking with you."

"Think nothing of it, Jim," he answered. "It's a pleasure seeing you. You Mounties are a mighty fine bunch...mighty fine."

James hurried back up the street to the station. The train was waiting, smoke curling out of the tall smokestack, an engineer oiling around the drive wheels from a can with a long spout. Carts were drawn alongside the baggage cars and clusters of people were gathered around saying their goodbyes. As James was about to climb up the steps into a coach he heard a strong voice behind him.

"What kind of a gawdam uniform is that?"

James turned around. A few feet away was a tall, broad shouldered American army officer, one of those he had noticed in the tavern. To James he looked a few years older than he was. His long, dark blue riding coat had two rows of brass buttons. There were stripes on his shoulder straps and crossed swords on his lapel. He wore long black gloves and had a dispatch case slung over his shoulder. His wide hat was pulled low over his eyes. His left hand rested comfortably on his sword. James noticed the other two officers a short distance off. They were looking in his direction with grins on their faces. It suggested to James that they were expecting some kind of confrontation.

Without hesitation James stepped towards the officer and held out his hand.

"Constable Keyden, sir, North West Mounted Police."

The officer was somewhat taken aback. He had expected some other kind of response.

"North West Mounted Police," the officer repeated. "Are you one of those Redcoats from Canada we keep hearing about?"

"Yes, sir."

"You traveling alone…what did you call yourself?"

"Constable Keyden, sir. James Keyden."

"You travelling alone, Constable?"

"Yes, sir."

"Where're you heading?"

"Fort Benton. Then north into Canada."

"Fort Benton. Now there's a God-forsaken place," said the American officer. "Maybe we'll have a chance to visit a little, Constable. We've got a long ride ahead of us."

The officer turned and joined his friends. James watched as they had words together and glanced back in his direction. He watched them disappear up the steps two cars behind where he stood. He turned, climbed up into the coach, found a seat and made himself comfortable. In a matter of moments the train was on its way.

The coach was not quite full. There were three families but not too many children. Most of the occupants were men in their thirties and forties. They looked like tradesmen except that their clothes were a little more worn and rumpled than nearer the big cities.

James' stomach started to act up again. Whether it was the beer this time he wasn't sure. He had discovered early in his young life that for whatever reason, his system rebelled against beer. He tried not to drink it except in cases where it was too rude to refuse. He leaned his head against the window and tried to sleep. Eventually he did. When he awoke it was almost dark. He put his feet up on the opposite seat and settled in for the night.

23

James drifted in and out of sleep through the night. As the first rays of the sun were streaking across the sky behind them he got up, walked up and down the aisle to get the kinks out of his back and neck. He found the lavatory unoccupied and made good use of it. Then he patrolled the aisle a little more. Most of the other passengers were still asleep, or trying to be. The lanterns hanging from the ceiling were still lit and swayed with the movement of the coach.

Returning to his seat he removed his boots, stretched his legs and laid them on the seat opposite. Out the window, in the first light of dawn, he was astonished to see nothing but sky. The land was perfectly flat and in every direction disappeared into the horizon. There wasn't a tree in sight. His face was glued to the window as the sun splashed across this immense landscape and bathed it in a warm, welcoming light. It was a sky he had never imagined. It rose like a huge dome from the horizon, stretched over his head and down to the opposite horizon. The sun touched with a pale red the scattered clouds high above and other softer puffs of white closer to the ground. As the sun rose higher the clouds disappeared and the sky changed to a bright blue.

"This is the prairie," James thought to himself. "The captain was right. You can't imagine it until you see it."

As a parting gift, Arthur had presented James with a copy of a book which had become very popular. Most Easterners' ideas of the North West had been taken from it. The same Captain Butler who had authored the report he had borrowed from Captain Channer had written it. Looking out the window he understood why Butler had titled it "The Great Lone Land."

"Mind if I sit down?"

James looked up to see the blue uniformed officer he had met on the station platform in St. Paul.

"Not at all," he replied clearing his things from the seat beside him and closing his book. "I'd enjoy the company."

"Where're you from?" asked the officer.

"Scotland," replied James.

"Where in Scotland?" asked the officer.

"A little town called Gask, it's seven miles west of Perth."

"My mother's people came from Ayreshire a few generations ago," said the officer, "wherever that is."

"It's not that far from where I grew up," replied James. "In fact, no two places are very far apart in Scotland. Compared to this," he said pointing out the window, "it's a pretty small country."

"So you're from Scotland!" the officer repeated. "What brings you over here?"

"I've only been here a month," James told him. "I came to visit my sister in Toronto. While I was there I was offered a job in the North West."

"By the way," interrupted the officer, "the name's Rawlins, Matt Rawlins, Major, United States Army."

"Cavalry?" asked James, pointing towards the crossed swords on his uniform.

"Cavalry it is," he replied, "but a staff man now."

James told him about his father and the Scots Greys. That got them going into a lively discussion about horses, cavalry battles, jumping, racing and other horse talk.

"What brings you to the Wild West…what did you say your name was?"

"Keyden, sir, James Keyden."

"Do you like to be called James or Jim?"

"I prefer James."

"Okay, James it is," replied the major. "My name's Matthew but I prefer Matt."

"I've been sent out here to report on the situation in the North West," James told him. "I'm a reporter really, not a policeman. I'll be based at Fort Macleod."

"Where the hell's that?" asked Matt.

"About a hundred miles northwest of Fort Benton."

"That must be about half way to the North Pole," remarked Matt.

"I hear it can get pretty cold!" James replied.

"Well, I don't know a damn thing about what's going on up in Canada," continued the major. "But I can tell you a thing or two about what's going on down here."

"I'd be interested," said James, "particularly about the Indians."

"Indians!" exclaimed Matt. "What do you want to know about gawdam Indians for?"

"I guess most of us Old Country people are fascinated about Indians," he answered.

"Well, let me tell you about Indians," said Matt, pulling off his boots and putting his feet up on the opposite seat. "There are good Indians and there are bad Indians. The good Indians are doing what they're supposed to do and settling down on reservations. The bad Indians don't want to settle down and are fighting us every inch of the way. They've made the Bozeman Trail…. you know the Bozeman Trail?"

"I've heard of it," answered James.

"They've made the Bozeman Trail impassable. They've been raiding and killing along it for years. On top of that we've had to beef up our escorts along the railway lines to keep them safe. We've had to send some of our best cavalry troops to protect the surveyors for the new Northern Pacific Railroad. They're extending it west from Bismarck. With thousands of miners and other settlers pouring into this country the Indians are only getting in the way."

"Miners?" asked James.

"Yeah, lots of miners," answered Matt. "They found gold in the Black Hills and its crawling with miners."

"I thought that was Sioux territory" said James.

The major looked at him sideways, a hint of suspicion in his eyes.

"How did you know about that?" he asked.

"I did a little reading before I came out here," replied James.

"Yeah, the Black Hills were on the Sioux Reservation," Matt continued. "But the Indians have no use for gold so the government's offered to buy it back from them."

"Have they sold?"

"No, not yet. But they will."

"But the miners are in there anyway?" asked James pointedly. "I thought part of the deal was that the army would keep settlers and miners out of Sioux territory."

"You know quite a lot for a newcomer," said the major with a little edge in his voice. "Look, there is no way we can keep those hordes of gold crazed fortune hunters out of there. Whether the Indians like it or not, the miners are going to stay and the settlers are going to follow them."

"But the Sioux don't like it very much," added James.

"You're gawdam right they don't like it," said Matt with a touch of anger in his voice. "In fact, we're at war over it. They're shooting up wagon trains, raiding forts, killing whites wherever they find them. But not much longer. Everyone, from President Grant on down, has had it with them. We're going to force them back to their reservations or kill them."

"You'd do that? You'd kill them?"

"If we have to."

"That would be a massacre," added James.

"That's not a massacre," replied the major indignantly. "That's a skirmish. There are only a few hundred of them. "

"Sounds like a massacre to me," added James.

"Look Jim…James," said the major, turning to look James in the eye. "I fought at Antietam Creek and Gettysburg. Those were massacres. Thousands slaughtered in an afternoon. I was at Chancellorsville the day we got good and clobbered. Lee surprised us and smashed our flank and rear. With a force half our size he kicked the shit out of us. By nightfall, there were 20,000 dead men – half ours, half theirs. That's a massacre."

They sat in silence.

"Most of us officers who are out here went through that war," added the major, looking thoughtfully out the window, "Crooks, Terry, Miles, Custer, Gibbons, and most of our men. Killing a few hundred redskins is nothing compared to what we've been through."

Again, silence.

"Ever heard of General Sheridan?" continued the major.

"I've heard the name."

"He's the boss out here – Commanding General, District of the Missouri."

"District of the Missouri?" asked James. "What's that?"

"Sheridan is responsible for the whole of the west – from Chicago to the Rocky Mountains and from the Canadian border to the Mexican border. I'm on his staff in Chicago. I've been with him every day since April '64, when Grant put him in charge of all the cavalry in the whole damn Army of the Potomac. He was thirty-three years old. To look at him you'd never in a million years think he would make a great cavalry commander. He's five foot five and less than 130 pounds. He was a little curly haired Irish kid from Ohio who worked his way to West Point. He's one tough son of a bitch."

"West Point?" asked James.

"Our military academy, we're all from there. I was in the same class as Custer, only I never made general. He graduated last in the class but he's got a great knack for publicity – and turned out to be not a bad general. He's a hell of an Indian fighter. You know what Lincoln used to say about Sheridan? Old Abe used to say, 'He's one of those long-armed fellows with short legs that can scratch his shins without having to stoop over.'"

They both laughed at the thought.

"But he's a fearless bastard in battle," Matt went on. "I was with him outside Richmond when we swept around Lee's flank and shattered Johnny Rebs' supply lines. We killed Lee's best cavalry officer, Jeb Stuart, in the process. I was with him through the Shenandoah Valley...."

The major stopped in mid-sentence and gazed out the window.

"What happened there?" asked James.

Matt hesitated but went on.

"By that time the Rebs were on the ropes, but they kept on fighting. They were getting a lot of their provisions from the Valley and General Grant wanted it stopped. He ordered Sheridan to take the Valley and destroy anything that would feed man or beast. Through the middle of September we fought our way from one end of the Valley to the other. We took all the horses and cattle we could and killed those we couldn't. We burned every barn, hay stack and crop to the ground. We didn't leave enough grain for a loaf of bread. Sheridan used to say, 'If a crow flies through the valley he better bring his own lunch.' It wasn't as bad as Sherman in Georgia but it was pretty gawdam terrible."

"What about the people?" asked James.

"They suffered... Jesus, we all suffered."

Matt stared out the window in silence. James watched him intently. There was a depth of emotion in the major which startled him.

"Lincoln made Sheridan a general for what he did in the Valley," Matt continued, still looking out the window. "He gave him command of the whole Middle Army."

Matt turned back to James. "You know, that same summer some of the Rebs were using Canada as a base."

"I've never heard that," answered James.

"Damn right. They'd cross the border, make a strike, cause a fuss, and high tail it back across your border where they'd be safe. Same as the Indians are doing out here."

"The Indians do that in the North West?" asked James.

"The Sioux have been doing it for years." The major paused in thought. "You know what makes fighting Indians so gawdam difficult?"

James remembered what Captain Channer had told him but he wanted to hear it from Matt.

"They don't stand and fight like we do. They're all over the place. They hit you here and they hit you there and just when you think you've got'em cornered they vanish – into the mountains, into the plains and sometimes over that border into Canada. It's what makes Sheridan so mad. You know what he says about Indians?"

"No."

"Sheridan showed up after the Battle of Washita. You've heard of it?"

"No."

"It's when Custer wiped out Black Kettle's Cheyenne village. After the battle, the Comanche Chief, Turtle Dove, showed up. When he met Sheridan he said, 'I'm a good Indian.' Sheridan turned on him and said, 'The only good Indians I ever saw were dead.'"

"Does he really feel that way?" asked James.

"When he's mad."

"And he's mad now?"

"At the Indian? Never seen him so upset."

They both sat in silence and looked out at the passing prairie. The sun was rising behind them. For the first time James noticed the long prairie grass. It was moving like waves in the ocean in response to the gentle wind. He could see no end to it. Here and there among the grass were small hollows, some with shallow pools of water, some dry beds with cracked surfaces. There wasn't a feature on the landscape he could identify. From one minute to the next the sight was almost identical.

"I rode with Sheridan to Cedar Creek too," continued the major. "You must have heard of Cedar Creek?"

"Tell me."

"We were miles away when a scout brought word of a raging battle at a place called Cedar Creek. We went tearing off at full gallop. I thought our horses would drop under us. When we arrived on the scene, Johnny Reb was licking our guys good and proper. Sheridan galloped up and down the line and turned the retreating men around. He regrouped the cavalry. Then he attacked with everything he had. You know what?"

"What?"

"We beat those grey shirts and won the day." Matt sat silent as if reliving the moment.

"That was just a few weeks before the presidential election," Matt continued. "Lincoln needed a big victory to help him win and Sheridan gave it to him at Cedar Creek. If you ever wondered why Lincoln and Grant thought so highly of Sheridan, that's why."

Again Matt was caught up in the memory. "You ever hear this?"

> Hurrah! Hurrah! for Sheridan!
> Hurrah! Hurrah for horse and man!
> And when their statues are placed on high
> Under the dome of the Union sky
> The American soldier's Temple of Fame,
> There, with the glorious general's name,
> Be it said, in letters both bold and bright:
> "Here is the steed that saved the day
> By carrying Sheridan into the fight,
> From Winchester – twenty miles away."

"Never heard it before," James admitted.

"It's from 'Sheridan's Ride'. It was actually six miles but twenty sounds better in the poem. It was read from every Republican platform right up to Election Day. If you ask me, it's what got Old Abe re-elected."

They were both looking out the window. There was a huge white cloud forming in the distance stretching to a great height. James thought of what the experiences of the Civil War had done to the major. The stories gave him some insight into General Sheridan who was commanding the cavalry in the west and leading the war against the Indians.

"Then there was the day," Matt interrupted, "that President Lincoln steamed up the James River to Aiken's Landing to review our troops. Our men were all along the shore washing the dust and ashes of the Shenandoah off themselves and their clothes and singing and splashing and laughing. The President was on the deck in his long black coat, waving his high hat to the men who recognized his tall lanky figure and cheered as he sailed by.

"When the boat docked I went on board with Sheridan. The two of them shook hands for a long time.

"Remember," Matt said looking at James, "the President was six foot six and Sheridan, five foot five. Lincoln said something like, 'General, when this war started I thought a cavalryman should be at least six feet four inches high. But I've changed my mind – five feet five will do in a pinch."

The major smiled as he remembered the occasion. He had rested his head against the back of the seat and was looking at the ceiling of the car. He was almost talking to himself.

"A couple of days before it was over we captured Robert E. Lee's son. On the last day of the war, April 9, I was there and I'll never forget it, our cavalry stretched for half a mile across a hill in the path of Lee's army. If Sheridan had raised his sword we would have been down on him like a tidal wave. Lee looked up and saw us and decided then and there it was all over. And it was."

The major turned to James. "So you see, my friend, after four years of that slaughter, and make no mistake, it was a slaughter like this world has rarely seen, killing a few Indians and burning down a few Indian villages doesn't bother us a hell of a lot."

24

When Major Rawlins found out that James hadn't eaten much since he had left St. Paul he invited him back to his seat to share some of the rations he and his fellow officers had brought with them. He introduced the other two cavalrymen who were lieutenants on their way to Fort Abraham Lincoln, a few miles south of Bismarck. The major was headed for the same place, on special assignment from General Sheridan.

James was grateful for the bread, cheese and fruit. It seemed to sit well in his stomach. The American officers looked at each other and raised their eyebrows when James selected the sarsaparilla over the beer. Their conversation was light and casual and when they had finished eating, one of the Americans brought out a deck of cards. They were glad to have James as a fourth. One of the lieutenants, whose name was O'Neil and who had a long saber scar across one ear and cheek, seemed to have particular hatred for the Indians.

"I say we just round'em up and shoot'em all," he said provocatively.

"Isn't that a little harsh?" replied James.

"Don't be so gawdam smug," the lieutenant shot back. "You British. You're so bloody self-righteous. You sail into the ports of China, train your ships' cannons on the locals and force them to buy opium. If they don't, you open fire."

James was about to defend his country's actions but the lieutenant interrupted.

"You march into India. You think you're doing them a big favour by helping them build a few roads and railways. Hell, all you really want is to sell them more cloth from your Midland mills. Someone discovered diamonds in Africa a couple of years ago and your army's in there now shooting up the natives."

James knew it was true.

"You tried sucking the wealth out of this country and we wouldn't stand for it," the lieutenant continued growing more heated by the moment. "We told you to go home and when you wouldn't, we sent you packing. Who the hell are you to tell us to be nice to the natives?"

"Easy, O'Neil," said the major. "We know what the Irish think of the English."

"With bloody good reason."

Rather than provoke a confrontation with O'Neil, James took the criticism, studied his cards and played in turn. What he was beginning to understand was that in this country, formality and propriety, even if it was superficial, was set aside. People said what they thought. He expected that they did what they wanted as well. If it was gold in the Black Hills, they took it. If it was a place to settle they wanted, or land to raise cattle, they took it. God help anyone who got in the way. If the buffalo and the Indians had to go to make way, he guessed that's the way it would be. "Maybe that's what they mean," he thought, "when they talk about the American way of life."

25

The next day the scene out his coach window was exactly as it had been the day before. There were great billowy clouds rising high into the sky. James could see the pools of light on the prairie where the sun was breaking through the banks of cloud. He read, walked up and down the aisle and went back through the two cars to visit with his card partners of the night before. They invited him to join them. There was no mention of the harsh words of the night before. They talked horses. One of the lieutenants had not been west before and he was quizzing O'Neil about how to deal with the monotony, how to survive the fierce winters and where to find women.

"You've only got three choices," answered O'Neil. "Some of the officers have brought their wives out here. You'd better stay clear of them. If their husbands find out they'll feed you to the wolves. If you're near a town there are the saloon girls, but they're pretty busy and most of them are near worn out. Then there're squaws. Hell, you can buy a young one for a bottle of whiskey. Send her back to her folks when you leave. If you can't afford a bottle you can have her mother for a cupful."

James was disturbed by the tone of the conversation. He excused himself and walked down the aisle through the train. He stood by the metal gate at the back of the last car and watched the tracks converge in the distance. The rushing air revived him even though at times it was spiced with black smoke that was puffing out of the smokestack of the engine. Returning to his seat, he nodded to the now familiar passengers as he passed and they smiled back. Sometimes the children followed behind him, the bolder ones asking to touch his sword. They reminded him of William and Hermione and at times he missed his nephew and niece.

As the sun fell towards the horizon ahead of them, the major walked up the two coaches and joined James who was well into his book. Matt asked about it and they chatted idly for a time. A trainman passed through the coach, took down the lanterns one by one and lit the wicks. There was a puff of black smoke until he trimmed it, then placed the glass over it and hung it again from the ceiling. It gave off a comforting, low light and swung with the rhythm of the train casting shadows that moved across the faces of the passengers.

"Don't take what Lieutenant O'Neil said too seriously," Matt advised. "This is his second tour out here. Last time he hadn't been here three months before his patrol was ambushed by a Cheyenne war party. One of the Indians grabbed a saber from a dead trooper and took a swing at O'Neil. You can see what he did to him. The attack scared him to death. He had to be sent back east to get over it. He's pretty nervous coming back, but he knows if he's ever going to make captain he has to put in some time out here."

The sun had fallen below the horizon. There was a magnificent blaze of colour stretching across the horizon – yellow, touching orange, touching red, touching purple and deep blue. It changed every few minutes, the lighter shades giving way to the darker. The mothers in the coach were trying to get their children to settle down, wrapping them in blankets against the chill of the evening. One of the fathers had his harmonica out and was playing softly to help his children off to sleep. Matt and James sat silently watching the last rays of colour fade until there was only blackness. If he shielded his eyes against the reflection of the lanterns, James could see a few stars poking through the night sky.

"Is there someone back home waiting for you?" asked Matt

James took a moment to reply. "I'm not sure where home is. How about you?"

"As a matter of fact, there're two – two beautiful women."

"Two?" questioned James.

"One's my daughter," he laughed.

"Then you're married."

"To a beautiful Southern belle."

"Southern belle?" questioned James. "After what you told me about your fighting against the South? That must be interesting."

"Interesting from the first day we met," replied Matt.

"Where was that?"

"Charleston, South Carolina of all places, where it all began," Matt started. "I was there on War Office business, still on Sheridan's staff. It was three years after the war ended, but there were still signs of devastation all over the city. A Union uniform was still not a popular sight. I was staying at the home of a business friend I had made in Washington. He was an ex-Confederate army officer who had gone into the textile business after the war. The army was buying from him. I was negotiating the contract and had gone down to see his mill."

"The South was pretty badly damaged?" asked James.

"Parts of it were flattened," replied Matt, "absolutely destroyed."

"One night," Matt continued, "we arrived back at his home to find the place in a flap. He had a younger sister who I thought was absolutely beautiful but whom I knew wouldn't look twice at a Union soldier. Besides, Jeff, that's my friend's name, said she was all but engaged to a fellow called Blanton.

"Well, that night Blanton came down with the 'flu or something and was too ill to take her to a grand ball that was going on in town that night. She had just received a message from him a few minutes before we arrived saying he couldn't make it. She was nearly dressed for the occasion and there was no way in the world she wasn't going to go. Jeff turned to me and said 'Matt would you mind if I deserted you tonight to take my sister to the ball.'"

"I said, 'Not at all Jeff. I'll be fine.'"

"Then Carolyn Duke, that's her name – lots of Southerners have double barreled first names said, 'I'm not going to this ball with my brother.' Before I knew it she turned to me and said, 'Matthew, would you escort me to the ball?' Hell, I didn't even think she knew my name."

Matt paused to recall the moment. The other passengers were asleep or quietly resting. The swinging lanterns cast dancing shadows over them.

"There was a stunned silence in the room," he went on. "Carolyn Duke's mother was there and she didn't say a word. She just glared, too polite I guess, to say, 'I absolutely forbid you to go anywhere with a Yankee'.

"Jeff didn't know quite what to say. He didn't want to let on that I might not be welcome at the ball. Thankfully, Carolyn Duke's father wasn't there or that would have been the end of it. I didn't say a word. After a few seconds which felt like hours Carolyn Duke chirped up and said, 'That settles it, I'm going to the ball with Matthew,' and ran upstairs to finish getting dressed."

"What then?"

"The next half hour was a blur," Matt recalled, smiling a little. "The family had a black maid in the house. Rachel was her name. She was getting on in years. She was large with a laugh that made you smile just to hear it. She hustled me upstairs to my room, had my jacket, shirt, pants, socks and shoes off before I knew what was going on. She was in and out of my room I don't remember how many times, for my sword, belt and hat. She brought hot water, towels and fresh underwear, which I guess was Jeff's, ordering me around like a general. 'Get yourself washed, and good, and get these clean things on before I'm back – ya'hear? And shave your face.'"

Matt smiled at the memory.

"I've never seen my uniform look so good before or since," Matt chuckled. "There wasn't a wrinkle in it and the buttons shone. I could see my face in them. I still don't know what she did to my sword but it gleamed like a flash of lightning. My boots were so black and shiny I didn't think they were mine. 'Off you go then', commanded Rachel, 'You give Miss Carolyn a good time, ya'hear.' There was a wide grin on her face. As I left the room Rachel whispered to me. 'You have a good evening, Mr. Matthew.' Then she added something I never forgot. 'Those'll be the only nice words you'll be hearing all evening, but don't you mind.'"

"What did she mean?" asked James.

Matt didn't answer. He just carried on with his story.

"Going down the staircase I caught a look at myself in the mirror," Matt continued. "I felt like General Grant. Carolyn Duke was waiting in the front hall. She was dressed in a long white ball gown that skimmed the floor. It was cut low so that her shoulders and neck were bare. Her skin reflected the candles on the wall and her dark hair shone. She was so beautiful I had to gasp for breath."

The only sound in the sleeping coach was the clacking of the steel wheels as they passed from rail to rail.

"A carriage was waiting," Matt went on. "Carolyn Duke's mother, Jeff and Rachel were on the porch to see us off. The mother was stony faced, holding in her anger. She didn't say a word. Jeff shook my hand and said, 'You look wonderful, Matt.' But his expression was tight and there was no smile. Rachel stood behind them and said nothing. She was smiling and there was the smallest tear in her eye.

"'Thank you, Matthew, for escorting me,' Carolyn said as we were moving off in the carriage. It was the first time I had ever been alone with her."

"'It's my pleasure, Miss Carolyn,' I replied. I didn't even know what to call her."

"'Please, call me Carolyn,' she said. 'That's what Blanton calls me. I really wanted to go tonight. It's the biggest ball of the year in Charleston. I've been counting on it for weeks. Thank you for coming. It took courage.'

"I was a little taken aback. I didn't know quite what she meant. Was I courageous to go with her, a younger woman, who I hardly knew? Was I courageous to go at such short notice? I began to get a slight feeling of dread. This was the Deep South. This is where the Civil War began. I was wearing a Union uniform."

"'Whatever happens tonight let's enjoy ourselves,' Carolyn said. 'Right,' was my rather weak reply."

Matt leaned forward and stretched his neck and shoulders. He looked for a long moment at the pools of moonlight on the prairie grass.

"What then?" asked James.

"The ball was in a beautiful old Southern mansion," Matt went on leaning back on the hard seat. "It had a classic, two-storey porch across the front with four white columns holding up the roof. I could see where shellfire had chipped away some of the masonry. The entrance was ablaze in light and there was a line of carriages waiting to discharge their passengers. It was obvious from the moment we went through the front door that any person wearing the uniform I was in was to be treated as if they had leprosy. Most of the glances were not even subtle. I'm glad we looked so great because I certainly didn't feel great."

Matt loosened the buttons on his jacket.

"But you went in."

"Carolyn didn't hesitate for a moment. We joined the crowd moving slowly towards the receiving line. Each couple was announced as they entered the ballroom, then moved through the seven or eight couples who were greeting everyone. There was generally a smattering of applause from the crowd in the ballroom as each couple was announced.

"Carolyn whispered to me as our turn came to be introduced. 'Whatever happens,' she said, 'try to enjoy yourself.' She slipped her hand under my right arm as we stepped into the ballroom.

"There was a man in a long formal coat with high white collar who greeted each couple at the doorway. He looked like something out of the 18th Century French court. He asked our names. When he looked at me his eyes went cold and hard. 'Miss Carolyn Duke Calhoun. Captain Matthew Rawlins, United States Army', he shouted to the assembled crowd. He didn't attempt to disguise the contempt in his voice.

"The ballroom went dead silent. Not a whisper. Carolyn was great. I felt her other hand on my arm and she led me strongly towards the receiving line. She knew them all by name. 'Good evening Mr. Marshall,' she said to the man at the head of the line, 'I'm afraid Blanton became ill today and Captain Rawlins, who is visiting us from Washington, was kind enough to escort me at the last moment. I'm very grateful to him.'

"I raised my hand to shake Mr. Marshall's hand. His stayed deliberately at his side. He looked me straight in the eye and didn't say a word. I was aware of a screaming silence. There was no applause in the ballroom. '....I'm very grateful to him,' I heard Carolyn say to Mrs. Marshall. I raised my hand to her. Again no response. I got the message. I didn't raise my hand again. But the second last woman in the line, I missed her name at the time, did raise her hand which I shook. 'We're very pleased you made it possible for Carolyn Duke to come tonight, Captain Rawlins,' she said in a strong voice for more than me to hear. 'She is a favourite of mine. Tonight wouldn't have been the same without her.' She looked me straight in the eye. She gave me a kindly smile and there were tears in her eyes."

James was gripped by the story and glanced over at Matt's face as he spoke.

"When we reached the end of the line Carolyn took command," Matt continued. 'It's a very hot evening, Matthew,' she said. 'Shouldn't we have something to drink?' With that she tightened her grip on my arm and steered me towards a long table on the other side of the ballroom. She was in no hurry. She held her head high, smiled and nodded to friends who were standing nearby until we reached the table. I felt every eye in the place on us. If they had known I rode with Sheridan I'm sure they would have lynched me on the spot.

"As we reached the table a black man in a spotless white jacket had two crystal glasses of something waiting for us. I still don't know what it was. We took them, moved off into the crowd to watch others arrive.

"'Enjoying yourself, Matthew?' I heard Carolyn ask. I looked down at her. There was a touch of a smile on her lips but tears in her eyes. I choked up. She had known from the moment that she asked me to escort her what was in store for us. Walking across that ballroom floor arm in arm with a Union officer had shown more courage than Pickett's men at Gettysburg."

Matt paused at the thought.

"We had every dance together. No one cut in on Carolyn and no one spoke to us. Twice during the evening I caught the eye of the woman who had shaken my hand in the line. She smiled at me both times.

"When we reached home Rachel was there to open the door. Then she disappeared.

"Carolyn and I stood in the hallway. She was looking at herself in the full-length mirror. To me she looked more beautiful than ever.

'I'm sorry, Matthew,' she said, speaking to my image in the mirror. 'I didn't mean to hurt you.'

"'I'm all right,' I told her. 'I was very proud to be with you. You knew what was going to happen. Why did you do it?'

'Because it's time to bury the past,' she said firmly. She reached over to me, put her hands gently on my neck, drew my head down and kissed me. There were tears running down her face.

"'Good night, Matthew,' she said. 'Thank you for a wonderful evening."

"I couldn't take my eyes off her as she went up the stairs. I couldn't sleep that night nor concentrate for days. I was completely smitten. I'd never met any woman with that much beauty and that much courage."

"When did you get married?" asked James.

"A few months later. One day I received a letter from Jeff saying he was coming to Washington and he wanted to see me. He mentioned that Carolyn was coming with him. After a dinner party with Jeff, Carolyn and I went for a long walk. By the time we arrived back at her hotel we were engaged."

"You weren't married in Charleston," said James.

"Hell, no!" replied Matt. "Jeff accepted our engagement but her parents were furious. They wouldn't hear of it. So with Jeff's help we were married in Washington. No family from either side except Jeff and a friend of Carolyn's who was working in the Capital."

"Your family weren't there either?" asked James.

"My parents both died when I was young," replied Matt. "I have a brother who works a farm west of Philadelphia. He lost an arm in the war. My sister and her husband have a place in Indiana and they couldn't make it."

"So it was just the four of you," said James.

"That was it," replied Matt. "When the news that we were married reached Charleston we received only one letter. It was from the same lady who shook my hand in the receiving line. Her name was Mrs. Nell Woodward. She recalled in the letter what a handsome couple we had been at the ball and wished us well. It was only then that Carolyn told me that both her sons had been killed in the war. I can't comprehend where a person like her finds the strength to do what she did for us."

"And now you have a daughter," added James.

"One," answered Matt, "a girl. We call her Nell."

26

Next morning James raised his head from the back of the seat and starred out the coach window. The view was the same as it had been for the last two days. The land swept to the horizon in all directions. The sky seemed bigger and the clouds higher. There must have been a wind from the southwest because the thick black smoke from the locomotive was drifting across the fields in front of him and dissipating in the distance.

James was relieved that this was to be the last day on the train. They were due into Bismarck early in the afternoon. His back and neck were stiff, the seat seemed to be getting harder and he was looking forward to the stagecoach ride to Fort Benton even though Matt had told him it would be bumpy, dusty and long. Maybe the change would finally settle his stomach, which had started to act up again. He picked up the Butler book and opened it where he had left off.

"Almost finished the book?"

It was Matt. He looked as tired as James felt.

"Sleep well?" asked James.

"No." Matt seated himself beside James and rested his dispatch case between them propping his big boots up on the seat opposite. James marked his place in the book and set it aside.

"You might have a day or so in Benton on your own," said Matt. "It's a miserable, one horse town with nothing much to do. I'll give you a note to the officer in command at the fort. If you have some time to kill you could look him up."

"I'd appreciate that," said James.

There came a long series of blasts from the locomotive's whistle and the train jerked as the engineer applied the brakes, bringing it to a halt as quickly as he could.

"Buffalo," yelled a voice behind them.

They both leaned for the window. James could see several buffalo ahead of them. Then he noticed hundreds of dots in the distance and recognized a vast herd grazing as far as he could see. The whistle kept blowing, long blasts and short blasts. There were passengers on the other side of the coach who had pressed their faces to the windows. There were buffalo on their side as well. Some must be on the tracks ahead of them. The train came to a jolting, screeching stop.

"Let's get'em," yelled a man's voice from the back of the coach. James turned to see several men heading for the door. They were carrying their rifles.

"Want to see some fun?" asked the major.

"What fun?" asked James.

"Shooting buffalo."

"What for?" asked James.

"For the hell of it," he replied, smiling. "Come on. The fresh air will do you good."

James finally had to confess to Matt the explosive forces at work in his stomach. He thought he should probably stay close to the lavatory in case he had to make a run for it. Matt laughed and punched him playfully on the shoulder.

"Don't worry," Matt teased. "Everyone gets it the first time they're out here. It must be the water."

Matt got up from his seat, walked to the back of the coach and followed the men out the door. James watched from the window as the men ran across the field towards the buffalo. He saw Matt and the two lieutenants join up and walk in the same direction towards the herd.

The first shots came from the other side of the train. James rose to cross the aisle to see what was happening. As he did, his leg hit the major's dispatch case knocking it to the floor. The papers spilled out onto the aisle. James bent down to pick them up. His eyes fell on the document on top. It was titled, "Sioux Pacification Campaign, Summer 1876. Lieut. General Philip H. Sheridan, Officer Commanding, District of the Missouri."

James looked up and down the aisle. There were some mothers and a few small children still in the coach but all the men and the older children had gone outside. He looked out the window. He could see the three blue uniforms standing far down the field watching the action. He picked up the papers on the floor, stuffed them back in the case but kept the one on top. He opened it and started reading.

> *To: Department Commanders*
> *Brig. Gen. George Crook, Omaha*
> *Brig. Gen. Alfred H. Terry, St. Paul*
>
> *On February 1, 1876, the Secretary of the Interior ordered that all Indians who have not retired to their reservations are to be declared as hostile. He has asked the Secretary of War to initiate whatever action deemed necessary to return them to their reservations.*
>
> *The following plan is in response to the Secretary of War's request. You are to pursue and engage the enemy until they are returned to their reservations or destroyed.*
>
> *Lieut. General Philip H. Sheridan*
> *Officer Commanding*
> *District of the Missouri*

James turned to the next page. It was a map of the campaign. It showed a three pronged attack on an area centered at the junction of the Bighorn and Yellowstone Rivers. General Terry was to attack west from Fort Lincoln.

General Crook was to attack north from Fort Fetterman on the North Platte River. Colonel Gibbon was to attack east from Fort Ellis.

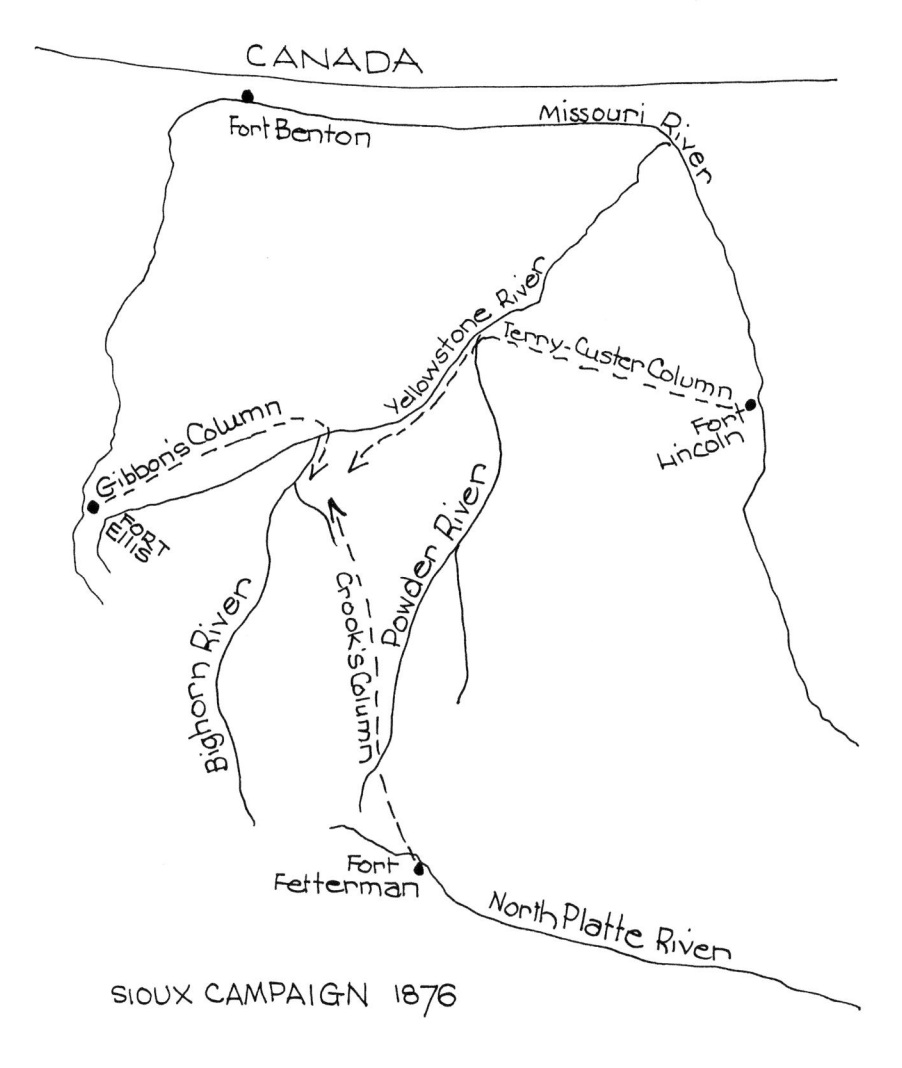

SIOUX CAMPAIGN 1876

James was glad he had spent as much time as he had studying the maps in the armory. He was able to place these movements quickly in the mind.

"When," he thought. "When will they attack?" He took a quick glance out the window. The blue coats were still standing where he had first seen them. He turned to the next page.

Disposition

Montana Column
Commander, Colonel John Gibbon
Action to commence, April 10, 1876
450 men of the 2nd Cavalry and the 7th Infantry
East from Fort Ellis, down the north bank of the Yellowstone River.

Crooks Column
Commander, Brig. Gen. George Crook
Action to commence, May 29, 1876
800 men of the cavalry and infantry
North and west from Fort Fetterman

Dakota Column
Commander, Brig. Gen. Alfred H. Terry
Action to commence, May 17, 1876
All 12 companies of the 7th Cavalry
2 companies of the 17th Infantry
1 company of the 16th Infantry to guard the supply train
150 wagons
1 detachment of the 20th Infantry with 3 Gatling guns
40 Arikara scouts
Total Force, 950 officers and men
Destination, West to the junction of the Yellowstone and Bighorn Rivers

James reviewed quickly what he had just read. "Jesus," he thought. "They're already on the move." He looked out the window again and saw the three officers turn and start back for the train. He reached for his notebook and began to sketch the map. Then he quickly copied the details of the disposition of the three columns. When he finished he put the document back in the dispatch case and rested it where he thought it had been. As he was putting his notebook back in his haversack he heard the men climbing up the steps into the train.

"Hey Lester, how many did ya get?" yelled one voice.

"Two for sure, maybe another."

"Hell, I got four for sure," said the loud voice. "Hit another but he ran off a ways."

"Good man," yelled Lester back to him. "Everyone counts. Every buffalo we kill means another starved Indian."

The men laughed.

The whistle sounded and the train started up again slowly. James was staring out the window absorbing what he had read in the report.

"I thought I left this with you," said Matt standing in the aisle beside the seat and reaching for his dispatch case. James was startled by Matt's sudden appearance.

"What was I saying before we stopped?" asked Matt. "Oh, ya. A note to the commander of Fort Benton." He sat down beside James. "Sorry you had to miss all the fun."

"What happens to all those dead buffalo?" James asked.

"The wolves'll get them. Maybe some drifters will skin them for the hides."

"Will the Indians take them?" asked James.

"Hell, no!" answered Matt emphatically. "They used to, but the wolfers sprinkle strychnine on some of the dead carcasses. Easiest way to get wolf pelts. Sometimes the Indians got there first and died as a result. Now redskins won't eat anything they haven't killed themselves."

"Seems like a waste," said James.

"Not really. There are millions of buffalo."

The major opened his case and noticed that the papers were a little out of place.

"Sorry," said James "I got up to see the shooting and I knocked it on the floor. Hope I didn't mess up anything."

"No, everything's okay," said the major, straightening the documents and reaching for some note paper. He wrote quickly, folded it and gave it to James.

"The officer in charge of Fort Benton is Captain Tom Davidson," he told James. "He's all right and will take good care of you. We're old friends."

"Thanks a lot," replied James. "If I have a chance I'll look him up."

Matt got up from his seat.

"See you at the station in Bismarck," said Matt. "And look after yourself. You're looking awfully flushed."

"Must be my stomach," replied James.

27

The six hundred miles and eight days it took to get from Bismarck to Fort Benton on the Montana Stage was the roughest, dustiest, most uncomfortable ride James had ever experienced. The stagecoach was just like the pictures he had seen in the Illustrated News. There were eight lean horses harnessed in pairs to a bulky, four wheel coach that had been beaten by wind, weather and torturous trails into as uncomfortable a vehicle as man could construct. Two men sat high up on a seat in the front with the baggage strapped to the roof behind them. One man drove the team of horses while the other watched, rifle at the ready, to ward off Indians, bandits or stray buffalo in their path.

There was room in the coach for eight passengers squeezed together on two seats facing each other. The seats had at one time been padded, but most of the stuffing had disappeared over the miles and James was sure that all the passengers suffered the same numb bottom that he did. Thankfully there were only four passengers on this occasion besides James headed for Fort Benton. There were two men in the transportation business, a representative of the railroad, a mystery man who said very little about himself or anything else and James. The horses were whipped into a gallop most of the time, except up inclines or through the streams and river fords. They stopped every fifty miles to change horses and allow the passengers to stretch their legs. The bumping and jerking kept James' mind off his stomach. The last thing he wanted to have to do was to yell to the driver to stop so that he could relieve himself in the middle of the open prairie.

Travelling fast had one advantage. It kept most of the mosquitoes and flies away from the coach. The first night out from Bismarck, as the sun dipped to the horizon, James had his first experience with prairie mosquitoes. When he stepped down from the stage for their periodic rest stop while a fresh team of horses was being hitched up, he was swarmed by the buzzing, stinging demons. He tried brushing them aside but it was hopeless. They were everywhere, down his neck, inside his jacket, up his sleeves, under his helmet. He couldn't run from them and he couldn't hide from them. Using the latrine was even worse. He was in and out in record time. The other passengers didn't seem to be as bothered as he was about it. They probably knew what to expect.

"Better get used to it," said the driver, noticing James annoyance. "If it stays dry for a couple more days they should die off pretty soon."

"Is it always like this?" James asked a fellow passenger. "Mostly in the spring and some years into early summer," he replied. "This isn't too bad, now. It's starting to get hot and mosquitoes don't like the heat. Another week or so, they'll be mostly gone."

After the first few days of bouncing over the bumpy trail, James began to think that the prairie would go on forever. He couldn't believe how endless the Great Plains were. His four companions, like himself, seemed to need all their energy just to keep themselves together. Conversation was spotty and always casual.

He did see his first Indians. He would have missed them except that the man on top with the rifle started shooting, the noise jarring him awake from one of the many times he had dozed off.

"Indians," yelled the railroad man, pointing out his window.

James could make out eight or nine riders on a ridge at least a quarter of a mile away. They were moving in the same direction that they were. Without the railwayman's description he wouldn't have known they were Indians.

"Why is he shooting?" asked James.

"What else do you do when you see an Indian?" replied one of the businessmen.

The next time James looked, the Indians had vanished.

The businessmen were travelling west to check on their investment in a freightline. They ran bull trains from Fort Benton to a town south of there called Helena.

"Helena used to be called Dead Man's Gulch," one of the businessmen explained to James. "The locals didn't think it a suitable name for a growing town so they named it after the only respectable woman in the place."

They told James that their freight business had prospered during the gold rush days of the 60's. When the gold dried up they had continued to do fairly well moving buffalo hides and wolf pelts to the steamer at Fort Benton for shipment to St. Louis. But the buffalo were getting scarce and the wolves were thinning out. The freightline owners had to decide whether to keep the bull trains moving or shut them down.

"Hear you're going to build a railway 'cross your plains to the Pacific," one of the businessmen said to James.

"Someday," he replied. "They haven't found a way through the mountains. It'll be a few years yet."

"Union Pacific's made a hell of a difference south of here," commented his partner. "When the Northern Pacific comes through here it'll be the end of the steamers."

Most of the long days were passed in silence. The men had tried to play poker but the cards scattered with every bump. They fought to breathe through the dust kicked up by the horse's hooves which swirled through the coach almost choking them. Mile after mile went by broken only by periodic stops and the never-ending battle with the mosquitoes.

As they approached Fort Benton, one of the passengers pointed to it with a shout. James stretched to look. There were a few ramshackled wooden buildings in the distance. He looked to see where the town might be but that was all there was of it. After weeks of travel he had reached his destination. It was a big disappointment.

The driver slowed the stagecoach as it reached the first shacks at the edge of town. They passed a string of harnessed bulls pulling a series of covered carts. The main street, if you could call it that, was a narrow dirt strip, deeply rutted with grooves of wagon-wheel tracks. It was hemmed in on each side with low, unpainted, rickety wooden buildings. James thought the whole place looked completely run down and in desperate need of repair. Small, one-horse carts were tied up in front of some building. Most of the wooden structures had flat fronts, with the name of the owner or its purpose lettered on the upper half. Other buildings had a covered porch with a raised wooden sidewalk often joined to the next building. It was like nothing he had ever imagined.

"This is Fort Benton?" James asked one of the businessmen.

"You're in it," he replied with a grin. "Two stores, a hotel, a few other businesses. The rest of these shacks are saloons."

The stage pulled up in front of a building with I. G. Baker & Co. written across its front. James remembered it as the name on one of the packets he was carrying. The passengers stepped down from the coach and were surrounded by a crowd of young boys eager to help. A rough looking man, bearded, in an old suit and a battered hat came out of the Baker store and chased them off. He had two young men with him. The man barked out orders. One of the young men climbed to the top of the coach and began untying the baggage. The man greeted the passengers as they emerged from the coach. James was the last one out.

"Constable Keyden?"

"Right," answered James.

"Welcome to Fort Benton," he said. "My name's Conrad, Oscar Conrad. One of your men asked me to keep an eye out for you. Which is your baggage?"

James pointed it out.

"Just the one? That's all you have?" asked Mr. Conrad.

"That's all."

"Your friends are expected here in the next day or so," Oscar told him. "They're picking up a shipment we're putting together for them. Would you like me to add your trunk to it."

"Please."

"They're expecting you at the Nugget Hotel," Oscar went on. "It's down the street on the other side. You'll find it okay for a night or two. Will you be wanting a horse, Constable Keyden?"

"Definitely," he replied, working his legs and stretching to get the kinks out of his shoulders.

"When you're ready," said Oscar, "I'm sure we've got one to your liking."

James watched as Oscar's boys carried his trunk into the store. The other passengers had moved on. He paused and looked around. It was the other end of the world from Perth, St. Andrews or Toronto. James shuddered. It was a rude welcome to the North West, but what did he expect. There was a strong wind blowing from the mountains. It kicked up the dust and swept it across the dirt strip in front of him carrying weeds and brush with it. The wooden fronts of the buildings lined the strip on both sides. There wasn't a woman in sight. The men he noticed were dressed in dusty shirts and well-worn trousers. They all had riding boots with high heels and spurs and broad rimmed hats. Some had scarves tied around their necks. He hadn't seen a man yet who wasn't wearing a handgun.

James walked down the street in the direction of the Nugget Hotel. On the way the men he passed said 'Hi' or 'Howdy' or gave him an almost imperceptible nod. He was pleasantly surprised. He had felt conspicuous in his scarlet jacket, white helmet and sword, but that didn't seem to make any difference to these men. The man behind the counter at the hotel was expecting him. He assigned him to Room 4. It was up some narrow stairs on the second floor at the back. The desk clerk said it would be quieter than the two rooms at the front facing the street.

Room 4 was as basic a room as James had ever seen. It had plain, unpainted wood walls, plain, unpainted wood floor, plain, unpainted wood bed, chair and dresser. There was a rusty pan on the dresser with some water in it. The door closed but didn't lock. The small, single pane window looked out onto an old barn that appeared to be on the verge of collapsing. It had been turned into a stable. There was straw and manure scattered all over the ground and the men standing in front of the stable didn't seem to be too concerned about cleaning it up.

Rough as it was, the room was the first private space James had had in weeks. The bed was a wooden frame with slats holding up a lumpy bag of straw. It was the first flat surface he had had to sleep on since he had left Toronto. It looked very good to him.

It was getting on towards late afternoon and James felt like stretching his legs. He knew the town was located on the Missouri River and after all he had read and studied about the great waterway he thought he would have a look at it. He asked the man at the desk for directions then set off and walked to the river. It was broad and swift-flowing and brought life to the town. There were trees lining it on both sides except where they had been cut away for the dock and the area around it. James felt refreshed just seeing it.

On the way back to the hotel he stopped for something to eat at one of the saloons. Then he delivered the envelope from the Dominion Bank to the clerk at the I. G. Baker store and picked up a few candles before returning to his room to write his first report to Mr. McLennan. With the information he had come across in Major Rawlin's dispatch case he knew it would be well received.

28

James wrote late into the night. He was pleased with the result and thought Mr. McLennan would be too. It was too late to write a note to Fiona and the children and he wanted to enclose one to his parents which he would ask her to forward. He smiled as he thought of his father and mother reading a letter from their son in Fort Benton. He could picture his father taking his well-worn atlas from the bookshelf. He would find the Missouri River but James was almost sure it wouldn't show Fort Benton. But sleep was catching up to him and the prospect of stretching out flat even on a lumpy bag of straw was too tempting. He would leave the other letters until morning.

Bright sunshine lit the scene out his window when James awoke. It had been the best sleep he had had in weeks and he felt much better for it. He looked across the courtyard below his window to the old barn, then over its roof as far as the eye could see. There was a jagged edge to the horizon with dots of white on it. The sight gripped him. It was his first glimpse of the Rocky Mountains. He followed the jagged line left and right. It went as far as his eyes could see.

James dressed, was careful to fold his report to Mr. McLennan and put it in his haversack. There was crispness in the air accentuated by the breeze blowing in from the mountains. The sun warmed him as he left the hotel. He walked through the town and back down to the river. He stepped out onto the dock alongside the river and watched the brownish, almost muddy water flowing swiftly by. Bending down, he picked up a piece of wood lying near his feet and threw it far out into the current, speculating how long it would take it to reach the Mississippi and then drift by New Orleans. He knew it would be a very long time.

29

There was a large rail-fence corral behind the Baker store. In it were twenty or thirty tired looking horses milling about deep in manure. James looked them over carefully. He was disappointed when none of them caught his eye. An old man was leaning on the fence near him also looking at the horses. James asked him if there were other horses for sale in the town. The old man told him to look behind Powers' store down the street. James went to have a look. He had the same experience and saw nothing that came anywhere near his expectations. James asked one of the boys feeding the stock if there were any other horses for sale. The boy told him that some half-breeds sometimes brought horses to the edge of town to sell. James followed his directions but there was no sign of half-breeds or horses.

Feeling discouraged, James walked back to Bakers to see if he would have better luck finding gifts for William and Hermione. On a shelf at the back of the store he found several pairs of doeskin moccasins decorated with beadwork. He selected two pairs, one with red beads and the other with white which he thought would fit the children and asked the clerk to hold them for him.

As he left the store a wagon, pulled by a team of horses and driven by a soldier in blue, passed in front. It reminded him of the letter that Matt had given him. He remembered the name of the Commanding Officer, something Davidson. James hailed the driver.

"How do I get to the fort?" James asked him. "I'm looking for Captain Davidson."

"It's a ways up the river," said the driver. "Hop on. I'll give you a ride."

James stepped up to the seat beside the driver. They bumped along together, along the rutted main street, out of the town and along the upstream bank of the river. Soon they arrived at the fort.

James learned from the driver that there were two companies of the 2nd Cavalry stationed at Fort Benton, that the men had very little to do and were bored to death. Like most soldiers, the driver thought the food was terrible. He couldn't see that things were going to get any better. The fort had had its hay-day during the gold rush. But the gold had run out three years earlier and the gold seekers had left. Since then the fort had become a forgotten outpost. The only excitement was the odd raid on the Indians. The driver had seen Redcoats before. He said they enjoyed a good reputation in the town because they bought most of their supplies there and paid their bills.

"But there's something we can't figure out," the driver added. "Redcoats never drink in the bars, never get in fights and never visit the girls in the saloons. What is it with you guys?"

This was news to James.

"Afraid I can't help you with that," he said. "I just got here."

They drove through the open gate of the fort. The driver dropped James off in front of a low building made of logs with a high flagpole in front of it. The flag with its stars and stripes flapped in the strong breeze. The driver pointed out the commanding officer's quarters and James went up the steps, across the wooden porch and knocked on the door. As he waited for someone to answer he noticed that there were a number of soldiers saddling up their horses across the square.

"Can I help you?" said a young soldier opening the door.

"I have a letter for Captain Davidson from Major Rawlins of Chicago."

"Captain Davidson is with the troopers," the young soldier said, pointing towards the men who were readying their horses. "If you'll follow me, I'll take you over to him." James followed the trooper towards the group of men some of whom stopped what they were doing to watch him coming. The trooper ran ahead, spoke to an officer who turned towards James.

"I'm Captain Davidson."

James handed him the letter which the officer opened and read.

"Just passing through then?" the captain asked.

"That's right," said James. "I have a few hours and I thought I'd pay my respects."

"I'm busy now," said Captain Davidson. "We're going to run some drills. You're welcome to watch if you like."

"Thank you, Captain."

"You don't have a horse?"

"No, sir. I just arrived last night by stage," replied James. "I'm hoping to pick one up in town before I leave."

"Corporal," the captain yelled at a nearby trooper. "Get this man a horse."

"The exercise field is a ways outside the fort," the captain said to James. "Ride out when you're ready."

The captain walked off to talk to his troopers. The corporal came out of the stable with a horse James thought was overdue for retirement. The corporal threw a saddle on its back and James went over to him.

"Can I give you a hand?" he said to the corporal. "Look's like you've got a lot to do."

It was James' first look at a Western saddle. It was quite different from the English saddles he had grown up with. He examined it closely and began to understand why it was more suitable for use in the North West. The leather of the straps was stronger. It provided more support for long hours of riding. James tightened the cinch strap. When he put on the bridle he noticed it had no noseband. He rubbed the horse's forehead and said a few words to it as he always did with a horse he was riding for the first time. He mounted up. It was the first time he had been on a horse since his rides with Captain Channer and Merrie. It felt wonderful except he wasn't sure he could get this horse to do much more than walk. James rode out of the fort and up the river towards an open flatland where he saw the troopers gathered. He rode up to the captain.

"You okay on a horse, Constable?" said the captain.

"Yes."

James had watched the Scots Greys in more parades and exercises than he could count. He was shocked at the undisciplined performance of this group of cavalry. The first column was led by a Lieutenant Erhart, two abreast, first walk, then gallop. The troopers were wearing sabers and carrying lances. It took them several minutes to get their lines straight and to begin to look like a company of cavalry.

The second column had divided into two groups, each lining opposite sides of the field. They were watching the first column go through its paces. James noticed that the troopers on the sidelines couldn't hold their positions in straight lines. Their horses moved back and forth at will. The men slouched in their saddles and talked among themselves.

"If these men were in my father's Scots Greys," thought James, "he's be furious. He'd have them matching in the square with full packs in the heat of the sun until they learned to do it right."

When the first column was finished running through its drills, the second went through the same exercises. James watched Captain Davidson. The commander did not seem too displeased and was talking to another officer beside him.

When the second column was finished, two troopers ran onto the field. They hammered two stakes in the ground beside each other and some distance apart.

The stakes were about four feet high and four inches wide. On top was a metal circle about four inches across. It was hinged so that when hit from the front it made a loud ring and sprung backwards on impact. While the troopers were fixing the stakes the columns were lining up on either side of the field.

Stakes in place, the captain raised his sword. He brought it down and the first pair of riders, one from each column, raced towards the stakes, their lances pointing at the metal. Both troopers raced by the stakes. There was no sound of lance tips hitting metal. Along came the second pair close behind them and the third and the fourth. James knew that if these were his father's men the Colonel would be raging mad. He had seen the Scots Greys go through similar drills but they used a small wooden peg, about four inches tall and two inches wide stuck in the ground. The lancer had to charge the peg, spear it and carry it off with him. James had run the drill hundreds of times.

The captain sent the officer beside him across the field to talk to the column commanders who in turn began dressing down their men. James couldn't hear the words but he understood the tone of voice. Lieutenant Erhart wheeled away from the troop, lowered his lance and attacked one of the stakes. A loud bang came off the metal disk as he hit it squarely with his lance. Not a cheer or even a word of praise greeted his feat.

"Not a lot of spirit here," thought James.

Lieutenant Erhart rode back to his men. He yelled a bit more and took another run at the stake. Again, he hit it squarely and again not a sound from his men. The lieutenant stopped at the end of the field, drew his saber and waved to the troopers at the opposite end. They broke off two by two and attacked the stakes. Those who hit it went to the right at the end of the field and those who missed went to the left. The troopers on the right repeated the action until there were only a few left.

"This is for a bottle of bourbon," said the captain to James. "Last man left without a miss gets the bottle. Do anything like this where you come from?"

"Yes, sir," he replied. "But we do it a little differently."

"How's that?" asked the captain.

"We stick a little piece of wood in the ground and carry it off," James told him, making it sound like there was nothing to it.

"Want to show us?" said the captain with a slight edge in his voice, calling what he thought was James' bluff.

"I don't think I could do it on this horse," said James.

The captain waved to the lieutenant who had been standing beside him. The exercises continued behind them and there were only a few troopers left in the game.

"Greenley," said the captain to the lieutenant. "This Redcoat wants to show us how they do it where he comes from. He needs your horse."

Greenley wasn't pleased with the idea but the request had come from his superior. He reluctantly got off his horse and traded reins with James who in one motion was on the horse.

"I'll need a lance, Captain," said James.

"Greenley."

The lieutenant got the message and handed his lance to James. It wasn't quite the balance he was used to but it would do. He felt the tip. It was sharp enough for the purpose.

"When this is over," Captain Davidson said to James, gesturing towards the charging troopers, "give us a demonstration."

"I'll find a couple of sticks," said James. He ran his horse towards the stockade of the fort where he thought he might find what he was looking for.

The competition was coming to an end. There was a little noise starting as the men began to cheer the riders from their column. James found what he was looking for and rode back to the captain.

"Why don't we make it interesting," said James, in a low voice to the captain.

"What do you have in mind, Constable?" asked Davidson suspiciously.

"I'll team up with your winner against the two lieutenants for the bottle of bourbon," said James with a slight grin. "If we lose, I'll buy the second bottle."

"You sure you want to do that, Redcoat?" replied the captain. "You saw what Erhart could do."

"I saw him," said James.

"Okay with me," said the captain with a smile. "We need a little excitement around here."

The winner of the competition was declared but hardly a cheer went up from the crowd. The captain noticed that James was a little puzzled by this. "Batsford always wins," the captain told James. "The men are getting tired of it."

Batsford was a grizzled veteran on a fast horse who looked like he had used a lance in battle more than once. He wheeled his horse towards the captain and rode over to claim his prize. As the winner stood before him the captain waved his officers in.

"Constable Keyden here from the Canadian Mounted Police says they do their drills differently where he comes from. He's challenged us to a match." James watched the men. Some laughed. Most sat unmoved on their saddles.

"Trooper Batsford and the Mountie," announced the captain, "against Lieutenants Erhart and Cairns. The team with the most hits wins – for the bottle of bourbon, except now there will be two bottles of bourbon, one for each man on the winning team."

Batsford was about to shout something in anger as he thought he saw the bottle he had already won disappear before his eyes. There were smiles on the faces of the two lieutenants.

"Three runs at the metal," ordered the captain. "Then we'll do it the Mountie's way,"

Word of the match raced down the line of troopers. They moved closer to the edge of the course. James rode over to Batsford and stuck out his hand.

"Constable Keyden. I think we can take them."

Batsford scowled at James and spat over the side of his horse. James lined up behind Batsford. Erhart lined up behind Cairns. Batsford and Cairns took off together and each hit the metal. James took off a few strides behind Batsford. His style was much different from the troopers. They sat straight in the saddle leaning forward as they attacked. James leaned low and far over to his right, his head was almost level with the horse's back. He aimed along the lance and hit the metal squarely. Erhart, who had been waiting for the captain's command came down after James and hit the metal as well.

The four competitors trotted back to the starting position. They turned and charged again in the same order, except that this time Erhart didn't wait. He followed close behind Cairns as James did behind Batsford. Again they all hit the metal. The crowd was getting into it and edged closer. They repeated it a third time and again they all hit the metal. The watching troopers were beginning to back Batsford and cheered him when he made his third strike.

"Okay, Constable. Your way now," yelled the captain. There was a little more respect in his voice.

James rode over to where he had laid the sticks. They were pieces of wood that had broken off the stockade around the fort. He jabbed down on one of them with his lance and lifted it up, the same with the second. They were about a foot long, pointed at one end and three inches across. James rode over to where the stakes were in the ground, dismounted and pushed the sharp ends of the sticks far enough into the ground so that they stuck straight up in the air.

"Show us how it's done, Redcoat," yelled Erhart. There was unmistakable contempt in his voice.

"The idea is to strike the wood, lift it out and carry it away," said James. "Like this." James went part way up the course, turned suddenly before he got to the start line and put his horse into full speed towards the stick. At the moment his lance hit the stick he lifted it up. The stick was fastened to the tip of his lance. James held it high in front of him. A cheer went up from the troopers. James rode back to the spot where the stick had been in the ground, dismounted and put it back in the ground. One of the troopers came over and helped him.

"You ride. I'll look after the sticks."

James caught a glimpse of the lieutenants. They were no longer smiling. But Batsford was.

"Five runs at the sticks," said the captain. "The team with the most lifts like we just saw, gets two bottles of bourbon." A cheer went up from the troopers who edged even closer. The contestants lined up for the first run. Batsford rode beside James and whispered.

"You go first. I wanna see how you do it."

James lined up beside Cairns. The captain waved his sword. The two charged down the course. James speared it cleanly, but Cairns missed the stick entirely. There were rumblings among the crowd of troopers. Batsford and Erhart moved up to the start line and charged the sticks. Batsford was a quick learner. He imitated James position, leaning low to his right. He hit the stick but couldn't lift it. Erhart kept upright, hit the stick but it bounced away from his lance.

On the second run James again speared it cleanly. Cairns hit the stick but it spun away. Batsford hit the stick but couldn't hold it. Erhart speared it cleanly. As they rode back for the third run, Erhart turned to James.

"Not so hard with practice is it, you gawdam show-off."

Third time James speared it again. Cairns had it in the air ahead of him but it dropped off. Batsford was getting the hang of it. He speared it cleanly and held it over his head to great cheers from the crowd. Erhart clipped the side of the stick and it spun off towards the crowd. As they were lining up for the fourth run James thought Erhart might put the lance through him.

"Maybe I am being a little hard on the lieutenants," James thought. "No one likes to be shown up in front of his men. I've done this drill a thousand times. But what the hell. The men need a little excitement."

Fourth time James got it again. Cairns got it high enough before it fell off that it was counted as a score. Batsford got his again and so did Erhart. They were beginning to get the hang of it.

Fifth and last run. James got it again. Cairns hit it but it spun away. Batsford's spun away and Erhart got it. Final score Batsford and James 7 Cairns and Erhart 4. The men were cheering Batsford who was smiling, having saved his bottle of bourbon. James moved up beside him and they rode together towards the captain.

"The bottles are waiting in the mess, gentlemen," Captain Davidson shouted, to cheers from the troopers. "Lieutenants, lead your men back to the fort."

Back in the mess the men were gathered around a bar relaxing and enjoying a little refreshment. Batsford held high his bottle of bourbon, which was quickly opened. After he had downed about half of it straight from the bottle he offered it to the men hounding around him. James was given his bottle to the cheers of the men. He knew he had overdone it a bit with Erhart and wanted to try to make up a little. Besides, he wanted an excuse not to have to drink the bourbon. His stomach was feeling a lot better but he didn't want to push it. James opened the bottle and walked over to where Erhart was talking with the other officers.

"Have a drink?" he said to the lieutenant.

Erhart turned away from him but the other officers held out their cups and James filled them to the brim.

"Here Erhart, the rest's for you," said James handing him the bottle.

"Keep your gawdam bottle," he said. "You won it." Erhart turned on his heels and walked out the door. James walked over to Batsford.

"Thanks for teaming with me," said James.

"Wasn't my idea," said Batsford. "But I'm glad we put it to Erhart."

James handed the bottle to Batsford. "Finish it." Batsford tipped the bottle to his mouth and drained it.

"I've got a present for you," said a loud voice behind James. It was Erhart. He was walking towards James holding something in his hand that dangled from long black strings.

"This is for you, Redcoat," he said, flinging it at James. "You've just taken your first scalp."

James flinched as the decomposed scalp of a long dead Indian hit him in the stomach. The crowd of troopers hooted with laughter. The hair of the scalp was tangled in James' sword handle, the scalp hanging near the floor. James reached down to untangle it. The scalp was shriveled and streaked with red. The hair was matted and stringy. It stank terribly.

"Thanks, Erhart," said James. "I think I'll hang it outside and pick it up when I leave."

The crowd hooted again.

James went out the door and hung it over a rafter of the porch. As he did he saw Captain Davidson running for the mess. There were several soldiers running behind him. The captain burst into the mess and yelled for attention.

"Quiet," he yelled in an angry voice. The noise fell to murmurs among the crowd of troopers.

"Message just in from headquarters," the captain shouted. "Five companies of the 7th Cavalry have been ambushed by the Sioux along the Bighorn River. They massacred General Custer and all the men who were with him."

There was a roar from the men and shouts of "No, it couldn't be true." "Don't believe it." "Not Custer, he knows how to handle Indians."

"It's from General Terry himself," yelled the captain, a wave of fury sweeping through the crowd.

"Company commanders," Captain Davidson shouted above the dim. "Have your men sharpen their sabers and tend to their horses. We're to be ready to move out at first light tomorrow."

The men started moving out of the mess at once. James saw Erhart draw his saber as he stepped out the door. He took a violent swing at the scalp James had hung from the rafter of the porch. The scalp was cut from the hair and sent flying out onto the ground with the force of the blow. Erhart strode over to it and ground the heel of his riding boot into the severed scalp.

"Gawdam savages," he said. "We'll get 'em this time."

James found himself standing alone in the square outside the mess as the troopers hurried to carry out the captain's orders. It looked like he was in for a long walk back to the town when Batsford rode up leading a second horse.

"Come on, Redcoat," he said, in a gruff, slurry voice. "Let's get you back to town." James mounted up and the two galloped off towards the hotel. Not a word was exchanged until they pulled up in front of the Nugget. James got off and handed the reins to Batsford.

"Thanks for the ride," he said.

"Good luck, Redcoat." Batsford wheeled his horse towards the fort, yanked the reins of the other horse so that if fell in beside him and galloped off.

30

From the desk clerk in the hotel James learned that the best place in town to eat was the Golddust Saloon down the street. His stomach was still feeling a bit tender but he needed something. He walked through the swinging doors and stepped into a large room finished with the same rough cut, unpainted lumber as his bedroom. There was a bar along one wall. A few men were gathered around tables in groups of two or three. Sitting alone was an old man he had seen in Baker's store. He walked over to his table.

"Mind if I join you?" asked James.

"Sit yourself down," said the man.

"James Keyden," he said introducing himself.

"Hamilton," said the other man.

"I noticed you in Baker's," said James. "Been around here long."

"A while."

James ordered a stew, which he presumed was buffalo and the two chatted. Hamilton loosened up as the meal progressed thanks in part to the liquor he was consuming. James learned that Hamilton had been in the region for years. He had come out first with the gold seekers, then traded in buffalo hides, then wolf pelts and finally liquor. But he assured James that his liquor trading days were over.

"That fellow Macleod has pretty well shut down the trade," said Hamilton.

"He's made it too expensive to get caught. If he catches ya he keeps all the gear – horses, wagons, the lot."

"I'm looking forward to meeting him," said James.

"He's a legend around here," said Hamilton.

"Why's that?"

"First winter you Redcoats arrived," explained Hamilton, "from what we heard your Redcoat friends were a sorry lot. Horses dying, not much food. Your fort wasn't finished until well into the winter, the men cold and freezing. Hell, from what we heard the men hadn't been paid since they left the East. The men were about to mutiny, or run off, or get out in some way. It was Macleod that held them together."

"How'd he do that?"

"It was the dead of winter," Hamilton went on. "Coldest, blowiest, snowiest winter in years. Even in town we hardly went out of doors. It was just before Christmas and out of the snow came Macleod and a few of his men. They had tried to ride but had to walk their horses through the blizzard most of the way from their fort. They were on their way to Helena to pick up some cash to pay the men."

"Walked?" asked James.

"Walked," said Hamilton. "We couldn't believe he did it but he did. We gave him one hell of a party, I'll tell you. Helped them thaw out their bones. I sold 'em some fresh horses."

Hamilton took another long drink.

"They only stayed long enough to get warm before they up and left for Helena. It was still blowing and howling and snowing. Before we knew it they were back with the money and on their way north. We'd never heard nor seen anything like it. Every body in these parts knows the name Macleod. You heard of Fort Whoop-Up?" asked Hamilton.

"Heard of it," replied James. "It was the worst of the whiskey trading forts from what I understand. That's where the Mounties were headed for when they first came out here."

Hamilton smiled and took a long drink from his bottle.

"Bet you didn't know that when it was first built it had another name."

"I didn't know that," said James. "What was it called."

"Fort Hamilton," said the old timer, "after me. I built it."

31

James wrote long into the night. He added to his report to Mr. McLennan the news he had heard from Captain Davidson. He told the banker that he felt the humiliation of the defeat of the 7th Cavalry would only raise the level of Sheridan's anger and intensify the Army's attacks on the Indians. He wanted to ask McLennan to pass on his greetings to his daughter but he thought better of it.

He wrote a letter to Fiona and Arthur and mentioned the gifts to the children. He would add them to the parcel when he gave the letters to the clerk. He smiled when he pictured them putting on their moccasins and dancing around the apartment. He enclosed a letter to his father and mother and asked Fiona to read it and then forward it on to them. It was a long letter that he had written to his parents. He included the military details for his father's benefit and tried to capture for them both the deep visual impressions that the journey had imprinted on his memory. He described the sweep of the prairies, the huge domed sky, the herds of buffalo, the dust and mosquitoes, his brief sighting of Indians and his first glimpse of the Rocky Mountains. He wrote much more than he had intended. It was with thoughts of his family and visions of endless stretches of prairie that he finally went to sleep.

32

Next morning James rose early. The sun was already up. The air was so fresh that the mountains appeared closer and clearer than they had the day before. At the I. G. Baker store James posted the parcels and letters. Hoping for better luck in finding a suitable horse, he walked back to the corral behind the store. He leaned up against the fence rails and studied the stock. It was pretty much the same as the day before. He heard some boys shouting behind him and turned around to see them walking towards town with what looked like a thick rope hanging from a stick.

"Look what we got, Redcoat," yelled one of the boys. James tried to make it out as the rope flopped about.

"A rattler," shouted one of the boys. "Look how big he is."

"Where'd you find it?" yelled James back at them.

"The edge of town," they yelled back. "There's lots of 'em out there." The boys ran off towards the town with their prize.

James turned his attention back to the horses. It was going to be difficult to find a good one among this bunch. Around the back of the barn came a stable hand leading a string of seven or eight more horses. He opened the corral gate and led them in. James walked over to the stable man.

"Are these for sale, too?" he asked.

"Yep," said the stable man. "The boss got 'em in a trade with some Injuns."

"I haven't seen any Indians in town," remarked James.

"No, and you probably won't neither," said the stable hand. "He got 'em to the east of here. Injuns don't come into town much now-a-days."

"Why's that?" asked James.

"Feelings running pretty strong against Injuns right now," said the stable man. "You know, Redcoat, we got laws in this town against harming horses, we got laws 'gainst swearing in front of women but there ain't no law 'gainst killing Injuns."

James turned back to the horses. There was a black in the new bunch that caught his attention. There were scratches across its chest, belly and flanks as if it had run hard through deep underbrush. Its coat, mane and tail were matted with mud. It was thin so that its ribs stuck out. But it had a broad chest and strong muscles. From its lines James knew that it was a very fine animal. James studied the horse. It was nervous and jumpy. He could see that with a little cleaning up and a lot of care, it would be just right for him. He had the stable hand put a rope around its neck and bring it closer. James went over the fence and had a closer look. The horse shied away. James took the lead from the stable hand and talked to the horse. He patted its neck, rubbed its forehead and calmed it. His first impression had been right. Although it didn't look it now, this was a very fine horse.

"I'll take this one," James said to the stable hand.

"You know horseflesh," was his reply. "This here's a good one."

James bought the black, a California saddle, bridle and halter. He felt hugely relieved to have found a horse that excited him. He led it to the blacksmith and had the hooves cleaned, trimmed and shoed. Then he led it back to the barn behind the Nugget. He gave it a good feed of oats and began cleaning it up – washing, currying and combing it. He was careful around the scratches. He trimmed the main and tail. The horse responded to the rubbing and scraping. He bobbed his head back and forth, nudging James whenever he got in range. When he was finished with the cleaning James saw that it was a very handsome animal. He wondered who the owner had been before the Indians got him. He looked it over carefully. There was no brand.

"What are we going to call you?" James thought to himself and considered the possibilities. "Your name is 'Mac'," he decided, "for McLennan. He paid for you."

James placed the saddle and bridle on him, adjusted the straps to fit and mounted up. Mac shied a step or two but responded to James' firm hand. James rode him at a walk out into the street and turned him towards the river, feeling the strength of the animal under him. He had seen how thin Mac was and didn't want to exert him until he had time to rebuild his strength. The trip to Fort Macleod would exercise him enough. He rode back to the Nugget, stored the saddle and put Mac in a stall with a generous supply of grass.

As James turned from the alley into the street on his way to the front door of The Nugget he saw a fine looking horse tied up in front of the hotel. In the scabbard on the saddle was a carbine just like his. James bounded up the front steps and through the door. Talking to the man behind the counter was a Redcoated officer. The man behind the counter pointed as James appeared. The officer turned around.

"Welcome to the North West," he said. "I'm Constable Webster, Mike Webster."

"Constable Keyden," responded James. "James. Very glad to meet you."

"They told me over at Bakers that you had bought a horse," Mike continued. "Ready to ride?"

"The horse is pretty rundown but he's ready if we don't push it."

"We're taking four wagons of supplies up to Fort Macleod," Mike explained. "The wagons'll be ready in an hour or so and I'd like to put in a few miles before sundown. Your horse will be okay. It's going to be a long, slow trip."

"I'll get my things and saddle up," said James.

"Meet me at Bakers when you're ready," said Mike.

When James arrived at Bakers the wagons were pulling into line. Mike suggested that James get his blankets, rifle and some ammunition out of his trunk. James filled the cartridge belt and the bandolier, which he put over his shoulder. He placed his Snider rifle in its scabbard and fastened it to his saddle. James hadn't fired a rifle in over a year. He had never fired a handgun. He was hoping he might get in a little practice before he had to defend the wagons from renegade robbers or rampaging Indians. But he said nothing to Mike. Just as they were about to leave one of the clerks rushed out of the store waving an envelope.

"Telegraph just in for Colonel Macleod," he shouted. Mike folded the message and tucked it inside his jacket.

The wagon train set off up the Whoop-Up Trail. It was easy to follow, marked as it was with deep ruts in the prairie from the numerous bull trains, wagons and Red River carts that continuously used it. They left the town behind and swung due west to skirt the Marias River towards the looming mountains and into the face of the relentless wind. James felt a sense of awe and almost nakedness as they moved into the open plain. Their small file was the only thing that moved as far as he could see in any direction, their wagons like small rafts in the middle of a shoreless ocean. The sky was overwhelming. He felt as if he were looking up at the ceiling of the gigantic dome of a cathedral. It was painted with an ever-changing fresco of high streaming and low billowing clouds, sometimes white, sometimes ominously dark. Behind the clouds was infinite blue.

They talked very little among themselves as they worked their way slowly up the trail accompanied always by the orchestral background of the wind sweeping through the grass, the creaking axles of the wagons and the occasional snorting of the horses. After several hours they turned northwest, stopped briefly to distribute a bite of hard, dried meat and a flask of water among them, then continued on.

As the sun began to set towards the mountains, the wind fell to a strong breeze. James' face and hands stung with the burning of the sun and wind. He couldn't take his eyes off the radiant streaks of reds, yellows, mauves and dark blues that streamed from behind the mountains clear over his head. The mosquitoes and small flies came out once again as the heat of the sun gave way to the coolness of dusk. They buzzed around his ears and crawled down his neck.

They bit him incessantly but nothing as bad as on the stagecoach journey. He hoped the mosquito season might mercifully come to a quick end.

The convoy had reached the beginning of a broad desert-like plain. The earth was caked, cracked and flaked with white dust. Mike called it Alkali Flats. Here they stopped for the night. There was a slight depression on the flatland and they drew their wagons into it for shelter from the wind. The drivers had the harnesses off their teams, the horses fed and tethered by the time the others had gathered some dried grass and buffalo chips to make a fire. The riders and drivers sat around it on the shifting, sandy soil of the gully laced with prickly cactus, the remnants of drifting sagebrush and shoots of grass. They ate a quick meal of more dried meat and washed it down with a hot drink they called tea. It wasn't the same drink James knew by that name.

"What's this we're eating?" James asked Mike, as he looked at the dark meaty roll he was handed.

"Pemmican," he answered, "strips of buffalo meat, dried and mixed with berries. What do you think?"

"It's all right," replied James after his first taste.

"Good thing you like it, it's about all we get out here."

James tied Mac on a long rope to one of the wagons and saw to it that he had some oats and a good supply of grass that they had brought with them. He was pleased to see that the scratches on the horse's legs were healing. His hide glistened with the sweat of the day and he was eating well. A few more days of this regime and he would be a very good mount.

Untying his blankets from behind his saddle James spread them down on the ground in the way he had seen the others do it. He was observing every practice and habit of his companions, learning as quickly as he could the pattern of their behaviour. The others were resting against their saddles or propped up against the wheels of the wagons. Some were talking in low voices, others idling away the minutes until the sun disappeared. They had put on their jackets against the coolness of the night air that accompanied the sun's disappearance. Besides himself, Mike was the only one clean shaven. The beards of the teamsters varied in attention from a month to a year. Their clothes were uniformly dusty and unwashed, in places crudely patched, their hats showing the stains of years of sweat and rain, their boots the style he had seen on every man in Fort Benton, pointed toes, high heels, some with elaborate leatherwork, all with jangly spurs.

The fire died, the men slid under their blankets and James looked up at the immense sky full of stars on his first night on the open prairie.

The fading glimmers of colour in the west seemed to last forever. The rays of reds and purples and blues darted between the low clouds that rested on the jagged edges of the mountain range which looked to James like the end of the world. He rolled himself in his blankets and rested his head against his saddle the way he had seen Mike do it. The burning on his face seemed to intensify. He studied the stars that glowed over his head and was conscious of every rustle of horse and man near him. The ground was hard under him but he was able to shift and squirm until he had worn a mould that fit the contours of his body. It was a long time before the memories of his first day on the prairie slipped from his mind and he was able to sleep.

33

JAMES AND THE SMALL BAND of wagons set out at first light. He was wakened by a gentle nudge from one of Mike's boots and the rays of the rising sun on the side of the gully. The fire was already crackling, there was more pemmican and tea and the teams were harnessed and ready by the time he had folded and strapped his blankets behind his saddle. He ate standing up while he brushed and saddled Mac and was mounted and on his way before he was fully awake.

It was as if he had never stopped for the night. The same ocean-like expanse surrounded him and he was swept with the same feeling of loneliness. The ground beneath them was sun-baked hard, the horses' hooves and the wagon wheels churning up swirls of bone-dry dust that caught in their throats before it was swept away by one of the never-ending gusts of wind. The water flasks were passed more often. The men on the wagon seats drew their kerchiefs over their mouths to try to keep some of the alkali dust from their throats. The fine dust clung to their clothes, its layers dulling the brightness of his scarlet jacket.

They didn't stop until they had crossed the Flats and reached the grass on its northern edge. They stopped to rest the horses and refresh themselves, brushing the dust from their shirts and breeches. But the sun and wind combined to suck the moisture out of man and beast and so the pause was short-lived. The sun was over the top but the wind whistled as before. The horses lowered their heads and walked on.

Towards mid-afternoon James was conscious of a sound he had never heard before. It started as a distant screech and grew to a horrifying wail. He could see nothing and looked at Mike for an explanation.

"Red River carts of the half-breeds," Mike explained, "wooden hubs rubbing on wooden axles with no lubrication. If they put some kind of grease on them they would get so clogged with dust that they would seize up in a minute. That's what makes that awful noise. The only lubricant they ever use is a dead gopher, but it only lasts a few miles."

When the wagons crested a rise they could see a line of Red River carts coming towards them. There were nearly twenty of them and they were travelling side by side across the prairie. There were a number of riders on horses surrounding them. It seemed like a strange formation to James. Mike noticed his consternation.

"If they traveled in file they would cut deep ruts in the soil making it hard on the carts at the end of the line. That's why they travel the way they do."

As the two fleets neared, James saw that the carts were piled high with hides and pelts. The carts were of simple construction, two large wooden wheels, almost as high as a man, hubs joined by a stout wooden axle. Sitting on the axle was a solid platform with thin wooden slats at intervals around the four sides forming a box. An ox or bull pulled it. The loads seemed huge for the single beasts pulling them and in addition, on top of the piles and hanging on to the sides of each cart were several women and children. They were waving, chattering and shouting as the two convoys met and stopped. The wailing of the wheels ceased and James could hear the laughter and shouts of the children.

"They're taking their winter's work to trade at Fort Benton," explained Mike. "They think they'll get a better price there than Fort Walsh. Besides, there's more excitement for them in Benton."

"Excitement?" exclaimed James recalling the dreariness of the town.

Redcoats were always looking for illegal whiskey and never passed up a chance to inspect a cargo. Mike rode over and James followed.

"Bonjour," said Mike to the lead driver. Mike asked him a few questions in a language that sounded to James something like French, but not the French he was familiar with. The cart people talked back and forth amongst themselves.

James recognized a few words but it was difficult for him to get a sense of what they were discussing.

Some of the nearby children were shouting and waving at James and he turned towards them. He was surprised at the differences in their skin tones and features. He remembered that Metis were the offspring of French Canadian fathers and Indian mothers. He tried to identify the origins of the characteristics he was looking at. Not having seen an Indian up close he could only guess.

The children were boisterous and full of life. They were laughing and teasing each other and shouting comments at Mike, James and the teamsters in their own lyrical language. Their clothes were a colourful mixture of buckskin and out of fashion men's shirts and trousers. The girls had rings in their ears and wore brightly coloured ribbons and sashes. Everyone wore moccasins. The men and boys had a comical variety of top hats, bowlers and wide-brimmed, high-crowned replicas of what he had seen the American cavalry officers wearing.

Up close the Red River carts reminded him of illustrations he had seen of French aristocrats being driven to the guillotine. The carts were the same shape and size, but the tall, heavy wheels were fashioned from several pieces of wood joined to the hub with wooden spokes. Rawhide was used to tie the pieces of wood together.

Mike looked around and under the hides in a number of the carts, carrying on a lively banter with the drivers and occupants as he went about his business. Finding no signs of the whiskey he was searching for, he waved at the drivers, mounted up and with James beside him rode back to the wagons. The shouts of the children continued until the screeching of the wheels against hubs drowned them out as the carts started on their slow march to Fort Benton.

"Wonderful people," remarked Mike. "They really know how to enjoy themselves. Trading in Benton is the big event of the year for them."

"Where are they from?" asked James.

"Several hundred miles northeast of here, along the North Saskatchewan," answered Mike. "But these ones spent most of last year on the move following the buffalo. They wintered near the Hills to the east."

"Do they get along with the Indians?" asked James.

"They're more like Indians than like us. Just as good hunters, too. Most of them speak one or more of the Indian languages and they live just like they do – on the land, on the move."

James and the wagons were following the Trail north towards the Milk River ford where they planned to spend the night. There would be trees and grass in the coulee through which the river ran with plenty of water for the horses and themselves. James learned that Mike had been recruited for the Mounties in the East and had been with them since its inception. He had signed on in the early summer two years earlier and was a veteran of the Great March.

"The Great March?" Mike answered in response to James' question. "It was more like the great disaster. No one in the East has half an idea how close we came to being wiped out, not by Indians and not by whiskey traders but by plain stupidity."

James looked incredulous.

"Colonel French, the Commissioner. You've heard of him?" asked Mike.

"Heard the name," answered James.

"He may have been a good artillery officer in Kingston," Mike went on. "But he was a menace out here. He wanted us to look like a British regiment on parade. He picked horses that looked good but couldn't pull a wagon over the prairie for the life of them. When we set out we had more machinery and cannons than food. We weren't five days out when the horses began to go lame. Some even died. If it hadn't been for the major, we all would have mutinied, deserted or died."

"The major…?" asked James.

"Major Macleod, the Assistant Commissioner," Mike answered. "He's really a colonel now but was a major when we started. We keep calling him Major and he doesn't seem to mind. We'd walk through a blizzard in our underwear for that man."

"Why's that?"

"He held us together across the nine hundred miles from Dufferin to Whoop-Up," explained Mike. "When a wagon got stuck he was there to pull it out. When someone got lost, he found him. When the horses stampeded in lightning storms – and I tell you, you haven't seen lightning storms 'til you see one out here – he rounded them up. When we were desperate he went off and found food for the horses and us. When French started playing high and mighty British general with us, Macleod stood up for us."

James sensed the anger that was still in Mike.

"Christ," continued Mike, "I remember one day towards the end when half the horses were dead or lame. There weren't enough good ones left to pull all the wagons. Our clothes were in shreds and there was little food for man or beast. French got on his high horse and charged some of the men with stealing biscuits of all things. Imagine, with all we had to contend with, he wanted to punish someone for stealing a biscuit." Mike shook his head in dismay.

"Macleod stood up to him," Mike went on. "With all of us standing there, Macleod said, 'Sorry, sir, you can't do that'."

"What did French do?"

"He was livid, but the major held his ground. He said, 'As a lawyer', you know Macleod's a lawyer from Queens…"

James nodded.

'As a lawyer, your action is a breach of the law,' Macleod told French. 'You have no authority for such action.'"

"Macleod said that to French?" James asked.

"In front of us all," Mike replied. "French lost control and shouted at him, 'The guilty one must be punished.' Macleod answered, 'There is absolutely no proof. Besides, we've got a lot more serious problems than a few missing biscuits. I won't allow this.'"

"What did French do?"

"He just stood there dumbfounded," Mike told him. "The major hadn't raised his voice but his determination made French stop. I think French meant to arrest Macleod until he looked at the rest of us. We were as steely-eyed as Macleod. French knew that if he pressed the point he would have a mutiny on his hands. He didn't say a word, nor did anyone else. Finally Macleod said, 'Right then, sir, we'll get the wagons ready to move out.' From that moment on, Macleod has been the real leader of this Force."

"What happened to French?" asked James.

"He was fired eventually," answered Mike. "I remember the last time I saw him. After struggling over hundreds of miles of prairie we were completely lost. We didn't have any idea where our destination, Fort Whoop-Up, was. The horses were on their last legs and the food had all but run out. We stopped in the Sweet Grass Hills, over there," Mike said, pointing to the east.

"What happened?"

"French, the major and some others went off to Fort Benton to get some help while we just waited. At least we had a little grass and water."

"What then?"

"One of the men rode back from Fort Benton with orders for us to move due west where we were to meet up with Macleod. A few days later French arrived with fresh horses he had bought in Benton. You know what he did with them?"

"No."

"He loaded most of the food and grain we had left into some wagons, took those wagons and all but one of the fresh horses he had just bought in Benton and a few men and high-tailed it back to Dufferin."

"You're not serious?"

"He left us on the plains with lame horses and damn near no food," said Mike with contempt in his voice. "Two days later Macleod showed up with supplies. We cheered him 'til we were hoarse. He had food for the horses and us. He also had a guide with him called Jerry."

"Jerry?" asked James.

"Jerry Potts, the best damn plainsman you'll ever meet."

"So what did you do?"

"Jerry knew exactly where we were and where we wanted to go. He took one look at us and knew we were damn near finished. He pointed us in the right direction and disappeared."

"Disappeared?"

"Yes, just up and left us," replied Mike. "Near sundown we topped a small rise and there in front of us was Jerry and some Indian women. They had a fire going with a buffalo calf roasting over it. It was all we could do to keep from running and hugging them. It was the first hot meal we could remember."

Mike smiled as he recalled the moment.

"Next day Jerry changed our course a bit to the northwest," Mike continued. "In a few hours we came to the clearest water we had seen since we left Dufferin. After that we trusted whatever Jerry said. We still do."

"He's still around?" asked James.

"Sure is. You'll meet him at the Fort sooner or later."

"And Macleod?" probed James.

"He's the best damn commander any man could have," Mike continued. "He did a couple of things for me I'll never forget."

"Like what?"

"During the first few weeks on the March most of us got the trots," Mike told him.

"Trots?" questioned James.

"Diarrhea. Loose bowels."

"Oh, that!" answered James. He smiled knowingly.

"Must have been the water," said Mike. "One day I just exploded. Right in my saddle. I made a hell of a mess. When it came time at the end of the day to make camp I didn't want to get off my horse and have the men laugh at me. So I rode down by a small creek that we were camped beside. I was waiting 'til it got a little darker so I could get off and clean up a bit without the others seeing me."

James smiled at the thought.

"Macleod rode up and noticed what had happened. 'I can fix that,' he said, 'Get off your horse.' I got off beside the stream and Macleod bent down and picked up handfuls of mud and smeared them on my backside and down my pants. 'No one will know the difference,' he said to me "They'll think you fell in the creek. Come on, Webster, let's get something to eat.'"

"What was the other thing?"

"After Fort Whoop-Up," Mike told him, "we moved up the Old Man's River to set up our winter quarters. Jerry helped the major pick the site. By this time it was well into October and starting to get really cold. The major had hired a gang from Fort Benton to come up to build the fort. When they arrived the major ordered that they build the stables first. When that was done he had the quarters for the men built. By this time it was well into December and the temperature was 'way below freezing most of the time. The men were living in a log building with a fire. Macleod and the other officers were still outside in tents. There were some days when we could hardly see them they were so covered in snow. One day we had a raging blizzard and their quarters still weren't finished. Macleod and the officers still stayed in their tents. Finally, just before Christmas, their quarters were finished and they moved in. That's Macleod for you. Horses first, men second, officers last. It was us – the men – that made him name it Fort Macleod."

"Some commanding officer," commented James. "He must be hard as nails."

"Strong, determined, firm, fair, all of them," said Mike. "But not hard. The truth is the man's dying of loneliness."

"What do you mean?"

"He's been engaged to a woman in Winnipeg for six years," Mike told him. "Every time they set a date some crisis comes up that he has to deal with. Never knew a man to miss a woman so."

The sun had almost reached the mountaintops when the wagons came to the rim of the coulee.

"Milk River," announced Mike. "We'll stop for the night down there."

"So that's a coulee," remarked James. "Where's the word coulee come from?"

"From a French word, couler. It means, to flow."

"Of course," replied James.

"Ever seen anything like that?" asked Mike.

"Never," said James. There was a broad valley stretching before them a mile wide and several hundred feet deep. The Milk River wound its way, back and forth across the flat bottom. The valley stretched off to their right and left until it disappeared behind the steep sides of the coulee. Clumps of tall, green trees bordered the river and filled the valley floor. In places there were broad gravel banks alongside the water and in other places broad open, grassy fields. The horses sensed the nourishing grass and the cool water. Their nostrils flared and they grunted noises of anticipation.

"We'll make camp in the trees on this side and ford the river in the morning when the horses are fresh," said Mike.

It was slow going down the steep trail to the river's edge. When they reached the bottom there was a flat, grassy field off to their left and they pulled the wagons into it and stopped for the night. James stripped the saddle and bridle from Mac, rubbed him down with some leaves and led him to the river's edge where the horse drank its fill. Between gulps, Mac rubbed his nose against James' leg, and wagged his head from side to side dripping water over him. James rubbed his neck and patted his flanks. There was a bond building between horse and rider.

After the pemmican and hot tea, James walked down to the river. He found a large flat stone, sat down, removed his boots and stockings and dipped his feet into the cold, swift running water. The current eddied among the boulders washing and soothing his tired legs. He draped his sunburned hands in the refreshing coolness and splashed his face, hair and neck trying to wash away some of the accumulated dust. The song of the water over the rocks and the breeze in the trees refreshed his spirit. He sat this way until the sun disappeared behind the edge of the coulee releasing the few remaining mosquitoes from their sleep and cooling the air noticeably. For the first time he was aware of the songs of prairie birds nesting in the trees. He stared at the water rushing by as he listened. The stresses of the long journey evaporated as his mind settled into hypnotic relaxation.

34

The wagons had crossed the high flatlands beyond the Milk River and were approaching the rim of the Old Man's River coulee. The sun was moving towards the mountains and the wind had picked up. They turned due west to follow the coulee upstream, straight towards the majestic Rockies which grew larger with every step they took. A near gale blew straight into their faces. The teamsters bent low to get as much protection as they could from the horses in front of them while James and Mike leaned forward in their saddles. Three riders, galloping hard, were almost on them before James heard the hoof beats and looked up to see them approaching from the direction in which they were heading. Mike yelled for the wagons to stop and they waited as the three came up to them.

"It's the major, Jerry and Richter," Mike shouted to James above the wind.

The three pulled up beside the lead wagon and Mike and James joined them.

"Sir," Mike addressed his superior, saluting.

James hadn't thought to learn to salute and didn't think this the appropriate time to start. Colonel Macleod looked in his direction and back to Mike.

"Constable Keyden, sir," he reminded the major. "He was waiting in Benton."

The major rode up to James and stuck out his hand.

"I'm Macleod. Very glad you've arrived. We've been expecting you. You're going to be a great help to me and you might as well start now." James was a little taken aback by the words but waited for what was next.

"We've had a report of whiskey traders doing some business down the Old Man's River and we're after them. Come along and I'll show you what we are doing out here. It will make a good story for your readers back in the East." Macleod turned to join Jerry and Richter and looked back to make sure James was following.

"Not sure this horse is up to it," he shouted to the major. "I just bought him and he's still not too fit."

Macleod took one look at Mac and knew James was right.

"Change with Webster," he ordered.

Mike didn't hesitate and was off his horse in a moment exchanging reins with James who, before he knew it, was riding hard to catch up with the other three. The wind was at his back now and Webster's horse was fit and ready for the ride. James didn't even have time to look back to see the wagons depart on their last leg to Fort Macleod.

They rode hard without a word for some time until Jerry signaled for them to stop. They reined up side by side on the rim of the coulee looking far down the valley to the east. They couldn't see what they were looking for and set out again. Before long Jerry drew up to the coulee's edge and looked eastward once again. James could make out faint wisps of smoke coming from behind some trees near a far bend in the river. It must have been the sign Jerry was looking for. He led the way down a steep gully between two hillsides of the coulee, Macleod, then Richter following him with James bringing up the rear. The horses slithered and slid through the shale of the gully. When they reached the bottom Macleod turned to see how James was making out and his face showed a flicker of surprise to see that James was right with them.

Once on the coulee bottom they galloped in the direction of the smoke, working their way through the trees, across the grassy flats and finally to a clump of trees near the river's edge. They were close to the source of the smoke. They slowed and followed the riverbank to a clearing. An Indian encampment was a hundred yards in front of them. It was a small camp of eight lodges. Three had been burned to the ground. Two were stripped of their buffalo hide covers exposing the lodge poles that had been knocked out of position. Three were still standing, their entrance flaps open. The only movement came from a few dogs that sulked around the tepees barking at the approaching riders.

Macleod and Jerry rode side by side into the center of the encampment, stopped and dismounted. The smell from the burning hides fouled the air. They handed the reins of their horses to Richter and James and walked slowly from lodge to lodge. They found what they feared. There were three bodies lying close together, one whose side had been blown away by a gunshot wound, another with blood caked on the back of his head. The third body was that of a woman. Closer to one of the burning tepees was another body, an older woman, and close beside her the body of a child. Jerry circled to the left and Macleod to the right, assessing the carnage. They met back at the horses.

"Three men, three women and one child," Jerry reported.

"Two men and two children," replied Macleod, a look of fury in his eyes.

Richter, looking beyond Macleod and Jerry sensed some movement in the trees.

"Behind you," he whispered, nodding in the direction of the movement.

The major and Jerry turned to see two women and several children emerge from the thicket. Behind them were several older people and finally two young men. They moved cautiously towards the Redcoats. Jerry walked towards them and spoke to them in their own language. His questions were short and the Indians' answers shorter. James caught Richter's eye. Then it struck him that the enemy that had devastated this camp was not the Cree from the north or the Sioux from the south but the traders from Fort Benton with their whiskey.

"Two wagons," Jerry translated for Macleod, "four men. They left a few hours ago after the trouble. They took all the horses and one of the women. If we leave now we can catch them at the Milk River ford."

"What about these people?" asked Macleod, gesturing towards the forlorn band behind him.

"They've already sent a runner to their friends on the St. Mary's – about two hours away. They'll have help before nightfall."

Jerry turned back to the watching group and said a few parting words. One of the women, her hair in tangles, her buckskin dress torn on one side with what looked like bloodstains down the front, came up to him, spoke with emotion and put a hand on his arm. There were tears in her eyes. She said something and Jerry answered her softly, putting both his hands on her shoulders. Whatever he said made her lower her head and hold on to him. He comforted her, said parting words to the group and reached for the reins of his horse.

"Her name's Rain Cloud," he said to Macleod. "Her son-in-law and a grandchild are among the dead. The whiskey traders have her daughter, Singing Bird."

35

The two wagons were travelling as fast as their weary horses could pull them over the flat prairie towards the safety of the border, the Medicine Line, as the Indians called it. Once into Montana Territory they knew they were beyond the reach of the Redcoats. The lead wagon, pulled by a team of four horses and piled high with buffalo hides, had slowed to a walk. The second wagon, lighter and pulled by a team of two was carrying kegs of whiskey, the group's gear and some old rifles and saddles the men had taken in trades. Tied to the second wagon was a string of horses tied neck to neck.

"Keep a'moving, Jess," yelled the driver of the second wagon to his counterpart up front.

"This here team's played out," yelled Jess in return, "and we've still got the ford and some miles beyond 'til we cross the Line."

Events that day had not gone as planned. They had spent the morning in the small Blackfoot camp eating with the men and trading – buffalo hides for whiskey, horses for whiskey and women for whiskey. But when the hides and horses were gone and the women had run away, the Indian men, already well into the fire-water, wanted more whiskey and became violent. The traders were used to this. It was easy to handle if there was a stockade to hide behind, but in the open, it was downright deadly.

When the Indians saw the traders harnessing up to leave, their guns came out. Jess, a savvy old-timer took the situation in hand. He whispered to his pals to keep harnessing and then get the wagons and their loot across the river and towards the border quick. Then he took a half-filled keg of whiskey from the wagon, hoisted it onto his shoulder and walked back into the camp inviting one and all to come and help him finish it. He didn't have to ask the warriors twice.

Making sure the Indians had all they wanted Jess took none. When he quietly slipped out of camp, taking the last remaining horse, none of the Blackfoot noticed. When he was half a mile away, just about to cross the river, he heard the gunfire. From the south rim of the coulee he saw the lodges in flames.

Jess caught up to the wagons a few miles south. They had planned two or three more trading parties with small bands of Blackfoot along the St. Mary's and Milk Rivers, trading for what remained of the whiskey. But Jess figured the gunfire and smoke might attract the Redcoats so he ordered his men over the border. Crossing the St. Mary's had taken longer than they wanted. They had to unhitch one team to help the other through the fast flowing water. Both teams were winded by the effort and they had to give them a rest before setting out again.

By late afternoon the fierce wind, strengthening from the west, was blowing dust across their faces. The horses, even at a walk, were pulling with their heads low. They were breathing heavily. One of the rear wheels on the first wagon was grinding fiercely and making a shrieking noise. As soon as they got over the border they would put some buffalo fat on it. They could see the edge of the Milk River coulee a mile off. It would be an effort to get across the river, but after that it was a clear, flat ten-mile run to the border. They didn't notice the Redcoats behind them riding hard for the river.

The trail down the coulee slope to the river was hard and dry, deeply rutted by previous iron-rimmed wagon wheels. It was the same hill James and the wagons had climbed coming the other way earlier that same day. The trees had been cleared left and right to make a wider approach. Jess guided his team down the slope, the wagon squeaking and shuddering under the heavy load of hides. His partner was pressing the brake pedal with as much strength as his old right leg could exert. The second wagon was close behind. The string of horses brought up the rear.

As Jess brought his team to a halt a few yards from the river he was startled to see a Redcoat, his carbine held loosely over his saddle, ride out from the trees in front of him. It was the major himself. Jess turned to see a second and third Redcoat riding down the slope behind the string of horses. They were Richter and James.

"Gentlemen, kindly step down from the wagons and place your firearms on the ground," said the major forcefully. "We're going to inspect your cargo."

"Nothing but trade goods," said Jess, eyeing Macleod carefully. The four men stepped over the wagon wheels and onto the ground. They took their handguns from their holsters and laid them on the ground in front of them.

"Now if you will just stand over there," said Macleod, motioning for the men to move to a position beside the trees lining the trail.

"Check the wagons, Constable," Macleod said to Richter, pointing his rifle in the direction of the four teamsters.

Richter dismounted and handed the reins of his horse to James, who had his own Snider rifle at the ready across his saddle. His heart was pounding as he found himself taking part in his first police action and wondering what he would do if he were called on to shoot one of the wagoneers. Richter carried his carbine in his left hand, circled the first wagon, then the second, reaching under the hides. When he came upon several casks he leaned his carbine against the wagon and reached for one of them. Forcing out the stopper he sniffed at the contents.

"Whiskey for sure," he shouted to Macleod.

"Where's the woman?" asked Macleod of Jess, in a voice that betrayed his anger.

"What woman?" said Jess indignantly.

"Search the piles of hides, Richter." Leaning his carbine against one of the wheels the constable climbed onto the wagon and began moving aside some of the heavy hides. He heard a faint moan.

"Sounds like she's under here," he reported. "She must be suffocating under this weight."

Macleod rode up to where Richter was now throwing hides from the wagon. Slowly a head appeared, then a head and shoulders.

"Is she all right?" asked Macleod with concern.

While Macleod and Richter were distracted with the young woman, Jess slowly reached behind his back and drew a small handgun hidden in his belt. Before he could raise it a shot rang out and Jess felt the heat of a bullet as it grazed his left ear. He turned to see his attacker.

"Jesus, it's Jerry," he gasped, knowing that for him and his gang, the game was up.

Jerry rode out from the trees where he had been watching the action. He had the wagoneers sit down beside the trail and motioned to James to guard them. James brandished his rifle in their direction and aimed it just over Jess's head. Jerry walked over to where the woman was huddled among the hides. He spoke briefly in her language. She answered faintly. He tried to help her up but she couldn't rise. She spoke again. Jerry reached for his skinning knife. Her ankles and wrists were tied to the floorboards. Four quick slashes and she was free. Jerry took her under the shoulders and helped her out of the wagon. She couldn't stand. He lowered her to the ground and rubbed her wrists and ankles. He walked back to his horse, standing just inside the trees, and took a canteen and a package from his saddlebag. He carried them back to the woman and gave them to her. She ate and drank gratefully. Macleod dismounted, walked over to where the young Indian woman was sitting and had a few words with Jerry. Then he turned to the men of the wagons.

"In the name of the Queen I arrest you for trading whiskey," Macleod said in a strong voice. "In this country it is against the law, as you well know. Tomorrow we will return the hides, horses and this woman to her people. Then we will take you to Fort Macleod where you will stand trial. If you are found guilty, your horses, wagons, firearms and goods will be confiscated."

Macleod and Richter mounted up, keeping their carbines at the ready. Jerry helped the woman to her feet. He made a comfortable place for her among the hides in the back of the wagon and helped her up, leaving his flask of water with her.

"She'll be okay," he said to Macleod. "They haven't touched her."

Jerry walked over to the old whiskey trader.

"Okay, Jess, turn these wagons around and let's get started."

The three Redcoats and Jerry took up positions around the two overloaded wagons and escorted them back towards the Blackfoot camp. They had not made the Old Man's River coulee by sundown but Jerry knew a small gully which would provide as much protection from the wind as they were going to get on the open prairie. It was there that they stopped. The four prisoners were tied together and to one of the wagon wheels. Singing Bird had taken some hides from the wagon and had disappeared from view. The major assigned guard duty for the night and James had his first experience as a sentry. He was so stimulated by the day's events that there was no possibility of nodding off.

Macleod assigned him the first watch of the night. The sky was clear, there was a quarter moon and myriad stars – giving off enough light to see his surroundings. He took up a position where he could watch the prisoners, his back firmly against the steep side of the gully. He had one blanket under him and another over his knees as he shifted against the sandy soil to carve out a comfortable seat in the dirt. He kept the rifle across his lap. He was astonished as he recalled the events of the day. The experience of the Blackfoot encampment and the capture of Jess and his outfit had already displaced the memories of his journey with the wagons. He had been drawn into a police action without an hour's training and on his second day on the prairies he had been expected to perform as any seasoned Mountie. The chief Redcoat of the North West had demonstrated a deep personal concern for the welfare of a very small band of Blackfoot and had led the pursuit and capture of four lowly whiskey traders so that justice would be done. In doing so he accepted all the hardships of one of his ordinary lawman on the Great Plains. James was impressed.

He looked over at Macleod who was already asleep. The blanket the major had thrown over himself had slipped aside in his restlessness. He had removed his jacket, folded it, and put it under his head as a pillow. He was a man of about six feet, strong in build. He had a full black beard. On horseback, the major reminded James of officers he had seen in the Scots Greys. Macleod was a man born to wear a uniform. The scarlet jacket with its gold trim, the sword, the breeches and boots, made him a dashing officer. James had noticed the ribbon over his left breast but didn't recognize the decoration it represented. The major was older than James had imagined. He had the features of a highlander and the firm eyes of a minister of the Free Church about to preach a sermon on sin. He was a no-nonsense kind of man. Hard to believe, thought James, in looking at him, what Mike had said about a man with a warm heart.

He was also impressed with Jerry and Richter. Jerry had been as relaxed in the saddle as a grandfather in a rocking chair, but the dark features of his face, shadowed by the brim of his well-weathered fedora, once the property of some city gentleman, had been etched with concern for the Blackfoot. From his position guarding the prisoners James could see Jerry in the moonlight. He was leaning back against a wagon wheel, his eyes closed, his rifle across his knees. He looked like he was sleeping but James was sure that with the slightest sound Jerry would have the gun leveled and ready in an instant. Jerry wore a buckskin jacket with fringes across the shoulders and down each arm. Across the chest were decorative figures of running buffalo. There was a handkerchief around his neck, the colours of which were hidden under countless miles of prairie dust. He had small eyes and an enormous mustache. On his feet he wore moccasins which reached almost to his knees with the cuffs of his trousers tucked in their tops. His trousers, James suspected were once the property of the United States Cavalry. They were held up by a thick leather belt to which was attached a long skinning knife with an antler handle. The rifle was a Winchester. There was a Colt in a black holster on his belt.

When Richter relieved James of the watch he was ready to stretch out. He moved a little way down the gully, wound himself in his blankets and was soon asleep.

36

The wagons with their escort reached the Blackfoot camp by late morning. Just as Jerry had said, help had arrived from a nearby band. The lodges were being repaired and the dead prepared for burial. There was an eerie wailing of mourning as they approached. Macleod had the wagons stop a short distance from the tepees. While Richter and James guarded the teamsters, Macleod and Jerry led Singing Bird and the horses back to the village. They returned with some of the men who removed a number of the hides from the loaded wagons and carried them back to the lodges.

This duty completed they turned the wagons west, forded the Old Man's River once again, made their way up the side of the coulee to the flatland above and headed for Fort Macleod about forty miles upriver. The major and Jerry rode together ahead of the wagons, James rode with Richter behind.

"What do you know about Jerry," James asked his companion.

"He's a legend," the seasoned Mountie replied. "He knows this country inside out. He speaks, I don't know how many, Indian languages. He can't read a word of print, but he can read signs on the ground, see movement in the distance, smoke over the horizon and know exactly what it all means. I don't think he's ever been lost in his life."

"Where's he come from?" asked James.

"His father was a Scots trader who worked in a trading post south of Benton on the Yellowstone River. His mother was a Blood Indian. When Jerry was about seventeen his father was murdered. Story goes that Jerry trailed the man who did it into a bar in Fort Benton and shot him dead. No one did anything about it because they knew what the dead man had done to his father."

"And his mother?"

"She was killed in a drunken rampage outside one of the whiskey forts," Mike told him. "Booze makes most redmen crazy. You saw what happened in that camp. They go completely wild. They end up burning down their own tepees and killing their own families. It's one of the reasons Jerry works with us. He hates the liquor trade with a passion because he's seen what it is doing to his family and his people."

"His people?" asked James. "Does he consider himself an Indian?"

"I don't think he cares," said Richter. "Indian, white, French. To Jerry there're only men that you can trust and men that you can't trust."

"You were talking about his mother," prompted James.

"Oh, yes," continued Richter. "Just like with his father, Jerry found out who killed his mother. This time it was an Indian. He laid in wait for him along a trail and shot him."

"Rough justice," exclaimed James.

"That's the only kind of justice there was out here before we arrived," answered Richter.

"Are the Indians still fighting each other?" asked James.

"Not like they used to. The last big battle between two tribes was fought just up the river. We just passed the place where it happened. Jerry was in the thick of it."

"How was that?"

"It was six years ago," Mike told him. "The Blackfoot were in a pretty bad way from smallpox and whiskey. A few of them were attacked by a large war party of Cree. Jerry rounded up a Blackfoot war party and they made him their war chief. He led the charge into the Cree and drove them into the river. The Blackfoot took a lot of scalps that day. When you meet Jerry you'll notice a piece of a bullet lodged in the lobe of his left ear. He got it that day. He's proud as hell of it."

"Does he live at the fort?" asked James.

"He spends a lot of time there but it's not his home," replied Richter. "He's got two Peigan sisters as wives. They live over the border in Montana, north of Benton. There are lots of kids."

"Strange existence," said James.

"Not out here," Richter told him. "People do what they have to do to survive. Jerry's been into everything. He's traded in buffalo hides, wolf and fox pelts. Probably even liquor. Before he joined us he was breeding horses. He likes working with us and we couldn't do our job without him. He's guide, interpreter, diplomat, go-between, negotiator and enforcer, whatever we need. Best thing is the Indians trust him."

"He gets along with Macleod?" asked James.

"Right from the start. I heard Jerry say once – and he doesn't talk much – that Macleod was the first white man who ever treated him as an equal. The major wasn't too proud to ask Jerry's advice on just about everything out here, especially about Indians. Jerry taught him how to behave in an Indian camp, about their ceremonies and customs. If one of us doesn't treat the Indians with respect the major is all over him."

"So the Force gets along well with the Indians?" asked James.

"One of the first things the major did when we arrived," Mike told him, "was to have Jerry set up meetings with the chiefs of the various bands. The major went to see the chiefs, not the other way around. He took Jerry with him to interpret."

"How'd it work out?"

"Jerry once told me," Richter continued, "that what most impressed him about the major was how he treated the chiefs with dignity. He'd never seen a white man do that before. The major has mastered their customs. He lets the chiefs talk first. When he talks about the law he makes no distinction between white men and red men. The Chiefs took to the major from the start. They even gave him an Indian name, Stamix Okotan."

"What's it mean?"

"Buffalo Bull's Head, the insignia on our buttons."

The wheels of the wagons kicked up dust and the wind wiped it into the faces of the two trailing Mounties. They moved closer to the rim of the coulee to avoid it but close enough to keep a watchful eye on the teamsters.

"Help me with something," James asked Richter.

"I'll try."

"When I was in Fort Benton I was talking with one of the American soldiers," James explained. "He told me that when Mounties were in town they never gambled, drank or visited the saloon women. Is that right?"

"It's right."

"Why?" asked James.

"Orders from the major," Richter told him. "He's impressed on us that we are representatives of the Queen out here. We're to behave like gentlemen. In public, no drinking, no gambling, no fighting, no visits to the brothels, no visits to the saloon girls and no sleeping with the squaws."

"He's that strict about it?" asked James.

"You're damn right he's strict about it, but he doesn't consider it strict, just proper behaviour for a British officer."

"No drinking at all?" asked James.

"We can drink in the fort when we're off duty," Richter told him. "Good thing too. The major is as fond of his whiskey as the rest of us."

The convoy had forded the St. Mary's and the Belly Rivers and was back on the open plains. The sun was touching the tops of the mountains when they drew up to the crest of the Old Man's River coulee once again. James saw the river winding through the bottom.

"The fort's just a few miles upstream from here," Richter told him.

"Who's the Old Man?" asked James.

"'Old Man' is one of the names the Blackfoot give to their god," explained Richter. "To them, this is God's river."

After some distance, the major fell back and rode alongside James.

"Can't tell you how glad I am to see you," said the major. James was taken aback by the warmth of his words.

"We've had the damnedest time communicating with Ottawa," he went on. "They don't seem to pay any attention to what I'm telling them. Sometimes I wonder whether they even open my messages. No pay for the men, no payments for supplies, and no answer to our request for more men and horses. So when I heard that they were sending you out in order to get better information, you can imagine how pleased I was."

James smiled and nodded.

"You can be sure I'll give you every opportunity to learn what we're doing out here. Look across the coulee to the opposite rim and tell me what you see."

James turned in his saddle, looked past the major and studied the prairie on the other side of the coulee.

"A little behind us," added the major. "See them?"

It took a moment but finally James spotted two riders moving in the same direction as they were but on the other side of the mile wide coulee.

"Two riders," said James.

"Blackfoot scouts," Macleod explained. "Canny devil, that Crowfoot."

There was a look of puzzlement on James' face.

"It was one of Crowfoot's chiefs that told us about these whiskey traders moving along the Old Man's River. We've told the Blackfoot since the day we arrived that we would put a stop to the whiskey trade. They continually test us to see if we are as good as our word. Those scouts will follow us until they see us pull into the gates of the fort with these wagons, then report to Crowfoot."

"Who's Crowfoot?" James asked.

"The senior chief of the Blackfoot and a highly respected leader of his people. I like to think of him as a friend."

James turned again to look at the Blackfoot scouts. They were still in their position of surveillance keeping exact pace with the wagons.

37

The wind was tearing at the Union Jack flapping at the top of a long pole high over the stockade and flinging clouds of dust at the two wagons and their escort as they approached Fort Macleod. The wagons jerked, squeaked and lurched as they made their way across the open field surrounding the barricade. James turned for one last glimpse of the Blackfoot scouts but the trees blocked his view of the far rim of the coulee. The sun was dipping behind the mountains that loomed larger on the horizon, the sky awash with a breathtaking array of colour.

As they approached the south gate of Fort Macleod, James could see that from the outside it wasn't much different in design from Fort Benton. But it was in much better condition. The stockade wall was straight and strong. The ground around was flat and cleared. Sounds of the evening's activities rose from the inside as they made their way through the gate. A series of low, log buildings lined the inside wall of the stockade.

The fort still had an air of newness about it. The original fort had been built two years earlier on a small island a half mile upstream, but the floods the following spring had made it impossible for the police to move to it or from it. When the waters receded, Colonel Macleod had had the fort rebuilt on higher ground.

There was a ten-foot stockade of lodge-pole pine and a wide courtyard surrounded by stables, men's quarters, officer's quarters, storerooms and a small jail. The two, three-pound cannons, hauled nine hundred miles from Fort Dufferin during the Great March, were positioned facing the main gate. They had never been fired in anger.

The wagons drew to a halt in front of the stables. Macleod gave orders to the men who met them to make an inventory of their captive's goods and equipment and to confine the four traders in the jail. James followed him to the stable where they handed over their mounts to the stable master.

"Tomorrow we'll put those four on trial," the major told him. "If they're guilty, and from what we saw of the barrels in their wagons, there doesn't seem to be much doubt, we'll water the prairie with their whiskey and confiscate their horses, wagons and hides. They'll spend the next six months with us unless one of their pals comes up from Benton and pays $50 each to get them out."

James walked back across the square with the major.

"Richter will show you where to get cleaned up," the major told him. "Then I'd like a few words with you in my quarters."

38

AFTER ATTEMPTING TO WASH SOME of the dust from his face James followed Richter up some steps and across a narrow porch. As he pointed out the door to the quarters of the Assistant Commissioner, Webster rushed up to join them.

"I almost forgot the telegram for the major," he said to James.

Webster knocked on the door and a loud voice invited them in. James stepped through the door with Webster. There were five officers seated around a table. Webster snapped to attention.

"Telegram for you, Major."

Macleod rose from his chair, crossed to where Webster was standing and took the envelope.

"Thank you Webster, you're dismissed. Excuse me for a moment, gentlemen, while I have a look at this."

The major returned to the table and stood behind his chair. He opened the envelope and read the message, a faint smile appearing on his lips. James waited in silence. The officers in the room were watching the major as he read the message. James was studying them. They were as impressive a group of men as he had ever seen in any officers' mess of the Scots Greys. In features, they were not dissimilar. They were definitely not spit and polish, commission-for-a-fee, parade square officers. Their boots were scuffed, their uniforms well worn and their faces and hands bronzed by the sun and wind.

The major burst into a broad smile.

"What is it, sir?" asked one of the officers.

The major handed the message to him.

"Read it out."

The officer took the message.

"It's from R. W. Scott," he began.

James recognized the name.

The officer read aloud.

> *It is with a great deal of pleasure that I hereby inform you that Lord Aberdeen, Governor-General of Canada, has approved your appointment as Commissioner of the North West Mounted Police, effective July 20, 1876..."*

The officer's voice was interrupted with loud cheers from the assembled group. They rose to their feet as one, shook the major's hand and clapped him on the back.

"Read on, Irvine," the major interrupted.

> *Lieut. Colonel French will be returning to duty with the Imperial Army. May I say, how pleased all of us here in Ottawa are with your ap-*

pointment. We understand the very great responsibilities we are placing upon you and know that you will carry them out with the same dedication and determination you have exhibited over the past two years. Our country's future in the North West rests largely upon your shoulders.

Irvine handed the message back to the major and shook his hand warmly. The officers were still on their feet.

"Thank you all," said the major to the assembled group. "Before we break up, may I introduce Constable Keyden. I mentioned to you that he was coming and as you know he is here specifically to report to Mr. McLennan and others in the East on the situation in the North West. It is my hope and I know yours too, that Keyden's presence here will significantly improve our communications with Ottawa. You all know how much we need that."

The officer's nodded their agreement.

"Please give Keyden every assistance. Anything we can do together to help Ottawa understand our situation is very much to our advantage. Keyden," added the major, "is there any news of special interest you have for us from your journey?"

"There is something I think will interest you, sir," replied James.

"Then carry on," said the major and he gestured for the officers to take their seats.

James took the notebook from his haversack. He began to relate to the group the information he had written in his report to Mr. McLennan. He started with the news he had heard at Fort Benton of the defeat of Custer's cavalry. This caught Macleod's and the other officers' attention and they hung on his words.

James told them of meeting the American officers on the train. He followed with the details of the U. S. Army campaign. Macleod and his officers exchanged glances as James spelled out the details of each column's strength and deployment.

The major turned to James. "Did the American officers on the train give you this information, Keyden?"

"Not directly, sir."

"But you saw the maps and reports."

"Yes, sir."

The major looked at James closely but did not press him on how he came by his information. He would find that out later.

"Repeat what General Sheridan said in his report," the major asked.

James read from his notes.

"…you are to pursue the enemy until captured or destroyed."

"You're sure he used the word 'enemy.'"

"Definitely, sir."

"Do you think that means that their cavalry will pursue the Indians over our border?" asked the major.

"I don't know, sir."

The major turned to his officers.

"Any questions?"

"Keyden," said the officer Macleod had called Irvine. "I congratulate you on the detail of your information."

"Thank you, sir."

"You said that all three columns were headed for the vicinity of the junction of the Yellowstone and Bighorn River," Irvine continued.

"Yes, sir, that's what the report stated."

"The news you heard at Fort Benton was that General Custer and the 7th Cavalry were defeated along the Bighorn River, right?"

"Yes sir."

"I think it is safe to assume, Commissioner," said Irvine turning to the major, and emphasizing the word 'Commissioner' to the smiles of his fellow officers, "that the United States Army and the Sioux will be engaged in a protracted battle. If General Sheridan's words are to be believed, the Sioux will be hotly pursued. I suggest, sir, that we can expect to see the first signs of the fleeing Sioux across our border in the very near future."

"No question about it, Irvine," replied the major. "We'll increase our patrols along the border from here to Wood Mountain at once. We'll let all our detachments know what's developing. We may need to move reinforcements from our northern outposts closer to the border. We'd better be ready for that. We may have thousands of Sioux on our hands before very long. We'll set that in motion tomorrow morning. Thank you, gentlemen."

As the officers left the mess the major asked James to remain behind. Macleod must have known from an earlier message, James surmised, that he had arrived recently from Scotland. The major invited James to sit down. He questioned him on the latest news of the Old Country. He pumped and prodded him for every detail of what was happening in Toronto.

"You know I grew up there?" said Macleod. "Born on the Isle of Skye, raised near Toronto."

James told him of Fiona and Arthur and that he had been staying in their apartment at Upper Canada College. He passed on the greetings of Mr. Wedd. The major was delighted to hear it. They talked for some time about Scotland, the Scots Greys, the College and Toronto.

"Keyden," said the major finally. "I understand you are to report back to Mr. McLennan at least once every two months. We'll see to it that you have every opportunity to see what is going on out here and to get to Fort Benton whenever you have your reports ready."

"Thank you sir."

"I'm counting on you to help us get through to the powers that be in Ottawa. The situation is very serious here – even more so with the news you brought. They need to understand that."

"I'll do whatever I can, sir."

The Commissioner rose from his chair and James followed.

"There's a place for you with B Company, Keyden. You should be comfortable there. Inspector Morrison is in charge. I'll be sure he understands your assignment and gives you every assistance."

James left the major and set out to find the quarters of B Company. The first man he met pointed them out. It was to the left of the cannons and next to the magazine. James stepped inside the low log building. There were seven or eight men inside. James introduced himself. They directed him to the unoccupied empty bunk. It was located at the end of a long, low single room. He guessed that it was about thirty feet long and twenty feet wide. It had a low ceiling of rough cut lumber. There were beds along the long walls facing the center aisle where a long table was set with several plates and mugs. The table was flanked on both sides with benches. There was a long shelf running high on the wall over the bunks. It was piled high with gear – belts, jackets, coats. At the far end of the room there was a large metal cylinder that looked like a barrel with both ends knocked out. It had a pipe running up from it through the roof. James guessed that it was the source of heat for the room in winter. Hanging from the middle of the ceiling was a single lantern. Some of the men had pinned pictures high up on the walls.

"So this is home for the duration," thought James.

The other members of B Company drifted in as James unpacked his things from the trunk that someone had already delivered to his quarters. The men were friendly in their greeting. Like the major, they wanted to know every scrap of news from the East. They were ecstatic to learn that the major had been promoted to Commissioner.

"Here's to Colonel French," shouted one of the men raising his mug. "May we never see his face again." The rest of the men cheered in response and joined in the toast.

Neither Webster nor Richter was in B Company. Someone had wind of the news James had given the officers and pressed him for details. The whole group listened intently as he told them what he knew of the American army's plans and their defeat at the hands of the Sioux. As James was finishing his story, the major and Inspector Morrison came through the door. James learned that it was the major's practice to visit each of the companies in their quarters every evening. Spontaneously, the men jumped to their feet and cheered.

"Here's to the Commissioner," yelled one of the men. The others responded with booming voices.

"Three cheers for the Queen," replied the major and the men followed his lead.

39

It hadn't taken the two Blackfoot scouts long to reach Crowfoot's camp on the Red Deer River. The Chief of the Blackfoot Nation and about seventy lodges of his tribesmen had made camp under the high bluffs of the coulees about thirty miles upstream from where the Red Deer River emptied into the Bow. The herds of buffalo were immense, the hunt was progressing well and the women were busy from sunrise to sunset with the processing of the meat and hides.

Several of the women were at the edge of the river as the sun came up on another day. They were washing up from their labours of the previous evening. There were young children and dogs running about among them. Absorbed in their work, none of the women saw the four warriors emerge from the trees on the opposite bank of the river and stop by the water's edge. It was one of the children who first saw them and shouted the alarm.

The women ceased their work at once, their eyes following in the direction the boy was pointing. The women recognized the riders as their enemies, the Sioux. Dropping what they were doing they ran back towards the encampment screaming alarm to the men in the lodges. Blackfoot warriors grabbed their weapons and ran for their horses, assembling as quickly as they could on the bank opposite the four riders who remained standing where they had first been sighted.

Facing the growing number of Blackfoot opposite them, one of the Sioux warriors raised his arm in the traditional gesture of peace. They wanted to confer, he signaled, with the Blackfoot chiefs. The Sioux leader dismounted, stood his rifle against a nearby tree and instructed the three with him to do the same.

The shouts changed to murmurs on the Blackfoot side. One of the chiefs edged his horse forward to the river and said in a loud voice.

"Are you four alone, or are there more of you?"

The reply came back, "Just us four, no more."

The Blackfoot chief sent one of his warriors back to the encampment. While they waited for his return the others faced the four across the swift flowing river.

The messenger was back shortly and on receiving his instructions, the chief signaled that they would be permitted to cross the river and could bring their weapons. There was a shallow spot a short distance upriver. The Blackfoot would meet them there and take the Sioux to their chief.

The Sioux took up their rifles, mounted and slowly rode their horses in the direction the Blackfoot had indicated. When they reached the ford they waded through the shallow water. The Blackfoot warriors parted to make room for them and took up positions on either side. The entire encampment – the young, the old and the women all watched as the Sioux were guided to Crowfoot's lodge.

Honour marks the ceremony of these meetings, the consequence of generations of tradition. Time is of little importance, understanding and consensus of great importance. The visitors were seated opposite Crowfoot, who was flanked by lesser chiefs and as many Blackfoot warriors as the lodge could accommodate. The leader and spokesman for the Sioux was Spotted Eagle, leader of the Sans Arcs and second in importance to Sitting Bull among the Sioux.

After the formalities, Crowfoot invited Spotted Eagle to speak. The Sioux chief, already known by reputation as a fierce warrior and brilliant military strategist, commanded their attention. Their eyes were drawn to his face with its piercing eyes, sharp nose with a deep scar running under it through his right cheek. His thick black hair was parted in the middle and ran in two matted braids down each side of his chest. A single eagle feather, anchored at the back of his hair, stretched over his forehead. There was a large bone medallion at his throat and below it, a beadwork design that took the form of a cross on his buckskin jacket. It was accentuated with a necklace of bear's claws.

Spotted Eagle stood to speak. His words were eloquent and his message simple. The white man's soldiers had pushed his people from their original homeland, through the Dakotas, to the valleys of the Missouri and the Yellowstone. The Sioux were at war with the Crows and under constant attack by the American cavalry that he called Long Knives.

"We are like a man sitting on a fallen log beside the river," Spotted Eagle explained to them. "We have been told to move over, and he have, and move over again, and we have, but now we are at the end of the log. If we move over one more time we fall in the river. All will be lost."

Spotted Eagle brought an invitation from his people to the Blackfoot Confederacy – Blackfeet, Bloods, Peigans, Stoneys and Sarcees.

"Come across the Medicine Line," Spotted Eagle implored. "Join us in our struggle against the Crows and against the Long Knives. If you do we will give you many horses and mules which we have taken from the Long Knives and many white women who are already our captives."

There was more to Spotted Eagle's message.

"If you will join us in our fight against the Americans," he continued, "as soon as the white man is destroyed on the other side of the border we will join you to wipe out all the white people on this side. We know how weak the white man is here. There are so few and we are so many. We have destroyed many American forts that are much stronger than the ones here. It would take us little time together to exterminate the white man."

Crowfoot sat motionless, his eyes fixed on Spotted Eagle.

The Sioux chief spoke to one of his men who reached in a bundle by his feet and handed the contents to Spotted Eagle. The chief opened it and placed it on the ground in front of Crowfoot. It was a piece of tobacco.

"I invite you to smoke this tobacco," Spotted Eagle said to Crowfoot, "as a sign that you will join us in our struggle against the white man."

Crowfoot remained silent, did not reach for the tobacco and looked Spotted Eagle in the eye. Spotted Eagle studied the great Blackfoot chief.

"If you do not smoke our tobacco," continued Spotted Eagle, his cold eyes fixed on Crowfoot, "after we defeat the Americans we will turn north and wipe out the Blackfoot along with the white man on this side of the border."

Some of the Blackfoot chiefs flinched at the words and there were murmurs among the warriors seated behind them. Crowfoot did not move. Spotted Eagle thanked Crowfoot for the opportunity to meet with him and invited his response. Then Spotted Eagle sat down.

There wasn't a sound among those assembled and all eyes turned to Crowfoot. The great chief sat expressionless, his eyes on the tobacco in front of him. His long black hair fell over his shoulders and partially covered his face, accentuating his firm mouth made distinctive by the indentation on his lower lip. He wore a necklace of buffalo horns and had a Hudson's Bay blanket over his knees. He was cradling in his arm a long eagle feather. A closed umbrella was beside him. There was a long silence. Finally Crowfoot spoke.

"We must think on this," was his reply. "We will send you our answer."

There was a flash of disappointment in Spotted Eagle's eyes. He had hoped for Crowfoot's agreement to take back to his besieged people. But Crowfoot had given his answer and Spotted Eagle knew he would have to accept it.

The concluding formalities began. Crowfoot invited Spotted Eagle and the other three to dine and rest before returning. Spotted Eagle thanked him, but said they must be back as quickly as they could. He thanked Crowfoot for the meeting, expressed his strong wish on behalf of his people that the Blackfoot join them in saving the buffalo and preserving their way of life. He looked forward to Crowfoot's answer and urged that it be soon.

Crowfoot rose and the two chiefs walked out of the tepee together surrounded by their warriors. The Sioux were handed their horses. Crowfoot ordered that they be given some dried buffalo strips for their journey home. The Sioux walked their horses to the bank of the river, followed by the Blackfoot warriors. At the river's edge they mounted, turned to Crowfoot and signed farewell. Crowfoot returned the sign. The Sioux wheeled their horses towards the ford and were off quickly. Crowfoot watched them go. As Spotted Eagle and the Sioux disappeared from sight Crowfoot called to one of his men.

"Take a message to Stamix Otokan," ordered Crowfoot. "Ask him to come as quickly as he can."

40

James was becoming familiar with the routine at the fort. He wakened with the sounds of the other men dressing in the barracks. The first rays of the morning sun were streaming through the one small window that faced east across the square. The first activity of the day, before eating or washing, was caring for the horses. He joined the men of B Company cleaning their section of the stables. Then he turned his attention to Mac.

The horse was responding to the exercise, the regular ration of oats and the generous supply of grass. His scratches were nearly healed. His coat, after much brushing and combing, shone. Mac had regained some weight and was beginning to look like the horse James had imagined when he first set eyes on him.

One morning, not many days after he had arrived, he was walking back to his quarters from the stables when one of the men came up to him.

"Keyden, the major would like to see you."

James knew that his present early-morning appearance would not satisfy the commanding officer of the Scots Greys. He looked at his dusty boots. He knew he smelled of horse and stable. But so did everyone else. He walked towards the major's quarters and knocked on the door.

"Come in."

James opened the door and found the major sitting behind his desk.

"I've sent Inspector Irvine with a party to Fort Walsh with the information you brought from Fort Benton. He will determine what we need to do to prepare for the arrival of the Sioux. I'm sure we'll see them sooner rather than later."

The major got up from his desk.

"I've received word from Crowfoot," the major said to James. "I've mentioned him to you before. He's the most important Blackfoot chief and the man we must do everything in our power to keep as an ally. He wants to see me right away. I'm going to meet him at his camp on the Red Deer River. I would like you to be there."

"Thank you, sir."

"I have work which will keep me here for a few days," the major continued. "Then I'll go straight to Crowfoot's camp. I would like you to leave today for Fort Calgary to give Inspector Walker and the detachment there the same report you gave us. After that you can ride over to Crowfoot's camp."

"Fine, sir. When do we leave?"

"You'll go alone, Keyden," said the major with a faint smile. "We are so few here that we can't spare a single person to go with you. It's a straightforward ride to Fort Calgary and then on to Crowfoot's camp. You shouldn't have any difficulty. I'll meet you there in a week or two."

The major smiled to himself as he watched James wrestle with the idea of his first trip alone across the prairie. He had seen the same reaction many times before in other men. He knew that the only way to initiate his policemen to life on the plains was to throw them into it. He would find out quickly enough what kind of an individual this Keyden fellow was.

"It will take you two or three days to Fort Calgary," the major told him, "a day to make your report and another four or five days to Crowfoot's camp. Leave as soon as you can."

The major looked down at his desk. James knew the meeting was over.

"Yes, sir. I'll be there."

As James was leaving the major called after him.

"Keyden, have Jerry give you directions."

James noticed the major's thin smile.

"Yes, sir."

Jerry looked even more improbable than the legend Richter had described when James found him just outside the west gate of the fort. Jerry was leaning against the stockade looking across the flat prairie towards the mountains. He had the end of an unlit cigar in his mouth and periodically spat bits of tobacco onto the ground. Jerry was short, his legs were bowed and he seemed unbalanced with a permanent lean to his right. He was resting on the barrel of his rifle, the butt against the ground. Jerry watched him approach but didn't say anything.

"The major suggested I ask you for directions to Fort Calgary and then on to Crowfoot's camp," explained James.

"That your black horse?" asked Jerry.

"Yes."

"Good horse," said Jerry

The scout squatted, leaning on his rifle. He smoothed the dirt in front of him. With his finger he drew a series of lines, the first, a straight-line north to south. From the top of this line he drew another touching it and running east. A short way down it, on the south side, he made an X. At the east end of the line he drew another line running north. A little way up, on the east side of this line, he made another X. Jerry pointed to the first north-south line.

"The mountains," he said. Then twisting to his left, he pointed towards the peaks in the distance. "See that flat topped mountain over there?"

James scanned the skyline and saw a massive, almost square shaped mountain. Its right side sloped steeply to the mountain beside it.

"The big flat one."

"That's it," said Jerry. "Chief Mountain. Remember it."

Turning back to the map he had sketched in the dirt, Jerry continued.

"Chief Mountain is here," he said, jabbing his finger on the map. "We're here," he said, jabbing a little to the east of it. He ran his finger north, up the chain of mountains, then right on the line he had drawn.

"Bow River." His finger stopped at the first X. "Fort Calgary."

His finger continued moving east until it hit the line coming in from the north, then followed the northern line. "Red Deer River." His finger stopped at the second X. "Crowfoot camp." Jerry brought his finger back to the base of the first north-south line. He jabbed his finger half way up to the first X.

"One day," he said

He jabbed the first X.

"Two days if you ride hard, maybe three.

He ran his finger along the Bow River from the first X to the second X.

"Four days, maybe five, okay?"

"Okay," replied James, studying the primitive map in the dust and committing it to his memory.

"Mountains on your left until you hit the Bow," instructed Jerry. "Then follow the river east."

Jerry got up and started into the fort.

"Jerry," James called out. "What happens if it's cloudy or stormy and I can't see the mountains?"

"They'll still be there," replied Jerry as he walked away.

40

JAMES NEVER FELT SO ALONE. He had left Fort Macleod as soon as he had put a few things together, turned north when he left the gate of the fort, keeping the mountains on his left as Jerry had advised. Inspector Morrison had dropped by as he was saddling up and James suspected that the major had put him up to it to be sure he had packed what was necessary for the journey.

"Take pemmican for a few extra days," suggested the Inspector. "Never know when the weather will close in or you might get lost for a few days."

It was just what James needed to hear! His heart skipped a beat at the word 'lost'. No one had said goodbye to him. When he passed Jerry on the way out through the west gate, the scout didn't so much as wave.

"I'm going on a three hundred mile ride on my own through one of the most hostile climates on earth," thought James in wonder. "It happens every day out here. No one thinks anything of it."

James forded the Old Man's River just upstream from the fort, then up the other side of the coulee and onto the open plain. The ever present wind was sweeping down on him through the mountains. It had a chill to it as he left the fort but warmed as the day progressed.

"You need to start worrying when the wind stops," one of the men had warned him. "It usually means some kind of storm."

Great puffs of white clouds were racing over the mountains and directly above his head. A little to the east they thinned until the eastern sky was a cloudless blue. The sun lit up the landscape casting pools of light across the surface of the plains. James wished he had a hat with a wide brim like Rawlins. He, like the rest of the men, wore his pill-box forage cap when not on parade and out here in the open plains it gave him little protection. He felt the sun and wind already burning his face and ears.

The land was almost flat to the north, east and south but began to roll in foothills towards the Rocky Mountains. The only thing moving were a few gophers, standing up straight as sticks as he approached, then scampering down their holes as he came closer. He had seen them first from the stagecoach and since then had seen rabbits, deer and elk and even a few wolves and foxes. The men said that there had once been grizzlies on the plains, the most ferocious of the bears, but those that had survived the hunters had moved further to the north.

James, as an only son, with a sister seven years his senior, had spent a good deal of time by himself. His father had been away from home much of the time. There were few children who lived close enough to his home in Gask with whom he could play. He had passed much of his youth reading or walking through the Perthshire countryside. From time to time he had hiked alone into the Grampion Hills and stayed overnight. As he grew older, he often took one of his father's horses into the hills. They would spend hours together exploring. A horse had always been a friend to him. He was glad he had found Mac. The black was turning out to be every bit as good a horse as he had hoped and he had begun to feel a real affection for him.

About the time the sun rose to its height, James came upon a shallow gully with a small creek running through it. He led Mac to it and the horse had his fill. James sat on the slope of the gully, ate some of the pemmican and drank from the creek. The gritty, heavy soil was hot running through his fingers. He picked at the red flower atop a cactus near at hand and tossed some small stones into the gently flowing stream watching them sink through the crystal-clear water to the bottom. The low grass that grew alongside the creek was sprinkled with purple crocuses. He lay back on the grass stretching his arms and legs, tight from the morning ride, watching the clouds moving southeast high above him.

Towards mid-afternoon they came across a small herd of buffalo grazing across their path and rode slowly among the great, furry animals with their menacing horns. The buffalo watched James and Mac closely, parted to give them space to pass but did not panic or run away from them. James had seen buffalo from the train but at that time his mind had been on other things. He hadn't had the chance then to get a good look at these remarkable beasts. He watched them graze as he rode slowly by, the noses of their massive heads buried in the short grass. There were large bulls, smaller females and numerous calves. The bulls lifted their heads as James approached, watched him suspiciously as he passed and put their heads back down to graze as he moved on. He could see hundreds, perhaps thousands of buffalo farther to the east.

Towards nightfall they came to a small river. James estimated that they had come forty or fifty miles which would put them about half way to Fort Calgary. It seemed like a good place to spend the night. The wind was moderating but still strong and he settled on a place in the lee of a steep bank. Dinner was more pemmican. He lit a fire to heat water to make what he now called 'prairie tea', but getting it started was not as easy as the teamsters on the way up from Fort Benton had made it look. But with some dry sagebrush and dead grass he finally got it going.

James sat for a long time watching the sun go down behind the mountains, awed by the magnificence of the sunset – a blaze of colour over the broadest horizon he had ever experienced. He couldn't take his eyes off it and watched until the streaks of red and gold, orange and violet merged with the advancing darkness until night fell. The only sounds were the water gliding by, Mac's hooves stepping over the ground and the night breeze through the prairie grass. It was a perfectly clear night. The stars, brighter than he had ever seen them, glimmered and sparkled.

James lay there for some time swept up by the night sky. The anxiety of setting out on this journey alone that he had felt that morning was fading with the emergence of a new confidence even when it occurred to him that the nearest human being was likely forty or fifty miles away. He felt a sense of calm that mirrored his surroundings. His mind was clear and his recollections sharp. He pictured his parents in the comfort of their country home. His mind went back to his stay with Fiona and her family and he smiled at the memory of the laughter of the children. And then an image of Merrie surfaced – it was at the party after the concert and she was dancing with carefree joy, the yellow ribbon in her hair untied and streaming behind her. He thought of the photograph that she had given him at the station and touched the breast pocket of his jacket to be sure it was still there where he kept it. "Hurry home," she had written. James began to wonder where his real home was.

41

The second day was a continuous panorama of unbroken prairie with a sky that seemed like a dome over the entire world. Towards late afternoon James reached the rim of a broad coulee and looked down on the Bow River. It was flowing east just as Jerry had shown on his crude map in the dust.

"As simple as asking for directions in Edinburgh," thought James. "Walk a few blocks up Princes Street and turn right at The Mound. Except in this case, Princes Street is about a hundred miles long and The Mound nearly two hundred."

He rode east along the rim of the coulee until he found a gentle slope to the river bottom below, followed it down and then across the flats beside the water. As the sun disappeared over the high hills of the coulee behind him he caught his first glimpse of Fort Calgary. From a distance it was another Fort Macleod but in a much more beautiful setting. The mountains with their sharp, rocky peaks and large patches of snow were much closer, the river valley broader and lined with trees; the water, fresh from the mountain glaciers was crystal clear and icy cold.

Inspector Walker gathered the men who were at the fort together to hear the news that James had brought. There was one other officer and about twenty of the thirty-five men who were stationed there. The others were out on patrols.

When James told them that the major had been promoted to Commissioner they cheered long and loud, just as the men at Fort Macleod had. The men were silent as they absorbed the details of the military action against the Sioux south of the border. James had brought a letter from the major for Inspector Walker. After reading it, Walker summarized it for his men.

"The major....the new Commissioner...," said Inspector Walker, "expects thousands of Sioux to seek refuge from the American cavalry on our side of the border. There may be the need to reinforce Fort Walsh near Wood Mountain and establish smaller detachments to the east and west of there. Some of you are to be ready to move south on short notice."

These men prized information from the outside world. Most of them had been in the North West for nearly two years. The only news they had was from travelers like James whom they saw very rarely. They spent a good deal of their lives alone or in pairs on patrol, amusing themselves with their own thoughts. They pressed him late into the night for news of the East. Those who had recently come from Britain were anxious for any news of the Old Country.

The major had suggested that James spend a full day at Fort Calgary but the following morning Inspector Walker, his sub-inspector and most of the other men were leaving at first light on various patrols. When he heard that James was headed for Crowfoot's camp the Inspector suggested James join one of the patrols that was headed northeast. They would take him close to the Red Deer River on a shorter route to Crowfoot's camp.

"The route along the Bow is easier to follow and it's hard to get lost going that way," said one of the men. "But come with us and we'll save you at least a day on the trail."

James was grateful for the company. Harris and Ryan, the two constables he was travelling with, set a much faster pace than he had the two previous days. He was heartened to see how well Mac responded. They had no difficulty keeping up.

"We have patrols out all the time," said Harris. "We go as far east as the Red Deer River, then turn northwest and follow it to Fort Edmonton. After that it's straight south back to Fort Calgary. This is how we keep in touch with what's going on out here."

"When there's trouble," added Ryan, "it's usually the Indians who know about it first and tell us about it. Most of the chiefs hate the liquor trade. They know we're serious about ending it so they give us all kinds of help."

Both Harris and Ryan had come to the North West in the Great March. They felt the same way about it as Webster had. They had become accustomed to the endless sweep of the prairie, the long hours in the saddle and the loneliness of their task. They hardly noticed the elk and deer that raised their heads in the distance or raced across their path.

The three Mounties rode continuously from sunrise to sundown. They took a short break around noon and then nothing until they stopped for the night. James studied them closely learning every lesson he could that might help him survive in this land that was so new to him.

Harris and Ryan were like men dying of thirst for news of the outside world. They couldn't hear enough about life in Toronto and Montreal. Harris came from a farming family that lived outside the town of Fergus, sixty miles northwest of Toronto. Ryan's grandfather had been Irish, his grandmother French-Canadian. He came from Sorel, a small community east of Montreal on the south shore of the St. Lawrence River. He had spent two years in Montreal and wanted to know everything that James had seen in that city from the time his boat landed until his train left for Toronto. So James told them in detail of the busy Montreal harbour, the fleet of sailing ships and steamers that lined the docks. He described the bustling business life around the waterfront which he had observed as he walked through it. There were the large stone office buildings, the majestic cathedrals, the narrow, cobblestoned streets, the frantic railway station and the long trains waiting to depart. Ryan had a faraway look in his eyes as he pictured the scenes that had once been so familiar to him and which were now made faint after two years on the plains.

They described for James how difficult life was for a Mounted Policeman in the North West. It wasn't only the loneliness and isolation, they told him, but the dust, the wind, the monotonous diet and the endless demands on such a few men scattered over such a wide area. They had their own horror stories about the Great March. But their greatest horrors were the mosquitoes in spring and the cold in winter. From James' own short experience with mosquitoes he believed every word they said. He found it harder to believe some of their stories about the mountains of snow, the blizzards and the freezing temperatures. Both men had signed on for five years. Even Ryan, who had grown up in Quebec, questioned whether he would be able to make it through three more prairie winters. After settling down for their first night together, the three sat by the low fire. James asked them about life at Fort Calgary.

"Macleod thought the best way to police the hundreds of thousands of square miles was from a chain of small detachments scattered across the prairies," Harris told him. "Last year, the major sent Inspector Brisebois a hundred miles north of Fort Macleod to a beautiful spot on the Bow where the hills begin to roll towards the Rockies."

James learned that both men had been part of F Company that had been sent to establish the fort. It had been their base ever since.

"Brisebois already had a reputation for poor judgment, insubordination and sloppy supervision of his men," Ryan told him. "Things got a lot worse after we built the fort."

"Like what?" asked James.

"Brisebois took a young Metis girl to live with him in his quarters," added Harris. "That was the start of the trouble."

"Then he took the only stove and cooking gear we had for his own use," added Ryan. "You can imagine how we felt about that."

"Then he had the nerve to name the fort after himself," continued Harris. "None of us wanted the fort named after an officer who so flagrantly abused his position."

"We finally got so fed up we mutinied," Ryan continued. "We sent word to Macleod and even though it was the dead of winter he and Irvine came up right away."

"Macleod was great," added Harris. "He understood immediately what was going on. He brought us together and calmed us down. He told us every move Brisebois had made was the opposite of what he and the Force stood for. He relieved Brisebois of command on the spot and put Walker in charge."

"How did the fort get its name?" asked James.

"Macleod told us that our site reminded him of a place he used to visit on the Isle of Mull in Scotland," Harris explained. "He said the grassland and the rivers were just like it. That place was called Calgarry so that's what he named the fort, except he took one of the r's out of the name."

"And Brisebois?"

"Thankfully, we've never seen nor heard of him since."

During their three-day journey to the Red Deer River they met only one other group of travelers. Mid-morning of the second day they spotted a small caravan of Red River carts moving northwest. There were five of them, squeaking slowly side by side across their path escorted by five riders.

As James had seen on the trail from Fort Benton, the families sat on the cargoes. There were four or five middle aged women and two younger women whom James found very attractive. They had wild, long black hair and dark complexions. One was dressed in buckskin, the other in a long plaid dress. They had dark eyes, sharp noses and high cheekbones on wide faces. There were numerous children of varying age, all laughing and jumping about on the wagons.

While Harris inspected the loads of hides for signs of liquor, Ryan chatted in the local French dialect with the drivers and riders. They carried on for some time, gesturing and pointing as they talked. Watching them, James understood how news was passed from person to person over this vast territory. James listened but found it hard to catch the words and follow their meaning.

The children had moved to the sides of the wagons closest to the conversation. Some were waving their arms and making faces trying to catch James' attention. He turned and made a face back at them. They howled with laughter and intensified their antics. This game went on while Ryan was doing his best to gather whatever information he could. Finally, the carts moved on with the children shouting and waving at a smiling James. He and all the others waved as the two parties set off in opposite directions.

Ryan told James and Harris that this party of Metis was from the North Saskatchewan. They had moved there from the Red River after the so-called Rebellion. They had been on the move for almost three months hunting hides and furs. They told Ryan that the buffalo were very scarce where they had been and it had taken them much longer than they had expected to fill their wagons. They were on their way to Fort Edmonton to trade.

The Metis reported that they had seen several groups of Indians hunting. Only one, they thought, was a war party. It was a group of Assiniboines that was further west than they normally should have been, encroaching on Blackfoot territory. Ryan had asked the Metis if they knew the whereabouts of Riel. They told him that they hadn't heard of him for over two years. They thought he was still in the East somewhere. Other than the thinly scattered herds of buffalo and the Assiniboines, they hadn't seen anything else of interest.

That afternoon the three riders crossed a stretch of blackened earth that went on for several miles. The grass and brush were burned to the surface. Ashes rose from the horses' hooves with the dust and stuck in James' nose and throat. He had to sip from his canteen often to clear the choking feeling. Mac snorted to clear his nostrils.

"This is what a prairie fire does," Harris told him. "Pray you never get caught in the path of one of them."

"How do they start?" asked James.

"Lightning. Or just spontaneously with the heat of summer," Ryan explained.

"Sometimes the Indians start them," added Harris, "to force the buffalo in the direction of the hunters or to destroy an enemy camp."

They reached the coulee of the Red Deer River as the sun was setting. They descended to the bottom and camped at the edge of the trees beside the water. They saw to their horses, had a quick meal and settled in for the night. James' face was flushed from the sun and the wind. He fell asleep almost at once.

The next morning they went their separate ways. Harris and Ryan headed upstream to Fort Edmonton, James downstream towards Crowfoot's camp. Harris had told James that it was about a day's journey to the camp. He would find it on a broad flood plain on the other side of the river. Sometime in mid-afternoon he would come to a ford where he would be able to cross.

James had felt reassured in the company of the two experienced Mounties and appreciated the chance to observe them on patrol. He was beginning to feel more confident finding his way on the featureless plains and was not nearly as anxious as when he had left Fort Macleod only a few days before.

Mac was gaining strength with each passing day and James stepped up the pace on his way to the ford. From time to time he ran Mac hard when the ground was even and solid and was pleased at the power and speed that was developing in him. James kept an eye out for the ford but by late afternoon had not seen it and was beginning to feel a little uneasy. He slowed Mac to a walk and began to scan the ground carefully for signs that might lead him to it. When he realized what he was doing he laughed to himself.

"My God," he thought, "I'm turning into an Indian scout."

Eventually he noticed off to his right some grass in an open field that had been trampled. He rode over to it and discovered several large circles of grass that had been flattened. He surmised that they were the marks left behind where Indian lodges had stood. James circled the small camp and saw faint, parallel tracks through the grass. They led down to the river bank, progressed along it in the same direction that he was heading. He followed them for a mile or so and saw them turn left into the river. He had found the ford.

James rode slowly through the shallow, fast flowing water and stopped on the other bank to give Mac a chance to drink. The sun was moving towards the rim of the coulee and he was anxious to make Crowfoot's camp by nightfall. He picked up the pace as they followed the same sets of tracks along the grassy flats beside the river.

The sun was well below the rim of the coulee when James came upon a wide flood plain. On the far side of it in the shadow of the coulee hills were many tepees with smoke curling from their tops. People young and old were scurrying among the lodges and along the riverbank ahead of him. With a sense of relief on having arrived and a twinge of fear of what lay before him he patted Mac on the neck and together they moved slowly towards the encampment.

42

The children were the first to see them as they approached. Some ran in their direction followed by a pack of dogs. When James reached the first tepee he dismounted and led Mac slowly towards the center of the camp. The children circled around him and tagged along. He didn't know where he was headed but he thought someone might come to greet him.

He studied the lodges as he passed. They were over twice his height, with long poles sticking out through an opening in the top. The poles were covered with buffalo hides stitched together. The lodge entrance was another hide thrown back. Each tepee had different drawings on it, in blue, black, red and white paint. There were sketches of riders on horseback, buffalo, stick figures of people lying down and arrows flying through the air. Some tepees had thick horizontal lines circling the top. Alongside many of the lodges were long horizontal poles resting on forked sticks. Over the poles were strips of what he thought must be buffalo meat hanging to dry. The tepees were placed quite a distance from each other. Between some were smaller, tepee-like structures not covered with hides. More strips of buffalo meat were hanging on them. Horses grazed everywhere among the lodges.

Some women had joined the procession that was following him. The children were chattering, pointing at his sword and running ahead to get a better look. He could see some of the men who were tending the horses looking in his direction. Up ahead a stocky-looking man was walking towards him. James stopped and waited as he approached. The man stopped a little way off and raised his arm. James wasn't sure what the gesture meant but he thought best to imitate it. The man came closer and said a few words that James could not understand.

"Stxkotan," said the man, "Stxkotan?, Stxkotan?"

James remembered that the major had an Indian name and that it sounded vaguely like what he was hearing. As the Blackfoot were expecting the major, maybe that was what this man was asking. James dropped his reins and with both hands made a gesture around his face to suggest a big beard. The man smiled and repeated the names. The children and women giggled to see James acting this way.

"How to convey the fact that the major is coming later?" James pondered. He pointed to the west where the sun was setting, then to the east and made a shape with his fingers to resemble the sun and raised his arms to signify what he thought represented the sun rising – tomorrow – the major is coming tomorrow. The man looked puzzled and James repeated the action again and again. The children and women were now convulsed with laughter. One of the women said a few words to the man. He smiled and nodded his head up and down. He mimicked James' action to let him know he understood its meaning.

The man made a gesture for James to follow him. He picked up the reins and with Mac followed along, the children with him but the women dropping off and returning to their tasks. The man stopped in front of a lodge. He made a gesture suggesting that James could enter. James nodded his head and said "Thank you", which the man did not understand.

"I hope there's someone in this camp who speaks English," thought James.

The man pointed to a group of horses and gestured that James could add his horse to the group for the night, then turned and walked away. James looked around. He was near the center of the encampment. There were lodges on all sides of him. He led Mac behind the lodge, took off the saddle and bridle, put on his halter and tied its long rope to a stake. He wasn't sure where to leave his saddle. There were some beside the lodge but he would rather keep his inside. He picked it up and carried it to the door of the lodge. The hide covering the entrance had been pushed aside and he looked in.

The lodge was dark inside except for the light coming in through the hole at the top. James stepped inside and as his eyes adjusted he could make out two figures sitting on robes. They were an old man and an old woman. Their eyes met. There was absolutely no movement in the old people's faces. The old man raised his arm and pointed to a buffalo robe laid out on the ground. James took the meaning and carried his saddle over to the robe and placed it on the ground beside the robe and near the side of the tepee. The lodge had a very distinctive smell. It was partly the scent of buckskin, partly smoke and what remained must have had something to do with buffalo.

As James was trying to decide what to do next a woman slipped in through the entrance. She motioned him to follow her outside. She led him a little distance from the lodge to an open spot on the ground where she had a large black kettle hanging from a tripod of long sticks over a small fire. She pointed to the ground. James sat down and waited. He watched her work over what he expected must be the evening meal. He made gestures to suggest that he had his own food inside the lodge. She couldn't understand, or pretended not to and pointed for him to stay where he was.

James sat quietly and studied what was going on around him. There were numerous fires like the one in front of him burning throughout the encampment. Women were busy keeping the fires going, tending to what was in the pots and moving in and out of the lodges. The woman in front of him was dressed in a shapeless robe that combined a blanket with buckskin. She was short and stocky. She had long black hair that fell over her shoulders. Its ends were gathered into two braids. The top of her dress was decorated with quills and beads in a pattern that went up the front of the dress and around the neck. She wore a necklace of shells. Her feet were covered in moccasins of heavy buckskin. They, too, were decorated with beads, although some of the decoration had been worn away.

Soon children arrived around the fire. James assumed these to be her family. They were full of life and curious about the visitor in the scarlet jacket. Then the man who had greeted him arrived. He gestured to James to follow him inside the lodge. At the entrance he stopped and pointed to a large drawing beside the doorway. Three large buffalo were rendered in red paint. The buffalo were drawn in a way that suggested they were definitely male. The man pointed at himself then at the drawings. He repeated this action several times. James looked at him, pointed at the drawings and at the man. He got the meaning. This man was Three Buffaloes, or Three Bull Buffaloes, or Three Bulls.

The man led James into the lodge but made no effort to introduce him to the old man or the old woman. He hardly took notice of them. He gestured for James to sit on the robe where James had left his saddle. James did and again waited. He knew the man wanted to talk but they were helpless without each other's language.

The woman by the fire came in carrying a shallow wooden bowl with thick soup. She gave it to the man. She went out and back again and gave the second bowl to the old man. The third she gave to James and the fourth to the old woman. The children must have eaten outside. They didn't come into the lodge to eat nor did the woman who had prepared the meal.

Inside the lodge they ate in silence. The woman returned and lit a small fire on the ground inside a circle of stones in the middle of the floor. The smoke swirled round inside the tepee eventually curling up through the opening at the top. She went outside and adjusted some of the long poles that controlled the opening at the top of the tepee and smoke began to rise more quickly. The improvement in the draft cleared some of the smoke that had settled inside the lodge. The woman removed the bowls and Three Bulls lay down on his robe for a short nap. James watched it all in silence.

After a time, three men arrived at the entrance. The host rose from his nap, invited them in and the four of them sat in a circle around the fire facing each other. One of the guests had brought a handful of short sticks and small stones and they proceeded to play a game of some sort with them. They rolled the bones and sticks in front of them in turn and chatted and laughed as the game progressed, glancing at James from time to time.

As the evening wore on the children came in. They sat silently around the edges of the lodge. James thought of William and Hermione and how excited they would be if they were with him.

One by one the children in the lodge tumbled over on their sides and fell asleep. The old man and old woman had already done so. Finally the woman entered. She went to her spot on a pile of thick robes, lay on her side and watched the game. James took off his sword, belt and boots and placed them beside his saddle. Like the others he rolled over on his side watching the players by the flickering fire until sleep overtook him.

43

JAMES WOKE THE FOLLOWING MORNING having slept the night through. He could tell from the light coming in through the hole at the top of the tepee that the sun was already up. He had a foul taste in his mouth and could feel the smoke from the fire in the back of his throat. He noticed for the first time a number of objects dangling from the spot where the poles came together at the top of the lodge and recognized them with a shudder as scalps hanging by their hair. Around the walls were bows and clusters of arrows hanging from the lodge poles together with weapons that looked like small stone axes.

James raised his head and looked around. Three Bulls was still asleep on the thick pile of robes where the woman had been the night before. The old people and the children were asleep as well. The woman had left the lodge. James quietly put on his boots, left the lodge and walked into the trees to find a quiet place to relieve himself. Then he walked towards the riverbank where several women were washing small children, utensils and clothes but he didn't see the woman of his lodge. He knelt down by the edge of the river and washed his face in the frigid water, rinsed out his mouth and wiped his wet hands through his hair.

"It's probably about time I washed some of my clothes," he thought.

James wasn't sure what the etiquette of living with an Indian family was. He went back to the lodge and quietly picked up all his things except his saddle. Not to disturb those still sleeping, he went outside again, dressed, then led Mac along the river bank to where he had seen some tall grass. He wasn't sure when the major and his party might show up. It might be today, or tomorrow or the next day. As long as his host didn't mind, James would spend a quiet day and give Mac a chance to graze restfully. He sat down beside the water and had a breakfast of pemmican from his haversack. He took out his notebook and for the first time in a long time he had a relaxed time to sketch. It crossed his mind that if Merrie were here she would find any number of memorable scenes to photograph.

A short time later James noticed several of the men of the village preparing to depart. They did not appear to be in a warlike mood and he assumed it was a routine hunting party. The riders broke into two groups each setting off in a different direction along the river.

The sun was warm, the sky clear and the wind moderate. James sat with his back resting against a tree savouring the chance to sit quietly without interruption. He concentrated on drawing a scene that included the river, the trees on the opposite bank and the slopes of the coulee hills in the distance. The sun was high above him when the drawing was complete. He wrote at the bottom "Crowfoot's Camp on the Red Deer River". He had forgotten the exact date but he knew it was "August, 1876"

After the river scene, he had turned to capture the image of the encampment itself, with the river flowing into the background on one side and the trees on the other. James had always enjoyed drawing, although he didn't consider himself very good at it. He could get a reasonable likeness of landscapes. People and faces he found much more difficult.

The children discovered him and crept up from behind to see what he was doing. They peeked over his shoulder, took quick looks, giggled and ran off only to return and do it again and again. James did not discourage them. Soon there was a quiet group, some sitting and others standing around and behind him, watching.

He gestured to a small girl to sit in front of him. He turned to a fresh page in his notebook and began to sketch her. He didn't think it was a particularly good sketch, but the other children were impressed and wanted their pictures drawn too. He did several of them until his hand was tired. The children made gestures suggesting they wanted to keep their pictures, but James didn't want to lose this record of his visit so he kept them.

Around mid-day he heard shouts from the flats closer to the encampment. By this time most of the children had disappeared so he packed up his drawing things and walked Mac in the direction of the noise. Some older boys were riding on horses without saddles. They were playing some kind of game, throwing what looked like an animal's skull back and forth among themselves as they raced up and down the flats. James moved closer to watch. One team would attempt to carry the skull to the far end while the other team tried to head them off or wrestle it away from them. He was impressed by the boys' agility and how they managed to stay on the horses' backs, hanging on to ropes around their necks or the horses' manes.

"No wonder Indians are such good riders," he thought.

One of the boys saw James watching and gestured to him to come to join them. James took off his sword and laid it along with his bandolier and cap beside a tree. He swung himself up on Mac's bare back.

James hadn't ridden Mac bareback before but he had done it a lot growing up. The boys gathered around James and one threw him the skull. James thought it must have come from a dog or a wolf. He caught it and threw it back. The boy pointed to some of his friends and James took that to mean that these were his teammates. The others rode part way down the field and turned to face them. The boy threw James the skull and sped forward. James and his teammates followed.

It took James a little while to catch on but soon he was well into it. They raced back and forth down the field, throwing, catching, running interference for their teammates and trying to cut off their opponents. James enjoyed it thoroughly and so did Mac. Only once did James fall off when Mac, who seemed to have a sense of the sport from the start, veered to cut off a rider when James wasn't expecting it. The boys stopped playing, came over to be sure he was all right, laughed and continued playing.

As the afternoon progressed the sun grew hotter and the game went on. Finally James waved to them and left the field soaked in sweat. He led Mac to the river where he had a long drink and was content to graze in the long grass. James squatted at the water's edge and splashed his face. The water felt much warmer than it had in the early morning.

There were several women and children along the riverbank, some washing clothes, some washing children and others romping with the younger ones. He wasn't sure whether the women minding the children were their mothers or their older sisters. They all looked about the same age. Some carried babies in long tight-fitting baskets on their backs. Generally the women had attractive round faces, bright, wide-set eyes, high cheek-bones and long, beautiful black hair tied in long braids which fell over their shoulders. They wore long buckskin dresses. Only the ones with belts gave any hint of the shape of the body underneath.

James took off his boots and jacket and laid them by the riverbank. He took off his socks and shirt and undershirt and took them to the shallow edge of the river. The water felt refreshing on his feet. He bent down in the shallow water, washed his shirt as best he could and did the same with his under clothes. He squeezed out the water and laid the clothes on the nearby bushes to dry in the sun.

He was brushing the dust off his boots when he was startled by loud cries from some children far down the riverbank to his right. He stood up and was surprised to see two small dark brown bear cubs emerge from the trees and walk to the river's edge. They put their black noses into the water and began to drink. The children were shouting at the cubs and the women were hollering at the children, waving at them to leave the bear cubs alone and run back to them.

As James was watching, and the children and their mothers were frantically shouting, a huge bear of similar colouring walked out of the trees towards the cubs. It was a frightening animal with a small head for the size of its body and a large hump over its shoulders. James remembered the word "grizzly" and the description of it from his companions in the stagecoach and shuddered with alarm.

The women on the bank were shrieking at the children to run for the camp. The children didn't need to be coaxed. They ran for all they were worth towards the lodges. Two of the mothers remained, hollering and James noticed that there were two children on the bank beyond the bears who were standing as if frozen in their place. They had terrified looks on their faces. The bear swung its head back and forth, looking right and left assessing the danger to her cubs. Several of the children were fleeing past James towards the lodges. The bear turned away from watching them and starting walking slowly in the direction of the two children standing alone by the bank.

James could see the peril the two little ones were in. If he could divert the grizzly's attention from them they might have a chance to run for the encampment. James grabbed Mac's halter rope, swung himself up and raced towards the bear and her cubs. He meant to startle the mother, draw her and her cubs away from the river, if he could, and into the woods

The closer he rode towards the huge animal the more nervous Mac became. The horse, like James, sensed the deadly power of the great grizzly and didn't like the idea of being this close. James held Mac steady. When they drew alongside the cubs who were now following their mother towards the terrified children, James let out a yell that drew the mother bear's attention. The grizzly turned its head and snarled towards James. Seeing him riding hard towards her cubs she rushed to the attack. Mac instinctively lurched to the right and raced into the woods. James glanced over his shoulder and saw the huge bear right behind them astonished that an animal of that size could run so fast. James led the bear deep into the trees until it tired and dropped back. He kept Mac at full speed, circled around the grizzly and her cubs back to the river, racing towards the two children who were still standing where he had last seen them. He reined Mac in long enough to take each child by the arm and swing them up, one in front and one behind. Then he raced with them for the lodges.

Women, children and old people were anxiously waiting by the edge of the encampment. As he stopped in front of them two of the women ran up to take the children from him. They hugged the children tightly as they ran with them into the protection of the lodges. Some of the men who were still in the camp had run out to see what was going on. The women pointed towards the woods. James looked back but there was no sign of mother or cubs. Some of the men ran back towards their horses. After a few minutes James saw them speed off into the woods. Some of the women came up to James and put their hands on his shoulders. They were speaking to him in words he could not understand but he understood their gestures and the look of gratitude in their eyes.

44

Before noon the following day Commissioner Macleod, Jerry and two constables arrived at Crowfoot's camp. Three Bulls and some of the other chiefs welcomed them. The major was glad to see James, inquired after Inspector Walker and the force at Fort Calgary and asked him to join them for the meeting with Crowfoot. James had not yet seen the great Blackfoot chief and looked forward to the opportunity. While the Blackfoot chiefs were assembling, Macleod and his men sat by the bank of the river waiting to be called. James was interested to know more about Crowfoot and asked Jerry what he knew of him.

"This Crowfoot is the second son of a great chief," Jerry told him. "His older brother, Sapo-makikow, it means Crow Big Foot, journeyed to the Snake Indians in the south with a pipe of peace. But they killed him. This Crowfoot led a raid against the Snake's to avenge his brother and it was a great victory for the Blackfoot."

Jerry spit out bits of the end of his cigar between sentences.

"This Crowfoot was made a chief and given his brother's name," Jerry continued. "It was me who shortened the name in English to Crowfoot."

"What kind of a man is he?" asked James.

"Brave warrior," answered Jerry. "He's led his people to many victories. Loves horses. Has over 200. Great rider. Superstitious. He'll only ride a spotted horse. Won't let anyone else ride his best horse."

Towards late afternoon the chiefs were assembled and word was sent to Macleod and the others to join them. The lodge was much like the one in which James had been a guest. Crowfoot was seated on the ground and flanking him on both sides in a wide semi-circle were the other chiefs. Many more Blackfoot men sat behind the chiefs, filling the tepee. James noticed that his host, Three Bulls, sat on Crowfoot's right. Crowfoot motioned for the major to sit opposite him.

James studied Crowfoot, whom Jerry had called "Chief of Chiefs" of the Blackfoot. Crowfoot sat with his shoulders hunched forward, his long black hair falling around his face. He had small, sharp eyes, a large beaked nose and an indented lower lip. He wore a buckskin shirt and long pants and had a blanket wrapped over his shoulders and across his knees. His moccasins were highly decorated. He had a necklace of buffalo horns and carried a long, broad eagle feather in his hand.

The major turned to James and in a low voice said, "Sit next to Jerry and take notes. No sketches. The Indians have a strong superstition against someone taking their image." James was surprised to hear this and thought of the drawings of the children that he had made the previous afternoon.

The assembled group formed a large circle around a small fire, just like the one in the tepee James had slept in. He looked up and saw a larger collection of weapons and scalps than were in Three Bull's lodge. One of the chiefs handed Crowfoot a long pipe. Crowfoot stood up, adjusted the blanket around his shoulders and raised his eyes and the pipe towards the sky. He was much taller than James had imagined. Crowfoot turned to the four corners of the compass and repeated the action, mumbling words as he did it. Jerry did not translate. Crowfoot was praying to the Old Man. When Crowfoot finished he sat again. One of the chiefs took a stick from the fire and held it to the bowl of the pipe while Crowfoot puffed on it. When the pipe was lit, Crowfoot smoked it, blew the smoke towards the fire and handed it to Three Bulls.

"Who's that?" James whispered to Jerry.

"Three Bulls, Crowfoot's step-brother," answered Jerry, looking straight ahead. "Don't speak."

The pipe was passed around the circle in silence. Each chief drew on the pipe briefly and passed it to the person on his right. Jerry passed the pipe to James who held it the way he had seen the others do it. He had smoked from time to time but never regularly. He drew cautiously on the Blackfoot pipe and felt the raw smoke gag in his throat. He held his breath to keep from coughing while tears welled up in his eyes and quickly passed it to one of the constables beside him. For several moments his throat still burned. Much to his relief he was soon able to breathe again without coughing or gasping for air. He knew he had come very close to embarrassing himself in front of the major and the assembled group. When the pipe was returned to Crowfoot he handed it to the chief who had brought it out. Then he looked across the circle and began speaking. Jerry was translating to the major as the chief spoke. James strained to get every word.

"Welcome, Stamix Otokan, and to your men," Crowfoot began. "We are glad you have come. We have exchanged messages with the Sioux and we are unsettled."

James took a quick look at the major whose eyes were fixed on the chief.

"The Sioux brought us tobacco," Crowfoot continued. "They invited us to join with them in an attack on their enemies, the Long Knives and the Crows. They offered us horses, mules and white women. They said that after they defeat the Crows and Long Knives they would join with us and destroy the white man in our land. They think the Redcoat forts are weak and that they can be overrun easily."

James glanced at Macleod. The major flinched but he did not speak.

"I sent the tobacco back to the Sioux," Crowfoot told them. "I said we could not smoke it on their terms. I told them that the white people here are our friends and that we will not fight against them."

James saw the major nod his approval, but Macleod still said nothing.

"A short time ago we had a reply from the Sioux," Crowfoot continued. "They said that as we would not come to help them against the Americans they would come over to this side and show the Blackfoot that the white police were nothing before them. They said that after they exterminate the white man they will come against the Blackfoot."

Still Macleod said nothing.

"Here is my question to you, Stamix Otokan," said Crowfoot, looking straight into Macleod's eyes. "If the Sioux move against us, will you help us?"

All eyes moved to the major.

"If the Sioux cross the Medicine Line," said Macleod, choosing his words carefully, "without the Blackfoot giving them any cause to do so, we are bound to help you. You are subjects of this country and have the right to our protection as all other subjects have."

Crowfoot waited for the translation then nodded to Macleod and smiled.

"It pleases us to hear that," replied Crowfoot. "We intend always to be at peace with the white man and particularly with you Redcoats. We have seen the way you have dealt with us since you arrived in this country. We know you are our friends."

Crowfoot looked along the line of chiefs to his right and then to his left and then across at the major. His face grew hard.

"We all see that the day is coming," Crowfoot said, his voice low, "when the buffalo will all be killed. We will have nothing more to live on. Then you will come into our camp and see the poor Blackfoot starving. I know the heart of the white soldier will be sorry for us and you will tell the great mother. She will not let her people starve."

James turned to see the major's reaction. His face was also grim.

"We are being shut in," continued Crowfoot, his voice rising. "The Cree are coming into our land from the north, the white man from the south and east. They are destroying our means of living. Although we plainly see these days coming, we will not join the Sioux against you. We depend on you to help us."

There was another long pause.

"As you are willing to help if the Sioux attack us," Crowfoot went on, breaking the silence, "we will help you. If the Sioux attack you, we will send two thousand warriors to fight by your side."

"Thank you for your offer," replied Macleod. "As long as the Blackfoot are peaceful you will always find us your friend and willing to do anything for your good."

"You are a good friend," said Crowfoot. "We will keep our eyes out for the Sioux and do nothing against them without talking to you first and seeking your advice."

The major reached into a bag that he had placed on the ground behind him and took out a large piece of tobacco.

"Thank you," the major said as he handed it to Crowfoot.

The chief took the package, opened it, held it up in his hands to show to his chiefs. The one with the pipe opened the package, took some of the tobacco in his fingers and placed it in the bowl of the pipe. Crowfoot held up his eagle feather.

"Before we smoke the pipe of peace and you depart," said the chief looking at the major, "there is one more thing." The major glanced at Jerry who shrugged. Jerry didn't know what was coming either.

"Yesterday, one of your men did a very brave thing," said Crowfoot, pointing in James' direction. James had said nothing to the others about the incident with the grizzly. The chief went on to tell the story of the mothers and children on the riverbank, the grizzly cubs appearing from the woods and the grizzly mother threatening the children. He told of James racing towards the bear to divert its attention and circling back to rescue the two children. The chiefs all nodded and murmured their approval as Crowfoot ended his story.

The major looked in surprise at James.

Crowfoot waved his feather at James in a gesture that meant stand up. James rose and stood in his place. Three Bulls rose from beside Crowfoot, walked over and stood in front of James. Three Bulls stepped forward and put a necklace around James' neck. It was a string of rawhide and from it hung the claw of a grizzly.

45

After the meeting with Crowfoot, James moved his saddle and belongings from Three Bulls' lodge to a campsite near the river where the major, Jerry and the other two constables were preparing to settle in for the night. James had asked Jerry to come with him to speak to Three Bulls and through Jerry he had been able to thank the chief for his hospitality and his gift of the necklace.

As the sun faded behind the coulee hills it became almost too dark for James to write. He was finishing up his report to Mr. McLennan of the meeting with Crowfoot when he heard an angry argument taking place in the woods not far from where he was sitting. He got up and walked towards the voices. Before he reached them the arguing stopped. One of the constables emerged from the trees. Even in the low light James could see that he was flushed with anger. A few steps behind him was the major. Macleod saw the questioning look on James' face.

"It's all right, Keyden," said the major. "Go back to the camp." James was curious to know what had happened but thought better of pressing the major. He turned around and started back to where he had put his blankets.

"Keyden," the major called after him. James stopped, turned and waited for Macleod to catch up to him.

"You might as well know what this is all about," said the major. "You'll find out soon enough." They walked slowly together back towards the camp.

"It's the custom of some tribes, the Blackfoot among them, to offer their women as bed partners to their guests," the major explained. "It's part of their idea of hospitality. On occasion, they make the offer to a member of the Force as they did to the constable tonight. Some of the men and even some of our officers think it is all right to accept these offers. I know that Inspector Walsh encourages it. He thinks that accepting these women gives the Indians a good impression of our manliness and that they think little of a man who refuses."

James could sense the anger rising in Macleod.

"Manliness, for God's sake," said the major. "As if they needed added demonstrations of our manliness." They walked on in silence until suddenly Macleod stopped and turned to James.

"Nothing could be further from the true state of the case. Indeed, I think that Indians have a much greater respect for the man who lives as a white man and does not follow their practices."

"I take it the constable didn't agree," said James.

"He did not," answered the major. "I had to come down on him pretty heavily. Hell, Keyden, I understand him completely. It's a lonely existence out here. I've been engaged to be married for six years. Three times I've had to put off the wedding because of some crisis. I haven't seen my fiancée in Winnipeg for over a year."

James saw a glimpse of the warm-hearted commander Webster had told him about.

"Never forget, Keyden," Macleod said to him emphatically, "we are the law out here. God knows, our strength is not in numbers. All we have is our integrity and the Indians' trust. If we lose that, we lose everything."

46

"I want you to ride to Fort Benton," Macleod told James as they were breaking camp the next morning. "I have a report of our meeting with Crowfoot ready for Mr. Scott. I expect you have one for Mr. McLennan as well. Hopefully, one of them will be read. It's important that Scott and the others in the East understand Crowfoot's loyalty and how important it is to keep it. It's a critical factor out here."

James took the major's report and put it in a saddlebag beside his own.

"After that I want you to ride to Fort Walsh. Give Inspector Walsh, who is in charge there, a full report of our meeting with Crowfoot. He'll be most interested. I think you should stay there for the next few months where you will be close at hand when the Sioux arrive. Here's a letter for Walsh. I've asked him to give you all the help he can."

Jerry sketched another map in the dirt as he gave James directions to Fort Benton from Crowfoot's camp, then northeast from Fort Benton to Fort Walsh. Fort Benton, Jerry told James, was a three or four day ride due south from Crowfoot's camp. He would cross the Old Man's River, the Milk and the Marias. The rivers would be low. There would be several places where James could cross safely. When he reached the Missouri he could determine from the size of the mountains on the horizon whether he should go upstream or downstream to reach Fort Benton. Fort Walsh was a three or four day ride from Fort Benton. It would take him over the Milk River and Lodge Creek. He would find Fort Walsh near the southwest corner of the Cypress Hills at the headwaters of Battle Creek.

During the three-day ride to Fort Benton James didn't see a soul. There wasn't one Indian rider, tepee or Metis wagon. He did see signs of large buffalo herds but not one of the shaggy animals. The sloughs were pockmarked with hoof prints, there were buffalo chips everywhere and the grass was beaten down.

He did see small herds of elk and antelope. They would graze alertly until he approached and then dash off when he rode too close.

The land became drier as he rode south, the prairie grass shorter, until he was almost in a semi-desert. He saw creatures he had not noticed before, prairie dogs, mice, ferrets and jackrabbits. His eyes were becoming accustomed to the landscape and he was able to pick up even the slightest movement much more quickly than when he had first arrived. He had been wrong to think that the prairie was devoid of life and movement. There was a great deal of it, but it was close to or below the surface and it took patience and a keen eye to capture it.

One day towards evening he came upon a large marshy slough where, in spite of its openness to the wind, he chose to spend the night. There was grass for Mac and dead twigs and buffalo chips for a fire. It was earlier in the day than he had planned to stop but it was a pleasant setting. He lingered over his 'tea', sitting on the grass by the water's edge and watching the activity around it as the sun set. There was an array of bird life, on the water, in the rushes along the water's edge and on the surface of the heavy clay soil that formed its bank. Ducks paddled and quacked in and out of the tall rushes. Robins, meadowlarks, blackbirds with red patches on their wings and sparrows swooped over the pond and rested on the tips of the fat, brown rushes. Snipes ran along beside the waterline, stopped suddenly to dip their beaks into the still water. Hawks flew high overhead waiting to pounce and crows squawked loudly at each other across the pond. There was an equal variety of bugs, some flying about, some skimming over the water. Mercifully there were no mosquitoes as their session had passed.

The sounds of the life of the pond continued as the sun disappeared, frog voices gradually taking over from the birds. The light of the moon and stars reflected off the water, mesmerizing James so that he sat and gazed at it long after the sun was down. Finally he rolled himself in his blankets, staring at the sky until he fell asleep.

The next morning the sky was filled with dark, boiling, threatening clouds racing over his head driven by the wind from the mountains. Although he heard rumbling of thunder in the distance not a drop of rain fell. The wind howled and he watched for the storm he expected, but it never arrived. Although the sun broke through the clouds only rarely, the heat was intense. Dust, sagebrush and dead grass swirled around him as the wind gusted. Finally he wrapped one of the blankets around his head to protect his eyes and ears.

He was relieved to reach the coulee of the Old Man's River. It seemed like a familiar friend and it provided shelter from the wind. He rode slowly down the gully between the coulee hills to the bottom and made his way deep into the trees near the riverbank. There was a clearing ahead through which he could see the water rushing by. Although the trees still swayed with the breeze, there was no more swirling dust. He stripped the saddle and bridle from Mac, gave his sweating hide a good rubbing with leafy branches from the cottonwood trees and led him to a long drink in the river.

It was a good campsite. Mac had grass, they were protected from the worst of the wind, he could hear the rushing of the river nearby and there was plenty of wood for a fire. After he had eaten, James felt the need to stretch his legs after having been in the saddle all day. He walked to the river's edge, ran his wet hands over his face and through his hair then started walking upriver. He could see the valley winding ahead of him, its steep slopes rising, a mile apart on each side. He turned into the trees and walked to where the coulee bottom met the sloping hillside. He followed it along until he noticed an outcropping of black rock. Pieces of the material had broken loose and some were at his feet. He picked one up and recognized immediately that it was coal. He glanced at the seam above him. It was clearly distinguishable, showing through the side of the hill. Little did he realize he was standing on the site of a tropical rain forest and that the piece of coal in his hand had been formed 70 million years before. He looked again at the seam of coal and noticed that above it were clearly delineated strata of differing materials – sand, gravel and small stones. Above it was a layer of heavy soil and above that three more layers of sandy soil before it reached the surface.

James bent down and picked up other fragments of rock lying among the pieces of coal. He could see the imprint of fossils, time's fingerprints, of the sea algae, diatoms, corals, ammonites and marine reptiles that inhabited this region in prehistoric times. Had James not turned around and headed back to his camp, but continued another hundred feet along the coulee face, he would have seen the tips of dinosaur ribs poking through the surface of the hillside.

47

After the solitude of the plains Fort Benton was a welcome sight. James took a room at the Nugget and put Mac in the stable behind it with six pounds of well-deserved oats and a stall full of grass. He posted the major's report to Mr. Scott and his to Mr. McLennan and walked down the street to the Golddust Saloon. He wanted something other than pemmican to eat and was interested to learn what he could of the movements of the Sioux and the American cavalry.

It was early evening and the Golddust Saloon was almost empty. There were three trail-weary riders at a table on the far side of the room. Two other men were at another table near them. There was a man wearing a dirty apron tied around his waist behind the bar and a woman in a long, frilly, low cut dress playing an out-of-tune piano trying to inspire a little life into the surroundings. Another woman in a long, silky red dress was leaning against the bar talking to the man in the apron. A long, white boa was wound around her neck and fell over her shoulder. The woman in the red dress left her place beside the bar and walked over to James.

"What can I get you, Redcoat?" she asked in a jaunty voice.

"Anything but buffalo," said James.

"How would you like a nice, thick beef steak?"

"That'd be perfect," he replied.

"What to drink?"

"Water would be just fine."

"You gawdam Redcoats. What is it with you guys?"

"Just the rules, ma'am."

"I'm not ma'am, I'm Mademoiselle Heidi!" she said in her best-affected French accent. She had probably been quite beautiful at one time. James could only guess how many years ago. He wondered what disappointments and misfortunes had brought her, at this stage of her life, to a place like the Golddust Saloon. She was quite tall and had put on weight since her days of youth. She was not nearly as heavy as the woman at the piano. Heidi's hair was silver. How it got that way James couldn't guess. Although her face was painted, it didn't hide the pain in her lifeless eyes. Her red dress, which reached nearly to the floor, was loose fitting except for a broad black belt pulled tightly around her waist.

"Okay, Redcoat," repeated Heidi. "Beef steak and water it is." She returned to the bar, gave the barman the order, poured a tin mug full of water from a wooden pail and returned to James' table.

"So, what were you saying about rules?" she went on as she put the water in front of him.

"Rules for Mounties – no liquor, no cards, no women."

Heidi made a face to express her disgust.

"But we can talk," said James. "Would you like a drink?"

"I never say no," she replied as she raised her arm and held up one finger to the bartender. "He knows what I like." Heidi sat down beside him.

"Anything going on in town, Heidi?" James asked.

"Not a hell of a lot," she told him. "Seems every year the town gets quieter."

"How about the fort?" asked James. "The troopers must liven things up a bit."

"They do when they're in town," she replied with a grin. "Most of them left a while ago. Ordered out somewhere. They'd been sitting around for weeks waiting for something. They hardly came in here at all. Whenever we did see them they were mad as hell about something."

The bartender caught Heidi's last words as he arrived with her drink.

"Their cavalry got beat up a bit down south," interrupted the bartender. "General Custer got killed along with a couple of hundred of his men."

"That many?" asked James.

"All that were with him at the time," the bartender went on. "That's what the men at the fort were so mad about. There's an Indian chief called Sitting Bull who was responsible. They want to skin him alive."

"Did they catch him?" asked James.

"Don't think so. Not yet," he replied. "After they killed Custer the Sioux just disappeared. No one seems to know where they are. Some of the cavalry think they've crossed the line into your country, or are heading that way."

"Any Sioux around here?" asked James.

"Nope, not around here," answered the bartender. He turned and walked back to the bar. James' steak was ready. The bartender called Heidi who left the table to pick it up. She carried it back and placed it in front of him.

"There you go, honey," she said, bending down low to kiss his pillbox forage cap. "Thanks for the drink."

James ate the steak but hardly recognized the taste of beef. Maybe on his restricted diet he had forgotten what it tasted like. It could have been a buffalo steak for all he knew or elk or antelope. When he had finished he walked through the main street to the dock on the Missouri. There was no steamer in town and little sign of activity around the landing. He walked back to the Nugget and wrote a letter to his parents, touching on the highlights of his first days in the North West. He described his afternoon at Fort Benton with the American cavalry for the benefit of his father. He described the arrest of the whiskey traders and their arrival in Fort Macleod. He gave them his first impressions of the officers of the North West Mounted Police and told his father how impressed he was with them. He described the Blackfoot encampment and Three Bulls' family who had taken him into their tepee.

It was late into the night when James finished writing. Then he had another idea. He would send this letter to Fiona first so she could read it to her family before sending it on to his parents. He added a postscript to his note to Fiona and asked her to give the news in the letter to Merrie and pass on to her the enclosed sketch. He tore the drawing of Crowfoot's camp from his notebook and wrote on the back:

"Merrie – this is a place you would love to photograph. James"

Although he was weary and sunburned from the long hours in the saddle he couldn't sleep. There was a question looming in the back of his mind.

"Where were Sitting Bull and his Sioux warriors?" He didn't much like the idea of meeting up with them on his way to Fort Walsh.

48

What a difference it made to James riding northeast to have the setting sun over his left shoulder and the wind behind him. There wasn't much difference in the landscape, the prairie grass lengthened a bit as he moved east, he lost sight of the mountains, but other than that it was a continuation of the Great Plains. The trail to Fort Walsh was not as well marked as the Whoop-Up Trail but he was able to cross the Milk River and Lodge Creek without difficulty.

It was a ride not without its anxious moments. James had seen a cloud of dust rising from behind a ridge to the east. He was ready to spur Mac into high speed if it turned out to be a war party of Sioux. As he topped a rise he could see a few miles further down the trail that the dust was raised by a huge herd of buffalo. They were moving south and were spread across the prairie as far as he could see. The rearguard of the herd was directly in his path. Mac skirted around the grazing beasts who took little notice of his presence. It was only when two bulls close behind them went at each other that Mac jumped. The crash of their massive heads coming together frightened the horse, making him shy, almost throwing James to the ground.

At Lodge Creek James came upon two caravans of Metis. Their carts were not loaded with hides but had hoops stretched over them like covered wagons. Perhaps the women and children slept in them when the weather was bad. Their camp was on the flats beside the creek. It was a beautiful spot. The water wound its way between the high coulee hills on either side. Large stands of cottonwoods and aspens surrounded the flats between the curves in the riverbed. There was plenty of high grass for the horses.

James waved to them and they waved back. He rode over and exchanged greetings. He tried his St. Andrew's schoolboy French but they laughed at it and turned to English. They had come from the Cypress Hills near Fort Walsh and were spending the summer hunting for buffalo robes, wolf hides, or whatever they could find. They were excited by James's news that he had come through a very large herd of buffalo. Two of the men were mending one of the large wooden wheels, which lay in pieces on the ground. It looked like a large puzzle. They were assembling the pieces in the shape of the wheel and binding them together with shrunken rawhide. The women were busy over a fire, the children running about exuberantly. Some of the more curious ones ran up to him for a closer look. James expected that the men were surprised that he didn't inspect their carts for illegal whiskey. He wasn't sure what he would have done if he had found some. One of the women offered James something she was cooking. He accepted it, sat with them for a time chatting about the weather, the buffalo and the trail to Fort Walsh. The Metis knew nothing of Sitting Bull or the Sioux and seemed to have no fear that they might meet up with them. James was grateful for the company, especially for such a warm and hospitable meal, but being late afternoon he wanted to cover more ground before nightfall.

Although the Cypress Hills were only a series of larger-than-average bumps on the prairie, James caught sight of the bright green knolls from a long distance away. He was surprised to see as he rode closer that they were covered with clumps of trees. When he reached them the hills were much higher than he had at first thought. He was struck with the variety of vegetation. It was an oasis in the midst of the plains. There were spruce and tamarack, pine and aspen, creeping cedar, wolf willow and mountain orchids. As the light from the setting sun streaked through the tops of the trees he rode along the base of the hills, among the trees and through the underbrush. There were bushes full of berries everywhere. No wonder this was a meeting ground for Indians and Metis and a favourite place to harvest the ingredients for pemmican. There were chokecherries, pin cherries, saskatoons, bush cranberries, raspberries, gooseberries, buffalo berries and red and black currants. He noticed signs of antelope and elk. He knew he was close to the fort, but as the sun fell below the horizon he decided to stop for the night and find it in the morning. He stopped in a small clearing in the trees with grass for Mac and as he was satisfied from the meal with the Metis, rolled up in his blankets for the night and was soon asleep.

An eerie howling that sent shivers up his spine awakened him. One series of howls came from high up on the hill beside him. Others answered it much closer. Mac was restless and James got up to calm him. He wrapped an arm around the horse's neck and stroked his nose. As the howling continued he could feel the flashes of nervousness surge through Mac. James went for his rifle and kept it close at hand. Still the howling went on. Finally it faded and died. James stayed beside Mac until he felt the horse relax. Only then did he return to his blankets. Whether it was wolves or coyotes, or both, James wasn't sure. He did know it was a sound he would never forget.

49

James arrived at the year-old Fort Walsh just in time for morning inspection. As he rode through the gate of the log stockade he surveyed the inward facing log structures – quarters, stables, kitchen, bakery, magazine, blacksmith and carpenter shops, guardroom and quartermaster's store all whitewashed, clean and shining. It was about the same size as Fort Macleod but certainly different in appearance and attitude. In the square the men were in full dress uniform, mounted in three lines facing an immaculately dressed commanding officer on a black horse, its saddle and bridle polished so that they gleamed in the sun. The Commanding Officer had the stern face and posture of a typical British officer, a heavy black mustache and he shouted orders as if on a London parade square. The men were in brushed scarlet jackets, white helmets, buckskin breeches and shining boots. Their horses were equally well turned out. Not one man looked in his direction as he stood in the open gate.

The Union Jack flapped from the top of a tall pole located just inside the gate as James sat silently on Mac and watched the performance. The Commanding Officer, who James assumed was Walsh, rode down the front of the files as he inspected each man and horse. When he was finished he rode to his original position and issued orders for the day. Only when they were dismissed did the men break ranks and go about their daily tasks. One of the men took the reins of Walsh's horse while Walsh strode towards his quarters. James rode slowly towards him and only then did Walsh turn to acknowledge his presence. James dismounted, introduced himself and said he had been sent by the Commissioner to report to Inspector Walsh.

"Major Walsh," the commanding officer corrected him. James caught a twinge of discontent in the inspector's reaction to the word "Commissioner". Walsh ordered him to look to his horse then bring the report to him.

"And get some of that filth off your uniform before you come to my quarters," he said brusquely.

Walsh was certainly a different type from Macleod. He was cold and distant. James sensed an arrogant superficiality. Walsh was playing the part of a frontier commander and enjoying it. He wondered whether his men were.

Inspector Walsh was sitting behind his desk when, in response to James' knock, he ordered him to come in. Walsh did not rise from his seat. He pushed himself back from his desk, put one highly polished boot against the edge of the desk and rocked back on the legs of the chair. He looked James up and down with a critical eye.

"You are not up to the standards of Fort Walsh, Constable," were his first words. "I'll give you a day to get there. Now, the report you have to give me."

Inspector Walsh straightened up his chair and leaned forward as James described the meeting with Crowfoot. James described Sitting Bull's overture to Crowfoot to join an uprising against the white man. Walsh was noticeably relieved when he heard that Crowfoot had refused it. The inspector knew he was directly in the path of the fleeing Sioux and the last thing he needed were hostile Blackfoot at his back.

Surprisingly, James found Walsh deeply sympathetic towards the Indians. As the inspector questioned him about the meeting with Crowfoot he saw that Walsh recognized that their way of life was rapidly disappearing and sensed in him a deep sadness at their plight. The inspector reminded James of a British officer more than anyone else he had met in the North West. How Walsh kept his uniform so neat in these rustic quarters James couldn't understand. The inspector was groomed, his mustache clipped, his uniform crisp as if he were about to parade before the Queen. The fort was the most orderly and well-kept James had seen on the prairies.

When James handed the inspector the letter he carried from the Commissioner, Walsh wanted to hear from James what his assignment was in the North West. James suspected that he already knew, but wanted to discuss the subject. Walsh said he would be happy to see that James participated first hand in all their actions and offered to review his reports to Mr. McLennan if that would help assure their accuracy. James bristled at the suggestion but replied that he didn't want to infringe on the inspector's valuable time. Walsh said that it would be no trouble and that he would be glad to help. James silently determined that it would never be necessary.

After he had found his quarters and settled in, he asked one of the men who had been at the fort for sometime how he would compare the commissioner and the inspector.

"Macleod is a colonel and wants to be called Major," he answered. "Walsh is a captain and wants to be called Major. Does that answer your question?"

Walsh took great care to be sure that James fully understood the very important role that Fort Walsh was playing in the North West. He sent James on patrols along the border. He sent him with Star Child, the fort's guide and interpreter, into Indian camps in the vicinity to find out if anyone knew the whereabouts of the Sioux. There were occasions when James felt that Walsh was taking more personal credit than he deserved for the Mounties' peaceful relationship with the Indians and assigned to himself a role that was far more important in his own mind than in reality.

There was no question that Walsh was a courageous and determined officer. James saw first-hand how courageous he was when one day a lone Indian rider raced through the fort's gate. James watched as the rider jumped from his horse and burst through the door of Walsh's quarters. In seconds, Walsh called for Star Child and within minutes had summoned every man in the fort.

The inspector briefed the assembled force. The Cypress Hills were a popular camping ground for many tribes. There was the shelter of the hills, plenty of game, forests of lodge-pole pine trees that provided the framework for tepees, fields of grass for the horses and plenty of fresh, clear water. It was not uncommon for one tribe to camp beside another.

The rider, Walsh told them, had come with the news that a large encampment of Assiniboine, about two hundred and fifty lodges, was harassing a small camp of fifteen lodges of Salteaux beside them. The Salteaux had wanted to move on but a group of young Assiniboines had blocked their way. Tempers had flared and the young warriors had hurled insults and threats. When the Salteaux said they would call in the police to protect them the warriors had insulted the police. The Salteaux rider feared violence.

Walsh had a dozen men saddle up immediately, Star Child and James among them. The Assiniboine and Salteaux camps were a ten-hour ride east and Walsh wanted to be there by nightfall. They rode hard the entire day, stopping only once to water the horses at a small creek. James' admiration for the men of the Force and for their horses grew as he rode with them. There was not a complaint from rider or horse. James was glad that Mac was fully fit again. His horse responded to the pace and grew stronger as the day went on. It was well after dark when they stopped for the night. They tended to their horses then sat around in a group eating their pemmican.

Walsh stood up among them and addressed the group. "This is what we're out here for," he said, in his most authoritative voice, "to enforce the law. Nobody, not white, not red, not anyone, breaks the law and gets away with it. I don't care whether there are two of them, two hundred of them or two thousand of them."

James was wakened in the middle of a sound sleep by the gentle prodding of a riding boot. The moon was high above him. The stars were shining from every corner of the sky. The wind was strong, as usual. It whistled through the grass. The men were saddling up. James roused himself, folded his blankets and did the same. Before they mounted up Walsh called them together.

"We'll be at the Salteaux camp in an hour," he told them. "If the Assiniboine are still there we'll surprise them before sun up."

They rode hard for an hour before slowing to a walk. James was horrified when they rode cautiously over a rise and saw a number of burning lodges a short distance ahead of them. Walsh lead them at a gallop to the camp. There were Salteaux men, women and children milling about the burning tepees. Star Child spoke with them.

"Assiniboine, maybe as many as two hundred," Star Child said to Walsh. "They came in the night and set some lodges on fire. They have killed many horses and dogs. The Assiniboines fired many shots, but no one was killed. The Assiniboine camp has moved a few miles north."

Walsh brought his force together again. "We're going to arrest the Assiniboine war leaders now," he told them. "We could well be in a very dangerous position. Obey my orders no matter how severe they might appear. Be sure your weapons are ready."

Walsh had his men load and check their weapons. He and Star Child led them north, keeping to the low-lying areas between the softly rolling hills. Eventually they slowed to a walk. Walsh raised his right arm bringing the force to a halt. The men edged up beside him and looked over the rise. A large Assiniboine encampment was ahead. There was a soft glow of light in the east but the first rays of the morning sun had not yet broken over the horizon.

The encampment was laid out in war-camp formation with the war lodge in the center. In that lodge, Walsh knew, he would find the ringleaders of the raid on the Salteaux. Walsh signaled the men to follow. He moved slowly towards the camp. The men took their rifles out of their scabbards and laid them across their saddles. They loosened the flaps of their holsters covering their revolvers.

James took out his rifle but he didn't bother to loosen the flap on his holster. He had never used his revolver and he knew now was not a good time to start.

The men fanned out as they reached the edge of the encampment and advanced among the tepees towards the war lodge. The camp was silent. Not even the dogs were awake to announce their coming. Walsh pulled up in front of the entrance to the war-lodge. He signaled the men to surround it. Then he motioned Star Child to open the flap of the tent. Walsh dismounted with his rifle held across his chest. Star Child flung the hide covering the door aside. Walsh stepped into the entrance. In a strong voice Walsh told the men inside that they were under arrest. He had Star Child translate his words.

Walsh stepped aside as the sleepy inhabitants stumbled out. They stared in amazement at the number of Redcoats surrounding the lodge. Walsh had them stand in a line in front of the war-lodge while Star Child went inside to check that everyone was out. James counted nineteen Indians standing in front of Walsh, all of them young. Walsh motioned his force to close in around the Assiniboine warriors. He mounted his horse and led the way out of the encampment, the warriors walking surrounded by the mounted Redcoats.

The first rays of the sun were beginning to streak across the sky. Women were out of their tepees and talking in animated fashion, pointing to the group as they passed. The heads of men began popping out of their lodge entrances. They looked in astonishment at the Redcoats escorting some of their young men away from the camp. Walsh led the group to the outskirts of the encampment and into the plains. He found a small, flat-topped rise and stopped. He asked Star Child to tell the prisoners to sit. Walsh positioned his force around them facing the camp and ordered Star Child to go back into the camp and bring back some of the chiefs and enough horses for the prisoners. James could see that the young Assiniboines were bewildered.

"Whatever fight they had in them last night certainly isn't visible now," James thought. They looked contrite and frightened. James could see that they had not expected the Redcoats, certainly not before sunrise nor in the numbers that surrounded them now.

Star Chief returned with three chiefs and a number of horses.

"These young men have broken the laws of the White Mother," Walsh said to them sternly. "They are my prisoners. We will take them to the fort and try them for what they have done to the Salteaux village."

"We tried to stop them," said one of the chiefs. "But we could not."

50

The Redcoats set out immediately for Fort Walsh with their prisoners. It was a long ride back and Walsh wanted to be there before nightfall. As the sun rose high above them a strange colour appeared in the western sky. Streaks of yellow light filtered through dark grey clouds rolling towards them from the mountains but disappeared as the sky darkened. The grey clouds on the horizon grew thicker and swirled in the high altitude currents. Walsh, Star Child and the others watched it closely. Suddenly Walsh signalled the column to veer sharply to the left, away from the oncoming cloud, and spurred their horses to full speed. Before long they came to a deep gully carved into the flat surface of the plain. Walsh led them into the gully and they dismounted. James watched as the others took off their shirts.

"What's going on?" he asked the Mountie next to him.

"Dust storm coming," he shouted. "Throw your blanket over your horse's head, tie your shirt over yours, hang on to your horse's neck for dear life and face away from the wind."

As he spoke the wind began to shriek over their heads across the top of the gully, whipping down and swirling around them. It grew darker and darker. The horses were restless and the men did their best to calm them. Then the dust storm hit. It was as black as night and James tightened his hold on Mac's neck mostly for his own stability. The dust screamed over their heads and tore at them. James began to choke as the dust filled his eyes, ears and nose. He held the shirt more tightly around his head, trying to keep the dust away. He buried his face into the horse's neck and hung on. He lost all sense of space and all he could do was gasp for breath. Mac snorted, stamped and shook his head. The storm went on and on until James was sure he would suffocate.

Almost as suddenly as it started the wind calmed and the sky brightened. There were still swirls of dust in the gully, but the men took the coverings off their horses' heads and away from their own. James almost broke out laughing as he looked at the men around him and at himself. They were coated with a dirty brown dust from head to foot. It stuck to their faces, their hair and their uniforms. No one could tell police from prisoner except for their weapons. The men struggled out of the gully leading their horses up the steep incline. They stood on the flat of the plain, brushing the dust from their clothes, then from their saddles and the horses' coats. The sky had cleared in the west but the dark, menacing cloud could be seen racing away from them to the east.

They mounted up and rode slowly for some distance. The police fell in again around their prisoners. The horses snorted to clear their nostrils and the men tried to get the dust from their eyes and ears. Walsh stepped up the pace. When they came to a small stream they stopped, gave the horses as much time as they wanted to drink and rub their noses in the cool water. Walsh gathered the pemmican from his men and distributed it among the policemen and Indians. It wasn't much but everyone had some.

It was well after sundown when they reached the fort. The prisoners were locked in the guardroom and the men dismissed to their quarters. James was exhausted from two days of hard riding with little sleep. The dust under his clothes irritated his skin in every part of his body. He longed for a wash in the river but the exertion to do it seemed too much. He went to his quarters, collapsed on his grass filled tick and was asleep in seconds.

51

Inspector Walsh assigned James regular duty on the border patrol. He was expecting the Sioux to cross over the Medicine Line at any time and he had patrols out constantly to catch the first sight of them. He was convinced they would cross into Canada somewhere between Fort Walsh, at the base of the Cypress Hills and Wood Mountain, a three day ride along the border to the east. There were several one-man patrols operating constantly, setting out from the fort in various directions. James was on a patrol that travelled three days east to Wood Mountain then back to the fort. He continued this through late summer, fall, and was still at it as winter arrived. It was early December and still there was no sign of the Sioux.

James was in the fifth day of his regular patrol, one day away from the warmth and shelter of Fort Walsh. The temperature was far below freezing and although he had his buffalo robe coat pulled high over his neck so that it touched his fur hat the cold still reached through to his bones. The prairie cold was like nothing he had ever experienced before. In spite of fur coat, fur hat, thick blankets, fur mitts, several pairs of socks and moccasins he couldn't seem to get warm or stop shivering.

The men had warned him about winter, but he hadn't taken them too seriously until the first snowstorm hit which was now weeks ago. He still was not accustomed to the stinging, blowing snow on his face and the chill that seemed to never leave him. Riding west back to the fort and into the wind was almost unbearable. He had the blankets wrapped around his head and neck so that only his eyes were exposed. He marveled that Mac did much better than he did. The horse walked on, through snow and cold and seemed little the worse for it.

The plains in winter were even more solitary than they were in summer. The sky was often cloudless, the plains bathed in brilliant sunshine – so brilliant off the snow that it was blinding. Often James had to hide his eyes under his blanket to help them recover from the brightness. On other days dark clouds ran low over the prairies shutting out the sky. The wind blew the snow so that visibility was limited and his mind was fixed on the simple task of keeping warm and moving in the right direction. There had been several snowstorms. The drifts were deep in the lee of the slopes and in the gullies. But the wind continuously swept the open plains so that the grass still poked up in places through the thin layer of snow that turned the vast plains white.

James had seen nothing move during the patrols of the last few weeks. He had almost given up on the Sioux arriving during the winter. He didn't expect he would have anything to report to Mr. McLennan until spring. He had no idea what was happening with the American cavalry or the Sioux on the other side of the border. His mind wondered. He recalled the one letter he had received from Mr. McLennan. He could visualize Miss Rossiter typing it on her new Remington. Every word stuck in his mind.

August 27, 1876
Constable James Keyden
   I am in receipt of your letter dated July 2, 1876 from Fort Benton, which I received on August 10, 1876. We were pleasantly impressed

with the detail of your information and that you were able to supply it so quickly upon your arrival in the North West. It confirmed our confidence in you and in your mission. We look forward to future reports.
Angus McLennan

James wouldn't have described the last months as boring. There was always some new prairie experience and there was always the challenge of surviving. He would not say he was homesick but there were times that he yearned almost beyond endurance to walk through the streets of a city, walk into a pub or book store, see new faces and talk to different people. He shook the boredom of yet another day on patrol by recalling an incident that had interrupted his routine.

For months the entire force had been on the lookout for a fugitive who had escaped from Fort Macleod. He was a Blood, who went by the name of Pox – Woman's Breast who had been charged with killing his wife. The Blackfoot had always been cooperative with the police and had reported his presence in their camps several times, but when the officers arrived to capture him he had moved on. Pox had been seen several times near a camp whose chief was Little Black Bear. The chief sent a message to Fort Walsh saying that the next time Pox showed up he would have a feast and dance lasting several days as a means to entice Pox to remain in his camp.

A few weeks later Little Black Bear sent a message saying that Pox was back in his camp and that the feast would proceed. James was with the party that raced out from the fort to arrest him. They rode through one whole night and the following day and arrived at the height of the dancing. They captured Pox but were so enthralled with the festivities that they stayed to participate before escorting him back to the fort. James recalled the whirling, stamping and chanting of the warriors in their colourful garb, the women and children standing in circles beating on skin drums and chanting. There were warriors with magnificent eagle feather headdresses, shaking rattles, yelling and weaving intricate designs with their feet. He remembered it as one of the most entertaining evenings he had had since his arrival in the North West.

James was lost in the memory as he pulled the blanket more tightly around him. His thoughts were drawn back to that enjoyable party at Louise Graham's in Toronto, the warmth of the fire, the music, the dancing, the people. He thought of Merrie and Fiona and her family and realized that he missed them all. Strong gusts of wind whipped the snow into his face, blotting out the landscape around him. Through the blowing snow, something caught his attention to his left. It was a long way off, but he was sure there was something moving. James urged Mac up a slope for a better look. Far to the south, dark dots stood out through the blowing snow. There were hundreds of them. At first James thought they were buffalo grazing, but the dots were moving in a thin column in the opposite direction he was and angling north towards the line he had just travelled. He knew that at the angle they were moving they were just about to cross the Medicine Line into Canadian territory.

James turned Mac towards the column and moved cautiously forward. He found a spot in a dip between two slopes where he could watch the travelers through the blowing snow without being seen. He was near enough to count hundreds of people, most of them walking, dragging or carrying what possessions they had with them. He knew that no one moved in this kind of weather unless they were in grave danger. It might be that this group was being pursued. A few of the men were mounted but they looked as weary as those who walked. Women were leading other horses pulling travois, two sticks fastened to the horse's back and dragging them behind. On them were strapped the hides for their lodges along with their other effects. On some travois were people, covered in robes. Dogs pulled similar but smaller travois. Children rode on top of the loads or walked beside the women holding their hands and staggering forward. Men, horses, women and children were wrapped in an assortment of blankets and hides, all bent forward with the wind. They appeared to have been travelling for some time and were near the end of their strength. James knew right away that they were the long awaited Sioux.

In the excitement of his discovery, James forgot the cold. He turned away from the column to pick up his trail flanking the Medicine Line and encouraged Mac to move faster towards the fort. He kept to the low-lying areas between the slopes so that he was out of sight of the Sioux. When he was well away from them he turned west again and made for the fort. He had the news that Walsh was waiting for.

52

James had ridden as hard as the head-wind and blowing snow allowed. After a day and a half he had burst into Walsh's quarters with the news, frost covering the fur cap and blanket around his nose and mouth. Inspector Walsh listened without exclamation. He had expected for weeks that the Sioux would seek refuge across the border and now he was proved right. Walsh ordered him to take care of his horse then come back and describe to him every detail of what he had seen. When James returned Walsh wanted to know the line of travel, the number of mounted warriors, the number of travois, anything that would give him an idea of how many Sioux there were in the column.

"Get yourself something hot to eat," Walsh told him when he had finished his report, tilting his chair back to his customary position. "As soon as you and your horse are rested I want you to take me to the spot where you saw them."

Next morning Walsh rode out with Star Child and ten men. James rode at the front of the column with the inspector and the guide. It was almost two days of hard riding through blowing and drifting snow, but they had the wind at their backs and that made all the difference. When they arrived at the spot where James had first seen the column it was not difficult to pick up the trail of the Sioux. Though the wind was still strong and the tracks of the horses and travois were in some places covered by blowing snow, there was still enough of a trail to allow Star Child to follow it. With the wind constantly blowing from the northwest, it was natural that the Sioux would seek shelter on the east side of Wood Mountain. They needed as much protection from the wind and driving snow as they could get. Both Walsh and Star Child knew the best camp sites on that side of Wood Mountain. The Sioux must have known them as well for their tracks were heading straight for them.

After three more days of hard riding the Mounties sighted the first Sioux lodges exactly where they expected them. Walsh led them slowly into the encampment and when the first Sioux saw them they screamed in panic and ran for their weapons. James had never seen that reaction from Indians before when he had approached a camp. The flaps over the entrances of the lodges burst open and Sioux warriors rushed out with rifles at the ready.

"It's our coats," yelled Walsh, "They think we're Long Knives." The Mounties were wearing heavy dark buffalo coats with dark fur hats.

"Take off your coats fast," Walsh ordered.

Although the temperature was well below freezing and the wind was still whistling around them, the men did so at once. Their scarlet jackets stood out against the whiteness of the snow. The Sioux lowered their rifles and the women stopped their screaming. These were not blue-coated Long Knives that they so feared.

Walsh had Star Child ask who the chief was and where he might be found. The answer came back that Sitting Bull was not among them. Black Moon was the head chief and there were at least five bands of Sioux encamped together with as many as eight hundred lodges.

"That's over three thousand people," said Walsh in reply to Star Child's information. "Let's find Black Moon."

The force rode slowly through the encampment. Five tribes, all branches of the Sioux Nation, had set up camp one next to the other. The earlier cries of the women had brought men, women and children out of their lodges. They stood quietly watching the scarlet-jacketed force go by. Some of the warriors wore swords exactly like the one that Major Rawlins had carried. On the back of one horse James saw a battle flag with stars and stripes used as a saddle blanket. The warriors were tall, muscular men. They had strong faces and suspicious eyes. They looked battle hardened and very weary. Their clothes were an assortment of U. S. army issue and buckskin, badly worn, full of holes and hardly warm enough for the season. The women and children were equally badly clothed. The lodges too were battered and worn, many with crude patches hastily sewn.

Star Child led them to the lodge of Black Moon and Walsh dismounted. The chief came out of his lodge with several of his men to greet him and waved for the policemen to put their coats back on.

"Don't button them up," ordered Walsh. "Be sure the scarlet shows."

The chief invited Walsh into his lodge. Walsh had four men guard the horses and four more stand outside the lodge. James went inside with the inspector, Star Child and one other constable and at Black Moon's invitation, sat around a small but warm fire. Black Moon summoned his other chiefs and the four Redcoats waited until they arrived. The Sioux tepee was not much different from a Blackfoot lodge, except that there were no ornaments or trophies anywhere to be seen. James did notice an American cavalry holster and pistol hanging from a lodge pole and an American cavalry officer's jacket beside it. Bullet holes in the sleeve of the jacket were clearly noticeable.

When the other chiefs arrived they sat in a circle on the buffalo robes that had been laid out on the floor. Black Moon reached for his pipe, lit it from the fire burning in the center of the circle and puffed slowly. Walsh had dealt with Indians enough to understand and honour their ceremonies. He knew that smoking the pipe together was a good way to start. He had learned to be as patient as needed and he waited until the chief was ready to speak.

The pipe made the full circle. James had learned from his last experience with a peace pipe and drew gently on it. When the pipe was returned to Black Moon, he set it down beside him and rose from his place. Star Child sat beside the inspector to translate and James sat close by.

"We have been driven from our homes by the Americans and we have come here to find peace," Black Moon began. "Our grandfathers told us that we would find peace in the land of the British." Black Moon held out his open hand. In it was a round, dark coloured medal.

"We were once the people of the British," Black Moon continued, handing the medal to the inspector. "Our grandfathers fought side by side with you. You gave us this to show that we were friends."

Walsh studied the medal and handed it to James. James turned it over in his hands. It was a large, round brass medal, badly tarnished. On one side was a distinguished looking profile and the name, 'George III Rex'. On the other side was an inscription that read, 'God Save The King'. James handed the medal back to the inspector.

"We have not slept soundly for years," Black Moon continued. "We want to find a place where we can lie down and feel safe."

Black Moon went on to describe their war with the American army that had gone on, he said, for years. That war had intensified over the last months and they were tired of running. He did not mention the battle on the Little Bighorn River. The Sioux, Black Moon told them, had come because they knew that they would find peace on this side of the Medicine Line. When Black Moon finished, Walsh rose. He took off his buffalo coat and hat and stood erect in his impressive scarlet jacket. Walsh had the instincts of an actor and James smiled to himself as he watched his performance. The inspector paid his respects to

Black Moon and the other chiefs and thanked them for their welcome to him and his men. He handed back the medal.

"You are welcome in this country," Walsh told the Sioux chiefs, "as long as you obey the laws of the White Mother. You cannot use our country as a base to attack the Americans and then expect to come back to escape them. There is to be no fighting, against Americans or against any other tribes in this land."

Black Moon and the other chiefs understood the words that Star Child translated. They looked at each other, then back to the inspector and nodded in agreement.

"You will be allowed to keep the weapons you need to hunt," Walsh continued, "but any weapons you have to trade you must leave with us. You are to bring them to our fort, which is only a few days from here. We will issue ammunition to you so that you have enough for the hunt."

The chiefs listened to these words and talked among themselves.

"The White Mother's laws are for everyone in this country," Walsh concluded, "white men, Indians, everyone. We expect you to obey them and we expect you to help us enforce them."

Walsh sat down, wrapped his coat around his shoulders while the chiefs talked among themselves. When they were finished, Black Moon rose again.

"We want you to keep the Long Knives from this land so that we may live in peace and sleep in safety," he said to Walsh. "We will obey your laws. We will deliver our trade weapons to your fort and we will help you keep peace."

The pipe was lit once more and passed around the circle. James found it hard to believe that these were the savage 'Tigers of the Plains' that he had heard wild stories about. He found Black Moon thoughtful and articulate. James believed the chief when he said the Sioux wanted to live in peace and safety. If it weren't for the American cavalry weapons and army uniform he had seen about the camp he might have thought that the stories of their battles with the Americans were exaggerated.

When the pipe ceremony was concluded the Redcoats rose, left the lodge and mounted up. Walsh waved to Black Moon who stood with his chiefs outside his lodge and the Mounties rode slowly through the Sioux encampment. Hundreds of men, women and children watched in silence as they made their way among the lodges. James studied their faces and saw desperate weariness, fear and curiosity. He found it hard to imagine how they had survived hundreds of miles of travel through the depths of winter and how they would take care of themselves until spring.

It was a long, bitter ride into the blowing snow back to the fort. Not long after they returned Walsh brought the entire force together and realigned the patrol routes to keep a constant watch on the Sioux. As the men were returning to their quarters Walsh called James back.

"I want you to take word to Fort Macleod of the arrival of the Sioux and our meeting with Black Moon," he told James. "Be ready to leave in the morning."

53

James left Fort Walsh before the first, low rays of the winter sun appeared in the southeast. It was approaching the shortest day of the year and he wanted to take advantage of every minute of daylight. The brightest stars disappeared one by one as the sun peaked over the horizon. But for a few wisps of clouds on the horizon below the rising sun there was a cloudless sky. It was fiercely cold with a strong breeze. His route took James straight west through the open plains until he hit the Old Man's River. He would stop there for the night.

The snow on the plains was being blown straight at them but as long as they kept to the wind-blown crests, Mac was able to avoid the deep drifts. They had not reached the river by nightfall but there was enough starlight and reflection from the moon to guide them on their way. It took a few hours of travel in the dark but they finally reached the coulee and found shelter in the trees along the riverbank. James made a fire that warmed them and used branches to sweep away the snow from some grass for Mac. Then he settled deep into a snow bank, a buffalo robe wrapped around him. He slept fitfully and at each waking, added wood to the fire. He was more comfortable sitting close to the fire than resting against the snow bank. He thought of the Sioux, pictured them bent against the snow and cold and wondered where Major Rawlins and the American cavalry were at that moment.

James woke from a restless sleep before the sun was up and decided to set out. There was enough light to see his way across the frozen river and up to the rim of the coulee. He reached the plains and followed the course of the river towards the fort. It was still well below freezing and the wind from the west was gusting, biting his face as he buried it as deeply as he could in the blanket around his neck. As the sun came up James noticed with some alarm a bright dome of light arching above the western horizon. As the sun rose higher the arch became less distinct, but the wind rose noticeably, blowing more fiercely into their faces.

As the morning wore on his alarm subsided. Clouds had not gathered in the sky and there was no snow. In fact, the sky had cleared and the wind grew even stronger – and warmer. As the sun reached its height it beat down through the cloudless sky with warmth that forced James to open his coat and jacket and take off his mitts. The snow on the plains began to melt all around them and there were small rivulets of water streaming down the inclines. James could hardly believe the sudden change in temperature. He hadn't been this warm out of doors since late summer. They traveled in comparative comfort, enjoying the welcome relief from the cold and letting the brisk wind warm their bodies. There were places on the open prairie almost bare of snow and Mac broke into a run, his hooves splashing in the damp ground with each step.

As the sun set, the wind turned frigid with the same suddenness as it had warmed. The temperature dropped to where it had been in the early morning. James found himself once again tightening his blanket around his neck and shoulders and pulling his hat lower over his ears. The ground had frozen again and where the snow had begun to melt there were now sheets of ice. Mac found the footing difficult and James rode slowly and with more care. They continued their journey into the night and finally walked through the gate of Fort Macleod with the moon over their heads.

"It was a chinook," said one of the constables, when James described his day. "It's a warm wind that comes through the mountains. It's named after one of the tribes on the Pacific coast. The temperature can vary sixty degrees or more in a matter of hours."

"That was it," replied James. "That's exactly what happened."

"Be glad it was a chinook." the constable went on. "It's a lot more enjoyable than a blizzard."

54

Commissioner Macleod was somewhere in Eastern Canada and Assistant Commissioner Irvine had been left in charge. Early the following morning, James handed Irvine the report that Walsh had written of the meeting with Black Moon and the Sioux. Later in the day Inspector Irvine called James into his quarters and kept him for some time, probing for every detail.

"You know we've been expecting this for some time," Irvine said to James. "From what the report says Walsh has carried out his orders well but there is much that we must do. I would like you to make a copy of Walsh's report and post it in Fort Benton, along with a report that I am writing to Mr. Scott in Ottawa."

James smiled. "Just another routine ride in mid-winter across the snow-covered prairie," he thought to himself. "He makes it sound like there's nothing to it."

The Assistant Commissioner and James continued to talk about the developing situation. Irvine was most concerned about the influence the arrival of the Sioux would have on Crowfoot and his people. He knew the Blackfoot would feel pressed from the south by having their traditional enemies so close at hand. With the declining number of buffalo, he knew competition would be fierce among the tribes for those that remained. Irvine told James of his confidence in Crowfoot's loyalty and peaceful intentions and how he wanted to give support to the Blackfoot in every way he could. James spent the evening copying out Walsh's long report.

"Walsh must have been up the whole night before I left," thought James. His report was very thorough and very detailed. He was interested in how many references there were to the inspector's own role in events. It left the reader with the impression that Walsh had acted on his own when James knew that the orders for the patrols and the disposition of the men had originated with Macleod.

James also wrote a report to Mr. McLennan. It contained a good deal of information taken straight from Inspector Walsh's report. James added the details of the cavalry sabers and the American army uniforms he had seen among the Sioux. He summarized the speeches of the chiefs and their call for peace and safety for their people. He ended with his observation that the desires of the chiefs were real and that if the Sioux were not provoked they would remain peacefully where they were.

Irvine called James to his quarters again early the next morning.

"Here's a telegram I would like you to send to Scott ahead of the full report," said Irvine. "Send it the moment you arrive. These developments are too important for him to wait for the arrival of the post." The major handed the message to James.

"Read it, James," said Irvine, "you may want to include some of this in your report to Mr. McLennan."

James read the message.

> R. W. Scott
> Secretary of State
> Government of Canada
> Ottawa
>
> Sir: – I have the honour to report that a large band of Sioux Indians have crossed the boundary line and are camped at Wood Mountain. I have instructed Inspector Walsh to send a small detachment to Wood Mountain and another to the eastern end of the Cypress Hills. These detachments thus stationed will keep him continually informed of the movements of the Sioux and prevent the trading of ammunition and firearms except by permit.
>
> I beg leave to press upon the consideration of the government that no time should be lost in dealing with the Sioux as if they are allowed time to recuperate I fear they may cause some trouble and will not be so easily dealt with as they would be in their present enfeebled condition.
> I have the honour to be, Sir
> Your obedient servant,
> Lieut. Col. A. G. Irvine
> Assistant Commissioner, NWMP

"What did Irvine mean 'in dealing with'?" wondered James. "Was he proposing that the Canadian government evict the Sioux and send them back across the border?" He asked the Assistant Commissioner directly.

"No," replied Irvine, "but we should encourage the Americans to meet with the Sioux and negotiate their return. And when you're finished in Fort Benton I suggest you go back to Fort Walsh," Irvine said. "You'll be much closer to the center of things."

James took his leave and opened the door to go out.

"By the way, Merry Christmas, James," said Irvine with a smile as he shook his hand firmly. "I'm sorry you won't be able to spend it with us here but I'm sure you'll have a fine celebration at Fort Walsh. Have a safe journey."

55

It took James three days to reach Fort Benton. The snow was deep and had drifted heavily in places. Although it was bitterly cold, the wind was mostly behind them and the sun, when it was up, gave them a touch of warmth. The rivers were frozen except where the water ran particularly fast. James could hear it rushing under the ice and avoided the open spots and the areas around them where the ice was thin. They crossed the Belly, St. Mary's and Milk Rivers with no difficulty and arrived in Fort Benton late the third night. Baker's and its telegraph office were closed so James checked into the Nugget and put Mac in the stable. There was no heat in his room so he went across the street to the Golddust Tavern for some warmth and something to eat. It was empty but for the bartender.

"Heidi's not here?" James asked the bartender, looking around and not seeing her.

"Left for Helena weeks ago," he replied. "Town's emptying fast. Baker and Power are the only two doing any real business – most of it to your outfit."

James shivered through the night. It seemed colder in that hotel room than it was sleeping in the woods in front of a fire. When he awoke the water in the basin on his dresser was frozen solid. He went to the stable, gave Mac a good brushing and currying, saw to his feed and went down the street to Bakers. He was surprised when the man behind the counter brought out a letter from Mr. McLennan addressed to him. He saved it until he had sent the telegraph message and posted the letters. Then he went to a corner of the store beside a window and opened it.

Constable James Keyden
North West Mounted Police
Fort Macleod, N. W. T.
c/o I. G. Baker & Co.
Fort Benton, Montana Territory

James couldn't help but think of Miss Rossiter in her severe black dress leaning over her new Remington typewriter. He pictured the high vaulted ceiling of the bank building, the dark woodwork, the chandeliers and Mr. McLennan's deep, black chairs. He could visualize the employees in this warm and comfortable setting.

> *Sir: – I am in receipt of your report on the meeting with Chief Crowfoot and am heartened by your news of his loyalty and cooperation with authorities. We are greatly concerned that American military forces are moving against the Sioux in strength and that the Sioux might flee into Canada. We see this as a threat to the peaceful conditions necessary to construct the railway across the plains and would appreciate any further information you can send us concerning this development.*
> Angus McLennan
>
> *PS My daughter has asked me to thank you for the sketch of Crowfoot's campsite. It cheered her up at a time when she was quite ill. She contracted a severe fever and although on the mend, she is not over it yet.*

"…not over it yet," thought James, as he looked out on the blowing snow beating against the window, "I wish he had said more." His mind fixed on Merrie. How easy she had been to talk to. He stood looking out the window for some time. The main street of Fort Benton was about as far removed from King Street, Toronto as he could imagine.

James reached for his sketchbook and found the other drawings he had made at Crowfoot's camp – the second scene and the faces of the children. He tore them out and took another page to write an accompanying note to Merrie. He described the Red Deer River landscape and his experiences with the children – their giggles and laughter and serious expressions. Although he knew the letter would not reach her until well into the New Year he wished her a Merry Christmas and thought for a long time about how to end it. He finally wrote:

> *"Your father told me you have not been well which saddens me and I wish there is more I could send or say to brighten your day. Most of all I hope this finds you fully recovered.*
> *Ever your friend, James."*

56

The weather continued much the same as it had been for the previous week, very cold, steady wind from the northwest and bright sun during the few daylight hours. James knew the drifting snow and bitter cold would make the journey slow and difficult so had given himself four days to reach Fort Walsh. That would get him there in time for Christmas. He wasn't sure how they would celebrate it but at least he would be among friends.

The first night out James stopped in a small gully. Scraping away the snow he found enough buffalo chips, that when shaved with his knife, burned brightly enough to keep him from freezing. They spent the second night in the coulee of the Milk River, deep in the trees with a roaring wood fire. The next morning they started before dawn and when they climbed out of the coulee and reached the plains James was surprised that, though the clouds were high, the wind was still. He planned to make Lodge Creek, where he had met the Metis families during the summer, before dark. He remembered it as a sheltered campsite and it was only a day's journey from Fort Walsh.

Mac made good progress. The snow was lighter on the high spots on the plain, driven almost bare by the high winds of the previous days and he was able to run at times and cover much of the distance to the creek. As the sun began to sink behind them it began to snow lightly and the wind picked up again but, to James' surprise it was coming straight at them out of the northeast. Mac walked steadily on and James kept an eye out for the coulee of Lodge Creek that he knew was not far off.

The snow fell more heavily and the wind increased in force before James became aware that he could hardly see where they were going. Soon the wind was shrieking and howling, driving the falling snow vertically, stinging their faces. James couldn't tell where the ground ended and the sky began. He became totally disoriented. He lost all sense of where they were or in which direction they were headed. The raging wind drove through his layers of clothing until his body shook with the cold. He leaned forward and lay his head on Mac's neck, his face wrapped in the blanket and turned away from the wind. He let the reins hang loose. He felt dizzy and very sleepy.

Dreamlike, James felt himself as a young boy riding with his father, the Colonel's strong arm holding him around his chest. The security he had always felt in his father's arms comforted him. When moments of consciousness returned he tried to raise himself up but he could not. His body swayed with the motion of the horse's footsteps. He felt his body going numb. He was helpless to stop the frigid wind from lashing his body. As he lapsed into unconsciousness he knew there was nothing he could do but hang on. If he was to survive, it was now up to Mac.

57

T<small>HROUGH A DREAMY HAZE</small>, J<small>AMES</small> thought he recognized the soft light of day through the hole in the top of a tepee. Thick smoke filled the lodge and was being drawn out slowly through the opening. He felt pressed in on every side and could not move a muscle. Not that he wanted to. He was feverishly hot and raked with fatigue. He slipped back into sleep.

How much time elapsed before he woke again he didn't know. The weight on both sides of him and over him was crushing, hot and suffocating. The smells of buffalo hides and fire brought visions of Three Bulls' lodge. He tried to move his arms but couldn't. There was a weight on them that hemmed him tightly. His body was on fire. He lay there motionless, fighting for breath in the smoke filled space trying to understand his situation. But his mind failed him and he slipped back into unconsciousness.

Sometime later movement beside him wakened him. The weight lifted from his arm and he reached to touch what held him. A soft hand touched his hand, laid it at his side and murmured some words he did not understand. There was a person lying beside him and from the tone of her voice, a woman. A similar but younger voice answered from the other side of him. She also stirred. He felt the weight that had held him move aside, arms that had stretched across his chest lifted. He lay in silence as the two women, one on each side of him, rose from their places, slipped buckskin dresses over their heads and looked down at him. The old one kneeled and put her face close to his. She touched his face with her gentle fingers and smiled. She said a few words to the younger one, who slipped on moccasins, put a heavy hide over her shoulders and went out through the entrance of the lodge. The older woman poured some liquid in a bowl from a pot over the fire and brought it to James. She lifted his head so that he could sip the fiery broth. It was pungent and raw but it soothed him. She laid his head down again and pulled the robes tightly around his neck.

James remembered the blizzard. He remembered the agonizing cold driven by the relentless wind. He remembered feeling lost and helpless. He remembered nothing of how he got to this place. The young woman returned with a man and a very old woman. They stood over him and spoke softly together. The very old woman bent down beside him.

"Ah, Redcoat," she said, "we are glad you live. When you arrived we thought there was little chance." James was surprised to understand her words. She noticed and replied.

"I once lived among your people," she told him, "but that was many years ago."

"Where am I?" asked James. He tried to rise but he could not. "How did I get here?"

"You were delivered to us," said the old woman, smiling. "Your mitts were frozen to your horse's mane. He brought you right to our door."

"Whose door?" asked James in a thin voice.

"We are Peigans," she explained, "camped for the winter in the woods beside Lodge Creek. Crooked Tree here is our chief. But you have Rain Cloud and her daughter Singing Bird to thank for your life." James looked up at the woman and her daughter who were looking down at him.

"We thought you were dead," the old woman continued. "Your feet and hands and face were white with the cold. We put you under many hides and lit a big fire. You stirred but you would not stop shaking. The women got under the hides with you and pressed the warmth of their bodies against your cold skin. Finally the shuddering stopped and you slept. They saved your feet and hands from the death of the cold."

James tried to rise but again had no strength.

"You still blaze with fever as you have since you first came," said the old woman. "It will be many days before you can stand and walk."

The younger woman, who was called Singing Bird, brought more broth. Her mother held James head while she spooned it into his mouth. It warmed him until he had no strength left. He lay back and closed his eyes. He could hear them talking among themselves as he fell asleep.

For days Rain Cloud and Singing Bird kept the fire burning strongly in the lodge where James slept. When he awoke they fed him more of the same broth. They rubbed heavy fat on his feet and hands that were swollen and sore. From time to time a man dressed in elaborate garb stood over him, shaking a rattle and chanting in a loud voice. Gradually James felt his mind clear as his body won the battle with fever and fatigue. When the old woman returned he had many questions.

"Does Fort Walsh know I am here?" he asked her.

"No, no one. The snow is too deep to ride. Besides, you are not fit to travel."

"My horse?" he asked.

"He grazes with the other horses," she told him.

James knew there would be little concern at Fort Walsh. They were not expecting him and the people at Fort Macleod would think that he had completed his trip as planned. No one would be looking for him.

Finally the fever broke and James lay exhausted. The women supplemented the broth with strips of buffalo meat and continued to rub his feet and hands. He had blisters on his cheeks that they dabbed with the same fat. He had not been cared for in this way since he was sick as a child. The old woman returned at least once each day. When he had the strength to talk he asked her how she came to speak his language.

"When I was a very young woman a man called MacKay bought me for his wife," she told him. "He gave my father four horses and a rifle. He must have wanted me badly because that was a high price for a wife."

"Who was MacKay?" James asked.

"A trader with the Hudson's Bay Company," she said. "He took me to Fort Edmonton – a long way from my home. Then we moved to Rocky Mountain House where he was the factor. He was a good man, but away most of the time. I learned your language in the forts."

"Why are you back here?" asked James.

"I looked after MacKay's home and comforted him," she went on. "We had five children."

"Five children?" remarked James. "Where are they?"

"One died very young, two died of smallpox, the oldest boy died in a fight over liquor and Rain Cloud is my daughter – the only one still alive. Singing Bird is my grandchild."

"And Rain Cloud's husband?" asked James.

"He died last year – also a fight over liquor," she said sadly. "Singing Bird was carried off at the same time. It was the Redcoats that brought her back." Suddenly it clicked in James' memory. Singing Bird was the girl they had rescued from Jess and the other whiskey traders at the Milk River ford when he first arrived.

"What do they call you?" asked James.

"MacKay called me Victoria," she explained smiling, "after your Queen – the White Mother. My Indian name was too hard for him to say. People at the fort called me Vicki."

"Where is MacKay?" asked James.

"When he got old and it was harder for him to travel," she went on, "he went home to your Old Country."

"And you?" asked James.

"He told me to go home to my people," she said sadly.

"He left you nothing?" asked James.

"The children," she said. "We had only two left then, our son and Rain Cloud."

James looked at the deeply lined face and imagined the life she had lived, taken from her people as a young woman, living with and raising her children among strangers, discarded when she was no long wanted. It touched him that there was still a warm glow in her eyes.

Slowly James' strength returned. He was able to sit up on his own, then stand and take a few steps. He slept when his body called for it and was often awake during the long nights. Rain Cloud and Singing Bird slept on robes near him and kept the fire going day and night.

The care of the women brought back memories of his mother. He had been close to her as a boy but when he went off to boarding school she had faded into the background of his life. She was a small woman, much shorter than his father, not strong physically, but firm in her views. She came from an Irish Catholic family but her grandfather had married a Protestant, much to the disgust of his family. He had been ostracized and they had raised their family in the Free Church of Scotland. There were stories that the Catholic branch of the family had snatched away his children as infants and had them baptized in the Catholic Church. James didn't know the full truth of this. What he did know was that his family had no contact whatsoever with his mother's family.

James dwelt on the thought of his mother whose name was Mary. She loved music and played the piano beautifully. Many were the nights he went to sleep hearing her play in the drawing room. With his father, the Colonel, away a good deal, it was left to her to raise the children and run the home. She did it with a firm hand. On reflection, James knew he must have been a handful to bring up. He was full of energy, restless and into everything. In remembering, he admired his mother for the way she had raised him. She hadn't used force or threats of force. Whenever he was angry, frustrated or unmanageable, she would put her arms around him and hug him until his temper and restlessness subsided. Then she would suggest some diversion to focus his attention on something positive and on he would go.

James regretted that he had not said more to his mother before he left for Canada. He had been so preoccupied with details and so excited about the prospects of the trip that he had almost forgotten to say goodbye to her. He wondered how she was at that moment and hoped that she was well.

From time to time Crooked Tree came with Victoria to visit James. The chief wanted to know how he was and said he was glad that James showed such improvement. James asked him about the Sioux. Crooked Tree knew that they had come across the border and said that more Sioux were arriving all the time.

"The snow is deep," said Crooked Tree, "but they keep coming. They have lost many of their horses and lodges. They are worn out. That is why they come here, to stop running from the Long Knives."

One afternoon, as the wind whistled over the top of the lodge, James sat around the fire which blazed in front of them with Crooked Tree, Victoria, Rain Cloud and Singing Bird.

"We were warned," said Crooked Tree staring into the fire.

James looked up at him. "Warned by whom?" he asked.

"The Old Man who came from the south," the chief began, with Victoria passing on the story to James. "As he traveled he made the mountains, trees, rivers and plains. He covered the plains with grass and made roots and berries grow in the ground. He took mud from the river and shaped it into a man and a woman. He breathed life into them and called them Siksika, or Blackfoot."

Crooked Tree stared into the fire as he spoke.

"When the man and the woman asked Old Man what they were to eat he made another image of clay. It was a buffalo. He made more images of clay and made the antelope on the plains and the bighorn sheep in the mountains and all the other animals. He breathed life into them and said, ' This is what you are suited for.'

"One day Old Man decided to make a child. He took more clay, molded it and covered it with straw. When he took the covering off he said, 'Rise and walk,' and it did. The man, woman and child followed him to the river. 'I am Napi,' he told them, 'Old Man, Maker of all things.'

"'Will we always live?' the woman asked Napi. 'Will there be no end to it?'

"Old Man picked up a buffalo chip and threw it in the water," Crooked Tree continued. "'If it floats,' Old Man explained, 'when people die they will come back again in four days. But if it sinks, when they die that will be the end of it.' Old Man threw the chip in the river and it floated.

"The woman did not like the idea of dying, even for four days," Crooked Tree went on. "'No, we should not decide it like this,' the woman told Napi, and picked up a stone. 'If the stone floats we will always live,' she said to him. 'If it sinks, people will die forever.' The woman threw the stone in the river and it sank to the bottom.

'There,' said the woman to Napi, 'perhaps it is better for people to die for ever. Otherwise they would never feel sorry for each other and there would be no sympathy in the world.'

'Well,' said the Old Man, ' You have chosen. Let it be that way.'

"Not long afterwards," Crooked Tree continued, "the woman's child died and she went to the Old Man pleading with him to change the law about people dying.

'Not so,' said the Old Man, 'we will undo nothing that we have done. The child is dead and it cannot be changed. People will have to die.'"

James was watching the old man as he told the story that had been passed down to him from ages past. He was bent towards the fire, his head looming large over his frail body. His black hair was still thick, parted into two long braids that fell over his shoulders and hung down in front of him. His round face was deeply lined, his dark eyes sunk deep into their sockets. His elbows rested on his knees and his hands were clasped in front of him. He swayed ever so slightly back and forth as he related the tale of the Old Man. To James, he almost was the Old Man.

"The Old Man taught the people how to make bows and arrows and how to hunt the buffalo," Crooked Tree continued. "He showed us how to take their skins and make robes. He showed us how to set up poles and cover them with robes to make tepees."

Crooked Tree's voice grew quiet.

"Then the Old Man told the Siksika that it was time for him to move north and make more land and people. 'This land is for you,' Old Man told them before he went, 'from the foothills to the Cypress Mountains, from the tops of the Rocky Mountains to the headwaters of the Yellowstone River. Let no other people come into your land. It is for the Blackfoot, Bloods, Peigans, Gros Ventre and Sarcees. If other people come, use your bows and arrows to give them battle. If you let them stay and make camp, you will lose everything."

Crooked Tree paused in deep thought.

"For many moons," he continued, "the five tribes gave battle to all people who crossed the line made by the Old Man and kept them out. Then some bearded men with light skins came, bringing presents. They said they wanted to stay only a short time to trap furs. We let them camp."

Crooked Tree turned and looked into James' eyes.

"It was as the Old Man said we lost everything."

Crooked Tree had a medicine bag with him and from it he took a medal with a small ring attached to its top. "This was the beginning of the end for us," he said and handed the medal to James.

James turned the medal over in his hands. On one side was a head and shoulders profile with the words "T. H. Jefferson, President of the U. S. A. 1804". On the other side were two hands shaking, one hand with the cuff of a military uniform and the other hand with a cuff of Indian beadwork. Over the hands were crossed a woodsman's ax and a peace pipe. Inscribed were the words "Peace and Friendship".

James looked up at Crooked Tree.

"Our ancestors met these men on the Marias River many moons ago," Crooked Tree told him. "They said they came from the Great Father in the East and that they wanted to trade our robes and furs for their guns. They said they had already made trade treaties with our enemies. We did not want our enemies to have their guns so we fought these white men. They killed two of our braves and left this medal on the chest of one of them."

James handed the medal back to the chief and Crooked Tree placed it back in his medicine bag.

"Then we fought all white men until they arrived with whiskey," he went on. "The firewater made us crazy and we forgot what the Old Man told us. You Redcoats came and stopped the whiskey but it was too late."

58

THE DAYS BECAME LONGER AND warmer and with them James' strength returned. He walked about the encampment and visited Mac, who had survived the blizzard and spent the cold months with the Peigan herd. His horse was thinner, but surprisingly fit for the heavy snow and harsh, cold temperatures that he had endured. It heartened James to see his old friend again. Soon he was saddling Mac and riding short distances.

Word around the Peigan camp was that small bands of Sioux were continually arriving across the Medicine Line. It was not known whether Sitting Bull was among them. James learned that there had been many battles between the Sioux and the pursuing cavalry and many of the people in the bands that had made it across the Medicine Line were wounded, starving and in rags.

James was feeling increasingly fit. One evening as he was eating together with Rain Cloud and Singing Bird, as he had for weeks, he found himself studying the young woman's face. She looked up and their eyes locked for an instant. James was moved by the loneliness he saw in her. He was grateful beyond words for the care she had given him but he didn't want his intentions to be misread and feared that they were.

Late that night James awakened to find Singing Bird kneeling on his robe stroking his face with a warm cloth as she had done so often at the height of his fever. From the light of the fire he could see the sadness in her eyes which were misty with tears. He felt aroused. He sensed that if he were to raise the corner of the robe she would come under it beside him. The passions of his body raged against his concern for her. He wanted to ease her loneliness and in some way show her how much her care had meant to him. But he would not make Singing Bird another Victoria nor condemn her to a life like Ginna's or her mother's. James rose from his bed and took Singing Bird by the hand. He led her to the place where she slept, lifted the robe so she could get under it, tucked it around her and walked from the lodge.

At sunrise the next morning James left for Fort Walsh. Victoria and Rain Cloud hugged him as if he were one of their lost sons. James looked around for Singing Bird and saw her standing off in the background. He walked over to her and hugged her, wishing he knew something to say in her language to convey how much her care had meant to him. Crooked Tree sent two of his warriors with James. There was still some snow on the ground and heavy drifts in the low-lying areas. It would take two days to reach the fort. As he waved good bye, James felt as if he were leaving his family. They had cared for him as only a family would.

59

James' arrival at Fort Walsh was unexpected. When Inspector Walsh heard James' story he was astonished. No one had any idea that James had been near death such a short distance from the fort.

Much had happened during the time James had been with the Peigans. Commissioner Macleod had been married at Christmas in Winnipeg, had combined his honeymoon with a visit to the police fort at Swan Lake and then had left his bride to return to Ottawa on urgent business. She had stayed behind in Winnipeg refusing to leave her aged father alone. Mr. Scott and the cabinet were preparing to formalize the government's relationship with the Blackfoot and were drafting a treaty that was to be signed by the Blackfoot chiefs late in the summer.

Sitting Bull had crossed the Medicine Line three months earlier along with a hundred and fifty lodges of his Teton Sioux tribesmen. His was only one of many more groups of Sioux that had moved across the border during the winter. Sitting Bull had made his camp one hundred and forty miles east of the fort on an old Cree-Salteaux battleground called "The Hole".

James learned that after the battle with Custer a large body of Sioux had fought a rearguard action against the cavalry from the valley of the Bighorn, north and east across the plains of Montana Territory to the valley of the Missouri. As winter began and game became scarce they broke up into smaller groups to hunt and avoid the pursuing Long Knives. Each small band was to make its own way across the Medicine Line as best it could. Many bands had encountered the cavalry during their escape and been savagely attacked. Almost all arrived with few horses, many lodges lost and their people starving. Some had eaten their horses to stay alive.

Inspector Walsh made a point of explaining to James in detail his first meeting with Sitting Bull and how he had the situation well under control. As with Black Moon in early winter, Walsh had explained to Sitting Bull the laws of the Great White Mother. Sitting Bull had accepted the laws that Walsh set out and made it clear he wanted to live in peace and in compliance. Sitting Bull agreed to let him know if anyone came among the Sioux. Walsh provided him enough ammunition to allow his people to hunt and he could get more from the fort when he needed it. Walsh emphasized that because of his firmness and understanding of the Sioux, there had been no incidents with Sitting Bull or any other chief since Black Moon had arrived. James recoiled from the self-congratulations that poured from the inspector but he couldn't argue with his courage or his record in dealing with the Sioux if all that he said were true.

It wasn't many days after James' return that Assistant Commissioner Irvine arrived at Fort Walsh for a meeting with Sitting Bull. Jerry and four constables were with him and James was happy to see that Webster was one of them. The assistant commissioner was pleased to see James again and astounded at the story of his months with the Peigans. When James told him how they had saved him from the blizzard and brought him back to health, Irvine wanted to know every detail. Irvine's compassion for the Indians touched James.

James had been favourably impressed with Irvine from the moment he had first seen him in Macleod's quarters. Irvine was a slightly built, grey-eyed officer with a closely trimmed reddish beard. To James he was the epitome of British duty and honour. James knew little about him until one evening when he and Webster were lingering at the long table in their quarters finishing their tea. Two years before, Webster had accompanied Irvine on a trip to Helena, south of Fort Benton.

Webster's story of Irvine began with a brutal massacre in the Cypress Hills only a few miles from where the two of them were sitting. It had taken place the year before the Mounties arrived.

"A group of drunken Fort Benton wolf hunters killed several Assiniboine Indians," Webster told James. "Some say twenty Indians were shot; others say it was nearer two hundred. Nobody knows for sure. The Assiniboine were camped beside a whiskey trading post called Fort Farwell. It was just up Battle Creek from here. When news of the massacre reached Ottawa it put a spur in the butts of the politicians who were taking their time setting up the Mounted Police. Soon after that the Force was organized and Irvine was given the task of finding the wolf hunters responsible for the massacre and bringing them to justice."

"No small order," remarked James.

"Irvine took the train to Bismarck, steamboat to Fort Peck and stagecoach to Fort Benton," Webster went on, "in the disguise of a gentleman adventurer."

"That's the way I came," replied James, "only I skipped the steamboat and the disguise."

"When he got to Fort Benton he had no trouble finding out who had done it. The killers had been boasting about it for months. Irvine went to the authorities, told them who he was and had the killers put on trial in Helena. Irvine asked the court to send the killers to Canada to be tried for the massacre."

"Did they?" asked James.

"Are you kidding? The jury was stacked with local supporters who had no use for Indians. The trial was a mockery. Irvine's evidence was ignored and the killers were freed."

"Just let go?" remarked James.

"Not only were they let go, the townspeople held a torch light parade and made heroes out of them."

"So they were never punished."

"Not that bunch. But some of the other members of the gang were caught in Canada. We held them in Fort Macleod. The nearest place they could be brought to trial was Winnipeg, so Irvine, a couple of other constables and I escorted them nine hundred miles for the trial."

What happened?" asked James.

"They were acquitted for lack of evidence. But surprisingly, Irvine wasn't too disheartened by the whole experience."

"I would have been," replied James.

"Irvine is still convinced the whole experience proved to the Indians our determination to see justice done. He knows his efforts didn't go unnoticed by many of the chiefs and they still respect him for it."

60

The day after Irvine and his party arrived at Fort Walsh, two Sioux warriors rode in with news that three Americans were in Sitting Bull's camp. Sitting Bull had promised Walsh that he would keep him informed and the chief was as good as his word.

Irvine and Walsh set out at once to visit Sitting Bull. Jerry and the four constables who had come with Irvine from Fort Macleod rode with them and Irvine asked James if he were up to the trip. James said he was even though he had questions in his own mind. It was his first hard ride since the blizzard. After a few hours on the plains he was pleased that he felt as fit as he did and that Mac had no difficulty keeping up. They covered the hundred and forty miles arriving in Sitting Bull's camp late in the afternoon of the third day.

The old chief greeted Irvine, Walsh and the other Redcoats warmly. From the moment James saw Sitting Bull he was impressed with the great Sioux chief who was so feared by the Americans. Sitting Bull led them to a special council lodge that he had prepared for the meeting. Soon a number of lesser chiefs joined them. Sitting Bull invited the Redcoats to sit with them in a circle.

When everyone was seated on the robes stretched on the ground Sitting Bull introduced the other chiefs who had formed a semi-circle beside him. James sat next to Jerry and noted the names of the chiefs, as they were introduced – Pretty Bear, Bear's Cap, The Eagle, Spotted Eagle and Sweet Bird.

Inspector Walsh introduced Assistant Commissioner Irvine and told Sitting Bull that Irvine was now the highest chief of the Great Mother in the territory. Jerry sat beside Irvine and translated in a low voice. James counted more than a hundred men, women and children sitting around them in the lodge. He noticed a priest with two other white men sitting at the back of the crowd.

A peace pipe was lit and Sitting Bull took the first puffs. The chief stood and raised it to the four quarters then handed it to Irvine, holding the bowl of it as the Redcoat chief smoked.

"God have pity on me," said Sitting Bull when Irvine had finished smoking, "we are going to live with a new people."

Then Sitting Bull passed the pipe to the chief to his right and it made its way around the circle. Unlike other pipe ceremonies he had seen, James watched as the last chief to smoke stood up, took the pipe just outside the entrance of the lodge, dug a shallow hole and buried the ashes. He took the pipe to pieces and placed the pieces over the spot where the ashes were buried.

Sitting Bull rose. The chief's speech sounded to James like prayerful oratory. The words were distinct and the cadence rhythmic. James wished he spoke the language to get its full meaning. He studied Sitting Bull as he listened to Jerry's translation.

Sitting Bull was a short and stocky man who walked with a pronounced limp. He had a pleasant round face, a strong lined forehead, a large hooked nose and a determined mouth. His black hair was knotted in two braids that fell down his chest to his belt. Two eagle feathers stuck straight up from the back of his head. He wore a simple, fringed, buckskin shirt and trousers with no decoration or beadwork and soft moccasins. When he smiled, which he did often, James thought his face brightened wonderfully.

"Why are you following us," the chief said in a strong voice, pointing to the priest and the two white men. "I have no wish to fight the Americans, but you have stolen our horses and our land and we have no other choice. You ask if we will go back. Our answer is no. You will take everything we have and destroy all our people. We have come here because we want to live in peace."

The other chiefs rose one by one and expressed the same sentiments. When the chiefs had spoken Sitting Bull invited Irvine to speak.

"As long as you remain in the land of the Great White Mother," Irvine said, addressing the chiefs opposite him in the circle, "you must obey her laws."

Irvine, although he was not tall, stood ramrod straight in his scarlet jacket, a figure of strength and authority. He made James proud to be wearing the same uniform.

"If you do, you have nothing to fear. You must not cross the line to fight the Americans and then return. In the Queen's land we all live like one family. If a white man or an Indian does wrong he is punished. You were right to tell us these Americans were in your camp. I will find out what they are doing here and take them out of your camp. I am glad you are looking for peace. We will protect you from all harm and you must not hurt anyone this side of the line. You need not be alarmed. The Americans cannot cross the line after you. You and your families can sleep sound and need not be afraid."

When the chiefs heard Jerry's translation they nodded in approval. When Irvine sat down the priest rose and addressed Sitting Bull.

"I come with the words of God," the priest began. "If you come back with all your people and give up your arms the American hearts will be glad. If you come back to your reservation you will live well, here you will not."

Sitting Bull interrupted him. "What would I go there for, for the Americans to come after me again?"

Irvine rose and asked Sitting Bull if he could be excused for a few minutes to talk with the priest and the two other Americans alone. Sitting Bull agreed and Irvine walked over to the priest, shook his hand and walked with him out of the lodge. The two other Americans and the policemen followed Irvine and the priest. They walked to an open spot in the encampment and sat together. The priest was Reverend Martin of the Catholic Commission in Washington who had worked with the Department of Indian Affairs. The other two were the chief scout and an interpreter for General Miles, a no-nonsense, hard fighting cavalry commander who had been given the order by General Sheridan to pacify all the remaining hostile Indians.

The priest explained to Irvine that he had come on his own, not as a representative of the government, to try to convince Sitting Bull to return. The scout and the interpreter told Irvine that they had been sent to find out where Sitting

Bull was. They had come with the priest for protection. James listened as Irvine ordered the priest, the scout and the interpreter to leave the country promptly after the meeting and to tell their American employers that all further contact with Sitting Bull was to be through him. Then Irvine rose and walked back to the council lodge where Sitting Bull and the other Sioux were waiting.

"The priest has told me he has come here to see what you intend to do," Irvine said to Sitting Bull, "whether you will remain or return to the American side."

Before Sitting Bull could respond the priest jumped to his feet.

"I do not come to give you any advice at all," the priest said to Sitting Bull. "If you stay here that is all right. If you come to America you must give up your arms and horses. I don't want you to come back, but if you do I will try to make it as easy as possible for you."

"That is not what you said before," Sitting Bull shouted at the priest. "Why have you changed your mind?"

"After hearing what these officers have to say," replied the priest, "I think you are better off on British soil. If you wish to come back I pledge my life that your lives and liberties will be safe. You will not be killed or made prisoner."

Spotted Eagle, second in command to Sitting Bull, and a respected war chief of the Sioux, rose slowly.

"Did the Long Knives send you here?" he said to the priest, making no attempt to hide the anger in his voice.

"No," replied the priest, "but I am assured that what I promise will be carried out. Do you intend to return to the other side, or remain?"

Sitting Bull was thoughtful, then turned to Irvine. "If I remain here will you protect me?"

"I told you the White Mother would," replied Irvine. "As long as you behave yourself."

Sitting Bull turned to the priest with piercing eyes. His words were said slowly and his voice was hard.

"What would I return for? Once I was rich, but the Americans stole it all in the Black Hills. I have come to remain with the White Mother's children."

Sitting Bull gestured that the council was over. James noted the significance of no pipe ceremony to conclude it. He rose with the other Redcoats. Sitting Bull walked over to Irvine and invited him and his men to stay the night.

Sitting Bull and Irvine left the lodge followed by the others. James found himself walking beside General Miles' scout and interpreter.

"I guess that settles it," said James to the scout. "Sounds like the Sioux will be staying in Canada."

"The hell they will," said the scout defiantly. "This isn't over by a long shot."

James was stunned by the words as he watched the scout and interpreter walk to where they had left their horses. James turned to see Jerry talking to one of the chiefs. The conversation ended as James approached. Jerry had a slight grin and noticed James looking at him.

"What is it, Jerry," James asked him.

"Pretty Bear says that if they hadn't promised to let us know about any Americans coming to their camp they would have killed their visitors, not the priest, but the other two. They held them captive until we arrived."

Sitting Bull entertained the Redcoats to a long meal that lasted several hours. James was surprised at the good humour of the Sioux and how easily they laughed at what to him seemed to be tragic stories. Sitting Bull related how it had taken his tribe five months to travel north from the Yellowstone. They had lost all their lodges in a flash flood on the Missouri. Fortunately they had already crossed the river and the cavalry were stranded on the other side.

"If they had cornered us in front of the floodwaters," said Sitting Bull, "we would all be dead. Their orders are 'Kill all who talk.'"

The stories went on into the night, many of them grievances against the Long Knives. In spite of their bitterness, James had never seen a happier group of Indians. Perhaps it was because of what the old chief said as they parted:

"This is the happiest night we have spent in many a long moon," he told Irvine. "We can sleep in peace."

Remembering the words of General Miles' scout, James wondered how long that would be true.

61

After the council with Sitting Bull, Irvine asked James to ride to Fort Benton to post a report of his meeting with Sitting Bull to Mr. Scott. Knowing that Macleod was due back in the North West soon, he asked James to carry another copy of the report on to Fort Macleod to be there when the major returned.

James was glad of the opportunity. His last report to Mr. McLennan had been sent in late December and he knew the banker would be fuming not to have heard from him since then. He spent the day he arrived back in Fort Walsh writing his own description of the council meeting with Sitting Bull. He included a review of his activities since December hoping it would help the banker understand why this report was so late. He left the following morning for Fort Benton, glad of the chance to be alone on the plains again in the warmth of spring.

He had forgotten the mosquitoes and black flies. With the higher temperatures and the melting snow, the ponds and sloughs were full of water, the rivers overflowing their banks and the marauding insects out in their millions. They made the ride a misery. James covered himself as best he could but the stinging, buzzing beasts found a way up his sleeves, down his neck and into his hair. At night he covered his head from the circling throngs, but they still managed to make his life unbearable.

Intentionally, he traveled by way of the Lodge Creek campsite where he had lived with Crooked Tree and his people. Whether it was the clouds of raging insects near the creek or the need to replenish their food stocks that had made them move on he didn't know, but they were not there. He was sad to have missed them. The rivers were in flood and it took him miles out of his way at each river to find a place where he could cross safely. The Old Man's River was the most difficult. Its water was particularly high and flowing swiftly.

He posted Irvine's report to Mr. Scott and his to Mr. McLennan. There were two letters waiting for the major, which he picked up and took with him. The trip north was only slightly less miserable. The wind was strong from the mountains and it blew some of the insects away from him. They were bad again when he descended into the coulees, probably a combination of less wind and more water where they seemed to congregate. He spent the night in a shallow gully on the open plains where the wind was strong in hopes of escaping the stings but it didn't make much difference.

When he arrived at Fort Macleod James found that the major had already arrived and that his new wife was with him. Macleod was happy to see James and invited him to his quarters the first evening he was back. When the major introduced him to his wife, James was startled to see that she looked close to his own age. He had expected someone much older.

James found Mary a remarkable woman. She was short with thick black hair that was parted in the middle. It was swept tightly over her ears and gathered behind her head. She had a broad forehead, wide-set eyes, a sharp nose and a strong mouth. She wore a long black dress drawn in at the waist with a black belt. There was a white frilly collar around her neck. She wore long silver earrings and a heavy silver chain around her neck from which hung a pendant.

Macleod and his wife had only recently arrived. On his way west from Ottawa he had met up with Mary in Chicago. They had travelled by the same railway route as he had taken to Bismarck but then had taken the steamer up the Missouri to Fort Benton. Mary had adjusted quickly to life at the fort and was quickly putting her own stamp on it. The major's quarters looked totally different from the last time James had been there. Large pieces of furniture were placed against the walls, china plates were on display in shelves over one of them, curtains were on the windows and a rug on the floor. The couple seemed completely at home in their surroundings.

The door from the small kitchen opened and James was halfway out of his chair with surprise. Entering the room was a large black woman carrying a tea tray.

"I'd like you to meet Aunty," Mary said as she smiled at James' surprise. "We met on the steamer to Fort Benton and she has come to live with us."

Aunty beamed at James who smiled back. He waited for her to place the tray in front of Mary, then shook her hand.

"I'm very pleased to meet you," he said.

"An' me to meet you, sa," she said back to him with a wide grin. "Ya know, Miz Macleod and me – we is the first white women in this territory." She tapped James on the shoulder and laughed heartily.

The major had read Irvine's report with great interest and wanted James' description of every detail of the meeting with Sitting Bull. Mary was as interested as her husband. The major probed him for descriptions of the chiefs, the state of the tribesmen and the condition of their lodges. He was particularly interested in the informal conversations after the Americans had left. He questioned James closely about the remark of the scout that the issue of the Sioux remaining in Canada was far from settled.

"I think he's right," said the major, much to James' surprise. "Our government will not grant them land in this country. The buffalo are disappearing fast and we cannot afford to feed them. There is a large reservation set aside for them in the Dakotas. All they have to do is move to it."

"But will the American army allow them to pass unharmed?" asked James.

"That's a serious question. I don't know the answer. But if the Sioux hand over their weapons I would hope the cavalry would honour their word and escort them peacefully."

They sat for a moment pondering the situation of Sitting Bull and his people.

"We are obliged to protect them while they are with us," continued the major firmly, "and that we will do."

"I'm glad to hear it, sir," replied James.

"Nevertheless, their presence represents a real danger," continued the major. "Our most important task in the months ahead is to solidify our good relationship with Crowfoot and the Blackfoot. One of the letters you brought asks me to set up a council with as many of the Blackfoot chiefs as we can gather to negotiate a treaty. It will be difficult. This time of year the bands are scattered all over the plains."

When the major was satisfied that he had learned all he could from James about Sitting Bull and the Sioux the conversation moved to James and how he had spent the winter. He told them of the blizzard and his months with the Peigans. He had not had a chance to relate the whole story in detail to anyone and he was moved by the major and Mary's deep and genuine concern for him. They were interested in the smallest details of the Indian's daily life. James noted their compassion for the hardships and suffering of the people and sympathy for their uncertain future. He was astonished at Mary's knowledge of the Indians and their way of life.

When the evening was over James wished them good night. Mary walked him to the door and out onto the wooden porch. "James," she said, "that was a remarkable experience. We're both so grateful for the Peigans and that you made it through the winter."

62

JAMES TRAVELED WITH THE MAJOR and Jerry to Crowfoot's camp to explain to the chief that the White Mother's representatives wanted to meet with him and his people to discuss a treaty. They spent several days with Crowfoot, making sure he understood the purpose of the meeting, answering his concerns and seeking his approval for the council. It was to be held in late summer at a place called Ridge Under The Water on the Bow River. Crowfoot, remembering James, asked to see the necklace that Three Bulls had presented to him and was pleased to see that he was still wearing it. James had a chance through Jerry to tell him of the blizzard and how grateful he was for the care of the Peigans who had saved his life.

Horseracing was one of the Crowfoot's great pleasures. As a young chief he had prided himself in owning the fastest horses and being the best rider. He was older now, preferred to watch others race but still boasted that he owned the fastest horse among the Blackfoot.

When their discussions were finally concluded, Crowfoot made an announcement.

"In honour of the major," ordered Crowfoot, "this afternoon we race."

Crowfoot had the major sit on his right with Jerry and James seated behind them. There was a large crowd of men, women and children watching the event. In front of Crowfoot, several braves were standing beside their horses. Crowfoot shouted some commands and the first two lined up in front of him pointing their horses towards a rider who had stopped some distance away.

Crowfoot always carried an umbrella. Sometimes he would hold it open over his head whether it was raining or not. Now he had it folded and was using it as a starter's flag. He raised it over his head and brought it down sharply. The two riders shot forward and raced towards the distant rider. When they reached him they wheeled around him and sped back towards the line from which they had started. One was three lengths ahead of the other as he crossed the finish line and Crowfoot shouted his pleasure.

One pair followed another until all the warriors had completed their race. Then he had the winners race against each other until a champion was declared. Crowfoot turned to Jerry and had words with him while glancing at James.

"He wants you to race against him," said Jerry, nodding towards the newly declared champion. James looked at the champion and at the horse that had just completed his fourth race over the course.

"That horse is winded," said James. "Is he up to one more race?"

"That's Crowfoot's horse and he thinks he can race all day," said Jerry with a smile. "He thinks he could still beat you."

Mac was fully recovered from his hard winter. The horse had regained the weight and muscle he had lost and the long rides over the prairie had helped him back to his old form. James had never raced with him or asked him to go full speed over a long distance. He wasn't sure how Mac would respond but he was excited to find out. He knew there was a lot more to Mac than he had ever called on.

"Give me a minute to get ready," said James.

He went to where Mac was grazing on his long rope. James took the rifle and scabbard, saddlebags and blankets off the saddle to reduce the weight. He took off his own sword, belt and revolver, removed the bandolier of bullets from around his neck and led Mac to the starting line. Crowfoot, the major and Jerry and several of the other chiefs were on their feet, chattering among themselves.

"The betting's heavy on this," said Jerry, "what are your chances?"

"Mac's good but he's never raced," said James. "I think the other horse is tired."

"Don't count on it," said Jerry.

"Then we'll see," said James as he mounted up.

Mac knew something was afoot and James could feel him tense up. James leaned forward, rubbed his neck and whispered in his ear. As he mounted, James caught the eye of the champion rider who half smiled, half sneered at him. Crowfoot brought them to the starting line with his umbrella held high.

James shouted to Jerry, "Just like the other races, once down and back?"

Jerry had a word with Crowfoot. "That's right," said Jerry. "First one back across this line."

James found himself lined up on the outside. It wasn't the best place but that was where Crowfoot wanted him. Down came the umbrella. Mac knew exactly what was happening and he shot forward. The two horses were neck and neck towards the lone rider at the far end of the course. James held Mac even with the champion, feeling that there was still more under him when he needed it. They were fast approaching the motionless rider who marked the turn. James was still on the outside. He saw his chance.

At the speed they were running James could see that the champion would overrun the marker as he swung around him and turned for home. James held Mac back just slightly and at the precise moment swung in behind the champion and made a very tight turn around the standing rider and was headed for home with the champion two lengths behind him. James held Mac steady as the champion closed the distance. As soon as he drew alongside James let Mac go. The black shot forward and pulled steadily away from the champion, whose horse was feeling the effects of having done this four times before in the last hour. Mac streaked across the finish line a length in the lead to wild shouts from the crowd.

James patted Mac on the neck and rode him slowly to where Crowfoot and the others were standing. Crowfoot gestured him to dismount. The old Chief walked up to James and reached for the necklace around his neck. Out came the grizzly's claw on the rawhide string. Crowfoot opened his hand and in it was a white bead with a hole in it. James undid the knot in the rawhide and took off the necklace. Crowfoot threaded the bead so that it slipped down the rawhide next to the claw and said a few words. James looked to Jerry.

"What did he say?" asked James.

"Crowfoot said, 'Rides like the wind.'"

63

THE GREAT PLAINS HAD NEVER witnessed a gathering like it. Several days before James had arrived at Ridge Under The Water, eighty miles downstream on the Bow River from Fort Calgary, with a detachment of Mounted Police to lay out the areas where the various tribes would set up their camps. They thought a large number of Blackfeet, Bloods, Peigans, Sarcees, Stonies and Assiniboines would be there but they hadn't expected anything like this.

James rode among the lodges of the immense encampment. With the council due to begin the following morning, tribesmen were still arriving. At last count there were over a thousand lodges, shelter for more than four thousand men, women and children. James watched the activity of the late afternoon, the women with their household duties, the children rushing here and there. Many of the men were looking after their horses. Jerry had told him he thought there were at least fifteen thousand head. Even Jerry had never seen so many in one place. Horses were everywhere, scattered among the lodges and in herds on the surrounding plains. There were horses as far as the eye could see in every direction.

James saw Jerry standing with a group of braves admiring a beautiful spotted stallion. They were chattering among themselves and pointing to various horses, obviously comparing them. He rode up to them and dismounted to take a closer look. The stallion was not a tall horse, but it had a long neck on powerful shoulders and a proud head held high. It was white with patches of brown spots with a tan coloured mane and tail.

"Whose is that?" he asked Jerry.

"Crowfoot's. He has so many horses he can trade for the best. This is his own. No one rides it but Crowfoot."

"It's a beautiful horse. Is he fast?"

"At one time very fast," replied Jerry. "Crowfoot cannot ride the way he once did. This horse has not raced for some time."

James swung up on Mac and continued his patrol. A large council lodge had been set up on one side of the encampment. Close to it was the Redcoat camp, home to over a hundred members of the Force. Their plain white, bell shaped tents in straight rows looked sterile and drab compared to the painted images on the buffalo hides covering the Blackfoot tepees. James rounded the council tent and approached the Mountie section of the camp. The Redcoats' tents had their bottom flaps pinned up so the wind could blow right through. In front of the major's tent were the two nine-pound cannons that had been hauled all the way from Fort Dufferin and recently up from Fort Macleod. James wasn't sure they had ever been fired.

The section of the encampment set aside for David Laird, Lieutenant Governor of the North West Territories, and the group that accompanied him was beside the Police. Laird was to be the chief negotiator for the government. He had brought several officials with him, some from as far away as Ottawa.

James continued his rounds until nightfall. He was astonished that there could be so many Indians in one place, from several different tribes, yet there had not been a single incident since he had arrived.

The next morning the Indians, officials and police assembled. The sides were taken down from the council tent so that the crowd could see inside where buffalo robes covered the ground. Lieutenant Governor Laird and Commissioner Macleod sat across from Crowfoot, Old Sun, Bull Head, Three Bulls, Red Crow, with forty or fifty lesser chiefs flanking them. Behind the chiefs, in a huge semi-circle which stretched for what James thought must be a quarter of a mile, were the assembled men, women and children of the Blackfoot Confederacy. There were others in the crowd – a priest in a black robe, a minister of the church in white collar, bureaucrats from Ottawa who stood out in their suits, high white collars and ties. Mary Macleod was sitting with five other white women whom he took to be the wives of other officers and officials.

James sat behind and to the left of Macleod where he could see Crowfoot and the other chiefs clearly and beyond them the multitude of tribesmen. He was close enough to Jerry to be able to hear clearly. He had his notebook out and wanted to capture every word and, if he had time, sketch the event.

There was a festive atmosphere magnified by the large number of tribesmen and horses, the colourful Indian dress, the scarlet police uniforms, the cannons and Union Jacks flapping in the breeze. The bureaucrats had the only severe faces in the crowd. James doubted that the Indian people understood the true meaning of the gathering or how much their lives were to be changed by it. Even Crowfoot and the other chiefs, he suspected, failed to realize the impact the proposed treaty would have on them and their people. He knew Crowfoot and his headmen trusted Macleod and that was enough for them to trust the White Mother and her representatives.

Crowfoot lit a peace pipe, smoked and passed it to the chief on his right. James watched as it was passed hand to hand, studying the face of each chief.

He sought to understand what was going through each mind and wondered what the future would hold for them. He watched Laird, whom he knew to be a man of his word, sympathetic to the Indians yet responsible to make the North West safe for settlement. He watched Macleod, whom he had come to admire greatly for his personal integrity and fairness with the Indians. James glanced over at Mary Macleod. Her eyes were fixed on the major. He could read in her expression the pride she had in her husband. Laird rose and Jerry stood beside him, translating his words as he spoke.

"The Great Spirit has made all things," Laird began, "the sun, the moon, the stars, the earth, the forests and the swift-running rivers. It is by the Great Spirit that the Queen rules over this great country. The Great Spirit has made the white man and the red man brothers, and we should take each other by the hand. The Great Mother loves all her children…."

James watched the faces of the chiefs. They were expressionless. He looked out into the vast crowd. The children were restless, the mothers trying their best to keep them quiet, the men leaning forward to catch Jerry's words.

"….The good Indian has nothing to fear from the Queen or her officers," Laird continued. "You know this to be true. When bad white men brought you whiskey, robbed you, and made you poor, and through whiskey quarrel among yourselves, she sent the Police to put an end to it. You know how they stopped this and punished the offenders and how much good this has done…."

Some of the chiefs nodded their approval.

"The Queen has sent Colonel Macleod and myself to ask you to make a treaty," Laird told them. "In a very few years the buffalo will probably be all destroyed, and for this reason the Queen wishes to help you live in the future in some other way. She wishes you to allow her white children to come to live on your land and raise cattle…"

Some of the chiefs' eyes went hard and there were signs of anger and disapproval.

"….Should you agree, she will assist you to raise cattle and grain and thus give you the means of living when the buffalo are no more. She will also pay you and your children money every year…."

James could read on their faces that many of the listeners opposed the idea of allowing white people to come to settle on their land. Laird's detailing of the moneys to be paid, the cattle, farm implements, ammunition, grain, and potatoes to be given in payment was lost in their concern.

"….Chiefs will get a suit of clothes, a silver medal, a flag and every third year another suit. A reserve of land will be set apart for yourselves and your cattle, upon which none others will be permitted to encroach – for every five persons, one square mile…."

James was sure the chiefs were having difficulty absorbing the details. They understood white settlement, they understood that the buffalo were disappearing, but what reserves meant and payments….it was beyond them.

"…. The Queen's officers will permit no white man or half-breed to build or cut the timber on your reserves, but if required, roads will be cut through them. As soon as you settle, teachers will be sent to you to instruct your children to read books like this Bible, which is impossible so long as you continue to move from place to place."

The chiefs were beginning to murmur among themselves. They wanted time to hear this again, slowly and discuss it among themselves.

"I have spoken," concluded Laird, "I have made you acquainted with the principal terms contained in the treaty which you are asked to sign."

The chiefs sat with faces of stone. The bureaucrats whispered among themselves. Finally Button Chief of the Bloods rose in his place and turned slightly so that the officials and the crowd could hear him. Jerry moved over to stand beside him.

"The Great Spirit sent the white man across the great waters to carry out his ends," began Button Chief. "The Great Spirit, and not the Great Mother gave us this land. The Great Mother sent Macleod and the police to put an end to the traffic in firewater. I can sleep now safely. Before the arrival of the Police, when I laid my head down at night, every sound frightened me. My sleep was broken. Now I can sleep sound and am not afraid."

Several of the other chiefs spoke. When the last chief had finished it was decided among Crowfoot, Laird and Macleod that they would meet with their chiefs and officials to discuss the details of the treaty. The chiefs gathered around Crowfoot as the crowd dispersed. James moved forward to hear the discussion between the chiefs and Laird and his officials. He was impressed with how orderly the talks continued through the day. The Indians had great patience, allowing each chief to speak for as long as he wished. Jerry was taxed to the limit, translating chiefs to officials and officials to chiefs, dealing with details and explaining new concepts to people who were being introduced to them for the first time.

At sundown discussions were suspended until the following day. James went back to his tent to start his report to Mr. McLennan, but was interrupted with cheers coming from the edge of the encampment. He walked in the direction of the noise and saw braves racing each other on horseback. The air was thick with the smell of cooking fires. There was good-natured chatter around the lodges, the women stirring pots and feeding their families, the men talking horses, the children rushing about.

Talks between chiefs and officials continued through a second day. At one point James was amused to hear Button Chief suggest that the police should pay for all the wood they had used since they arrived in the North West, the price being $50 for each chief. Laird responded by suggesting that the Indians should pay for the services of the police to which the chiefs broke out in hearty laughter.

During the evening James needed a break from his report writing and went for a walk to get some air. There was the haze of hundreds of cooking fires in the air but the stillness with thousands of people so close at hand was astonishing. There were small groups of warriors seated on the prairie grass, others standing in groups, all talking, some using their hands to emphasize their words. He could hear the horses moving all around him and a lone naying here and there. It was a beautiful night, the sky was clear and the stars bright. A light wind ruffled the tents and lifted the smoke from the fires into the eastern sky.

Passing one of the tents in the Lieutenant Governor's area James heard loud voices in discussion. He peered into the entrance and saw the priest, the minister and two bureaucrats sitting together.

"Everything all right in here?" asked James.

"Come in Constable, come in," invited one of the bureaucrats. "Maybe you can help us settle this question."

"What question?" asked James as he entered the tent and stood near them.

"Should we teach the Indians to plow first or pray first?" one of the bureaucrats asked James.

James stuck out his hand. "James Keyden" he said.

"Dobbie," said the man who invited him in. "Ministry of Justice, Ottawa."

Then turning to those with him, "My colleague Brumwell, from Laird's office. I expect you know Reverend McDougall and Father Scollen, who works with Father Lacombe."

"Pleased to meet you," said James. He had heard much of McDougall who he knew had lived among the Stoneys near the mountains west of Fort Calgary for years. Father Lacombe he had also heard of but had never met. He knew he had lived among the Crees to the north and was trusted by them.

"I'm afraid Father Lacombe is quite ill," said Father Scollen. "He asked me to come in his place."

"Now then Keyden," interrupted Dobbie, "is it pray and plow or plow and pray?"

There were not many people whom James disliked at first sight but Dobbie was very rapidly becoming one of them. Dobbie was a middle-aged, short, little man, dressed as he would to go to his office in Ottawa. He had a dark blue suit with a pinstripe running through it, his high starched white collar looked like it had been changed that morning and his tie was tight around his thin neck. It was more than his English accent that annoyed James. Dobbie exuded an arrogance and an attitude of superiority that he found irritating and offensive.

"I don't understand your question," said James, "you'll have to explain."

"Now look here Keyden," Dobbie went on, "Once we settle these savages on their reserves we'll need to teach them how to plow so they can grow their own grain to survive. These gentlemen of the cloth feel that the Indians would do much better as farmers if they became Christians first."

James recoiled at the word 'savage' and the thought that the Indians would be influenced to become Christian angered him.

"I don't agree with your use of the word 'savage'," said James to Dobbie. "In fact, I find it quite offensive."

"How can you say that," replied Dobbie. "They fight among themselves, killing, burning, torturing and scalping each other. They do the same to whites whenever they get the chance."

"How long have you been in the North West, Mr. Dobbie?" asked James.

"I arrived about a month ago," he replied, "but I have read every report that has ever been written from this wilderness."

"Would you call Europeans 'savages'?" James asked him.

"Of course not," he replied.

"Haven't we fought, burned and tortured each other for centuries? You English have done it to us Scots and we've done it to you. We British have done it to almost everyone we've conquered over the face of the globe. The French do it to the Spaniards, the Spaniards do it to the Dutch, the Dutch do it to the Spaniards and around it goes."

"That's quite different, my dear man," said Dobbie.

"How is it different?" asked James.

"We are modern nations defending our homeland and our civilized way of life," replied Dobbie.

"Civilized way of life?" James shot back, surprising himself with the heat of his words. "We use our power to conquer and convert and call it the advancement of civilization and Christianity."

"Force is sometimes needed," Dobbie interrupted in his most superior tone of voice, "to lift native peoples to a higher level of civilization."

"Is that what you have in mind for these people?" asked James, gesturing to the thousands of Indians surrounding them.

"Fortunately, we have not had to use much force out here," Dobbie went on. "You fellows have seen to that. Good work, by the way. But now we must prepare this territory for settlement. If the United States is any example we will have millions of people wanting to settle here in the next few years. The only hope for these savages…Indians…is that they become like us as soon as possible."

James was horrified at the thought.

"Like us?" he exclaimed.

"Of course," Dobbie went on. "Reverend McDougall and Father Scollen agree with me. The Indian must be civilized."

James looked at McDougall.

"I don't fully agree with all you're saying, Dobbie," interrupted McDougall, "but treaty or no treaty, the Indian way of life is ending. It's a shame, but it's true. My work is to bring the word of Jesus Christ to these people so that their souls will be saved. This will help them lead peaceful lives, become successful farmers and live in harmony with their white neighbours. I happen to think we should teach them to plow – that is to say – to become farmers first. It's my belief that Christianity will follow quite naturally from that. The good father here believes that we should make good Christians of them first and then they will make good farmers."

"It saddens me deeply," added Father Scollen, "to watch the Indian way of life disappear. At their best they are a caring, hospitable, free-spirited people who have a close relationship to the god that they know. It is true that they will never know salvation until they are baptized but that is beginning to happen. The Blackfoot are the slowest to understand the way of Christ but little by little they are coming to it."

"Gentlemen," James cut in, his mind racing to try to find the words to describe how he felt, "you are forgetting that it is us, white people, who have brought an end to their way of life. It is us who are butchering the buffalo and it is us who covet their land. We can mask it in phrases of 'for their own good', 'higher civilization' or 'the ways of Christ' all we like, but it is conquest none the less. Our guns and our greed for their land will overwhelm these resourceful, gracious people, whose way of life has survived in this harsh land for thousands of years. It is a tragedy."

"Come now, Keyden," replied Dobbie, "this is a filthy, backward race who stand in the path of progress."

"Who was it that brought smallpox, syphilis and whiskey to the North West?" James snapped at Dobbie. "Filthy? Backward? Which of us best fits the description?"

"The sooner we settle them on reserves, Christianize them, teach their children English and assimilate them into our ways, the better this country will be," answered Dobbie, dismissing what James had said. "That's what we think in Ottawa."

"Then god help the Blackfoot, and god help us," said James and he left the tent, his anger at Dobbie's attitude overflowing and his words powerless to make any impression on the bureaucrat's thinking.

There was no sleep for James that night. He had surprised himself by what he had said to Dobbie, Brumwell and the two churchmen. Some of the heat of his words had been in reaction to Dobbie's manner, but the sentiments he expressed he had not fully expressed to himself let alone anyone else. When he had arrived in the North West he had shared the belief that Indians were cruel savages and that white settlement was the "civilized" way. But he had come to know Indians as people, different from himself certainly, but individuals with instincts and emotions like any other people. He greatly admired their skill in surviving this hostile land, and within the band how they cared for each other. He knew he owed his life to Crooked Tree's band of Peigans. Three Bulls, Crooked Tree, Rain Cloud, Singing Bird, Crowfoot, Sitting Bull, Jerry – they were all people he admired tremendously and would never forget.

The more he thought of the attitude he had heard expressed by Dobbie the more he began to feel that he was part of a betrayal of the Indian people. No matter how much he wished it weren't true, he knew that the Indian way of life was doomed. There was no holding back the tidal wave of settlement sweeping North America. He thought of the determination of Macleod who truly believed in the work that he was doing to protect the Indians from debauchery and the ruthlessness of the lawless. Now he wondered if the same distress that he was beginning to feel lay behind the grimness he had noticed on the major's face.

"Were the terms of the treaty the best way for the Blackfoot," James wondered, as he lay restless through the night. "Certainly not if they are administered by men like Dobbie. Or was the treaty the first step in robbing these people not only of their land but of their way of life?" He was still searching for answers when the sun broke over the horizon.

The day dawned with a cascade of colour leaping out of the east. The wind from the west was warm. James emerged from his tent to find the great encampment alive with activity. Lodge fires were lit, wisps of smoke flowed gently from the openings in the tops of the tepees, children and dogs chased each other among the lodges, women were busy about their work, the men tended their horses. This was scheduled to be the final day of the council, the day, it was hoped, that the chiefs would sign the treaty. James had a sense of foreboding but he knew the die was cast.

He walked towards the council lodge where the crowd was already gathering. Men, women and children from the lodges were scurrying to find places on the ground where they could hear the speakers. On his way we was pleased to see Mary Macleod walking in the same direction. He was surprised to see that she was pregnant.

"Mrs. Macleod," said James. "I didn't expect to see you here."

"I came up with the major," said Mary. "I'm to be one of the signers of the treaty – think of that!"

"Congratulations," said James. "Your name will live in history."

She laughed.

"I don't know how the chiefs understand all of it," she said. "I had to have the major explain parts of it to me over and over. I'm not sure I agree with it all, but there it is. Probably the best we can do under the circumstances."

"I hope so," said James, not at all sure.

James found a spot where he could clearly see the small, low table that had been set up on a robe stretched over the ground in front of the council tent. Laird and Macleod took their seats on chairs under the large tent, its flaps open so that all could see inside. Crowfoot sat on the ground directly in front of Laird and Macleod on the opposite side of the table with his chiefs flanking him. A mass of men, women and children were arrayed behind the chiefs in a large half-moon shape that stretched as far back as the grazing horses.

Crowfoot started with a solemn ceremony of the pipe. The chief lit it, smoked and passed it to the chief on his right. The chiefs were in no hurry to pass it to their neighbour, contemplating as they smoked. The pipe reached Laird, Macleod and back to the chiefs. When it was returned, James watched Crowfoot hand the pipe to one of the headmen who buried the ashes.

One by one the chiefs rose to speak. James was careful to note the name of each speaker, then tried to capture his words. One of the first speakers was Red Crow, head chief of the Bloods. His was one of the most powerful tribes in the Blackfoot Confederacy.

"Three years ago, when the Redcoats came to this country," Red Crow began, "I met and shook hands with Stamix Otokan at the Belly River. Since that time he made many promises. He kept them all. Not one of them was broken. Everything that the Redcoats have done has been good. I entirely trust Macleod and will leave everything to him. I will sign the treaty."

James studied the major. He looked grim and acknowledged Red Crow with a slight nod of his head.

"It doesn't matter what's in that treaty," thought James, "they trust Macleod, and if Macleod wants them to sign it, they will."

James caught a glimpse of Dobbie sitting behind and to the left of Laird. His anger flared again as he thought of the contrast in attitude between him and Macleod. He wondered if Macleod was aware of the prejudices in men like

Dobbie in Ottawa. He suspected that he did and that it was the reason for the foreboding look he saw in Macleod's eyes.

Many of the chiefs spoke. Finally, Crowfoot rose slowly to his feet. James watched intently as the great chief turned and raised his hand to the crowd and then turned back to where Laird and Macleod were seated. James felt that the old chief was aging in front of him. His tall frame was slightly bent. He spoke in a strong, slow voice, his tone modulating with the rhythm of the words.

"While I speak be kind and patient," Crowfoot began. "I have to speak for my people who are numerous and who rely upon me to follow that course which in the future will tend to their good." Crowfoot paused to look back to his people and over the landscape.

"The plains are large and wide. We are the children of the plains. It is our home and the buffalo have been our food always."

Crowfoot turned to Laird and Macleod.

"I hope you look upon us as your children now, and that you will be indulgent and charitable to us," he said directly to them. "My people expect me to speak for them and I trust the Great Spirit will put into their breasts to be a good people."

Looking towards Macleod, who had his eyes fixed with kindness on the old chief, Crowfoot continued.

"The advice given me and my people has proved to be very good. If the Police had not come to the country, where would we all be now? Bad men and whiskey were killing us so fast that very few of us would have been left today. The Police have protected us as the feathers of the bird protect it from the frosts of winter. I am satisfied. I will sign the treaty."

With Crowfoot's approval and the speeches of the chiefs concluded, the signing began. James was horrified to see that it was Dobbie who was the bearer of the treaty papers and the person who took charge of the signing ceremony. Dobbie took his position by the table. Laird and Macleod were the first to sign. Then it was the turn of six women, among them Mary Macleod. Dobbie motioned to Crowfoot. The old chief hung back and motioned for his other chiefs to go first. The chiefs lined up one behind the other in front of the table. James' anger flashed as he watched Dobbie take great pleasure in orchestrating the signing, careful not to get his fine suit too close to the chiefs' garments as he pointed his finger to the spot on the document where each chief was to make his mark. Dobbie blotted each X with a flourish and kept the next chief in line waiting until he was quite satified that it was dry.

James watched Crowfoot standing aside as his chiefs approached the table and realized that the great chief had chosen to be the last to sign. He saw a distant look in the man's eyes and an expression of resignation on his face.

There was a lump in his throat as James watched Crowfoot approach the table. Crowfoot bent forward took the pen in his right hand and while Dobbie pointed to the spot on the document the old chief made his X. Both Laird and Macleod rose to shake the great chief's hand. When Macleod grasped the old chief's hand they looked each other in the eye and held each other's hand for a long moment. James knew as he watched them that it wasn't the terms of the treaty that had brought the chief to sign the document. It was his trust in Macleod.

Following the completion of the ceremony there was great merrymaking. The police finally had a reason to fire the cannons, which they did, frightening the horses so that the warriors had to scramble to keep them from stampeding. A racecourse had been set up around the encampment. It was a long circular course that at one point ran along the bank of the Bow River. Soon the warriors were racing around the circuit – sometimes three against each other, sometimes more. The racing went on most of the afternoon with great shouts and celebrations at the finish line as the winner streaked across. James was watching the excitement when Jerry came over to him.

"Crowfoot wants you," Jerry told him.

James followed Jerry to where Crowfoot was seated on a buffalo robe looking over the start and finish line. His umbrella was open over his head. Some of the other chiefs and warriors sat around him. Crowfoot waved for Jerry and James to come near him. Jerry bent down to talk to the old chief and Crowfoot lowered his umbrella over their heads for a private chat. When the umbrella was lifted James saw Jerry smiling.

"He's going to bet big on his stallion," Jerry whispered to James, "and he wants you to ride him."

"Me?" said James, "nobody rides that stallion except him."

"Today you ride him," said Jerry firmly, "and you better win."

James had no choice. He smiled at Crowfoot who smiled broadly back at him. Then the chief rose slowly and shouted to those around him. James couldn't understand a word but he knew Crowfoot was putting forth a challenge. Some of the other chiefs shouted back at him and held up one finger, others two fingers.

"Must be some kind of a bet," he thought.

When the chiefs had finished their wagering some warriors ran off. James wasn't sure why they had gone until he saw them return leading horses – not just any horses, these were all beautiful animals, strongly built and fast. Finally a warrior showed up leading Crowfoot's spotted stallion.

There were 'Ohs' and 'Ahs' from the warriors as they had a close-up look at the magnificent animal. The warrior handed the reins to Crowfoot.

"Watch this," Jerry said, smiling to James. "They know he has the best horse and they think Crowfoot is going to ride but they think he is too old to win."

Crowfoot raised his arm to quiet the crowd and waved for James to come over to him. The crowd watched as he handed the reins to James. Then in a loud voice he shouted something which James thought must be the announcement that Crowfoot had chosen him to ride the stallion. Crowfoot's announcement was greeted with hoots from the other chiefs while Crowfoot had a great smile on his face. Suddenly, one of the chiefs stepped forward and exchanged strong words with Crowfoot.

"He says only Blackfoot can ride," Jerry said to James.

Crowfoot walked over to James, raised the rawhide string around James neck and drew out the grizzly's claw and white bead. The old chief lifted them as high as the rawhide string would allow for the others to see and spoke loudly.

"He says you are Blackfoot," whispered Jerry.

James smiled as he saw some of the chiefs sulk as they accepted Crowfoot's word. Some chiefs mounted their own horses and others had warriors ride for them. James took the reins of the stallion and moved to the front of the horse. He hadn't seen a horse of this quality since he had been with his father at parades of the Scots Greys. He was sure this animal must have belonged to some high-ranking officer in the American cavalry. James rubbed the stallion's nose and whispered in his ear. The horse was balky and James took enough time to calm him and get him used to the idea that he was going to get on his back.

James took off his weapons and laid them down beside Crowfoot. The chief was looking at him with a smile that said, 'I fooled them,' and eyes that said to James, 'Now you'd better win this race for me.'

James was up and getting the feel of the stallion. He walked him a little, trotted and let him gallop lightly. Satisfied and ready, James turned to the starting line. There were five other horses ready to race. Crowfoot held his umbrella, still open, high over his head. Down it came with a roar from the crowd and off they went. James had noticed in the other races that most of the horses were slowing as they approached the finish line. It was a long course and he wanted some reserve for the final stretch.

James kept the stallion up with the leaders. The horse had no difficulty with the pace and seemed to want to move into the lead. James held him steady with the leader as they came to the half way point of the circle. James could see them approaching the narrow strip alongside the river. Just as they reached it the horse on his left veered over towards him and forced the stallion into the soft dirt next to the river. The stallion slowed to get his footing and the leader and two other horses shot by them.

James brought the stallion back onto solid ground but there were three horses ahead of him. The stallion was angry at being behind the others and James was angry at the tactic that had forced him off the track. He let the reins out and touched the stallion in the flank with his spurs. The horse shot forward at full speed. He caught the horse in third place and went by it and was soon beside the horse in second. But the leader was the one that had pushed him and he was at least three lengths ahead. James could see the finish line coming fast. He talked to the stallion and urged him forward. They were gaining. James could see Crowfoot's umbrella in the distance. The stallion was going full out and the horse ahead was beginning to flag. James kept low on his neck. He could hear the crowd shouting. They were neck and neck with only a short way to the finish line. And then they were across. The stallion had won by a nose.

Cheers went up from the crowd. There was a multitude of men, women and children surging around. James rode the stallion slowly back towards Crowfoot and the crowd parted to let them through. The old chief was beaming. James knew Crowfoot was several horses richer. They would be added to his herd of over two hundred.

James got down and handed the reins to Crowfoot. Jerry didn't seem to be around and there was no way they could understand each other. James picked up his belt and holster, sword and bandolier. The old chief touched him on the arm and James turned to face him. The chief held out his hand and in it was another bead, just like the white one he wore around his neck except this one was blue. He handed the bead to James and folded it in his hand. With both his hands Crowfoot held James clenched fist. James looked up. The old chief was looking him in the eye nodding his head up and down in approval.

James made his way through the crowd towards his tent. His was the last race of the day and the Indians were returning to their lodges. James happened to notice two women standing quietly watching him from a distance. They looked familiar and he stopped. They stood silently still looking at him. He walked towards them. His throat tightened and his eyes filled as he recognized Rain Cloud and Singing Bird. They were smiling at him. James hugged the mother and then her daughter. Victoria was no where to be seen. James looked around for Jerry but couldn't see him. He turned to them and made gestures to suggest Victoria, moving his hands and fingers to look like mouths talking to each other. Their eyes grew sad. They understood. Singing Bird folded her hands and laid them beside her head. Then she moved her arm in front of her, parallel to the ground. James understood. Victoria had died. James put an arm around each of them and they drew close, standing silently together. Finally they drew apart and James reached for the necklace around his neck. He undid the knot and slid the white bead from the string. He reached into his pocket and took out the blue bead, which Crowfoot had just presented to him. He gave the blue one to Rain Cloud and the white one to Singing Bird, folding them in their hands the same way Crowfoot had done to him. He hugged them again. There was nothing he could say. There were tears in the eyes of all three.

James looked up to see Dobbie staring at them from a distance. The man in the suit sneered at James, turned his back and walked away.

The merriment in the encampment carried on into the night. James walked among the lodges and watched the singing, the drumming and the dancing. The warriors were in their finery, tracing intricate steps to the beat of the drums. They whirled and leaped and stamped, singly and together. James could have watched all night but finally made his way back to his tent.

As he reached the Redcoat area of the encampment he was surprised to see a warrior holding Crowfoot's stallion outside the major's tent. He looked in and saw the old chief sitting down with the major and Jerry. The major saw James and waved him in.

"Excuse me, sir, sorry to interrupt" said James to Macleod.

"No, no," said Macleod. "You've made the chief a happy man today." Jerry was translating as they talked.

"A happy day, but a sad day," said Crowfoot. The chief studied all three of them and thought for a long moment.

"Why is it me, who is sitting here?" asked Crowfoot. "Why am I not you," he said to Macleod, "sitting where you are? It is the Great Spirit who decides whether we are Indian or white, man or woman, tall or short. It is he that says we will be born now, not earlier or later. Why was I born to be the leader of my people at this time, when the buffalo are disappearing and our way of life vanishing? We are people of the plains. We live by the buffalo. Will we survive when they are gone?"

James saw that the chief was drawn and tired.

"I am the chief and I have decided," Crowfoot said to them. "We must live together as brothers. I don't know what this treaty will bring. But I do know that I trust you, Macleod. We all trust you." Macleod grasped the old chief's hand and looked into his sad eyes.

"I pledge my word," he said to Crowfoot, "that as long as the rivers flow and the grass grows in spring, the Queen will live up to the treaty."

64

James wrote late into the night. He knew that Mr. McLennan would be aware that a treaty was to be signed with the Blackfoot but he wanted to give him a full account of the events that led up to it. He added a summary of the discussions that took place, the colour of the unprecedented gathering of thousands of Blackfoot, Peigans, Bloods, Sarcees, and Stoneys with the Mounties and the representative of the Queen. He included a summary of his conversation with the bureaucrats and expressed his misgivings about what he heard from Dobbie. He wanted Mr. McLennan to understand that as far as the Indians were concerned the treaty was not a legal framework but a pledge of trust.

There were so many thoughts and recollections chasing each other through James' mind that the glow of the late summer sunrise was showing itself in the east and he still had not slept. Some of the other Mounties were up already beginning the process of breaking camp for the trip back to Fort Macleod. James gave up the idea of getting any sleep at all and joined them. He was brushing Mac when the major came up to him.

"I expect you have your report ready to send to Mr. McLennan," said Macleod.

"Yes, sir," replied James, "I was hoping I might have a chance to post it in Benton after we get back to the fort."

"I'm sending Webster with my report straight to Fort Benton now," replied the major. "Send yours with him as well. I want you to come with me to Fort Walsh. I just received this." Macleod handed James a telegraph message.

Ottawa
15th August, 1877
Lieut-Col. James F. Macleod
care I. G. Baker
Fort Benton, Montana Territory

Important that Sitting Bull and other United States Indians should be induced to return to reservations. United States Government has sent Commissioners to treat with them. Co-operate with Commissioners but do not unduly press Indians. Our action should be persuasive, not compulsory. Commissioners will reach Benton about twenty-fifth instant. Arrange to meet them. Reply.
R. W. Scott
Secretary of State

James handed the telegram back to the major.

"The American government is sending General Terry to meet with Sitting Bull," Macleod explained. "He's coming to try to convince him and the Sioux to go back to the reservation that they have set up for them in Dakota Territory. Ottawa wants Sitting Bull to leave. In spite of this treaty that has just been signed, they think the Sioux might incite the Blackfoot, Cree and Assiniboine to rise up with them against the whites."

"Do you think that's possible?" asked James.

"Possible, but unlikely," the major replied, "but I haven't met Sitting Bull myself yet, and I want to see what frame of mind he is in. We also have to convince him to meet General Terry."

James remembered General Terry's name from the plan he had read on the train.

"General Terry was Custer's commander in the summer offensive against the Sioux," James reminded the major. "If the Custer defeat was as bad as reported then General Terry has a score to settle with Sitting Bull."

"All the more reason for us to meet him at the border and escort him to Fort Walsh," replied Macleod. "I don't think Sitting Bull will know that Terry was involved in the Bighorn battle, but we'd better be there to be sure nothing flares up between them."

Before handing his report to Webster and joining the twelve other Redcoats who were travelling with the major to Fort Walsh, James took a last ride through the sprawling Blackfoot encampment. The Indians were in no hurry to leave. The women were busy about their domestic tasks, the children ran in and out among the tepees and horses grazed as far as the eye could see. Here and there a hide covering a tepee entrance was thrown back and a sleepy inhabitant blinked into the rising sun. He was hoping he might run across Rain Cloud and Singing Bird again but they were nowhere to be seen.

As the detachment set out from Ridge Under the Water, James took a long last look at the Blackfoot lodges that were retreating into the distance. It was a scene of peaceful serenity, light smoke rising from the lodges, horses grazing, warriors, women and children moving among the tepees. "If only it could stay this way," thought James.

But he knew it couldn't.

65

Major Macleod and his force arrived at Fort Walsh late on the third day. Nearing the fort they had passed through a deafening thunderstorm with streaks of lightening that seemed to strike the ground beside them. They had found what shelter they could in a hollow between two rises. It wasn't much but it shielded them a little from the driving wind. Surprising to James, there was only a brief downpour followed by a few splatters of raindrops and then only the wind. Before long the black clouds raced southeast and the sun came out from behind them. They and the ground they travelled over were dry again before they had ridden another half-hour.

When they arrived at the fort, they found that Inspector Walsh had already been informed of the coming of the American Commission. He had left a few days earlier to confer with Sitting Bull to try to convince him to meet with General Terry and the other Commissioners. No word had come back from Walsh so the major made plans to meet the Commissioners and escort them back to the fort while hoping to hear of Walsh's success with Sitting Bull.

Two days after their arrival the major called James to his quarters to tell him that he had received a message from General Terry to say that the Commission had been held up. Their transport was needed to convey supplies to General Miles who was pursuing Chief Joseph and a band of Nez Percé and had them hemmed in against the mountains. The Commission would arrive at the border ten days hence.

Rather than wait around the fort the major decided to go after Walsh and meet Sitting Bull. He took Jerry, six others and asked James to join them. James was restless waiting around the fort and was glad for the activity. Sixty miles east of the fort on their way to Wood Mountain they came across Walsh, Sitting Bull and about twenty of his chiefs. They were sitting on the ground in a circle, smoking. A few of the women who were with them were preparing a meal. When the major and his party arrived Walsh left the circle and walked over to greet them.

"What's this all about, Walsh?" asked the major.

"They're not sure they want to meet the Americans," replied Walsh.

"Why not?"

"I'll show you."

Walsh went back for his horse and waved the major to follow him. The company of Redcoats rode after Walsh. They had not gone far when James saw a group of Indians sitting at the edge of a grove of trees ahead of them. As they rode closer it was obvious that several among them were wounded with bloodstains on their clothes. All of them looked bedraggled and exhausted. They hardly looked up as the Redcoats approached.

"Who are these people?" the major asked Walsh.

"A band of Nez Percé who have just crossed the border," explained the inspector. "They escaped during a battle with the Americans. They told Star Child that they had been pursued for weeks until finally the cavalry caught up to them. Their leader, Chief Joseph, has been captured and many of their tribesmen killed."

Macleod got off his horse and waved for Jerry to follow. They walked among the surviving Nez Percé, the major asking questions through Jerry as he bent to talk with them. Macleod was obviously shaken by the deep saber and gunshot wounds on their bodies and the look of fatigue and desperation on their faces.

Macleod walked back to his horse.

"Tend to these people with whatever bandages and medicines we have," he ordered four of the constables. James and the others opened their saddlebags and took out the meager assortment of medical supplies they each carried and handed them over.

"This is why Sitting Bull doesn't want to meet the Americans," Walsh told the major as they rode back to the Sioux. "He thinks General Terry is bringing a force to attack the Sioux."

When the major and the others arrived back at the place where Sitting Bull and the Sioux were sitting they dismounted and joined the circle. Walsh introduced Macleod as the White Mother's head chief and Sitting Bull rose to shake his hand. James thought the old Sioux chief had aged since he had seen him several months earlier. His face still radiated strength but his shoulders sagged. He was gracious to the major who responded with respect for the old warrior.

Sitting Bull gestured for Macleod and Walsh to join them in their circle. James and the other Redcoats sat down behind them. Sitting Bull started the peace pipe, rose, presented it to the four winds and prayed to his Great Spirit. The familiar ceremony began again. The major smoked in turn and exercised great patience while the pipe made the full circle. When it reached Sitting Bull he handed the pipe to one of his men who buried the ashes. This done, Sitting Bull invited the major to speak.

James noticed that although Macleod's words were in English, he had learned the slow, rhythmic cadence of the Indian. He spoke in short sentences that made it easier for Jerry to translate. The major spoke of the Great Spirit and the land in much the same way as he had heard Crowfoot and others begin their speeches.

"You need have no fear of the Americans," the major told Sitting Bull. "When you cross the Medicine Line there is a great wall that rises up behind you that your enemies dare not cross. I assure you, that as long as you behave yourself in this country you will be protected."

As the major continued speaking, James could see the stony expressions on the faces of the chiefs warm. It was some time before they agreed, but when the major had finished speaking and the council was over the chiefs mounted up. Escorted by the Redcoats, they rode without further incident to Fort Walsh. But when they reached the gates of the fort they would not go in.

"I have never been in a fort and I will never go in a fort," said Sitting Bull. "We will camp outside."

Macleod signalled his men to wait where they were with the Sioux and rode alone through the gate into the fort. Sitting Bull and his chiefs watched anxiously. In a few minutes the major returned with the entire garrison walking behind him. He had each of the men walk up and shake hands with Sitting Bull and then with each of his chiefs.

"I give you my word," Macleod said to Sitting Bull, "there are no Americans inside this fort."

The old chief walked his horse slowly to the gate, stopped cautiously and looked inside. Then he turned to Macleod.

"I believe what you have told me," he said. "We will go in."

The following day the major received another message from General Terry saying that the Commission expected to be at the border the following evening. Macleod left with six Mounties to escort the Commissioners back to the fort. James stayed behind to write up his notes of the meeting between Macleod and Sitting Bull. Jerry, Walsh and the rest of the garrison remained close by to reassure Sitting Bull and the rest of his party that they would come to no harm.

Soon after the major and the escort were out of sight Sitting Bull became restless. He gathered his chiefs around him and they talked together for some time. Eventually they got up and started for their horses. James saw them saddling up and ran to let Walsh know what was happening. The inspector and Jerry hurried out to talk with them and James followed.

"There is no use seeing the Americans," Sitting Bull said to Walsh as he started towards the gate. "No matter what terms they offer we will not accept them. We do not believe anything they say and have no confidence in their promises."

Walsh reassured Sitting Bull that he and his men would come to no harm.

He said that the Queen wanted him to meet with the Americans to hear what they had to say. He suggested a council to talk about it.

Reluctantly Sitting Bull and the other chiefs got off their horses. The next hours were spent in a council, Walsh and Jerry doing everything they could to hold the Sioux until the major and the Commission returned. Walsh provided as much tobacco as was needed to keep the peace pipe circulating while the chiefs talked back and forth. After much discussion and much persuasion, Sitting Bull decided to stay.

It was dusk the following evening when the Commissioners arrived at Fort Walsh. James watched from near the gate of the fort as the Americans set up camp on the flats some distance away. The Mounties who had stayed with the Sioux made a show of standing between the Indians, who were camped in the square inside the fort, and the Americans so that Sitting Bull and the others would see and feel their protection. James was up most of the night walking about with several other Redcoats. Their presence would signify to Sitting Bull that he and his chiefs could sleep in peace.

As the sun came up James walked across the flats to take a look at the American camp. He could see a number of dark blue uniforms of the American officers and a number of men in civilian clothes. Word had spread around the fort after their arrival that there were some newspapermen with the Commission, some from as far away as New York and Washington.

"Sitting Bull is a notorious figure in our country," one of the reporters had told a Mountie, who had escorted the Commissioners. "This is the first meeting with him since he killed General Custer. There's a lot of interest in this story."

James saw one of the civilians setting up a camera and he walked over for a closer look. It was a standard box camera, a large wooden instrument sitting on a tripod with lens and glass plates. The photographer was assembling it and testing the shutter. James was absorbed in watching him when he heard a loud voice behind him.

"What kind of a gawdam uniform is that?"

James recognized the voice instantly. He turned and saw Major Matt Rawlins, last seen on the station platform in Bismarck, smiling at him. They shook hands and greeted each other warmly.

"I never imagined you were still in this part of the country," said James. "I thought you had gone back to Chicago long ago."

"I would have except for what happened at the Little Bighorn," replied Matt.

"Little Bighorn?" questioned James.

"Custer – the Sioux – you must have heard about it," said Matt.

"We heard that the cavalry were pretty badly mauled," said James.

"Mauled!" exclaimed Matt. "Five companies were completely wiped out."

"That bad?" remarked James, not lettting on how much he knew.

"Custer had been fighting Indians for ten years and had beaten them every time," Matt went on. "He thought he could do it again, disobeyed his orders and attacked before the other units were in position. We had no idea there were as many Sioux as there were. Before we knew it Custer and more than two hundred and fifty of his men were dead."

"Why do you think he attacked early?" James asked.

"I have my own theory about that," Matt replied. "Custer was a very ambitious man. He knew that military glory could lead to the Presidency – you just have to look at Washington, Jackson, Taylor or Grant to see that. I think he wanted to be President. I guess he thought that if he beat the Sioux all by himself he would end up in the White House."

"Were you near the battle when it happened?" asked James.

"No, but General Terry was. He arrived the next morning and saw the slaughter. You can imagine what he thinks of Sitting Bull."

"So you've had to stay on?"

"Unfortunately," replied Matt. "Sheridan wants all the hostile Indians back on their reservations now. Sitting Bull and his Sioux are the last hold out. The General wants reports on their every move."

"The last hold outs?" asked James.

"The last ones," echoed Matt. "We caught up with Chief Joseph and the Nez Percé a couple of weeks ago and had to beat them up pretty badly before they surrendered. They are being escorted back to their reservation now."

"I know," said James. "We saw some of them up here."

"Some Nez Perce?" asked Matt with surprise.

"About a hundred of them, in bad shape," James told him. "They must have escaped and are camped east of here with the Sioux."

"Son of a bitch," exclaimed Matt. "We thought we had them all."

Matt walked James around the American camp and introduced him to some of the Commissioners. General Terry and General Lawrence were in conference but James met the two colonels who were their aides and a newspaperman from New York, another from Chicago. The newspapermen plied James with questions and tagged along as he walked with Matt but James was reluctant to say much and they finally left.

Matt had work to do before the council with the Sioux so they agreed to meet later in the day. James began a report to Mr. McLennan using the background on the Commission that he had learned from Matt. General Alfred H. Terry, like all the commanders in the west, was a veteran of the Civil War. He was the hero of the Battle of Fort Fisher, the largest amphibious military operation of the war. As Matt told James, General Terry had been furious that Custer had ignored his orders and was deeply humiliated by his defeat. From General Sheridan on down all the commanders of the American army in the west wanted the war with the Indians finished. As Sitting Bull was the only hostile chief left, Terry wanted him disarmed and back on his reservation in Dakota Territory just as soon as possible.

A large tent had been erected outside the stockade of the fort in which the meeting was to be held. It was a beautiful, hot, October day. The sun shone strongly and the wind was light. Generals Terry and Lawrence sat behind a long table on one side with their aides behind them. James saw Matt standing off to one side. The newspapermen were standing near the back of the tent behind the Americans. Macleod and Walsh sat on the opposite side of the tent leaving room in the center for the Sioux who had not yet appeared. James and several other Redcoats stood in a half circle behind Macleod and Walsh giving the appearance of protection to the Sioux.

The men in blue uniforms on one side and the men in scarlet uniforms on the other waited in silence. James knew that both Macleod and Walsh had been talking with Sitting Bull up to the last minute, reassuring him of his safety and convincing him that it was important for the Sioux leader to meet with the Americans. Yet the old chief had not appeared. James studied the generals, then his aides and then the newsmen who had stopped their whispering and were anxiously watching the entrance. He caught Matt's eye. His friend looked grim.

There was a soft sound of footsteps approaching. All eyes turned to the entrance. Sitting Bull was the first to enter followed by his lesser chiefs. Macleod and Walsh stood as Sitting Bull approached the center. James could see the reluctance in Generals Terry and Lawrence to stand but finally they did. Sitting Bull walked over to Macleod and shook his hand warmly. He did the same with Walsh. The great chief hardly looked at the Long Knives and deliberately refused to approach General Terry or General Lawrence. Sitting Bull sat on the robes laid on the ground in front of the table facing the generals. Jerry was beside him, Macleod and Walsh behind him. The chiefs flanked their leader on both sides.

Sitting Bull turned to Jerry and spoke in a strong voice.

"The Chief of the Sioux would like the table removed and the visitors to leave," said Jerry, pointing at the newspapermen standing behind the blue uniforms.

There was an awkward silence until Macleod signaled two of his Mounties who moved quickly to carry the table out of the tent. The newspapermen, reluctant to miss the proceedings, lingered, but one of the policeman moved towards them and shepherded them quietly but firmly from the council tent. The Sioux sat in silence until the last of the angry newsmen disappeared from view. Macleod rose, welcomed Sitting Bull and the chiefs to the council and introduced the American Commissioners. He looked at Sitting Bull with the expectation that the chief might speak first and hopefully start a pipe ceremony but it was clear Sitting Bull was there to listen and he sat motionless. Finally, General Terry rose. He had in his hand a written statement, which he began to read.

Glancing up at Sitting Bull and the chiefs, he began.

"We are sent to you today by the President of the United States and the Government of Canada. The President has instructed us to say to you that he desires to make a lasting peace with you and your people. He desires that all hostilities will cease and that all shall live together in harmony. He wishes this not only for the sake of the whites alone but for your sakes, too."

James was immediately impressed with General Terry and not just for his physical appearance. The general was at least six foot six and looked magnificent in his full dress uniform. He wore a long dark blue coat with epaulettes at the shoulders, two rows of shiny silver buttons down his chest and more buttons on his cuffs. He wore dark blue riding breeches with highly polished black boots, an ornate silver-on-black belt with gleaming sword. His familiar cavalry hat lay on the ground beside his chair. James knew from his conversation with Matt that, like Macleod, Terry was not a professional soldier but a lawyer. Having distinguished himself in the Civil War he was made a Brigadier General and later assigned to command the Department of Dakota. General Terry had not only proved an able military commander but was well liked by his officers and men. It was more than General Terry's appearance that caught James' attention. The commander had a gracious manner and a kindly face, not common in a veteran field commander. He spoke with sincerity and James hoped that it registered with Sitting Bull.

"I am instructed to say," continued General Terry, "that if you return to your country and refrain from further hostilities, a full pardon will be granted to you and your people for all acts committed in the past, and that, no matter what these acts have been, no attempt will be made to punish you or any of your people. What is past shall be forgotten and you will be received on as friendly terms as other Indians have been received."

James watched Sitting Bull to see what his reaction was to these words. There was not a crack in the hard expression on the chief's face. He stared intently at the general as he spoke.

The general looked straight into Sitting Bull's eyes.

"Of all the bands that were hostile to the United States your band is the only one that has not surrendered. Every other band has come into its agency. Of these bands that have come in not a single man has been punished. Every man, woman and child has been received as a friend and all have received food and clothing for their use."

Still, there was no reaction on the old chief's face. His mouth was hard and his eyes narrowed.

"It is true that these Indians have been required to give up their arms and their horses," General Terry continued, "but part of these have been sold and the money received from the sale of them will be used for their benefit. Already six hundred and fifty cows have been purchased for the use of the Indians on the Missouri River. If you abandon your present mode of life the same terms are offered to you."

Not one of the chiefs moved. Some had their eyes fixed on the general, others looked at the ground in front of them as they absorbed through Jerry every word that was said. James hoped that the general's manner and the terms offered might crack their distrust and open the way to their peaceful return.

"The President cannot, nor will not consent to your returning to your country prepared for war," General Terry told them. "He cannot consent to your returning prepared to inflict the injuries you have done as in the past. He invites you to come to the boundary of this country and give up your arms and ammunition and go to the agencies assigned to you, and give up your horses except those required for peace purposes."

James noted with alarm that Sitting Bull was on the verge of getting up to leave but the old chief restrained himself.

"Your arms and horses will be sold," continued the general, reading from his notes and lifting his eyes to look at Sitting Bull, "and cows bought with which you can raise herds to supply you and your children long after the game have disappeared. In the meantime, you will receive clothes and provisions, the same as other Indians."

Anger flared through Sitting Bull's face but he held it back.

"Of one thing it is our duty to inform you," General Terry read on, "that you cannot return to your country or your people with arms and ammunition. If you do so, you will be treated as enemies of the United States."

Sitting Bull's eyes tightened to slits and his face flushed.

"We ask you to carefully consider what we have told you," said the general raising his eyes from the papers he held and looking at the chiefs, "and take time to weigh the matter well. When you have done so we shall be glad to meet you and await your answer."

General Terry nodded to the chiefs and to Macleod and sat down. There was a long silence in which no one moved. Everyone waited to see what Sitting Bull would do. Finally, he rose to his feet. James was struck by how small the chief appeared compared to the general. Although he was thick in the chest, Sitting Bull was more than a foot shorter than Terry. The old chief took a step forward on his lame leg and began to speak. Jerry was beside him.

"For sixty four years you have treated my people badly," said Sitting Bull, looking straight at General Terry. "What have we done that caused us to depart from our country? We could go nowhere so we have taken refuge here. It was on this side of the line that I first learned to shoot. I was raised by Red River half-breeds and for that reason I shake hands with these people."

He pointed at Macleod and Walsh.

"We did not give you our country," said Sitting Bull, turning back to the general. "You took it from us. Look at these eyes and ears. You think me a fool. But you are a greater fool than I am."

James watched the general, who remained calm showing no reaction. His aides however were less controlled. They made no effort to hide their growing anger. James noticed that Matt's reaction was different. His friend looked sad and resigned.

"This is a Medicine House," continued Sitting Bull. "You come to tell us stories and we do not want to hear them. I will not say any more. You can go back home. That part of the country we came from belonged to us and you took it from us. Now we live here."

Sitting Bull sat down and before anyone else could speak something happen that took everyone by surprise. One of the chief's wives stood to address the Commissioners. It was rare for a woman to speak at any council let alone a council of this importance.

"I wanted to raise children in your country," she said to the General in a soft voice, "but you gave me no time. I come to this country to raise my children."

And she sat down. After another long silence, General Terry rose and spoke directly to Sitting Bull.

"Are we to say to the President that you refuse the offers made to you?"

Sitting Bull's eyes flared.

"I have told you all I have to tell you," replied Sitting Bull. "You can go back to where you came from and stay there. This part of the country does not belong to you, all on this side belongs to these people," he said, waving again towards Macleod.

"Then I have nothing more to say," said the General and he rose and walked from the tent followed by General Lawrence and their staff.

Sitting Bull waited for the Americans to leave and then rose himself. His people followed him. Macleod whispered to Walsh. Walsh walked quickly to catch up with Sitting Bull and Macleod disappeared out the entrance. When James emerged from the tent he noticed Macleod talking to General Terry as Walsh walked into the fort with Sitting Bull. Matt was standing off to the side looking in James' direction. James went to meet him and they walked slowly for some distance together.

"What happens now?" asked James.

"I hope Sitting Bull's smart enough to accept our offer," replied Matt. "The general's going to wrap this up one way or the other."

"What do you mean, one way or the other?"

"We know your government isn't going to give the Sioux land up here and that you want them out of here as much as we do. We know you're afraid of the influence they might have on your own Indians and the trouble that could come from that. You're not going to feed them and the buffalo are disappearing fast."

"So?" asked James.

"So if they don't come peacefully now, they'll come eventually and in a lot worse shape than they are now."

"They could survive up here for years," said James.

"Maybe three or four years, but not more."

"What makes you say that?" asked James.

"Starvation," said Matt flatly. "They'll come back eventually, or they'll starve to death."

66

Macleod, deeply disappointed that Sitting Bull's refusal had come so quickly and in hopes that the negotiations could be salvaged, asked General Terry to stay over another day. Macleod wanted a chance to talk with Sitting Bull without the Americans present. The general agreed and Macleod found Walsh and Jerry and together they set out to confer with Sitting Bull. The major asked James to join him.

The Sioux were preparing to leave the fort immediately to return to their camp. The women were stripping the hides from the lodge poles when Macleod arrived to talk with Sitting Bull. The old chief was still angry from his confrontation with the Americans but after much persuasion agreed to sit with Macleod. Sitting Bull put a halt to the packing of the lodges and summoned his chiefs once again. Macleod, Walsh and Jerry stayed with Sitting Bull and accompanied the Sioux chiefs back to the council tent. There was no peace pipe ceremony. The major started speaking the moment they were seated.

"Today you heard what the Americans had to say," Macleod said to Sitting Bull and the chiefs, "and you have given them your answer. I wish to tell you that this answer is of the greatest importance to you."

Sitting Bull and the other chiefs listened carefully to the translation of Macleod's words but they showed no wavering in their determination.

"The Queen recognizes you as American Indians who have come to this side for protection. The answer you have given the Commissioners prevents your ever going back to America with arms and ammunition in your possession. I wish to tell you that if any of you or your young men cross the line with arms and attack the Americans, then we become your enemies as well as the American."

Sitting Bull was studying Macleod intently, suspicion beginning to show in the lines around his eyes.

"You must remember that you will have to live by the buffalo on this side of the line," continued the major, "and that the buffalo will not last forever. In a very few years they will all be killed. After the buffalo are killed you will have to seek some other method of living as all that you can expect from the Queen is her protection."

Macleod, with a gesture to the old chief, invited him to speak. Sitting Bull rose, stepped forward to where Macleod and Walsh were sitting and shook hands with them both.

"I tell you the truth," Sitting Bull began. "Since I was born I have done nothing bad. The Americans tried to take our country from us. Our country, the Black Hills, was full of gold. They knew that the gold was there. I told them not to go in but they did."

James studied the craggy face with its deep lines and small, dark eyes and tried to imagine the life this old war chief and medicine man had lived leading up to this moment. Sitting Bull had seen his people relentlessly driven from their traditional home, further and further to the west, until they could go no further. His people had been promised and then forced from the Black Hills – the most cherished of their sacred landmarks. He was the leader of his people at the time when thousands of white settlers were replacing the thousands of buffalo which had provided them with their livelihood since the beginning of their existence. He was presiding over the death of their way of life. He wanted to postpone that death as long as he possibly could.

"The Americans kill ten, twenty of my children every day for nothing," Sitting Bull told the major, his voice strong and defiant. "I see on the plains no more deer, elk or buffalo. All is blood. Today you heard the sweet talk of the Americans. They would give me cattle and when they get me across the line they will fight me. The Americans have robbed, cheated and laughed at us. I could never live over there again. We want to be friends with all while we are here. You can come to our camps anytime. We like the Redcoats very much and it is only for this reason that we came to see the American Commissioners and hear what they have to say."

Sitting Bull again shook Macleod's hand. The major rose to meet him and held the outstretched hand for several moments while looking directly into the old chief's eyes. Then they both sat down again. There was silence until Macleod finally spoke.

"Then I am to understand that you have been driven from your country?"

Sitting Bull and the other chiefs nodded their assent.

"I have every confidence that you will do what you have promised," Macleod continued. "I want you to carry back to your camps the words that I have spoken. Be sure your young men understand. If trouble comes there is no telling where it will end. You can trust me."

The chiefs nodded as they heard the major's words through Jerry.

"We told you that you would be safe if you came here," Macleod went on. "We will take you back to your camps and give you provisions and tobacco for the journey. You may trade in any part of the country but you must have Inspector Walsh's permission to trade ammunition."

The chiefs smiled at the major's words.

"Now," concluded the major, "can you tell me where you will camp for the winter?"

Sitting Bull conferred with his other chiefs.

"No," replied Sitting Bull, "the man who settles our camping ground is not with us here."

Macleod rose and shook hands with Sitting Bull, the chiefs and each one of the Sioux present including the women. They smiled and nodded as they shook the major's hand. It appeared to James that they were trying to thank him in ways other than words. The major stopped at the entrance of the tent and gave an order to a constable who set off in the direction of the quartermaster's store.

As he passed James, Macleod motioned him to follow.

"Come with me," the major said to James in a tense voice. "I want you to get down every word."

Walsh and Jerry stayed behind with Sitting Bull. Macleod walked to the American camp with James. They found General Terry with his staff conferring in the open. The setting sun was still hot but there was a cooling breeze. When the Americans saw the major approaching General Terry rose to meet him. Matt was nearby and he nodded at James as he approached.

"Any progress?" asked General Terry.

"We had a frank talk," replied Macleod. "I tried to impress on them the importance of their answer to you. I also told them that if they or their young men crossed the border with hostile intent they would not only have the Americans as their enemies but us as well."

"And?" asked the General.

"We talked about the buffalo," Macleod continued, "and that they would soon be gone. I told them they could expect nothing from the Queen's government except protection."

"Do you think they understood?" asked the General.

"Yes," replied the major. "They stuck to the answer that Sitting Bull gave you. They promised to obey our laws."

"Well then," said the General. "I guess that answers that."

"I don't think you need have the least anxiety about any of these Indians crossing the line," the major said to him, "at any rate not for some time to come."

General Terry and General Lawrence looked at each other. The men in their staff had anger etched on their faces.

"Thank you for your hospitality, Colonel Macleod," said General Terry shaking the major's hand. "We have done what we could. We will be leaving first thing in the morning."

The major exchanged polite words with the generals and some of their men while James went over to talk with Matt.

"So you'll be leaving in the morning," said James.

"First thing."

"Will we have a chance to talk before you go?" asked James.

"We've got a few plans to draw up, it should take an hour of two," said Matt. "Why don't you come around here again at sundown. Better that I not go too near the fort while the Sioux are still there."

As James walked through the gate of the fort the Sioux lodges were directly ahead of him. Sitting Bull had put off leaving until the morning and the women were occupied with their evening tasks. His attention was diverted when he saw Webster coming out of the major's quarters. Webster was walking towards James and waving something in his hand. James remembered that he had been to Fort Benton.

"Letter for you," said Webster, handing James the envelope. James walked out the gate of the fort across the field and sat down, leaning against a tree. He opened the familiar envelope from the Dominion Bank of Canada.

> *Staff Constable James Keyden*
> *Sir:*
>
> *We received with great interest your dispatches of December 20, 1876 concerning the arrival of the Sioux on Canadian soil and April 2, 1877 reporting the arrival of Sitting Bull. We understand from your description that the winter was particularly severe and are gratified that you have come through your ordeal and are able to continue your duties.*
>
> *We have word that a treaty will be signed between the Government of Canada and the Blackfoot Confederacy towards the end of summer which includes the allocation of certain lands to various tribes. We see this as a positive development for the continuation of the railway from Winnipeg to the Rocky Mountains. The situation with the Sioux close to the American border, on the other hand, is still of grave concern to us.*
>
> *Towards the end of the year we are expecting bankers from London to visit us here with a view to investing in the next phase of construction of the national railway. It would help our cause considerably to have a person attend these meetings who has first hand knowledge of the situation in the North West. There are other assignments that I have in mind for you as well.*
>
> *Consequently, would you please return to Toronto as quickly as pos-*

sible after receiving this letter. The railway will be complete as far as Winnipeg by late September. I recommend you return to Toronto by this route, as it will be faster than via the American route and you will be able to give us your impressions of traveling over the recently completed line along the north shore of Lake Superior. I will expect your telegram from Winnipeg advising us of the date of your arrival.
Angus McLennan

James was caught by surprise at Mr. McLennan's instructions and was trying to absorb the fact that he would be leaving almost immediately for the East.

"Good news?" asked Matt, coming up beside him. "We finished sooner than I thought so I came looking for you."

James got up and they walked back towards the American camp. He told Matt about the contents of the letter and that he had instructions to leave as soon as possible for Toronto.

"That's great news," replied Matt enthusiastically.

Matt wanted to stop by his tent. While James was waiting for him, he could hear Inspector Walsh talking nearby with a group of reporters from the American papers. Walsh was speaking in an animated way, his voice loud, his words boastful. What he was saying must have been noteworthy. The newspapermen were writing frantically capturing his every word.

Matt and James picked up something to eat from the American mess tent and walked down towards Battle Creek. It was still warm and the last rays of the sun touched the riverbank. They found a spot at the edge of some cottonwoods and sat down, resting against two trees. They ate, watched the sun go down and chatted. They talked about the army, the Mounted Police and the future of Sitting Bull and the Sioux. James asked about Matt's wife Carolyn and his daughter Nell.

"If you have a family you really love, don't join the army," said Matt. "When I left Chicago to go to Fort Abraham Lincoln I thought I'd be away a few months at most. It's been over a year and I can't wait to get back."

"You should be able to go back soon," said James. "This meeting winds things up with Sitting Bull."

"Not completely," replied Matt.

"What do you mean?"

"This is between you and me," said Matt, "but the President, General

Sheridan, General Terry – all of them want Sitting Bull and the Sioux on a reservation. There are thousands of settlers pouring into the west and the only obstacle is Sitting Bull. They won't be happy leaving him here no matter how peaceful he says he's going to be. We're going to force him to come back."

"How can you do that?" asked James.

"We're going to make it so tough for him to feed his people that, little by little, they'll abandon him and make their own way south," Matt explained. "It may be a band at a time and it may take a couple of years but eventually Sitting Bull will come back too."

"Return to the your side?" said James. "I don't think there's a chance."

"You wait," answered Matt. "You'll see."

"How will it happen?"

"Starting tomorrow, we're putting cavalry units all along the border. We'll stop everything that's coming into this country, food, horses, feed, guns, everything. We're going to stop all Indians and half-breeds from moving freely between our countries. We're going to burn the grass along our side of the border from the Rockies to Dakota Territory so that the buffalo will have nothing to eat and they won't move north. There will be no buffalo for the Sioux."

"Or for the Blackfoot," added James with a note of criticism.

"Unfortunate, but true," replied Matt.

"So that will be the end of the war against the Indians," said James.

"It's over now," replied Matt. "The rest is just a question of time."

"So you'll be going back East as well?"

"Just as soon as I can get there," replied Matt happily. "Tomorrow we start for Fort Peck then I'll travel with General Terry to Fort Lincoln, wrap up my reports and head for Chicago."

The wind was rustling the leaves above them, the birds were singing their last songs of the day and the water in the creek was tumbling over the stones beside them. After some minutes James looked over at Matt.

"Your war against the Indians is over and we've settled with the Blackfoot. And now we are both going back East. I'm not sure what I'm going to be doing next but I expect Mr. McLennan has something in mind for me. Have you enjoyed your career in the army?"

"Enjoyed is not the word. I've been a cavalryman for sixteen years and to tell you the truth I'm tired of the killing, James. All I want to do is go home to my family and find something worthwhile to do."

The two sat in silence as darkness fell.

"I'm almost asleep," said Matt finally. "It's crowded in our tent. I think I'll just roll over and spend the night here." He edged away from the tree he was leaning against, lay down on the high grass next to it and stared at the sky.

"You're crowded!" said James. "Our quarters are so full I've been sleeping on the floor. I'll join you."

James lay awake a long time. The sky was clear, the stars shone brightly and he could see the shadows of the leaves high up in the trees swaying in the breeze. Every time he thought of going back to Toronto his heart skipped yet he was aware of how much he would miss the Great Plains.

He had dozed off when he was wakened by shouts close beside him. They were garbled but they sounded like "Get out! Get out!" Then he remembered Matt. James rose on his elbow and looked beside him. In the soft glow of the starlight he could see Matt walking around waving his arms frantically. He was shouting words that were unrecognizable. There was a look of terror on his face. While James was watching, Matt shook his head violently back and forth then seemed to relax and he rested his face in his hands. James wasn't sure whether he was awake or asleep.

In a few moments Matt's hands fell away and James saw him walk towards the stream. When he reached it he stood there for a long time just watching the water flow by. Finally Matt knelt down, held his hands in the cold water and splashed his face. James was alarmed. He got up and walked quietly to where Matt was kneeling beside the water and put a hand on his shoulder. Matt did not react.

"You okay?"

There was no answer. Matt stayed where he was and continued to stare at the water.

Finally, he replied, "Yeah, I'm okay." Matt continued to let the cool water run through his hands. He rubbed them on his face, took several deep breaths and stood up. James followed him back to where they had been sleeping and they sat down.

"Bad dream?"

Matt was silent a long time. "I have it from time to time," answered Matt. "Same one." James said nothing and Matt leaned back against the tree.

"It started just after we had Nell," Matt told him. "Did I ever tell you about the Shenandoah Valley?"

"You mentioned it on the train," replied James.

"Grant ordered Sheridan to destroy everything in the Valley that might be useful to the Southern army," Matt said, his voice far off. "It was one of their main sources of food and grass. So we did. We started at one end and fought our way to the other. We drove out the Rebs, rounded up the horses and cattle, herded them out and burned the barns and crops. One morning early, I was leading a company of cavalry through the woods and we came to a small village. I sent the scouts ahead to see if the enemy was around. They weren't so I sent them back to warn the villagers that we were coming. Then we went in. The men did what they were ordered to do – burn the barns, burn the crops but leave the houses. The whole place was in flames."

Matt paused and looked into the darkness.

"As I was following the troopers through the village I looked up at one of the burning barns and to my horror I saw a woman holding a little girl standing behind a window up in the loft. I couldn't hear her but I could see her screaming and banging on the glass. I jumped off my horse and ran to the barn to see if I could get them out but just as I got there the flames burst up the side of the barn and I had to back away. When I looked up again I couldn't see them. Then the roof fell in and the barn collapsed in a flaming heap. In my dream the woman at the window is Carolyn and the girl she's holding is Nell."

67

There was little sleep for James for the remainder of the night. There was too much going on in his head – the thought of leaving the North West, the day's events with Sitting Bull, the plan to starve them into submission and Matt's nightmare. Matt had nodded off beside him. A tall American cavalry officer standing over them awakened them both.

"Time to mount up, Major," said a loud voice. "General Terry wants to get an early start." James and Matt roused themselves and walked slowly together back to the American camp.

"It's been a real pleasure seeing you again," said James.

"Likewise," replied Matt. "Good luck back in Toronto."

"I hope we'll meet again," said James as they shook hands.

"If you're ever in Chicago, look me up," said Matt. "If you can find General Sheridan you'll probably find me – for two more years anyway."

James watched his friend disappear into his tent. He turned towards the fort and as he walked through the gate he saw the Sioux packing to leave. Their lodges were down and the women were folding the hides to load on travois which were already harnessed to some horses.

James walked to the door of Macleod's quarters and knocked. The door was ajar but there was no answer. James pushed the door slightly and saw the major sitting forward in his chair behind his desk, his head propped up on his hands. He was looking straight ahead.

"Oh, sorry to disturb you, sir."

"No, come in Keyden," he replied.

James opened the door and stepped inside.

"You look like you didn't get much sleep last night," said the major.

"You're right, sir. Too much going around in my head."

"I didn't sleep either," confided the major, "too much going around in my head, too."

James looked at him but didn't reply.

"This is not for publication, James," said Macleod, forgetting his rank and speaking as one man to another, "but I have come to a very disturbing conclusion."

The major got up from his chair and walked to the window where he could see the Sioux preparing to return to their camp.

"The Americans have treated their Indians as enemies while we have chosen to deal with them in the spirit of British justice. In spite of our different approaches I fear the result will be the same."

James was puzzled but did not interrupt the major who was still looking out the window.

"In a very short space of time," the major went on, almost talking to himself, "the Indians on both sides of the border will be confined like prisoners to very small parcels of their own land. Their traditional livelihood will be destroyed and they will be starving. It is too much to expect them to adapt to our ways in such a short time. I have made promises on behalf of the government, but governments have been known to betray promises when it is in their interest. I find this very unsettling."

Macleod stood by the window for several moments watching the Sioux. Finally he remembered James, who was shaken by the major's words, and turned back to his desk. When he was seated James stepped forward and handed him the letter he had received from Mr. McLennan.

"This came from Mr. McLennan yesterday. I thought you should see it."

James handed it to the major who unfolded and read it.

"So he wants you back in Toronto right away," said the major, resuming his authoritative bearing and looking up at James. "Needs your help to raise more money for the railway. Costly business, this railway, and it hasn't even reached the mountains."

The major handed the letter back to James.

"There must be a lot of pressure on McLennan," continued the major. "He's about to lay steel across the prairies and they haven't even found a pass through the Rockies yet. There may not even be one that's suitable for a railroad."

The major walked back to his desk and sat down.

"It's a good idea for you to go back by way of Winnipeg. The first trains will be running in the next few weeks and it will be faster than going via Chicago."

The major was speaking automatically, his mind elsewhere. He scanned some sheets in front of him.

"I've finished my report of our meetings yesterday for the Secretary of State. Take it with you. I expect you've written your own report for Mr. McLennan."

"Not yet, sir," replied James, "but I will before I go."

"I'll leave this open for you to read," said the major handing his report to James. "There may be something in it you want to include in your own report."

He handed the report to James.

"When had you thought of leaving?"

"As soon as I finish my report and can get my things together," replied James.

The major got up from his chair and walked around his desk.

"You know, James, it's so easy to condemn the Indians and force our will upon them with no appreciation whatsoever for how devastating life has become for them. It is going to take our best efforts to see them through this."

68

The Americans with several Redcoats had already left for the border by the time James stepped out of the major's quarters. Sitting Bull and the Sioux were packing and about to depart with another escort. James walked to the long table in the barracks and sat down to write his report to Mr. McLennan. He read what the major had written and was struck by its last paragraph, which he added to his own report:

> *I think the principal cause of the difficulties that are continually embroiling the American Government in trouble with the Indians is the manner in which these Indians are treated by the swarms of adventurers who have scattered themselves all over the Indian country in search of minerals before any treaty is made giving up the title. These men always look upon the Indians as their natural enemies, and it is their rule to shoot at them if they approach after being warned off.*
>
> *I am satisfied that such a rule is not necessary in dealing with the worst of Indians, and that any necessity there might be for its adoption arose from the illegal intrusion and wrong-doings of the whites.*

James described for Mr. McLennan Commissioner Macleod's straightforward, fair treatment of Crowfoot, the Blackfoot and now the Sioux and how the major's attitude, reflected in other members of the Mounted Police, was largely responsible for the peaceful relationships between Indians and whites. He did not repeat the fears expressed by Macleod that Indians, both American and Canadian, would before long be in a desperate struggle for survival. As he reread his report and recalled his sixteen months in the North West, he realized how much it had become part of him and how much he would miss it.

"McLennan paid for your horse," the major reminded James when he went to say goodbye. "Take it with you back to Toronto. And this."

The major handed James a sealed envelope addressed to Mr. McLennan. "It's my evaluation of your time with us. I think you will be satisfied with it."

The sun was breaking over the eastern hilltops as James rode Mac out the gate of Fort Walsh. He rode past the spot where the Americans had set up their camp, entered the woods on the slope overlooking the fort and threaded his way up through the trees to the top of the hill. The wind was sharp out of the northwest and blew waves through the tall grass on the open plain.

James stopped to look back at the valley that stretched out behind him. Below in the distance was the whitewashed stockade of Fort Walsh. Scarlet tunics were moving between the buildings. He could pick out the door to the major's quarters. The image of Macleod sitting with his head in his hands, agonizing over the future of the Indians he had done so much to help, was sharp in his mind. He looked to the south where Matt and the Americans were riding for the Medicine Line. The Sioux, he knew, were ahead of him to the east. James turned his eyes west to where the Great Plains met the sky. He couldn't see the mountains but he knew they were still there.

69

It was a ten-day ride to Winnipeg and there was more than enough time to review and evaluate his time in the North West. James was up each morning with first light and rode until dusk. The days were getting shorter and he wanted to reach Winnipeg before the first snowfall. Although the wind was at his back it carried the chill of winter and he couldn't forget how deadly a prairie blizzard could be.

There were few incidents to interrupt his thoughts. On one occasion he saw four or five riders in the far distance that he took to be half-breed hunters. There were small groups of buffalo and elk but he suspected most of the smaller animals could sense that the cold weather was coming and were finding comfortable homes for the winter. As Fort Walsh fell further behind and Winnipeg grew closer his mind shifted from the memories of the past to the possibilities of the future.

"What is it that Mr. McLennan has in mind?" he thought over and over again.

Riding down the broad streets of Winnipeg felt very strange – the crowds of people, the well kept houses, the shops full of goods. He attracted much attention in his scarlet jacket, riding on a very fine horse in the peak of condition. Then it occurred to him that some of the interest might be the result of his rather scruffy appearance and tattered uniform. It certainly was not as fresh and crisp as when he walked around Chicago or Fargo on his way West. He hoped whoever met him in Toronto would not be too disappointed.

Then the thought crossed his mind, "Who will meet me in Toronto?"

He was sure Mr. McLennan would be too busy. Hopefully he would get word to Fiona and family and they would be there. Then his heart skipped a beat.

"I wonder if Merrie will be there?"

It was not difficult finding the train station. It was an impressive new building with distinctive architecture. Fortunately for James there was a train leaving the afternoon of the following day for the East arriving in Toronto four days later. He sent the telegram to Mr. McLennan announcing his arrival and set out to find a place where he and Mac could spend the night. If it were a place with a bath so much the better.

The train ride took some getting used to. Having travelled exclusively for over a year on horseback it was a strange sensation to sit back on padded seats and watch the landscape flash by. The leather cushions still had a scent of newness. The coaches were well appointed and much better illuminated than those on which he had travelled west. There was the same mix of travelers though the coaches were not full.

Late the first day out from Winnipeg the familiar prairie landscape began to give way to woods and lakes with outcroppings of rock scattered across the surface of the land. He wakened on the second day to the sight of a body of water so wide he could not see the other shore. The forest pressed in on both sides of the train and through breaks in the trees all he could see were massive formations of rock along the near shoreline. To stretch his legs James walked to the end of the train. Standing in the vestibule of the last car he watched the tracks recede into the distance and marveled at the effort it must have taken to cut a railway line through this rugged country.

Images of the Great Plains were replaced by James' memories of Toronto. There was the concert in the St. Lawrence Hall and the carriage ride that preceded it. There was the party at Louise Graham's, and he recalled with a smile the look on Captain Channer's face watching him dancing, his uniform thrown on the floor. He thought of his long walk to town after meeting Mr. McLennan for the first time – and Merrie. Strangely, he thought, most of the occasions he recalled were with Merrie.

James opened his breast pocket and took out the photograph that she had given him on his departure. There was a crease across one corner but the strong backing had protected it from further damage. James turned it over. The words Merrie had written on the back were still clear "Hurry home, Merrie".

"Where is home?" questioned James. He thought of his mother and father in Gask. Although he could picture every detail of the home where he had grown up it seemed very far away. He thought of all the places he had stayed in the past year – the barracks at Fort Macleod and Fort Walsh, Three Bulls' tepee and the weeks with Rain Cloud and Singing Bird beside Lodge Creek. There was the Nugget Hotel in Fort Benton. But what stood out most from the last months were the star-filled nights on the open plains, the sound of the wind through the prairie grass and the gentle whisper of the water flowing in the rivers and streams. If only Merrie had been there to see it all.

As his train neared Toronto James knew that one uncertainty in his life had been resolved. He had come to love this country and its people. There were the major and his wife Mary; there was Crowfoot, Rain Cloud and Singing Bird, there was Jerry the scout and the half-breed families on their colourful, squeaky carts, there were his fellow Redcoats from whom he had learned so much. There was no question of returning to the Old Country. His future was here.

Now what next? He recalled the words of Mr. McLennan in his office when he had accepted the offer to go West. "If you carry out this responsibility well there is no limit to what you can do in this country." He was more than anxious to find out what the banker had in mind for him next.

There was one other gnawing anxiety that loomed larger than all the others as the train passed Duck's Hotel on the outskirts of the city and slowed as it approached the station.

"Is Merrie well? Will she be at the station to meet me?"

It was a thought he couldn't keep from his mind as the train slowed, forced the excess steam from its valves and came to a halt. He pressed close to the window but the coach he was in was near the end of the train some distance from the station. He grabbed his pack from the rack over the seat and headed quickly for the door. There were a few passengers in front of him and he could see very little over their heads and through the doorway as they got off. He was taking his last step onto the platform when he caught sight of William racing towards him. Not far behind was Hermione. They shouted for joy at the sight of him and flung their arms around him. Grabbing James by the arms they hurried him through the crowd of passengers back towards the station. And then – there they were - Fiona and Merrie standing together waiting for him.

James knew he was truly home.

Epilogue

CROWFOOT (1830-1890) WAS CONFINED TO a reserve like the rest of his Blackfoot tribesmen. In spite of his disillusionment with the federal government and its Indian agents Crowfoot continued to trust the Mounties and refused to join the rebellion in Northern Saskatchewan in 1885. The following year Prime Minister John A. Macdonald invited him to Ottawa in recognition of his loyalty but he was forced to cut his visit short due to ill health. He died of tuberculosis on April 25, 1890 and is buried at Blackfoot Crossing.

Colonel James F. Macleod (1836-1894) left the North West Mounted Police in 1880 to become a circuit judge. In 1887 he was appointed to the Supreme Court of the North West Territories, a position he held until his death in Calgary on September 5, 1894. His funeral procession was several city blocks long and was observed by hundreds who lined the route to Union Cemetery including many Blackfoot. Their mournful cries broke the silence. One of the letters written to the family was from a former colleague in the NWMP, Colonel Sam Steele. He wrote, "*The Blackfeet regarded him as the personification of truth and honour.*"

Sitting Bull (1831-1890) finally gave in to starvation and returned to the United States with the remainder of his band. He surrendered at Fort Buford, Montana Territory on July 19, 1881 and was the last of the Sioux to surrender his rifle. For two years he was confined as a prisoner-of-war at Fort Randall and then moved to the Standing Rock reservation in South Dakota. In 1890 the army sent a detachment of Lakota policemen to arrest him as a precautionary measure against further uprisings. He and his followers resisted arrest and in the struggle Sitting Bull was shot and killed. He died on December 15, 1890. He was buried at Fort Yates, North Dakota and in 1953 his body was moved to Mobridge, South Dakota where a granite shaft marks his grave.

Lieutenant-General Philip H. Sheridan (1831-1888) was made General of the Army in 1883, the highest military office in the United States. He died on August 5, 1888 and is buried in Arlington National Cemetery.

ISBN 141206869-X